Praise for Paul Gitsham

'Once again Paul Gitsham has produced an
utterly gripping thriller'

'Brilliant from start to finish. Love this series'

'Paul never lets you down'

'Beautifully written, well plotted and well researched'

'Up there with the best series'

PAUL GITSHAM started his career as a biologist working in the UK and Canada. After stints as the world's most over-qualified receptionist and a spell ensuring that international terrorists hadn't opened a Child's Savings Account at a major UK bank (a job even duller than working reception) he retrained as a Science teacher.

Also by Paul Gitsham

The DCI Warren Jones series

The Last Straw
No Smoke Without Fire
Blood is Thicker Than Water (Novella)
Silent as the Grave
A Case Gone Cold (Novella)
The Common Enemy
A Deadly Lesson (Novella)
Forgive Me Father
At First Glance (Novella)
A Price to Pay
Out of Sight

Time to Kill

PAUL GITSHAM

ONE PLACE. MANY STORIES

HQ
An imprint of HarperCollins*Publishers* Ltd
1 London Bridge Street
London SE1 9GF

www.harpercollins.co.uk

HarperCollins*Publishers*
1st Floor, Watermarque Building, Ringsend Road
Dublin 4, Ireland

This paperback edition 2022

1
First published in Great Britain by
HQ, an imprint of HarperCollins*Publishers* Ltd 2022

Copyright © Paul Gitsham 2022

Emojis © Shutterstock.com

Paul Gitsham asserts the moral right to be
identified as the author of this work.
A catalogue record for this book is
available from the British Library.

ISBN: 9780008395322

MIX
Paper from
responsible sources
FSC™ C007454

This book is produced from independently certified FSC™ paper
to ensure responsible forest management.

For more information visit: www.harpercollins.co.uk/green

Printed and bound in the UK using
100% renewable electricity at CPI Group (UK) Ltd

To Emmeline. Welcome to the world!
One day I will write a book with three intrepid
heroes named Hugo, Oscar and Emmy.

To my beloved Cheryl.
Finally!

Prologue

Gaining access to his victim's home was as simple as ringing the doorbell.

Weeks of preparation and planning paid off; she was surprised but delighted he had popped over, on this of all nights.

She even made it easy for him by asking him to remove his shoes before he came in; no footprints at the scene.

He followed her into the kitchen, having accepted her offer of a drink, and that was where he struck – from behind, before she even had a chance to open the cupboard.

Killing her was easy. He was almost a foot and a half taller than her and more than double her weight. Both elbows on her shoulders, gloved hands in just the right place across her forehead, a jerk back, and her neck snapped like a twig. It was even easier than it appeared in the videos he'd watched on the internet; mind you, they assumed your victim was a muscular enemy combatant, not a bird-like octogenarian with osteoporosis.

She died without uttering a sound.

Wrestling her into the canvas decoy bag was a bit trickier than he'd anticipated. He'd placed a plastic refuse sack in there, in case of leakage, and it got tangled up with her body as he tried to manoeuvre her in.

He'd remember that in future.

An insistent scratching at the kitchen door reminded him of something else he needed to deal with.

As expected, the tiny dog's tail was wagging; as far as Benny was concerned, this was all some sort of game between his owner and the visitor he'd become accustomed to recently. The victim's choice of companion was a fortunate one for the killer; miniature poodles shed less fur than other breeds, limiting the risk of the animal's coat linking back to him prematurely.

Nevertheless, the dog was a loose end that could potentially scupper the whole plan if its barking alerted neighbours too soon. He'd need to deal with it.

That done, he was free to walk around the small bungalow. Doubtless his socks and the carpet were busy swapping fibres, but again, he'd planned for that.

Returning to the decoy bag, he placed her handbag, coat and clothing in with their late owner and pulled the drawstrings tight.

He swung the bag over his shoulder; it was heavy but not challenging. How much had she weighed? Six, seven stone?

His quiet grunt of effort was enough to draw the attention of Benny, who was otherwise occupied with the three days' worth of food and water that the killer had spread out on the kitchen floor. It should be enough to keep him going until somebody noticed his owner's absence and decided to stop by. At least the tiny dog could use the cat flap to relieve himself in his favoured corner of the garden; finding the dog shut in, starving and his crap all over the house, would have raised questions prematurely.

'Enjoy,' the killer muttered quietly, as he left through the front door, locking it behind him with her keys, before walking briskly down the garden path to the side street where he'd parked the car.

After popping the boot lid, he heaved the canvas bag in. The quiet thump of the body against the metal was drowned out by drifting music from the house party across the street.

He quickly disrobed and stuffed his outermost clothing in a garden *refuse sack and placed it in the boot. That done, he retrieved the plastic bag from the passenger footwell.*

Suddenly, the music from the house party stopped. He could hear voices now, counting down.

Shit! He looked at his watch and was shocked to see how much time had elapsed.

The counting reached one, and a fraction of a second later the hiss of a rocket startled him so much he dropped the bag of new clothes he was planning to wear over his undergarments. A moment later the sky ignited with a shower of bright pink light, followed by a series of rapid-fire crackles and pops.

Calm down! he counselled himself. Across the road, drunken voices launched into 'Auld Lang Syne'. Even if everyone gave up after the first couple of verses and decided to get some fresh air, he had time enough to put on his shoes and drive calmly away. The car was in good condition, he was a careful driver, and he hadn't touched a drop of alcohol. If the police pulled him over to breathalyse him, there was no reason to look in the boot.

Driving away, he was careful to keep his speed close enough to the limit not to raise suspicion. As he did so, he cursed his poor timekeeping; it could have scuppered everything.

He vowed to watch that in future.

In the rear-view mirror, the flashes of celebratory fireworks continued.

Wednesday 28th February

Chapter 1

Detective Chief Inspector Warren Jones' stomach tightened as the car approached the farmhouse.

'This is going to be a really bad one,' muttered Detective Inspector Tony Sutton, scrolling through his emails in the passenger seat.

It was the third time he'd mumbled his misgivings during the short journey from Middlesbury CID; whether he was preparing his friend for what they were about to see, or just speaking to himself, was unclear.

Warren pulled to a stop behind a pair of Scenes of Crime vans parked with their side doors open. Ahead of them, he recognised Detective Constable Moray Ruskin's car parked beside an ambulance. From the accounts they'd received, there was little for the paramedics to do. A half-dozen police cars were at the far end of the driveway.

Either side of the house's front door were four-wheel-drive vehicles: an older model Land Rover and a much newer Volvo SUV.

Stepping out of the car, he was greeted by DC Karen Hardwick. She'd unzipped the front of her paper suit and pushed her hood back. The chill wind whistling over the flat fields had turned the tip of her nose pink, but her complexion was otherwise unhealthily pale.

'How is it, Karen?' asked Warren.

She shook her head. 'Even Moray's lost his appetite.'

'That bad, huh?' said Sutton. Moray Ruskin had a famously sturdy constitution; however, the reports they'd received since the gruesome discovery suggested that even he would be challenged by the scene in the master bedroom.

'Where is Moray?' Warren asked.

'He's with the son in the back of the ambulance,' replied Hardwick. 'The poor man's being attended by the paramedics. Moray's trying to get a basic statement off him now, in case they need to take him to hospital.'

A familiar-shaped figure stepped through the open door of the farmhouse. A look of relief passed across Hardwick's face; with the arrival of Crime Scene Manager Andy Harrison, there would be no need for her to go back in to show the DCI around the incident.

'Thanks, Karen. Why don't you get changed and find some coffee?' said Warren as Harrison made his way over. 'Tony, go and introduce yourself to the son and find out what you can from Moray, then have a proper chat with Karen. I'll speak to Andy—' he gave a sigh '—and then go and have a look for myself.'

* * *

'First impression: murder-suicide,' said Harrison. The ordinarily jovial CSI was sombre; the sight before them was not only graphic, but also saddening.

'Tell me about the shotgun,' said Warren.

'A basic, double-barrelled, side-by-side. The sort used for vermin control and bagging the odd bunny.' He gave a grunt. 'Good enough for this though.'

The elderly couple sat upright in the bed, the woman on the

left, her husband on the right, their hands entwined. They both wore nightwear, and they'd removed their glasses and hearing aids. Their bedside lamps still glowed.

All apparently normal.

If you ignored the blood of course.

A technician dusted a glass tumbler for prints on the table to the right-hand side of the bed. On the opposite side, another technician was sealing a clear, plastic evidence bag containing another tumbler; a second bag contained an empty plastic screw-cap pot, with a white prescription label stuck to it. On the husband's side of the bed, a 70cl bottle of Teacher's Highland Cream Whisky was almost empty.

'The tumblers smell of spirits and the label on the pot suggests there were some pretty heavy-duty painkillers in there,' said Harrison. 'There's some residue in the bottom of both glasses, so it looks as though they were dissolved in the drink. I'll leave it up to the prof to determine if they took enough that this—' he gestured at the horror show before them '—wasn't actually necessary.'

'Maybe there were only a couple of pills left and they were worried that wouldn't do the job?' said Warren.

The wife's head lolled to one side, her eyes closed, her skin a waxy pallor. It was impossible to say which of the blood spatters on the wall behind the couple had come from the gaping hole in her chest, but the bits of skull and brain matter had definitely come from her husband.

'The angle was a bit awkward, obviously,' said Harrison, 'but as you can see, he was able to place the barrel under his chin, then hook his thumb around the trigger.'

Warren looked at the man's hand. It was far better to stare at that than the remains of his head. Thank goodness he'd decided to skip lunch when the call came in.

Harrison was right. At first glance, it appeared to be a murder-suicide. The husband shot the wife, then took his own life. It looked as though they had consumed pills and alcohol first.

9

The question was why? An argument? A mercy killing, followed by remorse? A suicide pact? Did the woman drink the pill-laden whisky voluntarily, or had her husband tricked or forced her into consuming it? Had she known what was going to happen?

For the sake of the man waiting in the back of the ambulance, Warren hoped she had been a party to it; it was the only circumstance in which he could envisage any sort of comfort, no matter how cold. At least the bedroom door had been closed, stopping the family dog from wandering in. Pets were notorious for contaminating a scene. Or worse.

Warren looked at the radio alarm clock on the husband's bedside table. It was already mid-afternoon. Until they knew exactly what had taken place in this bedroom, he and his team would be working flat out.

Even if he made it home before his wife turned in, he'd be sleeping in the spare room.

There was no point his nightmares keeping them both awake.

Chapter 2

Warren called a team meeting immediately after returning to Middlesbury station.

'Indications are murder-suicide by shotgun, instigated by Mr Culverhouse, possibly with pills and alcohol involved. The post-mortem is scheduled for tomorrow morning.'

Ruskin took over. 'I spoke to their only son, Derek. Apparently, his mother was terminally ill with bowel cancer, but had decided to forgo treatment. After surviving breast cancer twenty years ago, she couldn't face going through radiation and chemo again. That would seem to be a compelling motive, but they were due to celebrate their fiftieth wedding anniversary next month. She was really looking forward to it; her sister was flying in from New Zealand especially. The whole family knew it would be her farewell party, and Derek can't understand why his father would kill her now.'

'Karen, get on to the couple's GP and see if anything had changed lately,' said Warren. 'Maybe Mrs Culverhouse's prognosis worsened, and they decided to go out on their own terms. Check his records also; caring for a terminally ill loved one takes its toll. He might have been undergoing a mental health crisis.'

He turned to DS Pymm, the unit's 'officer in the case' who

was in charge of coordinating the flow of information through the investigation and keeping the HOLMES2 database up to date.

'Rachel, can you take us through the background we have so far?'

Pymm pushed her glasses onto her nose and read from her tablet computer.

'The house has been the Culverhouses' family residence for the past forty-odd years. It was a farmhouse originally, but the neighbouring farm bought the land off the previous owner. The nearest residence is almost half a mile away, with no direct line of sight to the bedroom. Nobody reported any gunshots or suspicious activity.'

'The windows were double-glazed and closed, along with the curtains,' confirmed Hardwick. 'You'd need to have been standing on the driveway to hear anything or see the muzzle flash.'

'How well did the neighbours know the couple?' asked Sutton.

'They knew them to chat to,' replied Pymm. 'They confirmed what the son said about his mother's illness. The last time they spoke to Mr Culverhouse was a couple of weeks ago in the local supermarket. He said the couple were looking forward to the warmer weather and mentioned their wedding anniversary. Again, the implication was that it would be one last celebration.'

'Do we have anything more on the gun?' asked Warren.

'It's been sent off to Forensics, to confirm it was the weapon used,' said Pymm, 'but the description, a Webley 12 bore, matches the sole gun registered to him. He's had a licence for forty-odd years and the last spot inspection revealed he kept it in a suitable gun cabinet, with the keys inaccessible to the grandkids. No concerns or reports about him in all that time.'

'Speaking of grandkids,' said Warren, 'what was the family set-up?'

'Just the son, no other children,' said Pymm. 'Mrs Culverhouse had a sister in New Zealand; Mr Culverhouse a younger brother. The rest of the extended family live some distance away; they keep in touch but don't visit regularly. Those we've contacted so far were surprised and shocked; they all mentioned the anniversary party and none of them had heard of any change in circumstances.'

Murder-suicides could be a mess to deal with, but much of that burden would be borne by the coroner. The focus of his team's investigation would be establishing the sequence of events and ruling out any foul play. Determining the motive would ultimately be the goal of the inquest.

'Keep plugging away, see if anything turns up,' Warren ordered. A thought occurred to him. 'Hutch is back in tomorrow, isn't he? Hand over coordinating the inquiries to him; ease him back in gently.'

Pymm smirked. 'Delighted to; it'll be a lovely way to welcome him back,' she said.

'Hmm,' he responded, eying her suspiciously. The woman was up to something.

Thursday 1st March

Chapter 3

'Here he is,' announced Pymm, as the escalator doors pinged open.

'Welcome back,' Sutton greeted DS David Hutchinson as he gingerly stepped out of the lift. Warren heard the commotion outside and exited his office to say hello.

'Don't worry, your desk is how you left it,' said Mags Richardson, as she hugged her fellow sergeant. 'There should be a lovely layer of mould on your coffee cup, just the way you like it.'

'We were going to run it through the dishwasher,' said Ruskin, 'but we didn't want to damage it. We know how rare a cup with Newcastle United on the side is.'

'Funny man,' grumbled Hutchinson as he lowered himself into his chair. Watching his beloved football team play was the one of the few times his native Geordie accent resurfaced.

'Well, we've missed you,' said Pymm. 'So, I've baked a cake to welcome you back.'

'You shouldn't have,' said Hutchinson as Hardwick removed a large Tupperware container from beneath Pymm's desk. 'Oh, you absolute git,' he groaned as Hardwick removed the cake, an iced sponge in the shape of a motorcycle helmet with 'midlife crisis' iced on the side.

'Very, funny,' he groused as the team laughed. 'Well anyway, this is the last I'll be seeing of a motorbike helmet.'

'Mrs H won the argument, did she?' asked Sutton.

'Yes, and the kids backed her up. According to my lovely daughter: "Old men have no business travelling on anything with fewer than four wheels."'

'Well, don't say I didn't warn you,' said Richardson, squeezing his shoulder.

'Couldn't afford to anyway – the bike's a complete write-off and the insurance money's been earmarked for a family holiday.'

'Probably for the best,' said Warren. 'How's the ankle?'

'Sore. I'm still hobbling a bit, but they've given me some physio. I'll be back to normal soon.'

'You can borrow my mobility scooter,' said Pymm. 'You won't even need a helmet.'

'Well, at least your cake-cutting arm still works,' said Hardwick, handing him a knife.

Despite the teasing, everyone was relieved to see him back at work; his recent motorcycle accident could have been far worse. Over the past few years, the team had lost several members, and had a few near misses. The thought of attending another friend's funeral had caused the resurgence of the troubling dreams that had plagued Warren since the sudden, violent death of Gary Hastings three and a half years previously.

After taking his slice of cake, Warren carried it back to his office. He'd more than earned the calories he reasoned, after squeezing in fifty lengths at the local pool that morning, but he decided to save it for later. Experience had taught him that an empty stomach was the best preparation for what was to come next.

* * *

Warren hated autopsies. And this one was going to be *really* horrible. As senior investigating officer, it was up to him to attend or assign someone else in his place, but as the appointed hour drew near, the office became suspiciously empty, with only the desk-bound Pymm left. He had jokingly asked DSI Grayson if he fancied joining him, just for old times' sake, but the superintendent had so far managed to dodge even looking at the more graphic crime scene photos and he'd been given short shrift.

Professor Ryan Jordan, the American-born Home Office licensed pathologist serving North Hertfordshire, had transported the remains of the Culverhouses to his morgue in Stevenage the evening before, and had now completed his preliminary examinations.

'Both killed by gunshot. Fragments of pellets retrieved from both victims are consistent with the shotgun found at the scene and cartridges stored in the downstairs gun cabinet. They were both alive at the time of the shooting.'

Warren nodded, exaggerating his head movement so he could be seen behind his personal protective equipment. The last part of the verdict was important; if the couple were dead at the time of the shootings, it would indicate somebody else had been involved, rather than it being a murder-suicide.

He suggested as much.

Jordan shook his head. 'I'm not ready to accept that yet.'

'You've found a discrepancy?'

'Perhaps.'

Warren followed him to the head of the trolley Jemima Culverhouse lay upon, trying to conceal his reluctance.

The elderly woman's eyes were now closed. With the skilful ministrations of an undertaker, she would be presentable enough for an open casket, should the family wish. It was more than could be said for her husband, whose near-headless corpse was now behind Warren. He tried not to remember what was underneath the sheet.

'If you look closely at her top lip, you can see there is some residue coating it. It could be foundation, but that seems unlikely

19

given that they were both clearly ready for bed and there is no evidence of any other make-up. I've sent it off to toxicology.'

He gently reached into her mouth, pulling the lips back. A bottom front tooth was chipped.

'I found the fragment in her stomach, along with whisky and more powder. She had also aspirated some of the spirit.' He turned her jaw slightly. Under the bright overhead lights, the darkness on the skin was visible. 'Looks like her jaw was held.'

'She was forced to drink it,' concluded Warren. 'Which is consistent with her husband drugging her before shooting her.'

He sighed. He knew that if he was in Derek Culverhouse's shoes, he would have been praying his parents had decided to end their lives together; that Stanley Culverhouse had ground up his wife's pain medication and dissolved it in whisky, perhaps holding it to her lips to help her drink it. But if Stanley Culverhouse managed to chip his wife's tooth whilst feeding her the pills-laden whisky, then perhaps he was doing it against her will.

'I believe so,' said Jordan, 'but there's more. Mr Culverhouse also had some whisky in his lungs, although for obvious reasons, I can't tell if the glass was forced against his lips.'

'It could just have gone down the wrong way,' said Warren, trying not to think about the headless corpse. 'If we're correct, he was drinking neat whisky with medication dissolved in it, and he'd just forced his wife to consume it against her will. If he was crying, that could have made him choke.'

'Possibly, but come and look at this.'

He headed to the trolley holding the morgue's other occupant. Warren steeled himself as his stomach flipped. Thankfully, Jordan ignored the misshapen, covered lump where the man's head had been, and instead lifted the right hand.

'Mr Culverhouse was in reasonable shape for a man of his age but he was on blood thinners after a minor heart attack, and he bruised very easily.' Jordan carefully extended the index finger. 'This is probably the finger that would have been used when pulling the trigger to shoot his wife. If you look here, under the nail and on the finger pad, there is evidence of the early stages of bruising.'

Warren suddenly felt as if the temperature in the chilled morgue dropped even further.

'Could he have caught it on something earlier in the day?' he asked.

'If he did, it was only a few minutes before he died. The bruising is only visible under close examination.'

Jordan flipped the man's hand over, showing the back of his thumb. 'See this scratch? It hasn't broken the skin, just scraped the top layer of cells off. I think it came from the inside of the trigger guard. He needed to use his thumb to pull the trigger, because the shotgun was pointing the wrong way. He could have been pretty intoxicated by this point and a bit clumsy ...'

'Or somebody could have forced his thumb into that trigger guard,' finished Warren.

Chapter 4

Warren and Sutton were driving back out to the Culverhouse residence to meet again with CSM Harrison. As usual, the car radio had burst into something entirely inappropriate the moment Warren started the engine. This time his friend's teasing had been more muted than usual.

'If we have to listen to Eighties music, perhaps something by The Cure – rather than "Walking On Sunshine" – would get us in the right mood?'

'Or make me wrap the car around a tree at eighty miles per hour,' Warren countered. The banter had become a comfortable routine over the years and Warren secretly looked forward to Sutton's taunts.

'Did Andy say what was bothering him?' asked Sutton.

'Not really. Inconsistencies at the scene was all he said,' replied Warren. He thought back to the morning's autopsy. He'd just finished relaying Prof Jordan's finding to the rest of the team when Harrison called.

It was rare for an officer of Warren's rank to be so hands-on in an investigation. A senior investigating officer ordinarily remained at the station whilst junior officers fed back to them. They would certainly visit the scene of a high-profile murder, but it would typically be after the initial scene processing had been

22

completed, and the crime scene manager would be unlikely to call the SIO directly. As for interviewing suspects and going to visit witnesses – that was highly unusual.

But then Middlesbury CID wasn't the usual sort of place. The major crime teams for Hertfordshire, Bedfordshire, and Cambridgeshire constabularies had merged some years previously and now operated out of Hertfordshire's Welwyn Garden City headquarters. But vehement lobbying by Warren's predecessor had resulted in Middlesbury CID gaining a reprieve as a local 'first-response' CID unit, serving Middlesbury and the surrounding towns and villages in the northernmost tip of Hertfordshire.

Detective Superintendent John Grayson was in charge, and invariably delegated SIO duties to Warren, deftly taking credit for the team's successes, whilst carefully dodging any blowback from their rare failures.

Of course, such an arrangement was expensive, and there were those who felt that in these times of ever-shrinking budgets but increasing workload, Middlesbury's existence was a luxury the force could ill afford. The threat of closure had hung over the unit for the almost seven years Warren had worked there. Warren's predecessor had been passionate that Middlesbury retain its unique role, a position Warren had come to agree with. As long as they continued to deliver their enviable results, then DSI Grayson would use his clout in Welwyn to maintain the status quo.

But the future wasn't written yet, and Warren was conscious that with the changes on the horizon, his time doing the aspects of policing he loved the most – but which his peers had discontinued several promotions ago – might be coming to an end.

He glanced over at Sutton, wondering how many more times the two of them would be heading out to a crime scene, or breaking the will of a suspect with their good cop, bad cop routines.

He vowed to enjoy it whilst he could.

* * *

'It doesn't smell right,' said Harrison. The veteran CSI had processed thousands of crime scenes and Warren knew to listen when he spoke. 'First off, the pills.'

They were standing in the kitchen. The farmhouse was over two hundred years old, but the kitchen was brand new. Gleaming marble countertops, stainless steel fittings and modern appliances; a substantial amount of money had gone into its recent renovation. Warren and Susan were awaiting a new kitchen, having decided to get it done now, before a week of microwave-only cooking and washing dishes in the sink in the downstairs loo became impractical with their new arrival. Nothing in this room fell within their budget.

Harrison walked them over to the sink. On the draining board sat a black granite pestle and mortar. The depression in the mortar had a fine residue of faint green powder. The pounding end of the pestle was similarly dusted.

'We've already sent the powder off for toxicology, but I left this where it is; I wanted to see if you agree with what I think is wrong with the scene.'

Warren resisted the urge to pinch his bottom lip through his mask as he thought.

'They are both dry,' said Sutton. 'So, the whisky wasn't added to the mortar after the tablets were ground up.'

'That's probably not the most efficient way to do it,' conceded Warren, 'but he could have ground half the pills first, poured them into the tumbler and dissolved them in the alcohol, then repeated the action. He might even have done his wife before deciding to kill himself as well.'

'Quite possible,' said Harrison. 'But look again and tell me what is missing.'

'The pill container,' said Sutton suddenly.

'Which was sitting on Mrs Culverhouse's bedside table,' said Warren. He thought back to the transcript he'd read of Derek Culverhouse's statement.

'According to their son, the pills were locked in the bathroom

24

cabinet away from the grandkids. Mr Culverhouse was very strict about that, and he was in charge of doling out their daily meds. So why would he bring the tablets downstairs, prepare the pills, then take the empty container back to the bedside table? Why not leave it in the kitchen or remove the pills in the bathroom and leave the container in the cabinet?'

Sutton's eyebrows knitted together above his mask as he frowned. 'Again, it could be dismissed as him not being in the right frame of mind.'

'Then there's the whisky bottle. Same thing,' said Harrison. 'It was sitting on the bedside table. So, did he grind the pills in the kitchen, pour the powder into the tumbler and then add the whisky upstairs? That seems a strange order of events.'

'He could have done it down here, then taken the bottle back upstairs for a little more Dutch courage,' said Sutton.

'Have the fingerprints come back from the tumblers and the bottle yet?' asked Warren.

'Yes. Stanley Culverhouse's prints were on both tumblers and the whisky bottle, but his wife's were on neither, which fits the theory that he made her drink the mixture. There was an unknown set on the bottle. It could be significant, or it could be the sales assistant from where it was bought.'

'Both of their prints were on the pill container. There were no obvious prints on the pestle and mortar; we'll use cyanoacrylate back at the lab and see if we can lift anything useful.'

Warren pondered the findings. Harrison was right; the scene didn't smell quite right to him either. He asked for the high-resolution scene photographs to be sent to Pymm as soon as possible, the faint stirrings of an idea at the back of his brain.

'What else have you got for us, Andy?' asked Sutton.

'The gun cabinet.' Harrison guided the two detectives over to a door leading into a large utility room with an outside door. Standing on the threshold, he pointed to a green metal cabinet fixed to the far wall.

25

'Old man Culverhouse was assiduous about keeping his shotgun licence up to date, and the cabinet is fitted with a decent padlock.' Harrison turned to his left. 'But he kept the key with the rest of the house keys on these pegs. He even labelled them with a tag. The gun had been taken out, then the cabinet was relocked, and the key hung back on the peg. Now why would you do that, if the plan was to blow your brains out in the bedroom? Even if he originally intended to just shoot his wife and claim it was a home invasion, with the thief taking the shotgun with them, why would he lock the cabinet again? We've dusted the key for prints and there's nothing on there, not even his.'

'That is strange,' agreed Warren.

'Look, I'm not a detective, and I know there are plenty of rational explanations – not least that he was *irrational* when he did this – but it doesn't seem right to me,' said Harrison. 'I'm also not happy about the positioning of the shotgun.'

'In what way?' asked Sutton.

'Well for a start, it was still underneath where his chin used to be. His arms were just long enough for him to the manipulate the gun into position and pull the trigger with his thumb, but he wouldn't have been able to brace it against anything other than the duvet. The kick-back from that calibre shotgun should have sent it halfway across the room.'

Chapter 5

Warren called a team briefing immediately after a lengthy meeting with DSI Grayson.

'At this moment in time, we are still treating the death of the Culverhouses as "unexplained", but I am leaning towards double murder,' he started. 'Professor Jordan is confident that the bodies had been lying there for at least eight hours before we arrived on Wednesday, but they could have been shot any time before then, including immediately after their son's visit on Sunday. He can't be certain who died first, or if there was a significant delay between the two deaths.'

With the help of Tony Sutton, he ran through the discrepancies from the autopsy and the inconsistencies at the crime scene.

Karen Hardwick was the first to speak up. 'Something else is bugging me. I can accept that they may have decided to change into their pyjamas, because they wanted to die in bed together, but they had both removed their hearing aids. That suggests to me they had already gone to sleep for the night, before being woken up.'

'Not to mention one of Mr Culverhouse's aids is missing,' said Sutton.

'Hmm. Then let's start with who might have had a motive,' instructed Warren.

'I've got some preliminary background, but nothing jumps out,' said Hutchinson. 'Stanley Culverhouse was an engineer. He worked for the same small consultancy firm for his whole career, starting as an apprentice straight after school and working his way up to management, before being given a gold watch on his sixty-fifth birthday. He earned a good wage and had a generous pension; enough to pay off the mortgage. The firm still exists, and the woman running HR remembered him and said he was extremely well liked. She can't recall any unpleasantness whilst he was there.'

'He's been retired what, twelve years?' asked Sutton. 'That seems a long time to hold a grudge.'

'I agree,' said Warren. 'What has he done since then?'

'Nothing remarkable,' Hutchinson continued. 'He played bowls, although less so since his wife became ill. He kept up with a few of his friends, popping out for a pint now and again, otherwise he just seems … normal.'

'What about his wife?' asked Ruskin.

'She was a primary schoolteacher, up until she took early retirement after her first bout of cancer. Again, nothing stands out. Several of the current staff worked with her, and a couple were even taught by her, and nobody had a bad word to say. After she recovered from her first cancer, she played bowls with her husband and was a member of the Women's Institute for a few years, but that all stopped when she got ill again.'

'What about robbery?' asked Hardwick. 'Their house is pretty nice, and you said Mr Culverhouse had a decent pension.'

'You saw the scene,' said Hutchinson. 'It didn't look as if anything had been obviously taken. His gold watch was sitting on the dressing table, alongside some of Mrs Culverhouse's jewellery. They didn't own a tablet or any expensive devices, and the TV was untouched. They had mobile phones, but they were cheap, basic handsets. If it was a burglary, they're just the type a junkie might nick to sell on as burners, but they were sitting in

28

the kitchen, charging. They weren't into expensive art and there wasn't a safe.'

'The farmhouse was cheap when they got a mortgage on it, back in the Seventies,' interjected Pymm. 'They've done a lot of work on it, most recently a new kitchen. Financial records show they were comfortably off, with some investments ticking away and a few thousand in a savings account, but it looks to me like most of their money was being saved for a rainy day or their son's inheritance.'

'Speaking of which …' said Warren.

'That's where we may want to start looking harder,' said Pymm. 'They only have the one son, and presumably he stands to inherit everything. The farmhouse is worth a lot now, and it looks like he could use the money – they've been helping him out. Plus, somebody cared enough about the family dog to leave some food out.'

'What have you got on him?' asked Warren. If they were looking at a double homicide, then the first place to look was close to home. The farmhouse had a burglar alarm, but it was an old model and it didn't keep a log of when it was set and unset. Their son had disabled it when he went around and discovered the bodies. How many other people knew the alarm's code?

'They have been giving him handouts for the past few years. Five hundred quid here, a thousand there,' Pymm said. 'I ran the details for his nice, shiny SUV and there is a bank transfer of five thousand pounds to him just before he registered the car from new. That sounds like the sort of deposit a dealer might ask for on a new vehicle.'

'OK, we should be able to get a warrant for Derek's bank records,' said Warren. 'Whilst you're at it, get the records for all their phones and any linked to him. Hutch, start digging. Find out his work and family circumstances. We know they had grandkids so presumably they are his. Find out what the relationship was like with his parents. He seemed pretty upset when we spoke to him yesterday, but that could have been an act.'

He turned to Richardson, the team's video specialist.

'Sorry, sir, it's slim pickings. They had a basic alarm but no CCTV. The neighbours do have CCTV, but they are so far away it won't be any use. The cameras don't have sound either, so we can't even use the audio to put a time to the gunshots.'

'I suppose speed cameras and ANPR are out of the question?'

'I'm afraid so. The nearest cameras are on the A road a couple of miles away. I'll compile a list of drivers with a heavy right foot around the time they were killed, but the cameras are well signposted – there won't be many caught. I'll also put a call out for any mobile ANPR units, but the odds of a random patrol car recording a vehicle in that area during the period we're interested in are pretty low.'

'Coordinate with Hutch and see if we can pick up the son's car anywhere it shouldn't be,' said Warren. 'If he claims to have been in all night and we capture his licence plate out and about, we might be able to catch him in a lie.'

Friday 2nd March

Chapter 6

Warren was in the office early; his sleep the night before had been predictably poor, plagued with nightmares about headless corpses. It was coming up on forty-eight hours since Derek Culverhouse discovered his parents. The team all had their assigned roles and so he retired to his office, the door open. Experience told him that the pace of the case would pick up markedly once the forensic reports started coming in and his officers' investigations started to bear fruit, so he took the opportunity to clear his inbox. He had a court appearance for a previous case in a couple of weeks that needed preparation, so he focused his attention on that.

'I got the preliminary findings back from NABIS,' said Harrison, who'd called Warren directly, late that afternoon. 'I'll send the complete report through to you, but basically, they were both shot with the gun Mr Culverhouse was holding.'

The National Ballistics Intelligence Service had taken the gun as soon as Harrison's team had finished processing it. Warren didn't know how many favours he'd called in to get it looked at so quickly, but he was grateful.

'Not unexpected, but good to know,' said Warren. He couldn't think of a compelling reason why the couple would have been shot with a different weapon, when the Culverhouses' own shotgun was clearly available, but it was important to clarify such details if the case ever went to trial.

'But it's the evidence on the gun itself I'm interested in,' said Harrison.

'How so?' said Warren, immediately alert.

'We processed the gun for trace and found Mr Culverhouse's fingerprints on the trigger and the guard, as you'd expect. There were some skin cells on the inside of the trigger guard, consistent with the scrapes Ryan Jordan found on the back of his trigger finger. We'll have the DNA back from those cells soon. It's the blood spatter that concerns me.'

'In what way?' asked Warren.

'The end of the barrel had a spatter consistent with a close-range shotgun discharge, plus a bit of what we assume is Mr Culverhouse's brain. The blood and flesh will have hit the wall behind them with significant force, and some of it will have blown back. We're still waiting for DNA, but blood typing is consistent with Mrs Culverhouse's blood being on her husband's pyjama front, as if he sat opposite her on the bed, pointed the gun at her chest, and pulled the trigger.'

'OK.'

'Then it appears as though he turned around, climbed under the duvet, took his wife's hand, then placed the gun barrel under his chin. Again, the spatter on the bedding is consistent with that interpretation.'

Warren swallowed and bid him to continue.

'There is also lots of what we believe is his blood, not to mention flesh, on the gun barrel, his arms and the quilt. The shape of the drops indicates that at least some of them dripped from what remained of his head.'

Warren *really* wished Harrison would get to the point.

'All of that works. What doesn't work, is the blood on the gunstock.'

34

'What do you mean?'

'When he fired the gun at his wife, the wooden stock of the shotgun would have been facing him, probably pressed against his shoulder. Then, when he turned the gun on himself, the gun would have been rotated, so the wooden stock would have been away from him, pointing downwards towards the bed.'

'OK, I can picture that.'

'There were smears our preliminary blood-grouping has identified as Mr Culverhouse's on the butt end of the stock – on the opposite end where I'd expect it to be. As well as what looks like bloody mucus.'

'What are you saying, Andy?'

'Well, I can only suggest possible scenarios, but if you told me somebody had smashed Mr Culverhouse in the face with the butt of his shotgun before shooting him, perhaps breaking his nose, I wouldn't disagree with you.'

'And a point-blank shotgun blast to the face will pretty much ensure we can never be certain,' finished Warren.

* * *

'Share what you have on Derek Culverhouse,' instructed Warren. The team had gathered to share their findings about the Culverhouses' only child. If they were going to pursue a grieving family member as a serious suspect, Warren wanted them fully armed before they brought him in.

Moray Ruskin, who'd taken a preliminary statement from him at the scene and conducted a more detailed follow-up interview, started with a basic biography of the man.

'He's their only child. Forty-three years old and lives on his own in Middlesbury. He visits most weekends and usually phones them mid-week. It was them not answering the phone that caused him to eventually drive over Wednesday and find them.'

'What does he do for a job?' asked Hutchinson.

'Something in retail – he skirted over the details when I asked him,' said Ruskin.

'He works in Morrisons,' interjected Pymm. 'I have his bank records and he has received a monthly salary from them for the past nine months. I don't know what his job is, but even if he only earns minimum wage, he can't be working more than twenty-five hours a week.'

'Which would explain why his parents were bunging him cash each month,' said Hardwick.

'And he needs it,' said Pymm. 'A hefty chunk of his income goes on child maintenance.'

'An ex-wife with a kid, and two by his ex-partner,' said Ruskin. 'He's quite bitter about that; he doesn't see why he should be paying so much, now they are both married with husbands to support them.'

'What a quaint world view,' said Pymm.

'What was he doing before he worked at Morrisons?' asked Sutton.

'According to his bank statements, he was unemployed for almost twelve months,' replied Pymm. 'Before then he worked at SG Logistics – at nearly three times his current salary.'

'That ties in with what one of the uniforms reported back from the Culverhouses' bowls club,' said Hutchinson. 'Most of the members had little to say, but one of the players mentioned in passing that it was a shame, "after all they'd been through". The officer assumed he was referring to the wife's illness, but when she pressed, he suggested Derek had been causing them worry for a number of years. It sounded like Derek was fulfilling his filial duties, but it wasn't all plain sailing.'

'Any indication how he lost his job?' asked Warren.

'He didn't know,' Hutchinson replied. 'I'll give SG Logistics a ring after we finish.'

Warren pondered what they had been told. It was circumstantial, but there was the glimmer of a motive. When it came to murder, greed or desperation were two of the strongest reasons for killing. Derek Culverhouse may have been an outwardly loving son, but to a man in his position, waiting for his inheritance to come naturally might have taken too long.

'Bring him in.'

* * *

Derek Culverhouse was a grey-haired, white-skinned man in his forties. He looked exhausted when he arrived at the station, a faint miasma of cigarette smoke and cologne surrounding him. Warren and the team had spent much of the morning debating their interview strategy. They wanted the interview to appear informal, so that Culverhouse didn't realise he was a potential suspect, but anything incriminating that he said would be inadmissible as evidence if he wasn't interviewed under caution. Warren hoped he wouldn't be spooked and refuse to cooperate.

He needn't have worried. Culverhouse had simply shrugged as he declined a solicitor, clearly keen to get the whole ordeal over with.

Warren had sat across from many killers in his time and would be the first to admit that his initial impressions had been wrong on many of those occasions. Whoever had killed the Culverhouses had been clever enough to stage the scene to make it look like a murder-suicide. That had taken planning. Furthermore, several days had passed since the murder, giving the culprit time to cover their tracks and rehearse their responses, should law enforcement come knocking on the door. The question Warren found himself asking, was were the puffy red eyes and shaking hands on the man before him the natural response of a loving son confronted by an unimaginably horrific scene, or those of a killer trying to look the part?

Or was it a combination of the two? Derek Culverhouse may have ruthlessly planned the slaying of his parents, but it would be an especially cold-blooded killer who committed such an act and was unmoved by it.

'Tell me a little about your parents, Derek,' said Warren.

'Please, call me Des,' he said. For the first time, a bleak smile crossed his face. 'The only people who call me Derek are the bank manager and my mum when I'm in trouble.' The line was automatic, and obviously well used. The smile disappeared as soon as he said it, as if he realised his mother would never call him that again.

He gave a shuddering sigh. 'Where to start?'

Warren waited patiently whilst he gathered his thoughts.

'They were happy – that's why I can't understand why Dad ...' he started again. 'The last couple of years had been difficult, obviously, but they bore Mum's illness well. They weren't religious, but they kind of accepted that life happens, you know; generally speaking, they were "glass half full" sort of people. Mum especially. She always said that she'd been luckier than most. She'd dodged a bullet twenty years ago, and so everything since was a bonus. She retired when she was first ill, but once she was in remission, she started making the most of life. Women's Institute, bowling, book clubs ... she even learned to bake, since she'd never really had the time when she was a teacher. When Dad retired, they went travelling. Three months in New Zealand visiting her sister and a month in Australia.' Again he smiled. 'She called it their gap year.

'I guess that's why she decided to accept it when the cancer came back. The treatment knocked her for six last time, so she decided to focus on her bucket list. Better to have a couple more good years than five more shitty years, was how she put it.'

He smiled bleakly. 'When we entered the "end game" – or the "victory lap" as she liked to call it – she started to obsess about their fiftieth wedding anniversary. It was going to be so special ...'

'How did your father take the news?' asked Warren.

'Pretty well. They made the decision together and presented

it as a *fait accompli*. What I can't understand is the timing,' said Culverhouse. 'Look, I never for one minute thought Mum and Dad would kill themselves. Dad's older brother committed suicide when he was in his forties and I don't think Dad ever really forgave him. After what it did to him and the rest of his family, he was always vocal about people making that choice. He wouldn't have wanted that for me or his grandchildren.'

Culverhouse took a sip of water, before leaning forward in his chair. His shoulders slumped, and when he started speaking again, his voice was weary. 'But, having said all that, I guess your perspective changes when you're faced with something like this. Mum was suffering – I know that. She was on painkillers to manage it, but it wasn't going to get any better. I can see how they might decide to hasten things in the last few weeks, but Mum wouldn't want Dad to get into trouble. The only scenario that would make any sense to me is that she would say all her goodbyes at the party, then sneak a few extra pills before going to sleep that night.'

He shuddered violently, pain crossing his features as his eyes took on a faraway cast. 'A shotgun … why? I can't understand why Dad would do that. Even if he decided to go with her, it's just so violent. They didn't even leave a note …'

Warren thought back to the chipped tooth in Jemima Culverhouse's stomach. 'And you don't think your father decided to do it as a mercy?'

Culverhouse shrugged helplessly. 'I still can't see it. When they decided not to pursue treatment for the cancer, that was Mum's decision. Dad always respected her wishes; I can't believe he would then go against them.'

Warren gave him a moment, before starting again. 'Then did something change recently?' he asked. 'Something that made one or both of your parents decide they couldn't bear the next few months?'

'Like what?'

'A visit to the doctor perhaps? Maybe to tell her the cancer was progressing faster than expected?'

The team were still awaiting a reply from the couple's GP and Jemima Culverhouse's specialists. Warren would take careful note of the man's response to the question and compare it to the doctors' feedback.

'No, not as far as I'm aware. I think her last appointment with the oncologist and the palliative care team was a couple of weeks ago and Mum said they were as happy as could be expected. She even joked they would still have to pay the full council tax bill, as Dad wouldn't be eligible for the single-person discount yet.' His voice quietened. 'There was certainly nothing wrong with her sense of humour.'

Suddenly Culverhouse leant his elbows on the table and buried his face in his hands. His shoulders started to shake. 'Sorry,' he mumbled, his voice thick with emotion.

'No need to apologise,' Warren reassured him. 'I tell you what, why don't we take a few minutes. You go and get some fresh air, and I'll sort us out some coffee?'

The two men left the room, Culverhouse heading towards the exit, cigarettes in hand, Warren towards the staircase.

Time for some outside perspective.

* * *

'If he was the killer, you'd expect him to be pushing the murder-suicide angle harder,' said Ruskin as he handed Warren a coffee. Ruskin had initially interviewed Culverhouse and Warren was keen to hear his thoughts.

Warren had decided to do the interview alone, with his notepad closed and the lid firmly on his biro. He wanted it to feel like a friendly chat. If Culverhouse had killed his parents, detailed note-taking may have unnerved him, and so Ruskin had watched the interview feed remotely.

40

'He's leaving it wide open to the possibility that their deaths were out of character and should be investigated further. He could easily have said his parents were depressed and had been speaking about ending it all. Open and shut; grieving son comforted by a large inheritance.'

'Unless it's a double bluff,' said Hutchinson. 'Everybody watches true crime documentaries these days. If anything, criminals think we're cleverer than we actually are.'

'Speak for yourself,' interjected Pymm.

'The point I'm making,' continued Hutchinson, 'is he could have figured that staging a murder-suicide successfully is a big ask, so why not address it head-on? Send us down the wrong path for a week, until he's sure he's in the clear, then when we do finally figure out it was a set-up, push the theory that it was a robbery gone wrong, or a recently uncovered grudge.'

'So we should watch what he says and who he points a finger at in the coming weeks?' said Sutton.

'Exactly. I wouldn't be the least bit surprised if the moment we announce it's a homicide investigation he suddenly remembers a disturbing phone call his parents received, or some argument they had.'

Warren considered what they had said. 'If that's true, then the robbery gone wrong, followed by a staged murder-suicide, doesn't really make sense. Aside from there being nothing missing, surely it would have been far easier to go with the botched burglary in the first place? Come in, shoot them in their beds, and then nick some jewellery to make it look convincing. Why all the subterfuge?'

'Maybe he's going to try and frame someone else?' suggested Richardson. 'We should probably take any potential suspects he suggests with a large pinch of salt.'

'Or maybe he suspects who really did do it, and he's trying to push us towards investigating the case properly, without putting himself in the firing line,' said Ruskin.

Warren raised a hand to stop anymore suggestions. 'OK, folks,

I get what you're saying but let's not overcomplicate matters at the moment. The most straightforward explanation is he killed his parents to get a jump on his inheritance, and he staged the scene to make it look like they decided to check out early because his mum was suffering, and his dad didn't want to stick around without her or face the music.

'We'll keep an open mind, but for the time being, let's focus on Derek. He has motive, and he had the means – presumably he knew the alarm code, where the gun was kept and the details of his mother's medication. The question is, did he have the opportunity?'

Warren looked at his watch. 'He's had plenty of time to finish his fag. I'll take him down a fresh coffee and some biscuits and see if he has an alibi.'

He started walking in the direction of the communal urn, before pausing and turning around. 'You were wrong about one thing, Hutch. You said that because of TV, criminals think we are cleverer than we really are. Well Andy Harrison clocked that the scene was staged within twenty-four hours. I reckon even *CSI* would be proud of that.'

*   *   *

Derek Culverhouse took a grateful slurp of his coffee and reached for a biscuit. Warren had opted for a plate of supermarket-brand rich tea, rather than custard creams; he couldn't bring himself to offer decent biscuits to a potential murderer. The desk sergeant had reported that Culverhouse had stood outside the main entrance, smoking two cigarettes, one after another. A sign of nerves perhaps, but he'd seemed more contemplative than anxious, spending the time staring into space, not even checking his mobile phone. The experienced officer had seen hundreds of grieving relatives over the years, and even more guilty suspects. In his opinion, Culverhouse was the former.

'Before your parents were shot, it looks as though they took

42

pills dissolved in whisky,' said Warren. 'Do you know anything about that?'

'I guess the pills were Mum's,' said Culverhouse. 'She took oxycodone for the pain.' He gave a bleak smile. 'She used to joke that opiates get bad press, but the doctors figured it wasn't a big deal if she spent her last couple of years as a junkie.'

'What about the whisky?' asked Warren.

'I think it was in the cupboard downstairs. Mum hadn't drunk alcohol for years and since they put him on the blood thinners after his heart attack, Dad pretty much stopped. He had a glass of red wine on Christmas Day with his lunch – which is probably why he slept all afternoon.' He frowned. 'I think he may have had a whisky with his brother to see the new year in.'

If neither of the couple were big drinkers, it might explain why they had aspirated some of the liquid, thought Warren. If the spirit had been neat, mixed with the pills, it could well have made them choke. Again, Culverhouse would probably have known about the bottle, and if he had been careless enough to get his prints on it, he could easily explain them away. An idea was forming; he made a note to ask Karen to look into it.

'You may have been the last person to see them alive,' said Warren, carefully. 'You went out on Sunday; did they seem at all different to you?'

'Not really. Dad was talking about going to see Stevenage play in a couple of weeks if he could get someone to look after Mum. Mum was talking about the party; she wanted to order a cake from the bakery in town.' His brows knitted together in frustration. 'That's the thing. They were making plans. They didn't sound like they were intending to end it all in the next few days.'

'And did you drop them back home, or did your father drive?'

'I drove us. My car's more comfortable and Mum's wheelchair fits in the back more easily.'

'Did they say anything when you got back? Any throwaway comments that might not have seemed relevant at the time?'

43

'Nothing. Dad and I chatted about the weather on the drive home, whilst Mum dozed. I didn't stay long when we got back; I just helped Mum into the house. It was still early and she wasn't ready for bed, so we put her in her armchair with a fleece so she could have a nap. I let myself out and went home.'

'And you didn't go anywhere this week? You didn't pop to see your kids or go down the pub?'

'No, I tend not to visit pubs these days.'

'You told us you tried to call them at your usual time on the Tuesday?' Warren asked.

'Yeah, I called the landline. There's no point trying to get them on their mobiles. Even if they're charged, they're usually in the kitchen switched off.' He sniffed. 'I saw my parents on Sunday; they seemed normal to me, and that was the last I heard from them.

'I don't know why Dad did it, I really don't. I haven't slept for days. I keep on thinking about the last time I saw them, racking my brains for a reason why it happened. Something they said, perhaps some hint? Maybe I wasn't listening hard enough? Could I have stopped it from happening?' He sniffed again and fumbled in his pocket for a tissue.

'I'm really sorry for your loss, Des,' said Warren. 'My team and I just want to work out what happened, so you can move on.'

'No I'm sorry,' said Culverhouse. 'You've all been very kind. Especially that big Scottish lad – I didn't catch his name. Please thank him for me. I don't know what I would have done …'

'It was DC Ruskin, and I'm sure he'll be pleased to hear he was able to help. Do you have any questions for me?'

'I haven't really thought about it. When will the bodies be released? I need to start planning everything.'

'That's up to the coroner, I'm afraid, but we'll let you know as soon as possible.'

'Is that it?' asked Culverhouse.

'For now. I'll see you out.'

That done, Warren headed back up to CID. Culverhouse

claimed that he was home alone in the days before his parents'
death. That was his alibi.

Now they needed to confirm it.

* * *

The day's final findings came from Karen Hardwick.

'I've been following up that idea you had about the whisky
bottle; it's just what you suspected. I'll email you everything I
found.'

'Good. What else?' asked Warren.

'My hunch about the powder coating the pestle and mortar
looks like it may have paid off.'

'Go on.'

'Bear in mind we still haven't had the toxicology reports back
from the victims, or the chemical analysis of the residue in the
tumblers and the powder on the pestle and mortar,' she cautioned.

'But …'

'The powder on the pestle and mortar had a green tint.
According to the empty packet, the oxycodone tablets that Jemima
Culverhouse was prescribed were an off-white, buff colour.'

'If the ground-up pills, which were presumably the ones
dissolved in the whisky, weren't oxycodone,' said Warren, 'then
why was Jemima's empty pill container on the bedside table?
Coincidence? Or were there too few pills left for the killer to be
confident there was enough for both of them?'

The date on the pot had indicated that if she was taking them
as prescribed, then she was close to the end of her supply. In
which case, what had they used instead of the oxycodone and
where had it come from? It also indicated the killer might have
known exactly how many pills remained in the medicine cabinet,
again pointing towards their son.

'Given how the scene was staged, they're clearly forensically
aware,' continued Warren. 'Surely they would have known that

another drug could be picked up by a toxicology screen?

'That's where it gets interesting,' said Hardwick. 'I had a look online and oxycodone comes in several different strengths. Jemima Culverhouse was prescribed the twenty-milligram version, which are buff-coloured. There is an eighty-milligram pill, which is a pale green colour. Which also happens to be the most popular strength sold illegally.'

'And because it's still oxycodone, it won't show up as unexpected in the toxicology screen,' finished Warren. 'Clever bastard.'

Saturday 3rd March

Chapter 7

'How are the phone records looking?' asked Warren, addressing the early morning briefing. He'd arrived home at a decent hour the night before; he was taking advantage of the brief lull to spend some time with his wife. Quality time alone would be in short supply in a few months, so he was making the most of it. He knew he had a tendency to overwork during investigations; it was a fault he was trying hard to correct.

'I have records for the Culverhouses' mobile phones and land-lines,' said Pymm. 'Derek never uses his landline; he uses his mobile. His parents on the other hand rarely used their mobiles for anything other than texts. I also have the location data for all three phones.'

'Have you cross-referenced them yet?' asked Sutton. 'It might give an insight into the relationship with their son.'

'I have,' said Pymm, 'and "dutiful" springs to mind. It matches what he's told us so far. In a typical week he phones them on a Tuesday evening at about eight. The calls rarely last more than five or ten minutes at most. On the Sunday morning he usually texts them. Later on the Sunday, there may be a couple of texts sent between them. Based on what he told you at the scene, I suspect Tuesday night is his duty call and the texts on the Sunday morning are to let them know he's coming over.'

She swiped the screen on her tablet. 'For the location data, Derek's mobile typically leaves his house on the Sunday morning, immediately after he sends the text, and arrives at his parents' house, where it either stays for the next two or three hours, or sometimes leaves, along with one or both his parents' phones, and travels to places such as the local garden centre or a National Trust property. This Sunday, it looks as though they took a trip around the Ellacott Estate.'

'That matches what he told me,' interjected Ruskin. 'He said he'd sometimes take his mum and dad out on a Sunday.'

'Those are also the Sundays that they exchange text messages later in the day,' said Pymm. 'I'm speculating, but if it's anything like going out with my parents, the messages are probably along the lines of "Where are you? We've been waiting outside the toilet for ages." IT are looking through their handsets to see if the texts say anything more interesting. At least the phones are too old for encrypted apps like WhatsApp; they aren't even 3G.' She turned to Ruskin, the youngest on the team. 'Stop by my desk later, Moray, and I'll explain to you how once upon a time mobile phones could only be used to speak to people and couldn't connect to the internet.'

'No need,' Ruskin shot back. 'I did History Standard when I was at school.' He smiled. 'My teacher was probably almost as old as you.'

Warren joined in the laughter, until he remembered Pymm was only six months older than he was.

'Going back to the location data, I assume you'd have told us already if Derek Culverhouse's phone was located near his parents' house during the period we think they were killed?' said Warren. Pymm had a flair for the dramatic, but he doubted she would have held back such a key finding just to make a bigger splash.

'No such luck,' she said. 'His phone only moves between work and his flat during the week. He phoned them his usual time on the Tuesday night, but they didn't pick up. He called their landline and mobiles from work the following day at ten-thirty, again no reply. He tried again at twelve-thirty, and when they still didn't pick up, he hotfooted it over to the house. The time between his mobile arriving and him calling 999 is just under three minutes.'

'He wouldn't be the first person to leave their mobile phone at home whilst they committed a crime,' said Sutton.

'And we don't know when they were killed,' said Richardson. 'It could have been on the Sunday. That's his normal visiting time, so anyone seeing him wouldn't have been suspicious.'

'According to the location data on the phones, he didn't stick around long after they returned from the Ellacott Estate,' said Pymm. 'He didn't kick his parents out the car whilst it was still moving, but he also didn't stay for a cup of tea. It's hard to see how he could have staged the shooting within that timeframe.'

'Unless he had an accomplice,' said Ruskin. 'He, or they, could have killed them whilst the other carried the phones around the hall. Or perhaps he just dropped them off and slipped his phone into his old man's coat pocket before he left, to give him time to return to their house and prepare, before picking them up again? I accept it may be overcomplicating things, but we know the killer went to the trouble of staging the murders to look like a murder-suicide. I can't imagine they'd forget to sort their alibi as well.'

'If we're lucky, a staff member might remember them,' said Warren. 'There may even be some CCTV from the gift shop.'

'Speaking of gift shops, anything on the Culverhouses' bank statements?' asked Richardson. 'You know the National Trust; never one to miss an opportunity to flog you a tasselled leather bookmark. Plus if they went in the house there's an entry fee.'

Pymm tapped at her tablet. 'Nothing that weekend for the

parents.' She scrolled further. 'Aha, annual membership, so they won't have had to pay to enter.'

'What about Derek?' asked Warren. 'He'd need to pay if he isn't a member.'

They waited whilst Pymm looked it up.

'Nothing for him either and no membership.'

'So, either they didn't really go that day, only went in the free part of the gardens and didn't pay to go into the house, or paid cash for everything,' said Warren. 'Let's make clearing that up a priority.' He turned to Hutchinson. 'Next up, why did Derek Culverhouse get fired from his job?'

'Therein lies a sorry tale,' said Hutchinson. 'I spoke to a woman in human resources at SG Logistics. Culverhouse was employed for about eleven years until 2016. He was based in the warehouse, most recently as a supervisor. Unfortunately, he injured two of his co-workers when he lost control of a forklift. According to the Health and Safety investigation, several of his colleagues reported he often turned up for work smelling of booze, including on the day he had his accident. They couldn't prove he had been drinking that day, but he appeared hungover. It was enough that they gave him his marching orders.

'The two lads he injured were off work for three months. He was upset enough about what happened that he didn't contest the dismissal. Off the record, she heard rumours he saw it as a wake-up call and sought help for his drinking. No idea if that was successful, but his divorce happened shortly after.'

'Do we know any details about that?' asked Sutton.

'I pulled the court records, and it cited "unreasonable behaviour" on the part of Derek – read into that what you will,' said Hutchinson.

'What about his current employers?' asked Sutton. 'Do they know about the accident?'

'Apparently not, because he works mostly in the storeroom and uses the forklift. He claimed on his application form that his contract had ended, and the reference from SG Logistics was just a factual one, stating length of service et cetera. I suspect they were glad to brush it under the carpet.

'We've confirmed he was at work this week, and his manager said it was her who urged him to drive over when they still weren't answering the phone at lunchtime.'

'It sounds like his life wasn't going exactly to plan,' said Warren. 'It's a good motive, but we'll need more. I've spoken to DSI Grayson and we're going to defer publicly announcing that we are treating it as a murder. If the killer thinks they've successfully pulled the wool over our eyes, then they may relax and slip up.

'Hutch, assemble a team to get statements from his ex-partners and acquaintances about his relationship with his parents. And try and pin down his movements in the days before he found the bodies. Karen, get yourself out to the Ellacott Estate and check out his alibi.'

Chapter 8

Karen Hardwick led the afternoon briefing. 'The Culverhouses definitely went to Ellacott last Sunday. CCTV shows Derek using cash to buy drinks and cake in the coffee shop. I couldn't eyeball his parents, as they don't have cameras covering the seating area. However, according to the till receipts, shortly after the family's mobile phones arrived at the property, Mr and Mrs Culverhouse's National Trust membership cards were recorded as being used for entry to the house. The same transaction also had a cash payment, which I assume was Derek.

'Unfortunately, the entrance hall isn't laid out very well, so staff usually walk over to wheelchair users to serve them, and the CCTV cameras over the till didn't pick them up, but I think we're splitting hairs.'

'It would have been nice to catch him out in a lie,' said Sutton, 'but at least we now know they were alive Sunday afternoon.'

'There's more,' she said. 'Their doctor's surgery got back to me.' She read from her notes. 'They confirm that Jemima Culverhouse was suffering from terminal cancer and had declined treatment. Her prognosis was three to six months. Her oncology team prescribed oral slow-release oxycodone for pain relief. Her expressed desire was to receive palliative care at home if possible, with hospice care if her needs became too great. Macmillan Cancer Support were in contact and had helped her devise a care plan.'

'Slow-release tablets act much faster if they are crushed,' said Warren.

'Yes, it's an easy way to give yourself an accidental overdose,' said Hardwick, 'as is mixing oxycodone with alcohol, which it dissolves in quite well, according to what I've found online.'

She flipped over the page. 'The GP's last contact with her was a routine home visit a fortnight before her death. He notes that Mrs Culverhouse was in a largely positive frame of mind. They even spoke about the upcoming anniversary party. He reviewed her hospital notes and said there had been no changes to her prognosis.'

'So nothing to precipitate a sudden desire to end it sooner,' said Warren. 'What about her husband?'

'They had the same GP. Stanley had a mild heart attack eight years ago, for which he was prescribed warfarin to limit the risk of future coronary incidents.

'A specialist nurse practitioner spoke to him a month ago about his mental wellbeing and reported no concerns. She said he was well prepared for the coming months.'

'Well that confirms our suspicions,' said Sutton. 'The couple weren't suicidal and there was no change to their circumstances that support the murder-suicide theory.'

'Which ties in with what their son has been saying,' said Ruskin.

'There is a bit more,' said Hardwick. 'Stanley Culverhouse was due to have a routine medication review nine-thirty Monday morning, and the practice sent an automated text to remind him of his appointment on the Saturday evening. He never showed. Neither of them had previously missed an appointment in the nine years the practice booking system has been online. They texted him Monday afternoon offering him a new slot, but he never acknowledged it.

'I think they were killed Sunday night.'

Sunday 4th March

Chapter 9

Warren had successfully pushed aside the guilt he'd felt about using work as an excuse to skip mass that morning. His feelings were still ambivalent towards the church after his experiences on the Middlesbury Abbey case a few years previously, but he knew it was important to his wife, and his in-laws, so he'd recently started attending again.

'What have you got for me, Mags?' he asked, leaning against her desk.

Richardson took a swig from her water bottle before answering. 'So far, we have no evidence placing Derek Culverhouse's car near his parents' house on the Sunday night or any other evening that week.'

'Which ties in with the location data for his mobile phone,' interjected Pymm from her own workstation opposite Richardson's.

'However, one of the door-knockers reports that his next-door neighbour believes he was out Sunday evening,' continued Richardson. 'Derek's parking space is visible from the neighbour's front window. He remembers seeing his car there around ten a.m. Sunday morning, and that it was gone when they returned from church at about midday, which fits with Derek leaving to visit his parents. He noticed it was there again when he drew the curtains at dusk, which would have been about five-thirty, a couple of hours after we know Derek dropped his parents home. But it was gone again when the neighbour put the bins out about eight p.m. He thinks it was back in its usual spot when he left for work about seven-thirty Monday morning.'

'So Derek *did* go out again Sunday night.' Warren felt his pulse increase. 'He's been lying to us. We need to try and pin down those times more accurately. Bring in the neighbour and see if we can get some more detail out of him and assess his reliability. It's been a week – he may be mistaken. See if he remembers what was on the TV when he drew the curtains or put the bins out.'

'We can do better than that,' said Richardson. 'The house three doors up has a security camera with a partial view of the road. A vehicle that looks suspiciously like Derek Culverhouse's white Volvo is seen driving past at 18.02 and then returning at 20.48.'

'Bingo,' said Warren. 'I'll be interested to hear his explanation for why he lied to us about staying in.'

'And why he decided to leave his mobile phone at home,' finished Pymm.

* * *

Warren called a briefing to update the team on Richardson's revelations. The room was filled to capacity, with additional detectives drafted in from headquarters to supplement Middlesbury's core team. Even John Grayson had emerged from his office.

'So far, it looks as though Derek Culverhouse believes we buy the theory that his parents' death was a murder-suicide and that we don't have him in our crosshairs. I want to keep it that way, so we'll continue deferring announcing it as a murder.'

Warren turned to Hutchinson. 'What have you got from his former partners?'

'Interview teams visited his ex-girlfriend, Ellie Stanton, with whom he has his two eldest children and Anna Winterton, the former Mrs Culverhouse and mother of his youngest child.

'Ms Stanton sees little of him and hasn't spoken to his parents in years. Their two boys are now sixteen and seventeen, so they tend to meet up with him themselves, or just jump in and out of the car if he's playing taxi. She knew that he had lost his job, because of the change in child support payments. She heard that his parents had passed away but didn't know how they died.

Hutchinson grimaced. 'The interviewing officers didn't say anything, obviously, but their presence has made her suspicious. As far as she knew, Derek's relationship with his parents was fine.'

'Well it couldn't be helped,' said Warren. 'Hopefully, this won't tip him off. What about Winterton, his most recent ex? Their kid is what, five?'

'Yes, a little boy. She last saw him Saturday. We were right that the divorce was related to his drinking; the accident with the forklift was the last straw. She was keen to stress he was never violent or abusive, either to her or their son, but the alcohol was becoming a real issue. She also implied there may have been some other substances involved as well.'

'If he was using illegal drugs, then he must have had a dealer,' said Hardwick. 'Perhaps that's where those high-strength oxyco-done pills came from?'

'We'll keep that in mind,' said Warren.

'Anyway, Ms Winterton saw a bit more of his parents,' continued Hutchinson. 'His mum received her diagnosis a couple of months before the accident at work, and Derek tried to blame his drinking on that, but she said that was just an excuse.'

'What about his relationship with his parents?' asked Sutton.

'She says he was definitely worried about his mum, mostly because he didn't want her to suffer. Her father died from cancer three years ago and spent a very unpleasant last few months in a hospice.'

'And his own dad?' prompted Warren.

'Derek reckoned he was soldiering on, but was worried about what would happen when his mother finally passed, and he suddenly found himself at a loose end.'

'Did she say anything about Derek's frame of mind?' asked Hardwick. 'Saturday was only twenty-four hours or so before we believe they were killed.'

'She said he seemed his normal self.'

'What about the drinking? Did the interviewers pursue that any further?' asked Ruskin.

'She says he claims to have been sober for over a year. She takes that with a pinch of salt and insists he uses one of those disposable breathalyser kits you can buy at the chemist, before she lets him drive their son anywhere. Passes every time apparently.'

'Sensible woman,' said Hardwick.

Warren leant back in his chair and considered everything he'd heard.

'We know he needs money and that all his financial concerns will probably be solved overnight when he sells the house,' he said finally. 'We also know that he was worried about his mother's illness and the future effects on his father. He may or may not have alcohol problems that affect his judgement. That's two or perhaps three potential motives right there. Hell, he could even justify it to himself by saying he was doing them a mercy.'

'But if he did kill them, and went to the trouble of staging it as a murder-suicide, why is he so keen to pour cold water on the notion of his father killing his mother?' asked Grayson. It was the first time he'd spoken since the meeting had started, indicating that he had been paying at least some attention as he'd scrolled through his emails at the back of the room. 'He hasn't disputed the sequence of events as we've laid them out – and as the killer wanted them to seem – but everything he has said seeds doubt on any motive his father would have for killing his mother. That still bothers me. A lot.'

His statement was met with nods.

'Either way,' continued Grayson, 'as soon as he finds out we've been speaking to his ex-partners and neighbours, he's going to realise we're looking beyond his father as the killer.

'Bring him in again before he has the chance to hide any evidence or do a runner.'

Chapter 10

Moray Ruskin pressed the doorbell on Derek Culverhouse's flat, and then stepped back. Two uniformed officers in full kit flanked him; at the end of the short corridor, a further two-person forced entry team stood waiting, their 'big red door key' resting on the ground. Hopefully neither the additional officers or solid-steel door ram would be needed.

'It's DC Ruskin,' he called loudly. 'Can we have a word?'

'Yeah, just a second,' came a muffled voice, accompanied a few seconds later by the rattle of a security chain, then the snick of a lock.

The door swung open and Culverhouse stood there.

Looking towards the female constable next to Ruskin, he apologised for his scruffy dressing gown. 'I was about to shower. I'll get changed if you want.'

'That won't be necessary,' said Ruskin. 'May we come in?'

'Of course.' Culverhouse turned and headed back into the tiny apartment, thrusting his hands into his pockets. His parents' dog, a tired-looking Labrador, raised its head before going back to sleep. 'What's this about? I spent quite a bit of time with DCI Jones. I can't imagine what else you need to know.'

'There has been a development in your parents' case,' said Ruskin carefully.

'Oh?' Culverhouse turned back towards them.

Ruskin scrutinised the man's face and was shocked at how much he'd aged in the past few days. Dark smudges bruised the skin below his bloodshot eyes; his pale cheeks looked hollow and there was a tic in the man's right eye. Lack of sleep? Nerves? Or something else?

'We are now treating your parents' death as suspicious,' said Ruskin tensing.

At six feet five inches and eighteen stone, Ruskin was confident in his ability to handle himself; nevertheless, he was glad that he was accompanied by two colleagues dressed in stab vests, with fully stocked utility belts. If their suspicions were correct, the man in front of them had slaughtered his own parents, in a cold and calculating manner.

Culverhouse took a half-step forward, surprise on his face.

For the first time, Ruskin noted the shapeless, baggy nature of the man's dressing gown. There could be all manner of weapons in there he realised.

Beside him, PC Amy Cain clearly had the same thought, subtly interposing herself between Culverhouse and Ruskin.

Many men the size of Moray Ruskin would scoff at the very thought of letting a tiny woman like Amy Cain shield him from potential danger. Ruskin had no such qualms, taking a full step backward to give Cain room to manoeuvre. As far as he was concerned, the fifteen inches and ten-stone weight she surrendered to him was more than compensated for by the can of incapacitant spray and side-handled baton she carried, not to mention her years of near-daily grappling with violent thugs and drug users. He'd certainly wade in if it all kicked off, but he suspected Cain would have the situation under control pretty quickly.

Culverhouse started to remove his hands from his pockets; Cain and her partner placed their own hands on their batons.

Culverhouse raised his hands; they were empty, Ruskin realised, as the man lifted them to his face.

'Oh, thank God,' he said, as he started to sob.

* * *

'Suspicious. That's murder, right?' said Culverhouse.

He'd collapsed to the sofa, his head buried in his hands. It was hardly the reaction expected by any of the police officers in the room and they were still wary of what may be concealed between the cushions of the chair. Nevertheless, he seemed relieved.

'That's one possibility,' said Ruskin, unsure of what was happening.

'I knew it,' mumbled Culverhouse. 'I knew there was no way Dad would kill Mum and then take the coward's way out. Do you have a suspect? Do you know why they did it?'

He looked up at Ruskin, before casting his gaze around the room at the officers assembled in the tiny room. He paused as if seeing them all for the first time. His eyes narrowed.

'Hold on. You don't send a whole team to pass on news about developments in a case.'

Ruskin took a deep breath. 'Derek Culverhouse, I am arresting you on suspicion of murder …'

* * *

Culverhouse was dressed in a police-issue tracksuit and slip-on shoes before being taken to the station. Out on the street, his car was awaiting transport by a low-loader to the forensics garage in Welwyn.

He had sat in stunned silence throughout the journey to Middlesbury CID. It was only when the custody sergeant went through the arrest and caution again that his situation truly dawned on him.

He turned to Ruskin. 'This is madness. I don't need a solicitor, I need to go home. I'm supposed to be going to talk to the boys.'

Ruskin put a gentle hand on the man's shoulder. 'Des, mate, you really do need a solicitor.'

Chapter 11

Warren had seen many people arrested over the years. Those who protested the most vehemently were often the most guilty. If Derek Culverhouse was the killer, he'd had a week to prepare for the moment Ruskin arrived at his flat. But having heard the constable's account of the man's arrest, he could see why Ruskin was troubled.

'He seemed relieved that it was murder,' said Ruskin around a mouthful of protein bar. 'And it felt genuine.'

'Maybe he was relieved,' said Sutton. 'He wouldn't be the first killer so eaten up by guilt they were glad when they were caught.'

'Perhaps,' allowed Ruskin.

'I wouldn't bank on a confession though – especially after a chat with his brief,' said Hutchinson.

Culverhouse had finally been persuaded that availing himself of the duty solicitor was in everybody's interests; it was as much for the interviewing officers' protection as his. The last thing they needed was a canny defence team trawling through the interview recording and spotting a tiny procedural breach that deemed it inadmissible.

'Well, we'll get to see for ourselves soon enough,' said Warren standing and stretching. His back gave a series of small pops that brought a smile of relief to his face. He'd spent most of the past couple of hours preparing for the interview. After a long day, and an even longer week, he'd been looking forward to going home at a decent hour. Unfortunately, the custody clock had started ticking the moment Ruskin arrested Culverhouse, and they needed to do a preliminary interview under caution that night.

His smile faded; even if Culverhouse confessed everything, they were looking at several hours sitting on hard interview room chairs; his back was going to need more than a stretch to sort it out. Sometimes he regretted his insistence on conducting interviews himself.

'Ready when you are,' announced the custody sergeant when he rang through a moment later.

Thanking him, Warren clapped Ruskin on the shoulder.

'We're up.' He turned back to the team. 'Let me know as soon as those results come through.'

Hopefully they'd all be out of there before Sunday night became Monday morning.

* * *

They were back in the same interview suite Culverhouse had occupied previously. Gone were the biscuits and hot drinks, replaced by a plastic water jug and disposable cups.

Warren was now accompanied by Ruskin, and Culverhouse by the on-call duty solicitor, a short, black woman who Warren had worked with before. Their meeting in the corridor had been cordial as he apologised for ruining her Sunday night. She'd sighed but smiled briefly – it would likely be the last time she favoured him with such a look over the next few days.

'Why don't you start by telling us where you were last Sunday night?' said Warren, once all the preliminaries had been completed.

'No comment,' muttered Culverhouse, his gaze fixed firmly on the table in front of him.

So that was how it was going to be, thought Warren. Culverhouse had clearly listened to his solicitor.

'You told me earlier that after dropping your parents home, you went straight back to your own flat. And that you were in all night.'

'No comment.'

Unperturbed, Warren continued. 'Do you drive a white Volvo XC90?'

Culverhouse opened his mouth as if to say no comment, then changed his mind. There was no point denying something that could be checked with the DVLA.

'Yeah.'

'Does anybody else drive that car?'

Beside Culverhouse, his solicitor paused her writing, but said nothing.

'No, just me.'

A brief flash of disappointment crossed the solicitor's face, before being replaced by her professional poker face. She had doubtless advised her client to answer no comment to every question, no matter how innocuous, but like so many inexperienced interviewees he was unable to help himself. Guilty or innocent, the first instinct of most people was to at least appear helpful.

'According to a witness, your car left its usual parking spot that evening, before returning later. Can you explain that?' Warren pressed.

He was giving the man an opening – tell the truth, lie or no comment.

'No comment,' he said eventually. Catching him in a lie so early in the interview would have given them a powerful lever. A no comment was of limited use – was he trying to hide something or just heeding his solicitor's advice? The time-stamped photographs from the neighbour's CCTV would remain in the evidence folder for the time being; they may be of use later.

Warren leant back in his chair and pressed his foot on Ruskin's.

'Look, Des, it's late,' Ruskin said. 'DCI Jones and I are trying to work out what happened to your parents. We have a series of questions that we need to ask you about that night. Nobody in this room wants to believe that a loving son killed his mum and dad, but we have to do our job properly. If you can answer our questions fully and tell us what we need to know, then we will send you home to continue your grieving, whilst we work our hardest to figure out who is really responsible.'

He leant forward in his chair, catching Culverhouse's eye. 'Work with us, mate, help us do our job and clear up this whole thing.'

Culverhouse said nothing, but they could see him processing the words.

'Let's go back a bit, Des,' said Warren. 'Last time, you told me all about your parents. I like hearing that sort of thing. It makes the victims more real to me you know?'

Culverhouse gave a tiny nod.

'But I don't really know anything about you. You're an only child – is that right?'

'Yeah.'

'It must be really hard,' said Ruskin. 'All this and you have to cope with it on your own. I take it there won't be much support from your exes?'

Culverhouse snorted. 'No.'

'I know how it is,' said Ruskin. 'They're happy to ask you for support – money for school trips and new shoes – but it's a one-way street, when you need help.'

'You've got three kids, am I right?' said Warren.

'Yeah.'

Ruskin winced. 'That's got to sting. One's bad enough, but whoever works out your child support is probably taking you to the cleaners.'

'Which is why we know how much you valued your parents'

help,' said Warren. 'They were giving you a bit of a hand. Which is what parents do, if they can, and we know you were close to them. Did they get to see much of their grandchildren?'

The solicitor shook her head, but Culverhouse ignored her. 'Not as much as they'd have liked. My exes can be a bit difficult sometimes. That's why the anniversary party was going to be such a big deal. They haven't seen all three kids together since the Christmas before last.' He gave a sniff. 'It's been six months since I've had them under one roof.'

'That must be hard,' said Ruskin.

'Look, I don't like bringing this up,' said Warren, 'but you're obviously a bright bloke, so I've got to ask why you're only getting a few hours a week at Morrisons and relying on your folks for support? You were unemployed for a while, but you had a good job before then. What happened there?'

Culverhouse shifted in his seat. 'I got made redundant.'

'How come? You were there for years; isn't it usually first in, last out?' asked Warren.

'They needed to cut costs,' he said.

Ruskin sighed. 'Des, we need you to tell us the truth, or we can't help you. We know you weren't made redundant, as you didn't receive a pay-out. Instead, your wages just stopped. Come on, mate, what really happened?'

Culverhouse stared at the table, the tips of his ears turning pink. When he spoke, his voice was barely loud enough to be picked up on the recording.

'I got sacked.'

'What happened?' asked Warren.

Culverhouse cleared his throat. 'There was an accident. A couple of lads got injured. I was driving the forklift when it happened.'

'Seems a bit harsh,' said Ruskin. 'Accidents happen, and you'd been there for years.'

Culverhouse said nothing.

72

'How long has it been since you had a drink, Des?' asked Warren quietly.

'No comment,' he muttered.

'We know you've been drinking this week,' said Ruskin. 'Hardly surprising after what you've been through, but how long were you sober before then?'

Culverhouse remained silent.

'We spoke to your ex-wife,' Ruskin continued. 'She said that she thought you'd been sober for over a year.' He softened his tone. 'She was really proud of you. Is that true?'

When Culverhouse spoke, his voice was thick with emotion. 'Almost fourteen months. I woke up on New Year's Day last year with a hangover and memories of things I'd said the night before, and decided I needed to get my shit together.'

'And were your parents supportive?' asked Warren.

Culverhouse nodded. 'Yeah.' He sniffed again, before wiping his nose with a tissue from the packet his solicitor had placed between them. 'They were so good – Dad especially. If I was feeling desperate, I could call him and he'd talk me down.' His face crumpled. 'I don't know what I'm going to do without them.'

As if on cue, there was a quiet tap at the door.

'Why don't you take a moment whilst I answer this,' suggested Warren. He paused the recording and slipped into the corridor.

When he returned, Culverhouse had regained his composure. Warren gave Ruskin a small nod.

'If you're ready, we'd like to go back to when they were murdered,' Warren started, opening the file folder he'd placed before him. 'This is the bottle that was sitting on your parents' bedside table. Your father's fingerprints were found on the bottle, and on the two tumblers, as if he'd poured the drinks.'

Culverhouse gave a shrug. 'Well if they were murdered, maybe the killer put them on there after he, you know ...'

'We think that is probably what happened,' agreed Warren. 'But the thing is, your fingerprints were also on the bottle. But

73

you said you haven't had a drink for fourteen months. How is that?'

Culverhouse looked helpless. 'I don't know. That bottle could have been in the cupboard for years. I used to have a drink sometimes when I visited, back before, you know …'

'I'm afraid not,' said Warren. 'We traced the batch number on the bottle and it was distributed to Tesco in November of last year. We've also looked at your parents' Clubcard records and a bottle of this whisky was bought a week before Christmas. You've handled this bottle since then, even though you claim not to have had a drink in fourteen months. Can you explain that?'

'No comment,' said Culverhouse, shock on his face.

Warren opened the folder again. 'We have teams searching your flat as we speak. They've already found a couple of interesting things. Can you tell me what this is?'

Culverhouse closed his eyes in despair. 'No comment,' he managed.

'For the benefit of the recording, I have shown Mr Culverhouse a photograph of what officers believe to be a quantity of dried cannabis and two rolled joints. Can you explain why you have these drugs in your flat?' asked Warren again.

'No comment.'

Ruskin took over. 'Have you ever used oxycodone, Des?'

Culverhouse looked surprised. 'What? No.'

'So you have never bought oxycodone tablets?' Ruskin pressed.

'No, of course not, I ain't stupid. That shit's for losers.'

His solicitor cleared her throat and Culverhouse snapped his mouth shut.

'You see, here's the thing,' said Warren. 'You are in serious trouble financially. You've got three kids to support. Your parents have been bunging you a bit of money to help you out, but that won't even clear what you owe the payday lenders.

'Did they have any clue how much trouble you were in? Or did you tell them, and they refused to help?'

'No, it wasn't like that.'

'Then how was it, Des?' said Ruskin. 'I've seen their house, and I've seen your flat. You couldn't have all three kids over if you wanted to. But that big farmhouse … Easily enough room. And your parents have enough in their savings accounts to clear your debts.'

'Or maybe you weren't going to move in there,' said Warren. 'That would be a bit grim, what with your dad's brains all over the headboard in the master bedroom. But you could sell it, buy somewhere else, and pay off everything you owe. It was your idea to get the kitchen done, wasn't it?'

'The previous one was as old as me,' Culverhouse protested. 'They didn't even have enough plug sockets to use the microwave and the kettle at the same time.'

'Still a big job for an elderly couple in poor health,' said Warren. 'And expensive. But then the new kitchen has probably already increased the house's value by double what they forked out. No wonder you pushed for them to do it, even though your old man told his mates at the bowls club he was worried about the disruption. It's a win-win for you; a nice new kitchen if you decide to keep the house, or a bigger inheritance if you decide to sell.'

'No, I didn't kill them. I couldn't, you have to believe me.'

Warren raised his hands placatingly. 'Look, we understand. Your mum was ill; she was in a lot of pain. Your dad would never have survived being on his own. Some might see what happened as a mercy.'

'No, never.' Culverhouse turned an accusatory glare at the two officers. 'You're trying to stitch me up. To trick me into incriminating myself, to give you an easy arrest. Well you can piss off, the pair of you.'

'Des …' started his solicitor, laying a gentle hand on his arm.

He shook it off angrily and pointed a finger at Ruskin. 'And you should be ashamed. How do you even sleep at night? You act all nice, pretending to comfort a grieving son, whilst all the while you're getting ready to stab me in the back. Well you can fuck off. I'm not saying anything else.'

Monday 5th March

Chapter 12

'Early forensics from Culverhouse's flat are in,' said Pymm, first thing. She continued reading from her tablet. 'They haven't found oxycodone or other drugs, just the cannabis. They're going to dismantle his furniture, and they'll get the dogs in tomorrow, but they've checked the usual places. He won't have been able to keep the drugs at work. Staff lockers are first-come-first-served, and he didn't have his own workspace.'

'What about clothing?' asked Hutchinson.

'He doesn't have a massive wardrobe,' said Pymm, 'but unless we can work out what he was wearing that night, checking everything for blood and gunshot residue will take time and any matching fibres found at the scene will be easy enough to explain away, given his regular visits.'

Warren swallowed his frustration. There was a limit to how long they could keep Derek Culverhouse in custody without charging him, and everything they had so far was circumstantial.

'What about devices?' he asked.

'Just the mobile phone we know about, an old iPad and an ancient laptop. They've been sent to Welwyn for analysis – but who knows how long that'll take,' said Pymm. 'If I ask Pete Robertson nicely, he may send me an image of the hard drives so I can do some rooting around myself.'

'Don't waste too much time on it,' Warren cautioned. The amount of electronic data involved in investigations was increasing at an exponential rate, and the Digital Forensics Unit had a lengthy backlog; unless Warren could get authorisation to request a queue-jump, it could take months for any seized hardware to be examined. Pymm had attended some courses that meant she could at least have a look at copies of a device's storage, but it could be a tremendous burden on her time.

'What about social media?' he asked. A specialist unit dealt with that, but the whole team had been on refresher courses. Fortunately, Moray Ruskin and Karen Hardwick had taken a keen interest and received more advanced training. Warren was glad; it meant he could assign looking through thousands of vapid Instagram photos and obnoxious tweets to somebody who actually cared.

'Jemima and Stanley Culverhouse had no social media presence that we can determine,' said Ruskin. 'It looks as though text messages were about their limit. Derek was on Facebook. His feed seems to be mostly keeping in touch with old schoolmates and sharing dodgy jokes.

'Nothing stands out from the past few weeks, and he hasn't posted anything about his parents' deaths – or anything at all since he found them, for that matter.'

'Does he use any other platforms?' asked Pymm.

'Nothing we can find; he doesn't have apps for Twitter, Instagram, SnapChat, TikTok or anything else installed on his phone,' said Hardwick.

'I suppose it would be a bit much to hope he shared a video about killing his parents,' said Warren. 'Well, unless there's anything else, Moray and I need to prep for our next interview.'

* * *

Derek Culverhouse looked even more tired, if that were possible. But at least he was subdued, rather than in the combative mood he'd ended the previous day on.

'Mr Culverhouse has had time to reflect on yesterday, and wishes to make a statement,' said Culverhouse's solicitor. 'He feels it important that he tells you what happened last Sunday in his own words, as a way of facing up to the truth.'

Warren forced his face to remain impassive, but his pulse started to race. Were they going to get a confession? An attempt to justify his actions?

Culverhouse cleared his throat. After a brief pause he repeated the action, before finally starting again. 'I am an alcoholic. I stopped drinking on January the first 2017 but started again last Sunday. Last New Year's Eve, I had a wobble. I poured myself a drink from the bottle of whisky that my father kept in the cupboard, but my uncle came in and stopped me. I tipped it down the sink.

'On Sunday, after dropping my parents' home, I returned to my flat. I was agitated and smoked some cannabis to try and calm myself down. It wasn't enough, so I went for a drive. I ended up at the War Memorial Park and sat in the car park. I used to go there with Mum and Nan when I was a kid, and I find it calms me sometimes. It didn't.'

Where was this going? Culverhouse had just freely admitted to driving under the influence of cannabis. Was his admission made in the spirit of openness espoused by substance-abuse counsellors? Or was he trying to appear more believable by incriminating himself in a relatively minor offence that could never be tried in court, in the hope they would accept his later lies? Or was he just trying to set up his defence, with a view to pleading manslaughter on the grounds of diminished responsibility?

'After spending some time sitting in the car, thinking, I drove to the shops and picked up a small bottle of vodka and returned home, where I consumed the whole lot, before passing out. I awoke the next morning and went to work – I avoided using the forklift truck or any heavy machinery that day.'

'But you did drive?' said Warren, wanting to see if Culverhouse was willing to admit to that also.

'Yes, but I never went anywhere near my parents' house that night, I swear. I blacked out, but I woke up in exactly the same position I passed out in.'

'Why?' asked Warren. 'After fourteen months sober – or so you claim – why did you suddenly decide to get blind drunk? What was so different about this Sunday, compared to the previous sixty?'

Culverhouse covered his face with his hands briefly. When he removed them, there were tears shining in the corners of his eyes.

'It all got too much.'

'What got too much, Des?' asked Ruskin, his tone kinder than Warren's.

'Mum. Her cancer. Everything.' He gave a shuddering breath. 'After we walked around Ellacott on Sunday, we went to the coffee shop. Dad and I had a coffee and Mum had a tea. She hasn't been eating properly, so I got myself a slice of her favourite cake with two forks. I managed to persuade her to have a few bites.'

The tears started to trickle down his cheeks.

'I just wanted her to eat something, you know? She was wasting away in front of us.' He sniffed. 'Anyway, Dad went to use the toilet and suddenly, no warning, Mum was sick. She was really embarrassed, so I grabbed some paper napkins and wiped her down. She kept on telling me not to tell Dad, as she didn't want to worry him. I managed to get her all cleaned up before he came back. But I couldn't stop thinking about it.'

His lip started to tremble. 'When I got home, all I could picture in my head was me on my knees, wiping her down, like she did to me when I was a kid. And I realised, I'm going to lose my mum. And I'm not ready to lose my mum and I don't know what I'm going to do …'

Culverhouse put his face in his hands, his shoulders rocking as he sobbed. 'And now I've lost both of them,' he said, his voice so thick they could barely understand him.

Culverhouse's solicitor placed a comforting arm around his shoulders.

Warren gave him a few moments to compose himself, although he couldn't have said anything if he wanted to. It had been many years since his own mother's passing, but the memories were still there, locked in a box whose lid occasionally opened unexpectedly. Beside him, Ruskin shifted in his seat, the young Scotsman's expression inscrutable behind his beard.

'Where did you buy the vodka?' asked Warren eventually.

'The Tesco Express, up by the park. It was the first place I came to after I drove back.' He sniffed again. 'I hadn't even planned to buy any – I stopped off for some fags. But they keep the spirits next to the cigarette kiosk and there was a queue at the counter. As soon as I saw the bottles with their red labels, I couldn't take my eyes off them. By the time I got served, it was all I could think of.'

'We'll have to take your word for that,' said Warren. 'You left your mobile phone at home. Why?'

A stricken look passed across Culverhouse's face again, and his lip started to tremble once more.

'I couldn't face talking to Dad if he rang me and asked why there was sick on Mum's cardigan and blouse. I didn't know if I could lie to him.'

* * *

'What do we think?' asked Warren.

The team had gathered to go through Culverhouse's interview. There was no doubt that Culverhouse's feelings towards his mother's illness were genuine, but they had to look past that.

'If anything, it strengthens the argument that he killed his parents to spare them any more suffering,' said Hutchinson. 'And those tears may have been genuine, but they could easily be because he's killed his mam and dad.'

There were nods of agreement around the room; sometimes the truth was ugly.

'That last-ditch attempt before you ended the interview to get us to look elsewhere was pretty half-hearted,' said Ruskin. 'He couldn't even name the respite centre this "funny-looking bugger" supposedly drove his mother to once a month.'

'We'll look into it,' said Warren. 'But it smacks of desperation. Mags, what have you got for us?'

'I've sent someone over to Tesco to see if they have him on the CCTV. Unfortunately, it's possible to get from his flat to the park and then the Tesco and back without being picked up by any ANPR cameras, so we don't know if he really did make that journey, or he was lying.'

'And we already know he can get from his flat to his parents' house without being picked up, as long as he doesn't break the speed limit,' said Ruskin.

'We really need to know if he did drive out to War Memorial Park and sit in the car park, and at what time,' said Sutton. 'Do the council have cameras at the car park?'

'I'll check,' Richardson promised.

'Hutch, arrange a team to start canvassing the area around the park,' said Warren. 'Look for any businesses or houses with CCTV that may have picked him or his car up. Somebody using the park may remember someone in a white Volvo XC90 parked there doing nothing.

'Karen, can you contact the Ellacott Estate again and ask if anyone remembers an old lady in a wheelchair being ill? If that whole story is bullshit, I want to know.'

He looked at the wall clock. They had only a few more hours before they had to decide what to do about Culverhouse's detention. As things stood, they were light years away from reaching the charging threshold. In fact, Warren had grave doubts he'd even be able to extend custody by a further twelve hours.

By that evening, Derek Culverhouse could very well be on his way home.

Chapter 13

The clunkily titled Senior Investigating Officers Monthly Case Review had been informally re-christened the Monthly Monday Morning Murder Meeting as soon as it was set up. Started by Detective Chief Superintendent Andrew Fowlie, it kept all of the various Serious Crime Teams working across Hertfordshire, Bedfordshire and Cambridgeshire apprised of one another's most high-profile cases. Where necessary, officers from neighbouring forces would attend if cases overlapped with their jurisdictions. It had quickly become a valuable forum for bouncing ideas off colleagues, and unlike the similarly frequent budget meetings, Warren tried where possible to keep the slot free in his diary.

Today he had successfully conspired to drive him and John Grayson; although Grayson's top-of-the-range Mercedes was a joy to be a passenger in, it was less fun when Grayson was behind the wheel. It remained a mystery to Warren how the man had kept a clean licence for so long. The arrangement suited Grayson fine; he spent the entire journey down the A1 scrolling through his emails. Warren wondered if this is what being the parent of a teenager felt like.

'John, Warren, glad you could make it,' said Fowlie. A jovial man in his late fifties, with the lean build of a marathon runner, he had decreed from the outset that rank be left at the door; first names only.

The room was almost full, and Warren nodded to a number of acquaintances. Because of Middlesbury CID's unusual status within the Major Crime Unit, it was one of the few times Warren got to meet his peers, almost all of whom were based in Welwyn.

He scanned down the agenda for the meeting. He'd been allocated the final slot.

The meeting kicked off with an update on a recent spate of stabbings in north Cambridgeshire, possibly related to organised crime. This was followed by a summary of the progress in a domestic murder in Luton. Warren felt a twinge of sympathy for his colleagues in Bedfordshire Police; domestic violence cases were messy at the best of times, but suggestions that the victim and her abuser were already known to police had resulted in unflattering media scrutiny. Even more intense scrutiny was being directed towards Camilla Wong from the Missing Persons Unit, whose team were investigating the disappearance of a minor celebrity, and face of the popular teen cosmetics brand DzzleGrl, whose death bore similarities to the unsolved disappearance of the singer from the Welsh band the Manic Street Preachers. Finally, DCI Carl Mallucci from the drugs unit took the floor, to update everyone on the hunt for the brother of a drug dealer found shot in his car on the outskirts of Middlesbury.

When it came to Warren's turn, he started by outlining the inconsistencies that had led to their realisation that the Culverhouses' killings were staged, before moving on to suspects.

'Their son is the obvious prime candidate, and his alibi is shaky. With enough pre-planning, he could have made it to their house and back.'

'But …?' prompted Fowlie.

'He doesn't smell right,' said Warren. There were looks of understanding from his peers around the room. They had all been there; years of experience challenging what seemed like an obvious answer. It was a foolish officer who dismissed their instincts out of hand.

'If he is lying, then he's one of the best actors I've come across. He seems absolutely devastated by his parents' deaths.'

'Who else have you got in the picture, then?' asked DCI Ashley Roehampton.

'That's the problem,' Warren lamented. 'We've got nobody else with an obvious motive. Financially, he's the only person we've found who gains from their deaths, but we can't link him forensically to the scene; there's no way the CPS will authorise a charge at the moment. We're digging into the Culverhouses' backgrounds to see if there is anyone at all with a reason to kill them, but they seem too normal to have engendered that sort of hate. The only suggestion we have is the driver for some sort of respite club that his mother attended to give his father a break. Apparently, Stanley Culverhouse said the volunteer who picked her up each month was "a funny-looking bugger" and "a bit creepy". But Derek can't even tell us the name of the club, and she'd been too ill to go for months.'

'What about their son?' said Fowlie. 'Could he have got mixed up in something that resulted in his parents being killed?'

'That's something we're actively pursuing,' said Warren, 'but there's nothing so far.'

'You said you think the Culverhouses were sedated with additional oxycodone to that prescribed to Mrs Culverhouse,' said Mallucci. 'When you've got the analysis back on the residue, ping it my way. We may be able to trace it back to whoever sold it to the killer.'

Warren thanked him.

'So, if the killer wasn't known to the Culverhouses, then that leaves a stranger-killing,' said Fowlie, with a grimace. 'But it seems a bit elaborate. Which worries me.'

The room agreed. It wasn't a spur-of-the-moment decision. There would have been multiple opportunities for the killer to change their mind and abort their devastating course of action. If the person they were hunting wasn't Derek Culverhouse, then their killer had no obvious motive – at least none that would make sense to a rational person; they were dancing to their own tune.

And a person like that had probably killed before and would likely kill again.

* * *

The meeting wrapped with Any Other Business, then Fowlie announced one final item.

'As you are all aware, this will be the last time that one of us attends 5Ms.'

Grayson turned to Warren. 'Did you know about this, you git?' he hissed.

'I might have,' said Warren with a grin, as he opened the camera app on his phone.

'Come on up, John,' said Fowlie.

Shaking his head, Grayson made his way to the front to a round of applause.

'I know your official send-off isn't for a few more weeks, but you didn't think we'd let you get off that easy, did you?' asked Fowlie.

'You're buggers, the lot of you,' said Grayson.

After a short speech, in which Fowlie joked about Grayson's long service, including the 'good old days' before criminals studied *CSI*, he presented him with a large, framed picture; a caricature exaggerating his features to almost grotesque proportions, signed by all the regular attendees of 5Ms. To take the sting off the depiction, he was also given a bottle of his favourite single malt.

Grayson was uncharacteristically lost for words, managing little more than a few thanks. Sensing the man's predicament, Fowlie announced the meeting would conclude in the pub across the road.

'No excuses, John,' said Warren. 'Why do you think we took my car? First drink is on me.'

'And there was me thinking you didn't like my driving.' Grayson gave a wry smile. 'What? You think I didn't know?'

Laughing at Warren's discomfort, Grayson headed off to shake hands with a few of his soon-to-be-former colleagues.

Warren shook his head. 'And I thought I hid it so well,' he muttered to himself.

Looking around the room, Warren couldn't help wondering who in the room was in the running to replace Grayson as the head of Middlesbury CID.

Or more to the point, who Warren's rivals were.

Chapter 14

It was the odour that hit Warren's nose first; the rancid smell of decay and death. The body had been there some time. Around him, the forest seemed unusually quiet, the only sounds the rustle of paper suits and the muted voices of the CSIs. The crackle and squawk of a radio on the other side of the blue and white tape was indistinct.

The call had come just as Warren ordered a round of drinks for Grayson's send-off. He'd made his apologies, insisting that Grayson stay and enjoy the get-together. It was the usual story: a dog walker alerted to the find by his snuffling charge. Not for the first time, Warren reflected that the British public's love of dogs meant attempts to conceal a body in a remote piece of woodland were, as often as not, doomed to failure. Not that there had been much attempt at deception.

'The weather has been a bit rubbish, so he hasn't been out here since Friday,' explained Ruskin, who'd attended the scene as soon as CID were notified. The unfortunate member of the public who'd made the discovery was seated in a warm patrol car.

'And he thinks the dog would have found the body if it was here the last time they walked here?' asked Warren.

'Yeah, it's forever uncovering dead animals when they're out.'

'Well, we'll see what the pathologist has to say about probable time of death, but that at least gives us a potential window for when the body was left,' said Warren.

Rounding the clump of trees that was the focus of the forensic team's scrutiny, Warren caught his first glimpse of the body.

It appeared to be an elderly white woman, entirely naked, sitting upright against the trunk of one of the trees. Tiny in stature, she was hidden from the view of anyone walking along the path; but there was no disguising the smell. Warren would be using the showers back at the station and changing clothes before the briefing.

'I'll go out on a limb and say she was killed and left here.'

Warren recognised the voice of Meera Gupta behind the facemask.

'She definitely didn't wander here and die of exposure?' clarified Warren.

Given her apparent age and state of undress, Warren had to raise the possibility – however unlikely – that she had arrived under her own power; perhaps a confused resident from a local care home, although he didn't recall seeing any recent alerts about missing seniors.

'Doubtful,' said Gupta, squatting down with a torch. 'Her feet are spotless. Even if she'd walked here before the rain set in, there would be mud on them.'

She moved the torch to the woman's upper body. 'I'll leave it to the pathologist to determine cause of death, but the angle of her neck is suspicious, and that looks like bruising on her collarbones.'

Holding his breath, Warren leant in closer. The woman's head was bent unnaturally far back. Dark smudges on both collarbones were clearly visible against the deathly pale skin.

Warren had seen enough. Standing back up, he turned to Ruskin.

'Contact the station and get a message to DSI Grayson. I'm declaring it a suspicious death. Close off the path and that dirt track. Get a map of the area and identify any other access routes. If our victim didn't walk here by herself, then her killer must have brought her.'

* * *

Grayson had found a lift back to the station by the time Warren returned, having limited himself to the one drink. He agreed with Warren's assessment and started a murder investigation. After a shower and change of clothes, Warren joined him in the main briefing room. Warren had a feeling his twice-weekly, early-morning swim would be off the agenda for the foreseeable future and so decided against ordering in doughnuts; at least there were decent biscuits in the tin. Ruskin helped himself to several custard creams and a couple of Jaffa Cakes. It hardly seemed fair, but then he was under thirty and had already done a ten-mile cycle ride that morning.

Warren had asked Mags Richardson to secure any footage from the nearby main road, but the best they could hope for was a glimpse of any future suspect's vehicle in the area within the period they believed the body had been dumped.

'The crime scene has been pretty compromised by the weather, so the priority is identifying our victim and starting from there,' said Warren. 'We'll liaise with Missing Persons in the first instance; we have a reasonable headshot so they may be able to match her visually.'

'When's the post-mortem?' asked Grayson.

'Professor Jordan is prioritising it,' said Warren. 'He and Meera Gupta were unhappy with the state of the body; something wasn't quite right.'

'In what way?'

'He was reluctant to elaborate until he'd finished.'

* * *

Whilst kick-starting the investigation of the body found that morning was now the team's most pressing priority, they couldn't just drop their ongoing investigation. Tony Sutton and David Hutchinson were bringing Warren up to speed.

'He still had time to do it if he put his foot down and was already prepared,' insisted Sutton.

The CCTV from Tesco Express showed Derek Culverhouse entering the store, queuing at the kiosk, and then exiting with vodka and cigarettes. The surveillance footage of Culverhouse's Volvo from his neighbour had been authenticated, with the times it drove past verified.

'He leaves his house at 18.02, then we lose him. He doesn't reappear at Tesco until 20.34,' Sutton continued. 'That's a window of two and a half hours. It's a thirteen-minute drive each way to his parents' if you obey the speed limit, but more than half the journey is on an A road he's familiar with, on a quiet Sunday night. He could definitely have trimmed that time if he gave it some welly.'

'Look at him though,' said Hutchinson, pointing at the frozen image on the screen from the mini-supermarket. 'We're saying he's just killed both his parents with a shotgun, yet here he is queuing patiently for twenty Rothmans and a bottle of Smirnoff?'

'Anyone who can kill their own parents *has* to be abnormal,' said Sutton. 'If he is a psycho, then everything so far could be an act.'

Hardwick had spoken earlier to the coffee shop manager at the National Trust, who had confirmed an elderly lady in a wheelchair had been sick on Sunday afternoon, but couldn't remember at what time.

Unfortunately, the woman had been unable to say if those involved were the Culverhouses. So, whilst it suggested that Derek Culverhouse's story was true, as Sutton had immediately suggested, a skilled liar could have seen the incident happen to somebody else and adapted the story for their own purposes.

'We really need to know if Derek Culverhouse did go to War Memorial Park that night,' said Warren.

'No quick answers there,' said Hutchinson. 'Mags says the only camera near the park has been broken for months.'

'Then on the basis of what we have so far, we can't get an extension to custody,' said Warren. 'We'll charge him with possession over the drugs, but it was clearly for personal use, so we can't keep holding him. And it doesn't look good detaining a grieving son on circumstantial evidence. The *Middlesbury Reporter* would be delighted to ask Derek's thoughts on the matter, I'm certain.'

'What are we going to do with him then?' asked Sutton. 'Bail or RUI?'

Warren had already spoken to Grayson about the next step. A brief press conference had been well attended, and the shocking nature of the crime all but ensured decent coverage in the media. Hopefully that would bring forward witnesses. They'd revealed that they had made an arrest, without naming Culverhouse, but his age and a description of his car had probably identified him to those who knew him. That might jog a few memories, either from those who had seen him where he shouldn't have been or recalled a troubling conversation.

'Releasing Under Investigation buys us more time,' Hutchinson pointed out. 'We won't be bound by the new twenty-eight-day rule. There's a lot of forensics we still need to process, and you know what witnesses are like; they can take ages to come forward, especially if they're a close friend.'

'But if we RUI, we can't impose any restrictions on his movements,' said Sutton. 'At least if he has to turn up here and answer bail every week, we'll get a few days' notice if he decides to disappear.'

'Do we have enough to even justify bail?' asked Hutchinson. 'Especially now the CCTV from Tesco backs up his story.'

'*Partially* backs up his story,' clarified Sutton. 'We still don't know if he really did go to the park.'

'His solicitor will object either way,' said Warren. 'John agrees we'll go for bail. If we can't find what we need in the next twenty-eight days, we'll apply for an extension. In the meantime, let's not put all of our eggs in one basket. If Derek didn't kill his mum and dad, then the person who did is still out there – and they're a clever bugger. And I wouldn't be the least surprised if this isn't their first murder.'

Chapter 15

The whisper of the mortuary air conditioning seemed louder than normal; Warren wondered if it had been cranked up to reduce the smell of the decomposing body lying on the trolley.

It was already past eleven p.m. and Warren had driven down to Stevenage in old jeans and a T-shirt that could go straight in the wash when he returned home. His stomach gurgled, a combination of hunger from deliberately skipping dinner with his wife and nausea from the reason he'd opted not to eat.

'I know it's late, Warren, but something really bugged me about the body when I saw it at the scene. I managed to call in a favour from the histopathology lab and they confirmed my suspicions.'

'Thanks, Ryan I appreciate it,' said Warren.

'First of all, cause of death. Broken neck, deliberately inflicted.' He pointed to the woman's collarbones; under the bright lights of the morgue, the bruising was obvious. 'From the positioning, and smaller bruises on the forehead, I'd say the killer stood behind her, put his forearms on her shoulders, placed his hands on her forehead and pulled back. The vertebrae were misaligned to the point where they severed the spinal cord, and the phrenic nerve, leading to respiratory failure. She was frail and had low muscle tone, so it wouldn't have taken any great strength to overcome her. She also had osteoporosis, so her clavicles were both broken.'

He moved around the body and pointed at the woman's right-hand side.

'Livor mortis – after death she spent at least a few hours lying curled up on this side. You can see how the blood pooled. There's no mud or forest litter on the skin, so she wasn't killed at the scene and then propped upright against that tree.'

'She was killed elsewhere and moved,' Warren summarised.

'That'd be my guess, and that brings me to what's really worrying me,' said Jordan. 'The rate of decomposition at the scene looked a bit off and there was skin slippage reminding me of when a body has been submerged in water.'

'Could she have been killed in the bath?' asked Warren.

'No. I did wonder, but the histo lab looked at some of her tissue under the microscope. It's unmistakable. From the way in which the cells have burst open, and the fact she was still a couple of degrees below ambient temperature, I can only think of one explanation.

'She was frozen after death, stored and then left to thaw out.'

Tuesday 6th March

Chapter 16

'Winifred Palmer, eighty-two years old, known to her friends as Winnie.'

The screen behind Pymm showed a photograph of a smiling elderly woman, wearing a Santa hat. 'She's been missing since the new year. We found her picture on the Missing Persons database.'

'That's nearly two months,' said Ruskin. 'How come she wasn't flagged as a possible murder before then?'

'No compelling evidence of foul play,' said Pymm. 'She was a widow of twenty-odd years and lived alone with her dog. No kids or close family. She was recognised around the neighbourhood and St Mark's Church, but her main social activity was the "Wednesday Club" at Abbey Field's Community Centre. It was them that raised the alarm when she didn't turn up after the new year. When she didn't answer her phone, a couple of volunteers popped around to see if she was OK, and when she didn't answer the door, they called the police.'

'She was listed by Missing Persons as vulnerable,' said Sutton. 'I remember the bulletin and the search, but with no evidence she had been murdered or taken against her will, it never came our way.'

'It looks as though she vanished without a trace,' said Pymm.

'She's still on the active list, but they've had nothing. They couldn't be certain whether or not she left home willingly. Her coat was missing along with her handbag and purse. She tended to pay cash for everything and had made a large withdrawal a couple of days before Christmas, so there's no credit card activity and she had enough money to travel a significant distance if she so wished.'

Warren fought down a feeling of frustration. He knew the statistics; hundreds of people went missing every year in this corner of Hertfordshire alone, and some stayed missing. But it seemed strange that the elderly lady's disappearance hadn't been escalated.

'So, was she killed in her house, or was she killed somewhere else?' asked Hutch.

'There is a full SOCO team processing the house,' answered Pymm. 'The CSIs gave it a once-over back in January, but she was still a MisPer back then, so it didn't get the whole nine yards.'

'OK, everyone, Missing Persons may have dropped the ball on this, but now we know she was murdered, we need to focus on that,' ordered Warren, pushing aside his own recriminations. Missing Persons was as under-funded as every other department, and the festive season was their busiest period. Nevertheless, he wouldn't want to be working in that unit right now – doubtless an inquiry was headed their way and the results wouldn't be pretty.

'Whilst we're waiting for Forensics to finish, let's start with what we've got,' he continued. 'First off, when did she disappear?'

'Last confirmed sighting was about six p.m. on December 31st,' said Hardwick. 'Her neighbour said he saw her returning from the direction of the corner shop, dragging her wheeled shopping cart. That's confirmed by the shop's CCTV. She bought milk, bread, three tins of own-brand dog food and some cheese. All of them, aside from the dog food, were open in the fridge, but there was plenty left. All the dog food had been placed in bowls on the kitchen floor.'

'So she disappeared between New Year's Eve and Wednesday

the third,' said Warren. 'Can we narrow it down any more? I'm assuming somebody checked her freezer?'

There was a rustling of paper, before Hutchinson spoke up. 'No mention of it, but the photos show it was a miniature, on-the-counter job. There's no way she could fit in there.'

That was something at least; even though Missing Persons could have been forgiven for not thinking to look in a freezer for the house's missing occupant, the possibility Mrs Palmer had been in the house whilst they searched for her would have delighted the tabloids.

'Just make sure the CSIs check she hasn't got a chest freezer out the back or there's any evidence that one has been removed,' cautioned Warren.

'There were letters on the doormat,' said Hardwick. 'And the postie recalls delivering to her house on the Tuesday, the first day after the bank holiday. The letters were junk mail, so she could have left them on the floor, I suppose, but they believe she was a generally tidy person.'

'Then that suggests she went missing between the Sunday and the Tuesday,' said Sutton.

'Hutch, can you organise some door-knockers for the street again?' asked Warren. 'It's been a few months, but maybe we'll pick up somebody who saw something. I see from the report there were a couple of house parties that night. Try and track down attendees; somebody might have seen something. We're announcing her death and renewing the public appeal at lunchtime.

'The freezing and thawing has messed up the decomposition, so it's unclear how long she had been dead before she was frozen, which scuppers time of death. Was she held for a time before she was killed? There's no sign of sexual assault, nor injuries consistent with physical abuse or torture prior to death.'

'I'm assuming the temperature outside didn't dip low enough for her to freeze after she was dumped there?' said Hutchinson.

'No. Even if she was left there in January, and the dog walker somehow missed her last Friday, there were no lengthy spells of sub-zero temperatures that could have frozen a human body, and night-time lows for the last week have been above zero. The degree of decomposition would have been far greater if she was outside all that time. Plus, her core temperature was still below ambient. She was definitely dumped there recently, although there's no way to tell if she came straight from the freezer or was thawed out before being transported.'

'Then presumably her killer has access to a suitable freezer, or cold-storage facility,' said Ruskin.

'She was tiny,' said Hardwick. 'I reckon she could easily fit in a domestic chest freezer.'

'I'll look into recent purchases of freezers,' said Pymm. 'I'll also see what we have in the way locally of lock-ups with an electricity supply to power one.'

'Then let's find out everything we can about Mrs Palmer. Who she was, who she knew and what she did,' said Warren. 'And let's figure out who would want to kill an eighty-two-year-old widow and keep her body in a freezer for two months.

'Next up, the Culverhouses. Derek claims to have been parked up at War Memorial Park on the night his parents were most likely killed. Nothing we have found so far rules out him travelling to his parents' that evening. We need to pursue that. Hutch?'

'We have roadblocks near the park asking if anyone remembers a white Volvo parked there that evening,' said Hutchinson. 'Annoyingly, there are several routes he could have taken from his house to the park. We can exclude all the main roads with ANPR, but that still leaves a significant number of residential streets he could have driven down. I've organised teams to canvass every house and business in that area for CCTV. If we can get a glimpse of his vehicle at the right time, we might be able to exclude him.'

'Good. How's the search going?'

'Well underway,' said Sutton. 'The drug dogs have finished in the flat and the car. No sign of anything other than the cannabis we already found. They are testing his car with luminol and black lights. Andy Harrison reckons we could have a preliminary report by the end of play today.'

'Good, all in hand,' said Warren. 'Right, folks, I'm unavailable for the next couple of hours, so Tony is in charge. And if you don't think he's up to the job, either wait until I get back or go badger DSI Grayson.'

* * *

Warren had arrived with only seconds to spare. 'Sorry, sorry, sorry,' Warren repeated as he scurried across the waiting room. Susan rolled her eyes but accepted his kiss by way of an apology.

He'd spent the day so far juggling two different murder investigations, successfully distracting himself from what would happen next. Susan gave his hand a squeeze.

'It'll be fine,' she said.

How could she be so calm, especially after what had happened previously?

He took a deep breath and nodded.

Twenty-one weeks. They were past the halfway point – further than they'd ever made it before. He squeezed back and they headed through the door marked 'Ultrasound'.

* * *

Warren couldn't hide his grin as he returned to CID.

'They've got your eyes,' joked Sutton as he looked at the black and white photo. Warren was perched on the edge of his desk.

The sonographer had been very happy with the results of the scan, but there were many more weeks to go, and the couple had been cursed with bad luck and tragedy ever since they'd started trying for a baby.

Warren had largely come to terms with the fact that the couple's problems were almost certainly due to his reduced fertility. They had been fortunate that the clinic they chose employed one of the shockingly few male fertility specialists working in the UK, and so the root cause of the problem had been found sooner than it otherwise might have been.

Nonetheless, their journey had been stressful and lengthy. Their initial cycles had been unsuccessful, with the embryos failing to implant. When the couple had finally fallen pregnant with twins two and a half years ago, it seemed as though their luck was finally changing. Unfortunately, it wasn't to be.

'And you definitely don't want to know if it's a boy or a girl?' asked Pymm, as Sutton passed her the printout.

'No, it'll be a nice surprise,' Warren replied.

'How are Susan's parents taking the news?' asked Sutton. Warren's in-laws were strict Catholics. The couple's initial attempts at IVF had caused a rift with Bernice, Susan's mother, who ascribed to the Church's teachings on assisted reproduction techniques.

'Excited,' said Warren. 'Genuinely.'

It was a sad irony that the heartbreak from the loss of the twins had finally repaired the rift with Susan's mother, and Bernice and Dennis were excited at the prospect of becoming grandparents again.

Carefully placing the photograph back in his wallet, Warren stood up. There was enough time to make a coffee before the briefing, and this time he'd decided the team needed a pick-me-up, diet be damned.

* * *

'Forensics are in from Derek Culverhouse's flat and car,' Sutton told the meeting. 'They've found a fleece top with what appears to be bloodstains on the right sleeve. It's been through the washing machine, but they are confident they can get DNA.'

106

'Great,' said Warren.

'And they've found blood traces on the dashboard and the inside passenger door handle of his car. They've been wiped clean but showed up under luminol.'

'If it matches his parents, that's going to take some explaining. But if it's transfer from Derek's clothing, why would there be blood on the passenger side?' asked Warren.

'If he had blood on his fleece, perhaps he took it off before he got in the car?' suggested Sutton. 'He could have got some on his hands, and then transferred that if he put the fleece on the passenger seat.'

'Then why no blood on the seat?' asked Warren.

'Maybe he put his top in a carrier bag first?'

Warren tapped his teeth thoughtfully; something didn't feel quite right. 'OK, let's keep our powder dry for the time being and wait for the results to come back from the lab. Let's be certain the blood belongs to his parents before we bring him in again.'

Wednesday 7th March

Chapter 17

'We have two potential witnesses from a New Year's Eve house party a couple of doors down from Winnie Palmer's bungalow,' Hutchinson announced shortly after the morning briefing.

'Brilliant,' said Warren. Rachel Pymm had gone through the elderly lady's phone record and noticed an unanswered call to her house phone on New Year's Day, from an old friend trying to wish her a Happy New Year. It was another embarrassing oversight by the Missing Persons Unit, but it reinforced the team's belief that whatever had happened had taken place New Year's Eve.

'I wouldn't get too excited; by their own admission, they were rather the worse for wear. But they're willing to have a go at describing a man they saw loading something into the boot of a dark-coloured car around midnight.'

* * *

'I'm not going to lie, I'd had a proper skinful,' admitted Ashton Kirkby. The male witness was a broad-shouldered, dark-haired white man of thirty-two. Originally from Bolton, his heavy accent signposted his origins from north-west England.

His girlfriend, Sammy Eastley, was a petite, blonde-haired

woman, two years his junior, with a local accent. She admitted to being a little the worse for wear herself.

'We saw in the new year alone outside.' She touched her boyfriend's hand and smiled.

'Tell us what you saw,' Warren encouraged them.

'Well there were this bloke changing in the middle of the road a few doors down,' said Kirkby.

Warren blinked. 'Sorry, say that again.'

'This bloke. He were putting something in the boot of his car, dressed in just his undies. He took a tracksuit out of a carrier bag, got dressed and drove off.'

'I thought it was a bit weird, which is why we stuck around,' interjected Eastley.

'To be fair, I've seen stranger in Manchester on a Friday night,' said Kirkby.

'You said he was loading something into the boot of his car, did you see what it was?' asked Warren.

'No, sorry,' said Eastley.

'Can you describe him?' asked Hutchinson.

The couple looked at one another.

'Well it was pretty dark,' said Eastley.

'And I'd had a *lot* to drink,' added Kirkby. 'But he was big.'

'How big?' asked Warren.

'Over six foot.'

His girlfriend agreed.

'And what about ethnicity? What colour was he?' asked Hutchinson, scribbling in his notepad.

'White, definitely,' said Eastley.

'Hair colour?'

'Bald,' said Kirkby.

Eastley shook her head. 'I think he was wearing a hat, like a skin-tight one.'

'Aye, could have been,' admitted Kirkby.

'You said he was big – what was his build?' asked Warren.

112

'Chunky. Not fat, but not muscly,' said Eastley.

'Any tattoos or distinctive marks?' asked Hutchinson.

The couple looked at each other and shrugged.

'And how old would you say he was?' he asked.

'Forty to fifty,' said Kirkby, confidently.

'Twenties,' replied Eastley, equally confidently.

'Give over,' scoffed her boyfriend. 'He was bald.'

'No he wasn't, he was wearing a hat,' she replied. 'Sorry, it was dark.'

'And I was absolutely rat-arsed,' Kirkby reminded them.

'We'll record that as twenty to fifty,' said Warren, drily.

'Can you describe the car?' asked Hutchinson.

'Dark-coloured,' said Eastley.

'Yeah,' agreed her boyfriend.

'Did you notice the make or model? Or the licence plate, perhaps?' asked Warren, more in hope than expectation.

'I reckon it was an Audi,' said Eastley. 'I didn't look at the licence plate.'

'Nah, Beamer,' Kirkby contradicted her.

'Could have been. It was a nice one, I think.'

'What about its shape, then?' asked Warren patiently.

'Five-door,' said Kirkby.

'Hatchback,' said Eastley.

'Same thing, isn't it?' Kirkby asked.

'Close enough,' Hutchinson reassured them.

After a few more minutes of probing, he read back through the description they had given him.

'I'm really sorry,' said Eastley. 'It was dark, and the streetlights cast a shadow.'

'And I was absolutely wankered,' repeated Kirkby.

'Well, you've both been really helpful,' said Warren as he closed his notepad. They'd go through the pair's description and see what useful information they could glean from it; vaguer descriptions had yielded results in the past.

Eastley snapped her fingers. 'One more thing. When he turned his head, the streetlight caught his jaw. It looked a bit weird. Like it was twisted or something.'

'That's right,' agreed Kirkby. 'It were a bit like a bloke I used to play rugby with. Took a knee in the face. He were an ugly bastard to begin with, but it didn't help.'

Warren looked over at Hutchinson, who shrugged. It was all they had so far.

'Would you be prepared to sit with an artist and do an e-fit for us?' asked Warren.

'Sure, I've not got anything planned,' said Eastley.

'Me neither,' said Kirkby. 'Could be fun. Whilst we're waiting though, I could do with a fag and a pee. And any chance of some more coffee? Had a bit of a session last night.'

Chapter 18

'I was pretty borderline about authorising an e-fit until she mentioned his jaw,' admitted Warren, as he projected the newly completed picture onto the briefing room whiteboard. The person seen outside Winnie Palmer's house as the new year was rung in was their best – and only – hope so far.

The most distinguishing feature had been his jaw, agreed upon by both of the witnesses: twisted slightly to the left, with a notice-able overbite.

'I've seen worse,' said Sutton, 'but I think we're going to get a lot of hits with the description.'

He read from the page. 'White male, bald or wearing a hat. Over six feet, with a large build. Twenty to fifty years old. Clean-shaven. Deformed lower jaw. Seen driving a dark-coloured hatchback in the vicinity of Tollbooth Road at or around midnight. Was seen loading something into the boot of the car at midnight and getting changed into a dark-coloured tracksuit in the street.'

'Well, it's a start,' said Warren. 'Unfortunately, Mr Kirkby may have had a glass of shandy or two. Presumably our suspect's car was from outside the area, perhaps somebody recalls what time it arrived?'

'Good luck on New Year's Eve,' said Hutchinson. 'There were at least two house parties that night, with guests who were staying over.'

'I know what you're going to say, and my team is already on it,' said Richardson.

'And I know what *you're* going to say,' said Warren. 'Do the best you can. Any dark cars in the area. Prioritise hatchbacks. Could be an Audi or a BMW, but don't restrict the search terms. What's camera coverage like?'

'Nothing on her street, but there are a couple of nearby junctions with ANPR. Further out and there are some main roads with speed cameras and a couple of garage forecourts. Depending on the driver's local knowledge, he may have been able to dodge cameras. What sort of timeframe do you want to prioritise? The roads would have been quiet around midnight, obviously, but we don't know what time he turned up.'

'The neighbour spotted her at six earlier that day and doesn't think there was a dark car parked outside her house then,' said Warren. 'Try four p.m. until six a.m. Hedge our bets.'

It was little more than an educated guess, balancing the need to ensure they didn't miss the killer, without swamping the Video Analysis Unit down in Welwyn.

Winnie Palmer's body had been dumped in Beaconsfield Woods, almost a dozen miles from her home. In the intervening period, the killer had stored her body in a freezer. Did it make sense that the killer would transport her body a significant distance outside of the local area, before returning and dumping it? Any normal person would have wanted to minimise the distance and time travelled with the remains of somebody they'd murdered.

But then this person had killed a defenceless old lady for no apparent reason. They were hardly a normal person.

* * *

The e-fit compiled by the drunk couple was circulated at a hastily organised press conference, along with a description of the man's car. Warren was careful to describe him as a potential witness, rather than a person of interest, and appealed for more people to come forward. The couple weren't the most reliable witnesses; they really needed independent corroboration.

The killer must have been inside her house for at least a few minutes. Presumably, their vehicle had been parked in the street all that time. A better description would help them filter the hundreds of vehicles caught on ANPR that night.

Unfortunately, the twenty-four hours since the initial press appeal had given the reporters ample time to trawl through their archives and there were awkward questions about why the police had failed to follow up on the initial reports of an elderly, vulnerable woman, missing in the middle of winter. There were no good answers to that question and Warren was forced to deflect it with an agreed-upon statement that sounded weak even to his ears.

He was similarly evasive about the manner of her death, when they thought she had died, or how long she had been lying in the woods. These were valuable details that only the killer could know. He made no mention of her body being frozen, merely stating they were treating the death as suspicious and renewing their appeal for any sightings since she went missing.

When the conference finally finished, nobody in the room was satisfied, least of all Warren. It was no wonder John Grayson had uncharacteristically missed the opportunity to get himself in front of the cameras.

Thursday 8th March

Chapter 19

'The response from the e-fit is better than we expected,' said Pymm addressing the team briefing.

'Does anyone stand out?' asked Warren.

'You mean aside from our frequent flyers?' she replied. 'Batty Betty has suggested the funny shape of his jaw might be because he didn't have time to pull his human skin back on again.'

'Cup of tea and a biscuit?' said Hardwick.

'Yeah, although apparently she's not happy we don't give her custard creams anymore,' said Pymm. 'Community policing's not what it used to be.'

'Well let's assume that our killer isn't a lizard in disguise, and stick with the humans on the list,' said Warren.

Ditching the biscuits had been done to reduce costs and make the police station less attractive to those with a tenuous grasp on reality. It saddened Warren; Middlesbury nick was a community police station, and the desk team were proud to be a caring face for the lonely and troubled. But budget cuts had reduced the opening hours for the front desk, and they could ill afford the time to perform the parts of their job that couldn't be measured by performance targets.

'We have a total of twelve individuals named, four of them

121

more than once,' continued Pymm. 'Two of them are known to us. Of the eight only suggested once, two have records.'

All of them – and any new names that cropped up – would be investigated, but they needed to prioritise.

'Focus on the six named more than once or with records. We'll decide who to visit and in what order before lunch.' He turned to Richardson. 'How are we doing with the traffic cameras?'

'Lots of dark five-doors in the hours after the parties finished, mostly cabs,' said Richardson. 'We've run all the plates through the DVLA but nobody interesting has been flagged, and none of the indexes are on our system.'

'We'll come back to them if we have any suspects,' said Warren.

The public response to the e-fit had been encouraging, but the lack of detail was a concern. Warren suspected that any large white male with a crooked jaw within fifty miles of Middlesbury was likely to end up being shopped. On the other hand, the couple had been so unsure of key details it was quite possible that nobody would even recognise the person they were looking for.

Karen Hardwick was frowning.

'What's bothering you, Karen?' asked Warren.

'It's just a weird thought I've been having,' she said. 'The Culverhouses had a dog. And it looks as though the killer laid out a few days' food to make sure it was OK until it was found.'

Warren saw where she was going immediately.

'Yes,' said Warren. 'And it looked as though Winnie Palmer's dog had been left extra food also.'

'Surely that's just a coincidence?' said Sutton. 'Winnie Palmer's killer clearly wanted it to look as though she had left of her own accord and if Derek Culverhouse killed his parents, then maybe he just didn't want the family dog to suffer?'

'Derek claims the man who took his mother to her respite club was "a funny-looking bugger",' Hardwick persisted. 'Could that be a reference to a crooked jaw?'

'But the manner of death was completely different,' said Hutchinson.

'You're probably right,' said Warren. 'But let's not rule out a link entirely. If there is someone out there killing elderly people, then we need to know about it sooner, rather than later.'

*   *   *

'Who have we got?' asked Warren. It was coming up to midday and Rachel Pymm had commandeered the large table in the briefing room. She sat at the end, directing her indexers like a field marshal planning a battle, as they laid out individual piles of paper for each of the persons named by callers.

'Top of my hit list is Callum Harradine,' she said. 'Five different callers named him.'

The man in question was a hard-faced man of forty-three. Balding, with a flattened nose, the printout from the PNC described him as six feet two, with a large build.

'I recognise that name,' said Sutton. 'He used to be a low-level scrote; nicking cars, fighting, shoplifting, that sort of thing. Then he got involved in drugs and was done over with a baseball bat by a rival dealer – broken jaw as I recall. Didn't stop him sticking a knife in his attacker and getting five years though.'

'No mention of that distinctive hooter,' pointed out Hardwick.

'It was dark, two months ago, and as Mr Kirkby was so keen to stress, they were slightly tipsy,' said Hutchinson.

'Killing an old lady and sticking her body in a freezer seems a bit of an escalation,' said Warren.

'I'd agree, but that's not all he's been suspected of,' said Pymm. 'If you look at his file, he's also got a string of complaints against him for voyeurism and harassing behaviour. Nothing's ever really stuck, but it's enough for him to be on our watch list.'

'Hmm, violence, drugs and low-level sexual offences,' said Warren.

'And there's more. I called his previous probation officer,' said Pymm. 'After his last spell inside, he vowed to "go straight". She didn't believe him for a second, but there was nothing she could do. He's not stupid. He knows exactly what she needs and he delivers it; apparently, he's quite the charmer when he wants to be. Last she heard, he and an equally dodgy mate started up their own business doing house repairs and odd jobs. All by word of mouth and cold-calling. At least a couple of his former customers were burgled a few weeks after they completed the job. Unfortunately, there were no forensics linking back to them. Volume crime have them on their radar.'

'Winnie Palmer could have been a burglary gone wrong,' mused Ruskin. 'If he's as charming as they say, she may have had him in to do some odd jobs. If he thought she was going to be out that night, maybe she startled him?'

'If it was, then he did a very good job of cleaning up after himself,' said Warren. 'Mind you, if he knew her, that would explain why there were no signs of forced entry. He could have swiped her keys and made a copy.'

'And the neighbours didn't hear the dog,' said Ruskin. 'Apparently, he goes nuts normally when a stranger knocks. And there's nothing to say he didn't have an accomplice who wasn't seen by our witnesses.'

'What bothers me,' said Warren, 'is the way he then took her body and hid it in a freezer. Surely that's not the first thing you think of when you've accidentally killed an old lady?' He shook his head. 'My gut is telling me that this was premeditated. Either way we need to see if any of her neighbours remember any handymen or cold-callers in the area in the weeks before New Year. Rachel, find a headshot of his dodgy mate and pass it on to Hutch. Even if he wasn't involved in the murder, he may have been with Harradine when he was choosing his victim. If Winnie Palmer had any jobs done, I suspect she'll have paid cash, so don't count on a paper trail. Look into who did the Culverhouses' kitchen, whilst you're at it.'

Warren moved around the table to the next pile of paper.

'Eric Morton,' he read out, picking up the printout from the PNC. He scanned the offender details. 'Physically he fits the description, such as it is. Again, some violent offences, including domestic abuse of his ex-partner. Most recent was last month; he's currently on bail with a restraining order.'

'Three tips,' offered Pymm. 'Apparently, he used to be an amateur boxer. It looks as though he has an overbite, and his jaw is twisted slightly to one side. It's the opposite direction to what our witnesses said, but given their state, that's probably not a deal-breaker.'

'It looks as though one of these callers had a lot to say about him,' Sutton said, picking up two sheets of densely typed transcript.

'She certainly did,' said Pymm. 'Unfortunately, she wouldn't give her details to the call handler. I'm wondering if it's actually his ex, given how much she knows about him.'

'It says here that he works as a minicab driver, and off the books as some extra muscle at The Sidings nightclub,' said Sutton. 'Which is unsurprising – he'd never get a licence as a door super-visor with his record.'

'I don't suppose they said who he drives for?' asked Richardson.

'No,' said Pymm. 'She either couldn't or wouldn't name the firm. And again, given his record, he would have been off the books. I can't imagine the firm is going to give him up voluntarily. Stanley Culverhouse drove, but his son thinks a volunteer picked her up for her respite club.'

She looked at her notes. 'There are no calls to any taxi firms in Winnie Palmer's phone records, and she didn't have a mobile phone, so she can't have called an Uber. I'll double-check the Culverhouses, just in case.'

'Apparently Winnie used to walk to her social club or get a

lift from a friend,' said Hutchinson. 'And she caught the bus to Asda every few weeks for a big shop.'

'But how did she return?' said Hardwick. 'She was a tiny little thing; she can't have lugged that shopping trolley onto a bus if it was filled with groceries. When I was a student, I'd walk to the supermarket with my housemates once a month, do a big shop, then catch a taxi home. You didn't need a mobile to call for one, because they had a customer handset connected directly to the cab companies. You just pressed a button.'

'Get down there and find out which firms advertise their services,' said Warren. 'Let's also send some bodies to The Sidings and see if Morton was working New Year's Eve. If someone is willing to admit he was there at midnight, then he has an alibi. Do we have a current address for either of these upstanding citizens?'

'Both of them have somewhere listed, although Morton shouldn't be staying with his partner,' said Pymm.

'Well let's prioritise these two first,' ordered Warren. 'If they've seen the e-fit, it may have spooked them. We don't want them vanishing.'

He moved around the table again. 'I take it these are the two named only once that are in the system?'

'Yes, they are well down my pecking order,' said Pymm. 'Both of their descriptions are tenuous, and their criminal records are low-level, minor offences, with nothing recent. I reckon it's just pissed-off neighbours trying to get some payback for antisocial behaviour.'

'Right,' said Warren. 'Callum Harradine and Eric Morton are the priority. Do some digging into the other two jokers and find out if there is any conceivable connection to our victim, then check if they have an alibi. The remaining names have no record, am I right?' asked Warren.

'That's correct,' said Pymm. 'I've found names and addresses for most of the original twelve; no photos at this stage. I may be able to find a headshot from the DVLA. A name and approximate address might do the job. A couple of callers will need a call back, to see if they can be a bit more specific than "the weird-looking bloke who lives in my street". Most just had one call. Two were named by more than one person.'

Hardwick picked up the list of names, read down it and passed it over to Ruskin. If Pymm hadn't found their names on either the Police National Computer or HOLMES, the chance that anyone would recognise the names were slim.

The sheet continued to make its way around the table.

'We need to follow every lead,' said Warren, 'and these are all we've got so far. Welwyn have assigned us plenty of support, so use them.'

He was about to dismiss everyone when the sheet finally made it to him. He glanced at it automatically, before going to place it on the table. He paused and looked at the printout again.

'Spencer Aspinall,' he said. 'I know that name.'

'He was named twice,' supplied Pymm. 'The first caller said the description reminded him of the strange lad who lives down his road. He's confident on the name, because his old man has his name on the side of his van.' She turned to the next sheet. 'This one was a female caller. No address, but she named him and said the description reminded her of a lad she went to school with. Again, she said he was a bit of a weirdo.'

Warren's mouth felt dry. It couldn't be, surely? He did the sums.

'It says here that he's about twenty-one. How certain was she?'

'They were in the same year at school, so presumably she knows how old he is,' said Pymm, looking at him curiously.

'I don't suppose she mentioned the name of the school?'

Pymm's eyes flicked down. 'Yes, Riverview Academy.'

'I can't believe it,' said Warren. 'I think Susan used to teach him.'

Chapter 20

'Susan taught Spencer Aspinall biology A level when he was in sixth form, but had run-ins with him and his family as head of department when he was lower down the school,' Warren told Grayson after he'd called his wife. Warren had gone to him as soon as he realised there might be a personal connection with one of their suspects. Susan had been fairly sanguine, pointing out that she'd taught or dealt with literally thousands of young people during her career. 'I'm amazed this hasn't happened before,' she'd said. Nevertheless, any connection with his wife, no matter how tenuous, made Warren uncomfortable.

'In a nutshell, he was extremely bright, but very lazy. He did the bare minimum to avoid being kicked out of sixth form, but spent most of his time playing video games and, the school believed but couldn't prove, smoking weed.

'His home life was a cause for concern; his father was verbally aggressive at parents' evenings, berating Spencer for being lazy and squandering chances that he was never afforded. He was also hostile towards some teachers, blaming them for not being able to inspire Spencer to work harder. Eventually, he was banned from the school site.'

'What about his mother?' asked Grayson.

'The complete opposite. In Susan's words, he was "mummy's little soldier". He could do no wrong and the school was letting down "the brightest pupil they ever had". However, she wasn't as aggressive as his father and so the school continued to engage with her, although any communications were run past his form tutor first. She blamed all of his problems on bullying – either by pupils or staff.'

'God knows bullies don't really need a reason,' said Grayson, 'but was there anything specific?'

'Take your pick. In sixth form especially, he was very socially awkward and regarded as creepy by both female pupils and staff, with very few friends. It didn't help that he was somewhat averse to bathing. His mother claimed the bullying was because he had a mild speech impediment, caused by a congenital jaw deformity that caused it to be twisted to one side. Susan thinks the e-fit could be him if you ignore the age estimates.'

'He's definitely worth looking at, if only because the description matches,' mused Grayson. 'But is there anything else beyond him being a bit of an oddball with a stifling home life?'

'Nothing concrete,' admitted Warren. 'We know there were some concerns about him being left in the care of his grandparents for an extended period when his parents went on holiday. They were ill and not suited to looking after him; the school flagged it as potential neglect. He does have a history of violence – he apparently flattened the school judo champ a month before their final exams, when he objected to Spencer making a clumsy pass at his girlfriend. The school dealt with it internally; the lad's parents agreed not to call the police as long as Spencer was sent home for study leave, and not allowed to return until his exams.

'His mother blames this for him failing to achieve the grades necessary to go to university, but Susan disputes that. They'd been predicting him straight Ds for months because he wasn't doing enough work, and his teaching had pretty much finished by that point.'

Grayson tapped the table with his pen thoughtfully. 'A crap childhood, possible anger management issues and perhaps a chip on his shoulder. It ticks a few boxes, I suppose. OK, bring him in and at least check out his alibi.'

*　*　*

Spencer Aspinall wasn't the only one of their potential suspects who was ticking the right boxes.

'Eric Morton worked for Abacus Cabs,' said Hardwick. 'Not that they'll admit it. I visited all three cab firms linked to Asda's customer courtesy phone. All of them claimed never to have heard of him, but one of the Abacus drivers overheard me. He recognised Morton's first name and description. He also confirmed that he drives a black car, although he doesn't know the make or model.'

'Can we get hold of Morton's logs?' asked Warren.

'Not unless they admit employing him illegally. Apparently, legitimate drivers have their jobs recorded on the computer. But they have a few others they dispatch using word of mouth. They tell the customer the driver's wireless credit card reader isn't working so they have to pay cash. The unlicensed drivers get paid under the table, the cab firm doesn't declare that income for tax purposes, and they have the biggest pool of drivers in town. Everyone's a winner, except for the legit drivers who lose out on fares.'

'Sounds risky,' said Sutton. 'If any of those drivers are traced back to the firm, they'll be fined, and the council may suspend their operating licence.'

'Apparently, they have fake IDs and stickers to fool the punters, and it's an open secret the council cutbacks have decimated their enforcement department. Quite worrying when you think about it.'

It certainly was. There had been a number of high-profile murderers and rapists who had found their victims through driving taxis.

'Do we know if Morton was working on New Year's Eve?' asked Warren.

'He couldn't remember, but it's the busiest night of the year and they charge a fortune after midnight, so it's likely.'

'He wasn't working at The Sidings on New Year's Eve,' interjected Hutchinson. 'The woman we spoke to was delighted we are interested in him. Female servers are advised not to go out the back to change the barrels if he's on shift, as he can be "a bit creepy".'

'And she was certain he wasn't there that night?' said Warren.

'As sure as she can be,' said Hutchinson. 'There are always plenty of police about on New Year's Eve; the club hires additional licensed security and gives the freelancers the night off, just in case.'

'It would be an easy alibi,' said Hardwick. 'A couple of hours driving before midnight, clock off and kill Winnie Palmer, then clock back on so passengers remember your face.'

Warren turned to Richardson. 'Get onto the DVLA and see what he drives, then check where he was that night.'

'Already ahead of you, Boss,' she said. 'According to the DVLA he lost his driving licence eighteen months ago for drink-driving, so has no cars or insurance registered in his name. He owned a blue Ford Focus, but according to their records, sold it on shortly after he was convicted.'

'Hardly a deal-breaker,' said Sutton. 'That's probably why he's unlicensed.'

'Then we'll need to do some checking around and see if we can find the licence number of the black car he's using now,' said Warren.

'I just had a disturbing thought,' said Hutchinson. 'If he did go back on shift after killing her, it's possible he spent the rest of the night picking up punters with Winnie Palmer's body in the boot of his taxi.'

'You're right – that is disturbing,' said Sutton. 'Thanks for sharing, Hutch.'

There were now several suspects, all of whom needed interviewing. Warren decided to let the team gather more information on Eric Morton before they pulled him in, which left Spencer Aspinall and Callum Harradine, the career criminal who had also matched the e-fit.

He'd been mulling over what to do about Aspinall. He knew he had to keep some distance between the investigation and Susan.

Jones was a common-enough surname, but it was no secret at her school that she was married to a senior police officer; Warren had even spoken at careers evenings.

Aspinall was young enough that he may respond well to a more youthful officer, making one of the two DCs the obvious choice. However, largely built young men often felt the need to prove themselves when faced with an even bigger young man. They could do without excess testosterone sloshing about, so he decided Ruskin would be better suited to the more-seasoned Harradine. Hardwick could deal with Aspinall.

Ideally, he wanted their suspects at ease. The killer was clearly intelligent and hopefully would feel that if they kept their calm when interviewed, they could deflect the investigators' attention. If they felt threatened, they could shut down, insist upon a solicitor, and no comment their way through the whole process. Warren decided that they'd only arrest once they felt they had their suspect in front of them.

But he wasn't about to send his colleagues into the firing line alone.

* * *

Two uniformed officers accompanied Karen Hardwick to the smart, semi-detached home Spencer Aspinall shared with his parents. The driveway was empty.

The house was medium-sized but included a one-car garage with a roller door to the right of the front entrance. Hardwick pressed the doorbell and waited patiently. The bell had clearly sounded inside the house, but there was no pause in the noise of the violent video game drifting through the garage door. She was about to ring again, and dispatch one of the officers to walk down the narrow path between the garage wall and the neighbouring hedge, when a shadow appeared through the frosted glass.

A woman in her early forties peered through the gap in the door, surprise on her face.

'Mrs Aspinall?' queried Hardwick.

The woman's voice was quiet, almost timid. 'Yes.'

Hardwick introduced herself, then asked if her son was present.

'Yes. What's it about?' the woman asked, making no move to allow the officers in.

'We just need to ask Spencer a few questions,' said Hardwick favouring her with a smile.

'Why? He hasn't done anything,' she said, still not moving.

Hardwick recalled DCI Jones' briefing. Patricia Aspinall had been described as 'overprotective' in her interactions with the school – it seemed that three years after her son had left sixth form, little had changed.

'It'd be better if we speak to him directly. May we come in?' asked Hardwick, her tone polite but insistent.

Eventually, the mother stepped back. One of the uniforms casually moved a little further down the driveway, ready to respond if Aspinall decided to make a run for it out of the garage's side door.

Mrs Aspinall walked a couple of steps down the hallway to a wooden door set into the left-hand wall and knocked on it.

'Spencer? The police are here.'

The gunshots and shouts from whatever game was being played continued unabated.

'Sorry, sometimes he plays with his headphones on.' She rapped harder and repeated herself more loudly.

Hardwick wasn't really into video games; she wondered if

it was normal to wear headphones and also have the speakers turned up so loud.

Patricia Aspinall was about to knock a third time, when the sound suddenly stopped. A few moments later, there came the slide of a bolt and a key turning.

'Sorry,' she said. 'My husband insisted on installing decent locks when he knocked through the wall to the garage. There's no point having good security on the front and back doors, if somebody breaking into the garage can just kick in the connecting door.'

'That makes sense,' said Hardwick, although she did wonder why whoever was in there needed to lock the door if it was occupied – and why there was a bolt on the garage side.

Finally, the door opened. The smell of stale sweat, cigarette smoke and what might have been cannabis drifted out.

Spencer Aspinall wasn't as big as Moray Ruskin, but he filled much of the open doorway. Hardwick peered around him and could make out an expensive-looking computer setup; an image of a heavily armed soldier – apparently in the middle of a gun battle – glared out, 'Game Paused' blinking on the screen. To the other side of Aspinall, she spied dumbbells and other weight-lifting equipment. From her viewpoint she couldn't see a chest freezer.

'Spencer Aspinall?'

'Yeah?'

Aspinall's gaze flicked down to her trouser-clad legs then back up again, before settling on her chest. She was glad the cool weather meant she was wearing a thick coat.

'I wonder if you would be willing to come with us and answer a few questions?' she said, politely but firmly.

'What's it about? I'm busy,' he said.

'It's about New Year's Eve,' said Hardwick, interested to see his reaction.

He shrugged. 'I was here all night, seeing in the new year. Can't really help you.'

'We watched *Graham Norton* on the BBC and then watched the fireworks,' interjected his mother.

'Well, I haven't told you what I want to know yet,' said Hardwick. 'Why don't you come with us, and we'll have a little chat.'

Aspinall stared at her for a few seconds before giving a big sigh. 'Fine. I'll get my coat.'

'Should I call a lawyer?' asked his mother, wringing her hands together.

'Don't be silly,' scoffed Aspinall. 'I haven't done anything.'

'I'll call your father – he'll know what to do,' she said, heading back into the house, towards an old-fashioned telephone table.

'Don't worry, Mum,' snapped Aspinall. 'I'll be back home in a couple of hours. I probably just fit a description or something.' He turned to Hardwick. 'That's right, isn't it? Otherwise I'd have handcuffs on.'

Hardwick said nothing, just gestured for him to leave the house ahead of her. The two uniformed officers flanked him as he walked down the drive.

'On our way,' Hardwick radioed.

* * *

On the other side of town, Warren pulled to a halt behind the ambulance, his tyres grinding. The call had come in over the radio just minutes before, and after a moment's indecision, he'd leapt into his car, Tony Sutton beside him.

By the time they'd arrived, his heart was no longer in his mouth.

'We need to talk about this,' said Sutton quietly, placing a hand on his friend's arm before they exited the car. Warren nodded; Sutton was right. His reaction had been stronger than the situation warranted, and he was glad Sutton had insisted on accompanying him, relaying information from the open radio channel.

135

Despite the officer's measured tones, the call had been dramatic. 'Officer down, ambulance needed.'

Karen Hardwick already had Spencer Aspinall in the back of a police car. That left only one other person from Warren's team out on a job, and he instinctively knew the identity of his fallen colleague before he even heard the details from the dispatcher.

The flashback had been intense, catching Warren off-guard. It had been years since he'd made the same frantic call himself, covered in Gary Hastings' blood after his senseless death. The subsequent counselling sessions had helped deal with the lingering PTSD enough for him to do his job, but the thought that he may have placed another of his junior colleagues in danger still gave him bad dreams.

Moray Ruskin sat on the back step of the ambulance, holding a bloody cloth to his face. He looked up sheepishly when Warren approached.

'Looks worse than it is,' he mumbled. 'Bastard stuck a headbutt on me. Proper Glasgow kiss.'

'What happened?' asked Sutton.

Ruskin motioned towards the two uniformed constables who had accompanied him to Callum Harradine's address.

'He must have seen us through the window; he was out the front door and down the garden path before we even managed to park the car. Me and PC Cain gave chase.' He smiled ruefully. 'I was a bit quicker off the mark.'

'Harradine legged it down that alleyway,' said Cain, pointing towards the end of the row of houses. 'Mr Triathlon here followed.' She glared at him disapprovingly.

'Yeah, he was waiting around the corner,' continued Ruskin. 'Caught me off-guard with a shoulder barge and then finished the job with a headbutt and disappeared over a garden fence. They've searched the area, but he's vanished. Sorry.'

'By the time I got there, there was blood all down his shirt,' said Cain. 'I thought the silly sod had been stabbed.'

'Bloody hell, Moray, what were you thinking?' said Warren. 'You're not in uniform anymore. No stab vest, no baton or spray. You don't even have a decent pair of rigid handcuffs to wallop him with. Christ …' He took a deep breath.

Ruskin raised his hands in surrender. 'You're absolutely right, Boss. I fucked up. I should have let these guys handle it.'

'Yeah, you should have,' said Cain punching him lightly on the shoulder. 'If you were that desperate for a collar, I'd have let you put the handcuffs on him.'

Ruskin gave a laugh, followed by a wince.

'Well at least you're in one piece,' said Sutton. 'What's the prognosis?'

'I didn't hit my head and my nose isn't broken. Reckon I'll have a couple of shiners and some sore ribs, but otherwise I'm right as rain.'

'Off home with you then,' said Warren.

'No, seriously, I'm fine. I need to write everything up.'

'It wasn't a suggestion, Moray,' said Warren. 'Get yourself home and soak in the bath. Take a sick day and do the paperwork when you return.'

'Yes, Boss,' said Ruskin, his tone chastened. 'Sorry he got away,' he repeated.

'Not your fault,' said Cain. 'He was over those fences like a bloody gazelle.'

Warren gave Ruskin's shoulder a squeeze, before turning back towards Harradine's flat.

'Ahh, the impetuosity of youth,' said Sutton once they were out of earshot.

'It's not a laughing matter,' said Warren. 'What if Harradine had had a knife?'

'But he didn't,' said Sutton. 'Go easy on him. We've been through this before; you have to let them do their jobs, Warren. You can't wrap them up in cotton wool. Moray's an exceptional officer. He just got a bit overexcited.'

Warren said nothing, his gaze fixed on the middle distance.

But Sutton wasn't ready to leave the subject yet. 'I seem to recall it wasn't that many years ago that a newly minted DCI chased an armed murderer over some garden fences himself.'

Again, Warren said nothing.

'The same DCI then followed a serial killer into a darkened forest, without backup,' continued Sutton. 'And only a couple of years ago, two senior officers, who really should have known better, legged it after a killer up a flight of stairs. That didn't end so well, but we both survived.'

Warren pushed that image away; Sutton's stroke halfway through the chase still brought him out in cold sweats.

'Anyway, one good thing has come out of this,' persisted Sutton. 'We have the perfect excuse for a search warrant.'

Chapter 21

'I suppose he could fit the description,' mused Sutton, holding up the e-fit against the live feed on the briefing room monitor.

'He's thinning a bit on top, so he does look older than twenty-one,' said Warren.

He stared hard at the video of the man sitting in the inter-view suite on the ground floor. At the moment, Aspinall was just helping with inquiries and had answered all of the questions Hardwick had put to him. He'd not asked for a solicitor.

However, Warren didn't care for the man's sneer and the way he had stared at Hardwick as she leant across the table to pour herself some water. He could see why Susan and her female colleagues had found him creepy.

'You say that you were in all night New Year's Eve,' said Hardwick. 'Can you give me a bit more detail?'

'From when?' he asked.

'Oh, I don't know, let's say six o'clock onwards.'

Winnie Palmer had last been spotted as she returned from the corner shop at about this time.

'Well it was a Sunday, obviously, and just after Christmas, so we were all in the house,' said Aspinall.

'Who's we?' asked Hardwick.

'Me, my mum and my dad.'

'No grandparents, cousins, friends or family over?' she inquired.

'My grandparents are dead, and I don't have any other family,' he said flatly.

'I'm sorry to hear that,' said Hardwick. 'Please continue.'

'Mum and Dad spent the afternoon and evening watching telly and drinking. I was in the garage listening to music and playing *Call of Duty* online.'

'Is there any way we can see if he really was online?' asked Warren. 'Do Xbox or PlayStation or whoever keep logs of that sort of thing?'

'You're asking *me*?' scoffed Sutton. They both turned towards Pymm.

'I'll look into it,' she said.

'When was that until?' continued Hardwick.

'Dunno. Dinner time. We were still finishing the Christmas stuff, so I loaded up my plate and went back to the garage.'

'What about later?' asked Hardwick. 'I'm assuming you all stayed up?'

'Yeah, I went and sat with Mum and Dad and had a couple of beers in front of *Graham Norton*.'

'That finished at twenty past eleven,' said Sutton, who'd accessed the TV schedules. 'Just enough time to get over to Winnie Palmer's if he was prepared in advance.'

'I didn't watch the BBC that night,' Hardwick was saying. 'Did he see in the new year?'

Aspinall shook his head. 'No, there was some music programme on about half-eleven. Not my cup of tea, so I went back into the garage and spoke to a friend on the phone.'

'On it,' called out Pymm from behind her monitors, already accessing her records.

'Who were they?' asked Hardwick.

Aspinall looked down at the table. 'Just someone I met online,' he mumbled.

'Who called who?' asked Hardwick.

'She called me.'

'And how long did the call last?'

He shrugged. 'I dunno. Fifteen minutes? A bit longer? We just chatted and wished each other a Happy New Year.'

'And what then?'

'I went back into the living room to watch the fireworks on the TV and see in the new year with Mum and Dad. They went to bed a few minutes after. I went back into the garage to finish off a game I was playing then turned in myself about half-two or three.'

'OK, there's plenty there to work with,' said Warren as Hardwick pretended to receive a text and left the room. On the screen, Aspinall leant back in his chair, apparently relaxed.

'Did you get all that?' asked Hardwick, out of breath from her jog up the stairs.

'Yeah, it checks out,' called Pymm.

Everyone moved over to her workstation.

'Location data places his phone at his parents' address all day and night. It never left the house for about three days over the New Year period.'

'He could have left the handset at home,' said Richardson, who had only heard some of the conversation.

'No, he was on it only a few minutes before the suspicious man was seen outside Winnie Palmer's house. It's just as he said – he got a phone call at 23.35. It lasted for nineteen minutes, before they hung up. Location data places his phone bang on his parents' address throughout the call.'

'There's no way he could have got from his parents' house to Winnie Palmer's in time to commit murder at midnight,' said Sutton.

'What do we know about the number that called him?' asked Warren.

'Not much,' said Pymm. 'Unregistered pay-as-you-go, and it

141

only ever contacts him. That always makes me suspicious, but then I'm a cynical old bat. There are calls and texts between this number and Aspinall's phone from a couple of weeks before Christmas until the present day.'

'Nineteen minutes sounds a little long to be chatting to your dealer,' said Sutton. 'Girlfriend or boyfriend, perhaps?' suggested Hardwick. 'He looked a bit embarrassed. Maybe they're keeping it a secret?' She wrinkled her nose. 'I imagine they stand upwind of him.'

'Any location data?' asked Sutton.

'Coming through now,' said Pymm. She scrolled through the file, making noises in her throat as everyone waited impatiently.

'The phone moves about a lot; difficult to pin down where the owner might live. Looks as though they are local to Middlesbury though.' She clicked her mouse a few more times. 'The call made to Aspinall on New Year's Eve was miles away from Winnie Palmer's address.' She clicked again. 'He was also on the phone the night that the Culverhouses were killed. We'll have to check with the video game company to see if he was online that night.'

'I suppose it depends what time they were killed, but it sounds like he's in the clear,' said Sutton.

'Fancy giving him the good news, Karen?' asked Warren. He felt a sense of relief. The thought that his wife may have taught someone capable of such a brutal murder – even if it was years before – had troubled him more than he thought it would. He imagined Susan would feel similar.

'Shame,' said Hardwick. 'I really wanted to arrest that creepy bastard.'

Chapter 22

'The killer had to transport Winnie Palmer to the woods somehow,' said Grayson. 'Have Forensics finished processing the scene?'

The team were gathered in the office, discussing the day's events. Spencer Aspinall had long since been released.

'Almost,' said Pymm. 'They have some partial tyre tracks in a lay-by about two hundred metres from the dumping site. Best they can say is a mid-sized family car or van.'

'A van could be useful for transporting a body,' said Hardwick, 'but the witnesses from New Year's Eve clearly stated our suspect was using a dark-coloured five-door.'

'He could have used the car the night he killed her,' said Hutchinson. 'That would have raised less suspicion than a strange van parked in the neighbourhood.'

'See what other vehicles Callum Harradine has access to,' instructed Warren, 'and include his dodgy workmate. Do we have any mobile phone data from them?'

'No phones listed in either man's name,' said Pymm. 'Hardly surprising – they strike me as the burner-phone type.

'Forensics found some footprints next to the tyre track similar to partials near the body. Given we believe she was left after the recent rain, it would be quite a coincidence if the person who left the prints did so before she was dumped or wandered past and didn't notice her body propped up against that tree. Andy reckons men's Reeboks between size eleven and thirteen. They might be able to match them to a suspect's shoes if we can find them, and the soil specialists will probably be able to link them to the scene if they haven't been too thoroughly scrubbed.'

'Then for the time being, let's assume they are the killer's,' said Grayson. 'I don't suppose those same prints were found at her house?'

'They didn't look back in January,' said Pymm, 'so they'll be long gone by now.'

'What about fingerprints?' asked Sutton.

'Nothing, and the place is suspiciously clean, even of Mrs Palmer's prints.'

'The killer had the presence of mind to leave food for her dog and make it look as if she had left of her own accord,' said Warren. 'They wouldn't be careless enough to leave their prints. Although their decision to wipe the place down suggests they had concerns that they could have left evidence behind.'

'I think you're right that this person has probably visited her before,' said Grayson. 'It sounds like the dog recognised them, and there's no forced entry. I can't imagine she left a window open in January. Either they had a key, or she let them in. The whole operation seems too polished for someone randomly spotting her out and about and deciding to take a punt. We need to identify any acquaintances that she may have invited in.'

'I've been looking into that,' said Hutchinson. 'She was quite private; even her friends from the Wednesday Club rarely visited.'

'Andy reports they have found some unaccounted-for fibres on her carpet,' said Pymm. 'Bright red cotton, consistent with a blend used in socks. As far as we can tell, Mrs Palmer didn't own any red socks. The bad news is that the dye used in the cotton is extremely popular; the socks could have been bought anywhere.'

'So we're looking for a killer with large feet, who wears bright red socks and drives a family car,' summarised Sutton. 'Has anyone checked to see if Moray has an alibi?'

Everyone smiled at Sutton's weak attempt at humour. Ruskin had gone home and was no doubt trying to explain to his husband why he was sporting two black eyes and wincing every time he took a deep breath.

'Derek Culverhouse has size twelve feet,' said Hardwick.

'I don't recall seeing any Reeboks on the search report from his flat,' said Pymm. 'And we've yet to find a link between him and Winnie Palmer. Or any of our other suspects yet.'

Hardwick shrugged. 'Just throwing it out there.'

'There is a glimmer of good news,' said Pymm. 'The CSIs have confirmed there is no space in her kitchen or the utility room for a freezer large enough to store a body in, and no indications one has been removed. Because that would have been really embarrassing ...'

'Then tomorrow's priorities are as follows,' said Warren. 'Find Callum Harradine and/or his dodgy mate. Check if any of the dark-coloured cars caught on camera that night can conceivably be linked to either man.

'Hutch, continue the neighbourhood canvass. Try and place any of our potentials, including Derek Culverhouse, in the area on or before New Year's Eve. We need to establish any connection with Winnie Palmer. Given how she was successfully kept off our radar for nine weeks, there must have been at least some preparation beforehand. Keep Aspinall in the mix for the time being, just in case we missed something.'

'What about the other suspects from the e-fit?' asked Sutton.

'Aside from Eric Morton, the only others known to us have alibis. We're still tracking down the ones we don't know,' said Pymm.

'Ideally, I want Eric Morton picked up at that taxi firm,' said Warren. 'It gives us a reason to search his car; their records might also place him near Winnie Palmer's house or establish a connection between them. We'll wait twenty-four hours for him to turn up for work; otherwise go and knock on the door of his registered address.

'We are still operating on the assumption this mysterious man getting dressed in the middle of the road on New Year's Eve is our primary suspect, but don't get too fixated on that questionable e-fit.'

He changed gear mentally. 'Derek Culverhouse's alibi?'

'We've spoken to almost a dozen dog walkers and joggers who were in War Memorial Park when he claims to have been sitting in his car,' said Hutchinson.

'Anything?' asked Warren.

'Nothing concrete,' he admitted. 'A couple walking off their Sunday dinner remember seeing a white four-by-four, but they couldn't tell us its make or whether there was anyone in it. A jogger says she may have seen a vehicle matching his, but she's been there again since that night and admits she could be getting her days muddled.'

'What about CCTV from the surrounding streets?'

'More promising,' said Hutchinson. 'Forty-eight residences and nine businesses have cameras with a field of view overlapping the road. Almost all the routes he could have taken to or from the park have something. The Video Analysis Unit are securing it, but it's a motley collection; everything from high-definition full-colour to a vintage black and white on video cassettes. There's even a couple of smart doorbells.'

'Any timeframe?' asked Warren. The VAU would need to transfer the data to a useable format before it could be examined. Presumably, most of the footage would be side-on, so the licence plates wouldn't be visible, meaning it would need to be looked at by human analysts. Fifty-seven videos of up to two and a half hours in length could yield nearly 150 hours of footage.

'Assuming we don't get lucky and spot him early on, weeks,

unless we get authorisation for a fast track and recruit more eyeballs,' said Richardson.

'No chance,' said Warren. 'He's on bail. There's no evidence he's a flight risk, or a danger. Finding his car will confirm his alibi and eliminate him, but *not* spotting him won't prove anything. He might have driven there by a different route.'

Hutchinson headed back to the office and Warren leant back in his chair, rubbing his tired eyes. This was the bit they edited out in the fly-on-wall documentaries. The slow, steady grind. He had a feeling it was going to be a long, frustrating case.

Friday 9th March

Chapter 23

'Asda can't help us with the CCTV,' said Richardson. 'They delete the footage after eight weeks unless there's a court case pending. There's no way to tell if Winnie Palmer used the customer courtesy phone to call Abacus Cabs last year, so we won't be able to determine if Eric Morton picked her up that way. It's probably just as well; the Video Analysis Unit would have had kittens if I asked them to look for a connection based on what we know so far.'

'Then we'll do it the old-fashioned way,' said Warren. 'We'll bring Morton in for questioning and see if we can connect him to Winnie Palmer. Any luck tracking him down, Hutch?'

'His registered address is his brother's, because of the restraining order from his partner.'

'I still like the idea of taking him in for questioning when he turns up for work at Abacus Cabs,' said Sutton. 'We can seize his car as he won't be insured, then put the frighteners on the dispatchers to give us their logbook. They'll just think it's because they're using unlicensed drivers.'

It was a gamble; Morton could be planning to abscond after the e-fit's release, but Grayson had agreed that the benefits from catching him illegally driving a taxi outweighed the risk.

'I agree,' said Warren. 'If he can't give us a decent alibi for

New Year's Eve, and he matches the description, then given his history of violent offences we have reasonable suspicion to search his vehicle for evidence of Winnie Palmer.'

'We should also check his tyres to see if they match any tracks at the Culverhouses' home,' suggested Ruskin.

Warren turned to Hardwick. 'If your new friend doesn't give us the nod soon, we'll see if he's at his brother's.'

'We should have a search warrant ready for there anyway,' said Sutton. 'If he is the killer, he had to store her body somewhere.'

'Hutch, how are the interviews with Winnie Palmer's friends going? Any possible links to the Culverhouses?' asked Warren.

'No links yet. Most of the interviewees have largely repeated what they'd already told us. She had a small circle of friends, with a social life largely revolving around the Wednesday Club and St Mark's. I spoke to the vicar, and he said that when he saw her the week before Christmas, she seemed quite normal and gave no indication she was planning on going away. She and her husband had never really celebrated Christmas, so he wasn't overly concerned about her being lonely over the holiday period.

'However, he now remembers offering to arrange for her fence to be fixed back in November, but she told him not to worry, as she already had a friend who said he'd do it.'

The mood in the room shifted, slightly.

'Could this be a link to our two friendly builders?' asked Sutton.

'Unclear,' said Hutchinson. 'He keeps an eye out to stop his more vulnerable congregation being ripped off, but apparently the friend wasn't going to charge her as it just needed a few nails banging in.'

'Do we have a name?' asked Warren.

'He can't recall it and never met him. Another friend, living in a care home, also remembers her mentioning a "young man" back in November. Apparently, Winnie had a very bad habit of leaving her purse on top of her wheeled shopping trolley when she dragged it home. This young man had turned up on her

152

doorstep with the purse in his hand that evening, claiming to have found it in the street. He accepted a cup of tea and a slice of cake by way of a thank you and said she reminded him of his grandmother and that he hoped a stranger would be as honest as he was if she ever dropped her purse.'

'I'm not liking the sound of this,' said Sutton. 'For a start, how did he work out where she lived? She didn't drive, so she doesn't have a driving licence, and bus passes don't have addresses on them.'

'Exactly my thoughts,' said Hutchinson. 'Since then, he's done a bit of shopping for her and fixed a leaking tap.'

'I don't suppose the friend met him?' asked Richardson.

'I'm afraid not, and she suffers from memory problems. Even Winnie's description of him as a "young man" is a bit suspect, as she described anyone with his own hair and teeth in those terms.'

'Any other reports or sightings?' asked Warren.

Hutchinson shook his head. 'Nothing. None of the neighbours spotted him, and none of her other friends recall her mentioning him.'

'If this new-found friend did some jobs around the house, he may have left some trace evidence,' said Warren. 'Pass it on to Andy Harrison and get him to check her taps and the garden fence. He might have cut himself on a splinter or left his prints on the bathtub. Get them to double-check the crockery; if he pulled out a plate and saucer for his tea and cake, he might have touched the other ones in the cupboard. Check the biscuit caddy as well, in case she offered him a custard cream.

'Mags, it sounds as though he may have followed her home from the shops. What's the chance of there being any CCTV footage from November?'

'None,' said Richardson. 'Missing Persons seized some footage when she was reported missing in January, but none of it was from before December. Since she paid cash for everything, we can't even pin down the date she was likely to have visited the shops.'

'OK, folks, we may have a potential suspect. The fact he appears to be quite handy points the finger towards Callum Harradine again, so continue digging into him. Meanwhile, let's hope Forensics get lucky or one of her other acquaintances remembers a bit more about this new friend.'

Chapter 24

'The preliminary search has been completed on Callum Harradine's flat,' said Deputy Crime Scene Manager Meera Gupta. Warren had her on speakerphone. 'I'll write it up and send it over. There's plenty of evidence that needs to be processed, but I can give you the headlines now.

'The flat is the ground floor of a converted house, but there are three steps up to the front door. One bedroom, living room, kitchen, bathroom and an airing cupboard. There is one flat above him, with its own front door. There's no rear access.

'I'd say he lives alone. The bathroom only has one of everything; there are no women's clothes. I wouldn't go so far as to say the flat is dirty, but he'd have to put in a good few hours if he wanted to impress anyone he brought back. He does have a chest freezer.'

Sutton punched the air.

'But it's a very old, half-size version. Winnie Palmer could fit in, but she'd have to have been folded in half, not lain flat.'

'I'll speak to Professor Jordan and see if he thinks she could have been frozen in that position,' said Warren.

'If she was stored in there, it would have been awkward, though not impossible, for one person to have manoeuvred her in. The killer would have had to be pretty big and strong,' warned Gupta.

'He knocked Moray flat on his arse, so he's no lightweight,' said Pymm.

'The freezer didn't have much in there, just a few ready meals,' continued Gupta. 'We've seized it and its contents to analyse for trace evidence; if she wasn't wrapped in a plastic bag, there may be some transfer in amongst the stray peas and crumbs.'

'Her handbag was missing. Any sign of it?' asked Warren.

'No. But we found a treasure-trove of iPads, mobile phones and jewellery in a box beneath the boiler, along with what appear to be drugs. They're being catalogued at the moment.'

'That explains why he scarpered when Moray turned up,' said Richardson.

'His parole officer thought he might be using his household repairs business as a way of identifying targets to burgle,' Pymm reminded them.

'Identifying the original owners of those items might confirm that theory,' said Sutton. 'But what are the chances he held on to something that he stole from her or that would place him in her neighbourhood? He'll have fenced it ASAP.'

Warren drummed his fingers on the table in frustration. Even if they could demonstrate Harradine had been working near Winnie Palmer's house in the weeks preceding her death, it would be easily dismissed by the defence as a coincidence. They needed an irrefutable link between Harradine and the victim; either evidence he had been in her house or, even better, that she had been in his flat or vehicle.

'We're trying to match his clothing to the fibres found on the carpet at Winnie Palmer's,' said Gupta.

'If he was forensically aware enough to change his clothes in the middle of the road, we can probably assume he's got rid of them by now,' said Richardson. 'Any footwear?'

'Yes, it looks as though his shoe size is the same as the

impressions found near her body, but we haven't found any shoes matching their make.'

'Even if he's ditched them, he has to have bought them somewhere,' said Pymm. 'I'll get someone to trawl through his bank statements and see if he shopped at any shoe stores. If he paid by card, we may be able to link him back to the purchase.'

'Speaking of which,' said Warren. 'What have you found in the way of paperwork?'

'It looks as though he just chucked everything in a drawer. Lots of bills and receipts, some of them quite old. There are also some carbon-paper copies of handwritten invoices.'

'Those could be useful for identifying previous customers,' said Pymm. She leant towards the phone speaker. 'Can you bag all those and get them couriered over to me, please. I'll get a team cataloguing them immediately.'

After thanking Gupta, Warren ended the call. 'Hutch, where are we with his neighbours?'

'We've spoken to the people in the flats either side and the woman upstairs. Nobody seemed surprised the police were looking for him. The bloke in the flat on the right-hand side said, "Nice enough bloke, but you wouldn't trust him to take in a parcel for you."'

'Anyone remember what he was doing New Year's Eve?' asked Sutton.

'The woman upstairs was away. The neighbours to the right were having a party and didn't see him all night. The older lady to the left is deaf and had the TV up loud. Nobody remembers seeing him that day or the next. Unfortunately, there's no residential CCTV.'

'What about the days before her body was dumped?' asked Warren. 'He's a big man, but he'd have still had to lug her body down those steps. I can't imagine he did it in broad daylight.'

'Nobody remembers anything suspicious; no bumps in the night or anything,' replied Hutchinson.

'What about last Sunday? Did anyone see him over the period we think the Culverhouses were killed?'

'Nobody remembers.'

'Any luck finding him?' asked Warren.

'No family on file for Harradine, but we have a name for his dodgy mate,' said Pymm. 'Danny McCamphill. Naturally, he's not on the electoral roll, appears not to have paid any council tax this year, and the address on his driving licence pre-dates his last spell in prison. He's finished his last stint of parole, but the Probation Service will track him down for us.'

'Get a search warrant for his properties also,' said Warren. 'They could have been working together.'

* * *

'That's a lot of freezers,' said Tony Sutton, as he read down the list on Rachel Pymm's computer. It was shortly after lunch and Warren was trying not to feel jealous of his wife, who'd WhatsApped him a photo of the cake she was enjoying with her colleagues.

'And those are just the ones sold by the major retailers in the past twelve months,' replied Pymm, clicking a second tab on the spreadsheet. 'These are the second-hand freezers we've found listed online in the past year. I think we should park this until we have more details. I've requested a list of names for everyone who's bought one using a credit card or given their details, and I can search against it every time we get a new name.'

'I doubt it'll be that easy,' said Sutton. Warren agreed.

'There's no way to search the second-hand adverts, as obviously we only have the sellers' details,' said Pymm. 'But we could probably whittle the list down by discarding unsuitable models. I suppose you could fit an intact body in a large larder freezer, especially someone as small as Winnie Palmer, but it would be awkward and you'd have to secure the door so she didn't fall out.'

158

Pymm was probably correct, but would getting rid of some of the appliances listed on those grounds risk losing a valuable lead?

'That's a huge job,' said Warren. 'Hold on to the data for now; we can come back to it if we need to. I don't suppose you found a receipt for a large chest freezer amongst that paperwork from Callum Harradine's flat?'

'No,' said Pymm. 'But there are lots of handwritten invoices, some with partial addresses. Unfortunately, his handwriting is so bad that in another life, he could have been a doctor. I have a couple of willing workers trying to locate these customers and build a picture of his movements before Christmas. I'm fairly confident there are none for Winnie Palmer or the Culverhouses though, so either he didn't do any work for them, or threw those away.'

'That would have been sensible,' said Sutton.

'I have had a bit more luck with his mobile phones. He lists one as a business number on his tax return, such as it is, and he also chucked the cardboard inlay for a different SIM card in his receipt drawer. There's a serial number on there that the service provider might be able to link to a phone number.'

'That's great. Have you got any location and call data for the business phone?' asked Warren. 'If he's been using it recently, we may be able to use it to track him, or at least have a stab at guessing where his business partner lives. Even better, it may place him in Winnie Palmer's neighbourhood if he did some work in that area.'

'I'm waiting on it.'

'Any more?' he asked; knowing that Pymm liked to drip-feed her discoveries to make it more dramatic.

'Funny you should say that,' said Pymm. 'There is a receipt for a shoe store in town. Men's trainers, bought in November, fifty-five pounds. No details on the receipt, but there is a barcode. Unfortunately, he paid cash, so no direct evidence it was him who bought them, and I imagine the CCTV footage is long gone, but we handled the receipt with gloves, so we may find his prints on there.'

'Arrange for somebody to pop down there and confirm the make and size, first,' said Warren. 'If they match, then we'll arrange for fingerprinting. It's circumstantial but it builds a picture. If he isn't wearing them when we finally find him, then I'd like an explanation for why he chucked a pair of trainers away after less than six months.'

Chapter 25

Karen Hardwick's work phone rang a little after five p.m., as she was chasing Oliver around the bedroom, wearing a foam dinosaur mask. The toddler squealed in delight as she finally grabbed him, lifting him above her head.

'You are getting a little too heavy for this, my boy,' she muttered as she felt her back twinge. 'Bend your knees, not your back' also applied to squirming two-year-olds, especially those less than two weeks away from their third birthday and already wearing age four-to-five clothing.

'Eric's on the roster,' the taxi driver who'd recognised Morton said when she picked up. 'It's quiet tonight, so he'll end up back at the office to wait for fares and use the loo at some point.'

Thanking him, she hung up then relayed the information into the department. She felt a little disappointed that she wouldn't be present to pick Morton up and perhaps even have a go at interviewing him, if only so she could tease Ruskin that she had successfully brought in two suspects this week, to his none.

She felt her knee buckle, as a high-speed ball of energy clutching a stuffed *Tyrannosaurus rex* careened into her. Pulling the foam mask back over her face, she turned and roared. The shriek of her son's laughter reminded her that some things were more important than another collar.

*   *   *

Eric Morton was brought in for questioning just after seven-thirty, after getting out to stretch his legs and use the vending machine at Abacus Cabs' despatch office.

Not wanting to risk a repeat of the Harradine debacle, two unmarked cars boxed in Morton's black Vauxhall Insignia, officers moving swiftly to block all potential escape routes. Morton had sworn mightily at the appearance of the two uniformed officers either side of him as he retrieved his drink, but had agreed to accompany them to the station. The dispatcher had paled when presented with a search warrant demanding he turn over all his records, including those of the unlicensed drivers he kept off the books. Within fifteen minutes of the raid, his lawyer was heading over.

Back at the station, Morton availed himself of the duty solicitor. Richardson was already running the details from Morton's car through the computer and Pymm requested the phone records and location data for both the handset Morton had in his pocket and the one attached to his dashboard.

They had decided to arrest Morton on motoring offences. Since he was currently on bail, he would hopefully be more preoccupied with trying to avoid having that revoked than worrying about anything else they may be investigating him for.

Warren had texted Susan to tell her he would be late home, before nipping out for something to eat. Grayson had disappeared hours ago. If Warren did replace him, then late nights like this would become much rarer. He wasn't sure how he felt about that.

The warm smell of frying oil and vinegar drifted from the fish and chip shop on the adjacent street. Two uniformed constables were perched on stools in the window of the chippy, their car parked outside. One of them gave a wave of recognition with half a battered sausage as Warren walked past. He smiled politely, forcing his feet in the direction of the corner shop two doors down.

Five minutes later, Warren emerged with a container of chilled tomato and cheese pasta salad and a banana. The police car had gone; hopefully not called away before his two colleagues had a chance to finish their food.

Swiping himself in through the rear entrance to the station, Warren did his best to push aside images of salt-and-vinegar-soaked chips by mentally calculating how many calories he'd successfully forsaken with his choice of dinner. He'd probably save a couple more when he threw the lettuce in the bin.

It didn't work.

Ten minutes later, he found himself in the communal coffee area, waiting for the kettle to boil.

'The absolute buggers,' he swore slamming the cupboard door shut. The biscuit tin was as empty as the honesty jar for the coffee, and whoever finished the custard creams hadn't even had the decency to throw the empty packet in the bin.

'Sod them,' he muttered, retrieving his fifty-pence piece from the otherwise empty container. 'Let them buy their own bloody biscuits and coffee.'

It was an empty threat; he'd been saying it at least once a month for the past seven years.

* * *

Warren sipped a cup of decaffeinated coffee as he watched the interview on the monitor. No caffeine after seven was the new rule he'd finally agreed with his wife, in the hope it would help him sleep better – something he would doubtless appreciate in the coming months. He'd successfully negotiated an emergency clause in the case of all-nighters; however, unless Morton suddenly confessed to having murdered Winnie Palmer and wanted to get

163

it all off his chest, Warren doubted that tonight would necessitate its use.

Tony Sutton maintained that despite switching to decaf after his stroke, the mere act of drinking coffee still gave him a psychological boost. Warren thought he was spending too much time around Rachel Pymm. He'd tried his best to cut back when he and Susan were undergoing fertility treatment, but he'd largely failed.

'He matches the e-fit and is probably closer in age to the description than that Aspinall lad,' said Sutton. His shift had also finished, but he was as keen as Warren to catch a first glimpse of a potential suspect. If the man on the screen was unable to give a satisfactory answer to their questions, then he may become the focus of their investigation.

'He drives a black Vauxhall Insignia,' said Warren. 'That's a five-door hatchback. The witnesses suggested an Audi or a BMW, but it was months ago, they were drunk and it was dark. Modern cars all look the same these days anyway.'

'Give me a Ford Cortina or a Vauxhall Chevette, any day,' joked Sutton. 'No mistaking those for a Beamer.'

In the interview suite on the floor below, Morton scowled at the tabletop. He was accompanied by his solicitor, an older, grey-haired man. On the opposite side of the table, Mags Richardson finished cautioning him. She was alone.

Sending Richardson in with a second officer may have risked tipping Morton off that this was about more than motoring offences. But more importantly, Warren and the team felt they had the measure of Morton. A large, well-built man, he spent his life intimidating people – whether it be belligerent drunks at The Sidings or his tiny, waif-like pregnant girlfriend. A man like Morton would feel in control of the interview; not only was he physically larger than Richardson, he and his solicitor also outnumbered her.

Warren settled back in his chair, looking forward to seeing

Richardson disabuse him of that notion.

'I'm sure you know why you are here, Eric,' said Richardson.

Opposite her, Morton said nothing. He wasn't going to offer information unless it was requested directly.

'Who does the car belong to?'

'No comment.'

Undeterred, Richardson continued. 'The registered keeper of the vehicle is Kyle Morton. Does he know you are driving his car?'

Morton finally stirred. If he refused to answer, Richardson could easily claim that she suspected he had taken the car without consent and he wouldn't be going home that evening.

'Yeah.'

'And does your big brother know you are banned from driving? After all, that would invalidate his insurance.'

Morton scowled. 'No comment.'

'Is that your photo or Kyle's on the Private Hire Licence hanging from the rear-view mirror?'

Morton's jaw worked up and down. 'Kyle's,' he said eventually.

'So why were you using his car – and his licence – when we picked you up this evening?'

Warren and Sutton waited to see what Morton would do. Would he seek to explain, no comment, or lie?

'Doing him a favour,' said Morton.

Richardson said nothing, waiting for him to fill the silence.

'He was ill, so I offered to do his shift for him.'

'I see. So tonight was just a one-off?'

'Yeah.' Morton twisted his face into what he doubtless thought was a remorseful expression. 'We look like each other. I know I shouldn't have, but he has three kids to support; he needs the extra money. I couldn't let him lose his job because he was a bit under the weather.'

'Did Abacus Cabs know you were helping out your brother tonight?'

'No.'

Richardson pretended to consider his words. 'And what if I were to ask to see the cab firm's records? Would I find your name? Because that would mean you were lying to me.'

Morton shook his head vigorously. 'No, I don't work for them. They don't know who I am. I swear.'

'Nice one, Mags,' said Sutton, enjoying the show. 'You've caught him in his first provable lie.'

'That's strange,' said Richardson, frowning. 'A couple of the other drivers said they recognised you.'

'Like I said, I look a lot like my brother.'

'They said they know you as Eric. How would they know your real name, if they thought you were Kyle?'

A look of panic crossed Morton's face.

Richardson seized the advantage quickly, not giving him time to think up a more convincing lie. 'In fact, the cab firm have nobody called Kyle Morton working for them. Why is that?'

She gave him time to think through his answer. The wise thing to do would be to refuse to answer the question. His solicitor advised him to do just that.

'No comment,' said Morton, but Richardson could see he was fighting the instinct to try and explain.

'I think your brother Kyle is working off-the-books for Abacus. Am I right?'

Despite the conflict raging on Morton's face, he answered no comment again.

Richardson opened the folder next to her elbow and removed a sheet of paper.

'This is a transcript of the WhatsApp messages between the phone stuck to the car's dashboard and the dispatcher in the cab firm's office. It looks as though you did a half-dozen or more pick-ups before we arrested you and had another two pending. Don't they have a special app for arranging jobs? WhatsApp seems a bit low-tech.'

166

'Like I said, I was doing Kyle a favour tonight. I don't have the app.'

'And what about all the other nights?' Richardson gestured towards the folder. They hadn't had time to transcribe more than a couple of days' worth of messages, so she'd shoved a pile of blank paper sheets in there.

'The phone isn't mine – it's the one Kyle keeps in the car,' said Morton hastily.

Richardson frowned again. 'I'm confused. You said "I don't have the app." But now you're saying the phone is Kyle's and he keeps it in the car. Which is it?'

'That one. I meant the phone Kyle keeps in the car doesn't have the app. It just has Google Maps on it and WhatsApp.'

'So, it stays in the car permanently?'

'Yeah, he locks it in the glovebox when he's finished his shift.'

'And what about the other phone? The one we found in your pocket. Is that Kyle's as well?'

'No, that's my one,' said Morton.

Richardson took out a pile of stapled sheets. 'The car phone certainly travels about a lot,' she said, flicking through the pages.

Morton gave a shrug. 'Well yeah, he's a taxi driver.'

'And do you go with him? You know, to keep him company?'

'No.'

'Well that's strange.' She took out another sheet. 'Because wherever the car phone goes, your phone goes also. And not just tonight, every night.'

She placed the piece of paper down on the table.

'OK, time to stop lying to me, Eric. You've been full of shit since you walked in here.' She pointed towards the wall clock. 'It's getting late, and I'm running out of patience. Your brother doesn't drive for Abacus; you do. The car you drive isn't your brother's; it's yours. He already has two family cars; he started leasing that one two weeks after you were banned from driving and disposed of your own vehicle. I have enough to charge him with permitting somebody to drive without insurance. He works for a firm of solicitors; they aren't going to be happy he's breaking the law on behalf of his dodgy brother.'

Morton swallowed.

Richardson adopted a more conciliatory tone. 'I'll be honest, Eric, you and your brother don't really interest me. I'm far more interested in Abacus Cabs. You aren't the only driver they employ off-the-books. That licence hanging from the rear-view mirror is a fake, and they know it's a fake – they just use your brother's details so it matches the car's registered keeper and the sticker on the bumper. And that isn't your brother's photograph; it's yours, because, like you said, you look enough like him to deceive anyone who compares it to his driving licence.

'They use WhatsApp because it's secure and encrypted, and it means that your name doesn't appear on the job sheet they submit to their accountants.

'Now would be a very good time for you to stop lying and start helping us,' she concluded, sitting back and folding her arms.

Morton cleared his throat. 'I'm currently on bail. If I help you ...'

'Above my pay grade,' Richardson interjected. She softened her tone slightly. 'But I can't imagine it would hurt your case if you cooperate with us.'

'I need to speak to my lawyer,' said Morton.

'Don't take all night,' said Richardson.

* * *

'Fantastic work, Mags,' said Warren when Richardson entered the office. 'I'd offer you a biscuit, but some git already ate them all.'

'Don't worry, I've got an apple,' she said, before taking a long pull from her water bottle.

'You've got him where you want him,' said Sutton. 'Once he's admitted he drives for Abacus, see what he says about New Year's Eve.'

168

'Then hit him with Winnie Palmer,' said Warren. 'I want to see his reaction. I wouldn't bank on a confession.'

'What about the night the Culverhouses were killed?' Richardson asked.

'Not yet,' said Warren. 'It would be too much of a coincidence; if he is our man we don't want to tip him off.'

Biting into her apple, Richardson took the printouts offered by Rachel Pymm who pointed to a section circled with pencil. 'See what he has to say about that.'

Richardson raised an eyebrow. Before she could reply, her desk phone trilled. Sutton answered it. 'He's finished speaking to his solicitor.'

'Finish your apple and stretch your legs,' said Warren. 'Let the bugger sweat for a bit.'

* * *

'Yeah, you're right. I do drive for Abacus Cabs,' admitted Morton as soon as the interview resumed. 'But Kyle had no idea I was using the car as a cab.'

'But he did know that you are banned from driving when he bought you it,' said Richardson, unwilling to give Morton's brother a free pass, but ignoring the fact Morton currently lived with him and could hardly have failed to notice the large yellow sticker on the car's bumper. She'd hold that in reserve in case she needed it.

'Yeah,' mumbled Morton.

'OK, Eric, thank you for admitting that,' said Richardson, her tone business-like. 'It will help our case against Abacus if we can have some concrete details from you, such as how long you've been working for them, any dates or specific jobs you can remember, that sort of thing.'

Morton nodded, his expression one of abject misery. 'I just needed the money, you know? I can't get a job and my benefits are shit; my partner's expecting.'

169

'That would be the partner you pushed down a flight of stairs, when she was three months pregnant?' said Richardson. They needed Morton's cooperation, but she wasn't going to spend all night listening to some self-serving sob story.

Morton scowled.

'When did you start working for them?' she asked.

He pursed his lips. 'About eighteen months ago.' The date corresponded roughly with his brother purchasing the Vauxhall Insignia, meaning Morton had started working within weeks of the court-imposed three-year ban he'd received for a second drink-driving offence.

'What sort of shifts do you work?' she asked, keeping her face carefully neutral.

'Weekdays, mostly. A couple of night shifts. It varies.' His tone was slightly cagey, and Richardson made a note to go through the location data for the car phone with a fine-tooth comb; she had a strong suspicion his rest periods during and between shifts were probably shorter than legally mandated.

'And what about the holiday periods? Any specific dates you can give us to help jog people's memories?' she pressed. She really needed Morton to confirm he had worked over the New Year. The location data for the phone that he used when driving was useless on its own – it would be far too easy for his defence to claim someone else was using the vehicle on that particular night.

'I did full shifts on Christmas Eve and Boxing Day, and a few hours on Christmas Day itself. Triple time, mad not to.'

'I can see that,' said Richardson. 'What about New Year's Eve? That's got to pay well.'

'Yeah, of course. I did three or four hours either side of midnight. Easy money, and better than watching Jools bloody Holland.'

Richardson chuckled. 'What about regular customers? Anyone who could confirm they booked the cab through Abacus and recognise you as the driver?'

'Not really.'

'What about the supermarket run? My nan always gets a taxi back when she does her big shop.'

'Sure, they all have courtesy phones, but I couldn't tell you the names of any of the pick-ups.'

'What about social clubs?'

'Probably.' Morton stifled a yawn. It was getting late, and Richardson's more gentle questions had started to make him relax. Beside him, his solicitor also yawned, followed by Richardson.

'Sorry,' mumbled Morton. 'Been a long day.'

'Well just a couple more questions,' said Richardson. She opened the folder again.

'Does the name Winnie Palmer mean anything to you?' Richardson watched him carefully.

'Sounds vaguely familiar,' he replied. 'Couldn't tell you where from though.'

Upstairs, Warren and Sutton peered intently at the screen.

'I can't tell if he recognises the name or not,' said Sutton.

'He may not know it,' said Warren. Morton wouldn't be the first killer with so little regard for his victims he never bothered to learn what they were called.

Back in the interview suite, Richardson pushed a photograph across the table. 'Do you recognise this person?'

Morton stared at it. Next to him his solicitor sat up in his seat, a sudden look of shock crossing his face as he realised that the evening's routine call-out had suddenly become a lot more interesting.

'I've definitely seen her somewhere,' said Morton. 'Was she a customer?' His eyes narrowed. 'Wait, why are you asking me this?'

'Can you tell me what jobs you did on New Year's Eve, particularly in the hour or so surrounding midnight?' asked Richardson.

'I don't know,' said Morton. 'Look at the job list.' He pointed at the folder. 'It'll be on WhatsApp.'

171

'We did,' said Richardson. 'We also looked at your call history and the handset's location data. Why did you turn both of your phones off between eleven-thirty and ten past midnight?'

*   *   *

It came as no surprise when Eric Morton's solicitor requested a break to speak with his client, but Morton either didn't hear him or ignored him. It had taken a moment for the click of recognition, then his eyes had widened.

'Shit, that's the old bird that turned up dead in the woods.' He frowned as fragments of the story came back to him. 'I read about it. Didn't she go missing over the New Year?'

'Yes, she disappeared from her house on Tollbooth Road.'

'So? What has it got to do with me?'

'You match the description of a man seen outside her house around midnight.'

'You are joking? That bloody photofit on *The Reporter* website? It looks nothing like me,' he scoffed.

'A number of people think differently,' said Richardson. 'Anyway, if it wasn't you, we need to tick you off our list.'

'I would advise you not to answer any more questions, Mr Morton,' interjected his solicitor.

But Morton was having none of it. 'Is this what this is all about? You pull me in because some prick thinks I look a bit like some shitty picture in the local newspaper. For fuck's sake.' He slumped back in his chair, glaring angrily.

Back in the main office, Tony Sutton was unable to stifle a snort of derision. 'I think he's more pissed off about the unfairness of being caught driving illegally because of the e-fit, than he is about being identified as a potential suspect in a murder case. If he is our killer, then that's a tick in the narcissist box on the psychopath checklist.'

Downstairs, Morton was still ignoring his solicitor's advice to shut up and ask for a break to discuss the alarming developments in the interview.

'I never did any jobs in Tollbooth Road. Check the job list.'

'We did. Along with the location data for both of your phones. However, you turned them off for forty minutes within a mile of Mrs Palmer's house. Again, why did you do that?'

'I was on a break,' said Morton. 'It all kicks off after midnight when everyone's finished singing "Auld Lang Syne" and the fares go up, so I decided to have a piss and a bite to eat before the rush.'

'You still haven't told me why you turned off both your phones,' said Richardson calmly.

'Because I wanted some peace and quiet,' said Morton. 'Bloody WhatsApp was pinging like a submarine.'

'And your personal phone?' pressed Richardson.

'Same reason. I have WhatsApp on there as well, in case I get a job offer when I'm not already in the car.'

'So where did you go to get food?'

'I didn't. I had some sandwiches with me and a flask. I parked up in the lay-by next to the burger bar near the roundabout.'

'And the toilet break? Did you use their bathroom?' If Morton had gone into the fast-food restaurant, he would be on their CCTV, which could rule him out as a suspect. On the other hand, if he claimed to have used the facilities and didn't appear on their cameras, they'd caught him in a lie.

Upstairs, Sutton and Warren held their breath.

'No, I went for a piss behind some bushes.' Morton shrugged. 'Fast-food places are bad enough at midnight normally; on New Year's Eve they're wanker central. Besides, they won't let you use their toilet at that time of night unless you buy something.'

'Damn,' said Sutton.

Warren rubbed his eyes. 'Well it was always a long shot that we'd get anything useful tonight. We'll question him again tomorrow, then look at getting his bail revoked. At least we got the search warrants. He had to keep Winnie Palmer's body somewhere for

173

the past two months, and he also needed to move her around. His brother's house and the flat he shared with his ex-partner have been sealed, and both his brother's cars impounded.'

'I bet that went down well this time of night,' said Sutton. 'If he is our man, do you really think he'd be stupid enough to keep her body in a house with other people?'

'Doubtful,' admitted Warren. 'We'll need to see if there is anywhere else he has access to. Of course, that's assuming he acted alone. For all we know, he and his brother could have been working together. Big brother has been very obliging since Eric lost his driving licence. He's really put his neck on the line buying him that car and letting him use it illegally.'

'I still don't see a motive,' said Sutton. 'I know we don't necessarily need one to make a case, but it would be good to know he isn't just some random psychopath and Winnie Palmer was unlucky. That always gives me the creeps.'

'Me too,' admitted Warren. 'But I'll tell you what really worries me, is how much planning went into her death. Making it look like she went missing, then hiding her body in a freezer, before deciding it was time to get rid of her. He made no attempt to dispose of her body, or even properly hide it. He wants the world to know what he did.'

When Sutton spoke again, his voice was heavy. 'What if he was just clearing space in the freezer for more victims?'

Saturday 10th March

Chapter 26

Saturday morning started with two pieces of good news.

'We have the DNA back from the bloodstains found on Derek Culverhouse's fleece and in his car, and they confirm the preliminary blood group tests,' said Hardwick. She stifled a yawn. Oliver was old enough to sleep through the night now, so Warren wondered if there was another reason she was so tired. Out of the corner of his eye, he caught Richardson and Pymm's smirks. He'd interrogate the two sergeants later, but it looked as though Karen might finally have had some luck on the dating front. He was pleased; it had been over three years since Gary's death, and she was finally finding her feet again.

'The blood on the fleece is his, but the blood in the car is his father's?' Warren clarified.

'Yes.'

'Any sign of his car up near the park that night?'

'Nothing yet,' said Richardson. 'Could be days.'

'We'll hold fire a bit longer,' decided Warren. 'I don't want to tip him off just yet.'

'We also have that warrant for Callum Harradine's dodgy mate,' said Pymm. 'The parole officer reckons he's still living at the last known address, and Harradine's mobile regularly spends time near that property. It's not turned on at the moment, but it's somewhere to start.'

'That's great news,' said Warren. He turned to Sutton. 'Let's not take any chances this time – one bloody nose is enough. Arrange a forced-entry team; full recon of the property before going in. I'll speak to DSI Grayson and get authorisation for TASERs. I'm not risking him or his mate assaulting anyone else.'

* * *

The raid on Danny McCamphill's flat went smoothly; the appearance of several officers wearing stab vests, carrying bright yellow TASERs, took all the fight out of the man.

'He ain't here; piss off,' said McCamphill, a scrawny, rat-faced man who looked as though he needed a few good meals inside him.

'That's OK, we'll just take you down to the station to answer a few questions,' said Sutton.

'Am I under arrest?' he sneered.

'Would you like to be?' asked Sutton.

'Going to need some grounds for arrest,' said McCamphill.

Sutton held up a search warrant. 'I'm sure we'll find something.'

McCamphill's shoulders slumped and he scowled, before sitting back in an armchair and folding his arms.

Thirty seconds later, there came a series of bangs from upstairs, followed by the no-nonsense tone of one of the arrest team. 'Put that baseball bat down and get out of the wardrobe, or I *will* use my TASER.'

The response was muffled but didn't sound polite. A few seconds later there came a series of crashes and a yelp.

'TASER discharged,' came a voice. 'Send for paramedics.'

'I wonder who that could be?' asked Sutton, not bothering to hide his smile at the prospect of the man who'd left his colleague with two black eyes being given an electric shock. It was just a shame he hadn't seen it in person; he'd look forward to reviewing the footage from the body-worn cameras. Doubtless so would Ruskin.

A few moments later, one of the arrest team appeared at the living room door, a plastic evidence bag in his hand. 'Thinking of starting your own jewellery business, Danny?' she asked.

'Looks like you could also start your own pharmacy,' came a voice from the kitchen.

'I think we've got our grounds for arrest,' said Sutton.

Chapter 27

The team decided to interview Danny McCamphill first; Callum Harradine had been taken to hospital for a brief check-up after his electric shock and was only now meeting his solicitor.

'He looks pissed off,' said Sutton, as he watched the interview on the briefing room screen. 'But I wouldn't say he looks like a man who thinks he's on the hook for a murder.'

Beside him, Warren agreed. 'He's a serial burglar; he knows that if we trace any of that jewellery back to their original owners he's on his way back to prison. Those drugs aren't going to help him much either; there was far too much for personal use.'

'At least we know he wasn't the one who stored Winnie Palmer,' said Sutton. 'He only has a fridge and the CSIs reckon there's no indentations in the carpet to suggest he got rid of a freezer recently.'

The two men settled back in their chairs as Karen Hardwick started the interview. She was currently applying for promotion to detective sergeant, and Warren wanted to give her every opportunity to showcase her skills. Competition was fierce for the reduced number of posts available and, in Warren's opinion, she was as good a candidate as any he'd ever worked with – importantly, Grayson agreed with his assessment. Tragically, her late fiancé, Gary Hastings, had just successfully completed the process when he was killed, but never received his notification. He would never know it, but through the quiet intervention of Grayson, he had been awarded the promotion posthumously, his final rank recorded as DS in the ledger in the police memorial in the corner of St James's Park.

'Can you tell us where you got the jewellery we found in your flat?' asked Hardwick.

'No comment,' replied McCamphill.

Hardwick pushed on regardless. 'Did you and Callum Harradine fit a bathroom at twelve Winchester Road between the 20th and 22nd of February?' she asked.

McCamphill paused. Over the video screen, they could see his calculating look. He had to know that if they were asking about that job, then they had probably linked the jewellery back to a burglary that took place shortly after the work was completed.

The owners had paid cash for the two men to fit a bathroom after they undercut the seller's fitting fee by a significant amount. The following week, the couple had jetted off to Tenerife for a short break that they'd told the charming and chatty Harradine all about. Whilst they were gone they were burgled; the intruders clearing the house of anything of value, including a necklace and some gold rings matching items found in McCamphill's flat.

Unfortunately, although a forensic team had attended, there had been no evidence linking the burglary to the two men. And had the CSIs found anything pointing towards them, they had been in the house legitimately only weeks before.

'No comment,' he said eventually.

Hardwick carefully laid a sheet of paper on the table.

'This is a list of all the burglaries committed in Middlesbury and the surrounding area for the past six months. The ones I have highlighted in yellow all had jobs done by you and Callum in the preceding month. We are currently in the process of matching the jewellery in your house, and items found in Callum's flat, to property reported as stolen.

'So here's the offer, Danny. You play fair with us, save us some time, and admit to these burglaries, and we'll note your coopera-tion. You also need to tell us if you were working alone, or Callum gave you a helping hand.' She paused. 'Then we'll check if what you've told us, matches what he's been telling my colleagues.'

'And the drugs?' he asked.

'A separate matter.'

McCamphill licked his lips. 'I'd like a break to speak to my solicitor.'

* * *

'Nicely done, Karen,' said Sutton as the DC pulled the tab off a can of Diet Coke. 'If we can at least get him to admit to working with Harradine, then we're well on the way. Good call making him think Harradine might already be giving him up.'

'The prisoner's dilemma,' she said. 'I doubt he trusts Harradine enough to hope he keeps his mouth shut and doesn't pin every-thing on him.'

'Works for me,' said Warren.

'Any news on when Harradine will be ready for interview?' Hardwick asked.

'He's with his solicitor now,' said Warren. 'He's detained on suspicion of handling stolen property, possession with intent to supply and assault occasioning actual bodily harm after that headbutt on Moray, so he's got plenty to worry about. I'm going to wait until we've got more out of McCamphill before we go and rattle his cage. Let him sweat a bit and wonder what his mate is telling us.'

'Whilst we wait for McCamphill to figure out his options, would you like to see a short video?' asked Sutton. 'Dare I say it's quite *shocking*?'

Hardwick smiled. 'Love to.'

* * *

Danny McCamphill drew a horizontal line about halfway down the first sheet of burglaries. The first of the offences dated back three weeks.

'Me and Callum did these. He robbed them; I just looked after some of the gear until he could get rid of it.' He sat back with his arms folded.

'Bugger,' said Warren upstairs. 'He knows what they haven't fenced yet and that's all he's going to admit to. He's gambling the only thing we have connecting them to the burglaries is the stolen property they haven't managed to sell on.'

'But it does sound like he's prepared to chuck Harradine under the bus,' said Sutton.

'And what about these incidents?' Hardwick was asking, pointing to the remaining rows on the sheet.

McCamphill shrugged. 'Nothing to do with me.'

'It seems a bit of a coincidence that all of these people had you and Callum around to do some work and were then burgled a couple of weeks later.'

'The Lord works in mysterious ways,' McCamphill said, not bothering to hide his smirk.

Undeterred, Hardwick continued. 'For two of the burglaries that you've admitted to, we have a pretty good idea what time the break-in occurred. Yet on each of those occasions, both your mobile phone and Callum's were turned off during that period. Why? You never seem to turn them off at any other time.'

'Why do you think?' he sneered. 'We ain't idiots. It's like carrying around a fucking homing beacon.'

Hardwick repressed a smile. It was always gratifying when a suspect's arrogance tightened the noose around their own neck.

'We also have more burglaries earlier in the year, in properties that you worked at, each with approximate times. Again, both your mobile phones were turned off around then.'

'Coincidences happen,' said McCamphill.

'So you weren't involved in those burglaries?' said Hardwick.

'No.'

'Sure about that?' she asked quietly. 'Remember our deal. I only put in a good word if your account matches what we already know and what Callum corroborates.'

McCamphill looked over at his solicitor, who stared back passively. He'd discharged his legal obligations; he wasn't going to advise McCamphill to lie to the police or admit to any more offences. On the other hand, a no comment at this stage might be seen as a lack of cooperation. McCamphill was the only one who could make that decision.

'No comment,' he eventually said, his shoulders slumping in defeat.

Hardwick gave him a sympathetic smile. 'I'll tell you what, why don't I make it easier for you? I'll name a burglary and you can either admit to it or deny it and hope Callum hasn't copped to it. I'll take a no comment as a denial.'

McCamphill again looked at his solicitor. No help from there. He gave a sullen nod.

'Then let's begin,' said Hardwick, her tone upbeat.

'Sparrowhawk Lane. You did a bathroom fitting there on February 10th and they were burgled on February 12th sometime after 11.30 p.m. It's a seventeen-minute drive from your house to Callum's flat. You sent him a text message at 11.05, he replied within sixty seconds and then you turned your phone off. Nine minutes later, Callum also turned his phone off. At that time of night, it takes six minutes to drive from Callum's to the burgled house. The neighbour's dog went nuts at 11.35, probably when you broke the glass on the French doors. If you were in and out in ten minutes, you could easily drop Callum back home just before midnight when his phone was switched back on, then return to yours at twenty past, when your phone was turned back on.'

She smiled. 'How does that sound to you?'

McCamphill's face had fallen further and further as Hardwick recounted the evening in exacting detail.

'Yeah,' he muttered.

'Thank you, Danny. Let's try another one, shall we?' Hardwick said, in the voice she usually reserved for her son trying a new food.

'Broad Street. You did their downstairs toilet on January 24th, two weeks before they went away for the weekend to celebrate their wedding anniversary. According to their alarm – which nobody pays attention to as it's always going off – the house was broken into at 11.43 p.m., which neatly coincides with your phones being turned off.'

'Yeah, that was us,' said McCamphill, defeated.

She outlined a third burglary. By the time she finished recounting the sequence of events, McCamphill was nodding.

'Chancellor Street, January 11th,' said Hardwick, deliberately not giving any more details.

'Yeah.'

'Clematis Drive, January 6th?'

'Yeah.'

'Tollbooth Road, New Year's Eve?'

Upstairs, Sutton and Warren held their breath.

McCamphill frowned.

'Say again?'

Hardwick repeated Winnie Palmer's address.

McCamphill shook his head. 'Doesn't ring a bell. What job did we do?'

Hardwick dodged the question. 'Your mobile phones were turned off again, with plenty of time to get there and back.'

McCamphill's eyes narrowed. 'Like I said, doesn't ring a bell,' he said.

'Then why don't you tell me what you were doing that night?' asked Hardwick.

McCamphill sat back in his chair. 'No comment.'

* * *

'Sorry, I tipped him off,' said Karen, taking a bite of the Twix Pymm had offered her.

'No you didn't,' said Sutton firmly. 'It's not like we were expecting him to confess to being there that night.'

'Tony's right,' said Warren. 'You gave him every opportunity to admit to being elsewhere. He chose to no comment.'

Hardwick's tone was still doubtful. 'The moment I couldn't tell him what job they supposedly did, he knew we were fishing and shut down.'

'He was burgling houses before you were born,' said Sutton. 'I'm amazed you got as much out of him as you did.'

'Anyway, you've given us everything we need for our interview with Callum Harradine,' said Warren.

'Speaking of which, do you think he's sweated long enough?' asked Sutton.

'Oh yes,' said Warren.

Chapter 28

Callum Harradine sat with his arms folded; he knew the drill. He was a little taller than Warren, but had the bulky build of a man used to hard work. Could he have been the man seen dressing in the road outside Winnie Palmer's house minutes into the new year? His jaw had a decided twist to it, although Warren would have thought the squashed nose the more noticeable of his features. But then as the witness had been so keen to stress – they had both been *very* drunk.

'Why did you run when we arrived at your flat on Thursday?' asked Warren.

Harradine said nothing.

'Was there a reason why you assaulted our officer – he's all right by the way, thanks for asking,' said Sutton.

Harradine remained silent, but a smile tugged at his lips. His receding hairline did nothing to mask the bruise in the centre of his forehead.

Beside him, his solicitor cleared her throat.

'Pass on my best wishes,' said Harradine, his tone dripping with insincerity.

'I presume it had something to do with the items we found

at your premises,' said Warren, pushing a series of colour images across the table.

Harradine didn't even bother to look at them, turning instead to his solicitor.

'I am somewhat confused by the order of events here,' she said. 'The search warrant was authorised *after* you arrived to speak to my client. On what grounds was it issued?'

'You're right. We had no intention of searching Callum's property at that time; we merely wished to speak to him,' said Warren. 'However, his assault on DC Ruskin and his flight from the scene gave us reasonable grounds to suspect he had items in the property that we might be interested in.'

The solicitor pursed her lips.

'The magistrate agreed,' said Warren, shutting down her next objection. 'With that established, what can you tell us about these items of jewellery and these drugs?'

'No comment,' said Harradine.

Warren gave a dramatic sigh. Sutton opened the folder again.

'OK, Callum, if you want to play it that way, fine,' said Sutton. 'But before you no comment your way into a lengthy jail term for multiple burglaries – again – I think it is only fair to let you know that Danny has been telling us all about the little scam you had going.'

Harradine's scowl suggested he had no trouble believing that his so-called friend was busy saving his own neck.

'Frankly, Callum, we have you bang to rights,' said Sutton. 'Now you can waste everyone's time and sit there and no comment, but we'll charge you anyway. We've already confirmed that the jewellery we found in your flat and Danny's home, along with the iPads, laptops and a bread-maker, belong to homeowners burgled shortly after the two of you worked on their houses.'

'That's all circumstantial. You can't …' started Harradine.

'Shh, let me finish,' interrupted Sutton, raising a finger. 'We're fair-minded blokes, so we're going to offer you exactly the same deal we offered Danny. Admit to these burglaries, and if your story matches his, we'll note your cooperation. If it doesn't …'

He pushed the burglary list across the table.

'We'll give you some time to think it over,' said Warren, reaching over to pause the interview.

* * *

The interview recommenced less than half an hour later.

Like McCamphill, Harradine admitted only to the most recent burglaries, for which stolen property had been retrieved. But heavy hints that McCamphill had already admitted other offences meant that by the time they got to Winnie Palmer's address, he was positively seething.

'Not one of ours,' he said firmly. 'We never did any jobs in that street.'

'Are you sure?' asked Warren.

'Positive.'

'Then what were you doing on New Year's Eve, when you both turned your phones off?' asked Sutton.

'None of your business,' he said.

Warren and Sutton exchanged a glance. It was time to push a little harder.

'This house was owned by a little old lady named Winifred Palmer; Winnie to her friends,' said Warren.

'And? I told you, we didn't do any jobs in that street and we didn't burgle anyone.'

Next to him, his solicitor was frowning. The frown turned to one of wide-eyed recognition the moment Warren pushed the headshot of Winnie Palmer across the table.

'I'd like to take a moment to speak to my client,' she said.

Harradine turned to her, a look of surprise on his face at the interruption.

'We really need to speak,' she said.

'You heard the lady,' said Harradine. 'I'd like a break.'

'Of course,' said Warren.

* * *

'I know he's probably a psychopath, but he didn't seem to recognise her when we showed him her picture,' said Sutton.

'He's had two months to practise his reaction,' pointed out Hutchinson.

'Let's see what his response is now that his solicitor has joined the dots and informed him he could be in the frame for a murder,' said Warren. 'Then we'll take whatever he tells us back to McCamphill and see if he confirms what he's told us.'

Harradine was still towards the top of his list of suspects, but Sutton had a point. Nothing they had found so far ruled the two men out, but similarly, they had yet to find anything placing them in the area that night.

* * *

For the first time since his arrest, Callum Harradine wore an expression other than irritation, arrogance or sullen compliance. He looked positively sick.

'We weren't anywhere near Tollbooth Road that night, and I've never seen that woman in my life,' he said.

'So you said,' said Sutton. 'But we're going to need more than that, because so far you're looking good for it.'

'Based on what? A picture that doesn't even look like me? The report said the bloke was getting dressed in the middle of the road on New Year's Eve. The witness was probably off their tits and seeing things.'

'So where were you?' asked Warren. 'Give us an alibi we can verify and you're off the hook.'

'You're right, we was burgling that night. Up Templar Lane.'

190

Sutton scanned down the list of burglaries. There had been several over the Christmas and New Year period.

'Number fourteen?'

Harradine frowned in concentration. 'Yeah, that'd be right.'

'Well here's the problem,' said Sutton. 'One of the burglary team spoke to the homeowners and they said that they hadn't had any jobs done on their house. That's why it wasn't highlighted.'

Harradine sighed. 'They're right. We replaced some fencing next door. The old bird from fourteen came over for a natter when we were working, and I heard her saying she was going to Edinburgh for New Year. Figured we'd have a go.' He shrugged. 'House was empty and nobody gives a shit about burglar alarms these days. In and out.'

'So you expect us to believe that this one time, you decided to change a tried and trusted method and burgle the neighbour?' Sutton's tone was sceptical, bordering on belligerent, although Warren knew his old friend well enough to know that, like him, he thought it unlikely Harradine could have made up such a story.

'Wasn't the only time,' Harradine admitted. He marked a cross next to another burglary on the list. 'That one's across the road from a driveway we did. The owner asked us how much we charged and said he'd call us when he got back off holiday. Bastard never did.'

'How rude,' said Sutton.

Harradine resumed his habitual pose again, arms folded. 'There you go. I've done my bit; now you do yours. Charge me and release me. I want a fag and a piss.'

'All in good time, Callum,' said Warren as he turned off the recording again.

* * *

Callum Harradine and Danny McCamphill had been led back to their cells. They still had plenty of time before they had to decide

191

if they were going to ask for an extension to custody.

'We can charge them with multiple counts of burglary and possession with intent to supply right now,' said Warren, 'but we'll never persuade a judge to remand them in custody awaiting trial. Unless we can further arrest them on suspicion of murder, they'll be out the door.'

'Bad news and bad news,' said Hardwick. 'First, Callum couldn't have killed the Culverhouses. He got into a pub fight in Stevenage last Sunday. He spent the night in Stevenage nick.'

'OK, that's no surprise,' said Sutton. 'Rachel still hasn't found any evidence they did the Culverhouses' new kitchen.'

'Furthermore, McCamphill confirms Harradine's version of events for New Year's Eve,' said Hardwick. 'And I looked through the crime report for that night, and the alarm was triggered at eleven-fifty. There's no way they could have been burgling up Templar Lane at that time and outside Winnie Palmer's ten minutes later.'

He turned to Richardson. 'Do we have anything back on the vehicle searches?'

'None of the hire cars we've identified were rented by either man. As to the other dark vehicles, no link to them or anyone with the same surname, but they could have borrowed a friend's car.'

'What about Harradine's shoes?' There was no point asking about McCamphill's – his feet were at least four sizes smaller than the imprints found near Winnie Palmer's body.

'The ones he was wearing today match the ones listed on the receipt from back in November, but don't match the footprints found near the body deposition site,' said Pymm.

Warren looked around the room. 'That's it then. Unless anyone has any bright ideas or Forensics turn up something, we've nothing on them.'

Nobody answered.

'Right, I'll pass everything we have over to Volume Crime, let Drugs know what we've found, then bail them. One thing's for sure, I imagine they won't turn their phones off next time they go burgling, now they know it's a bloody great red flag that they're up to no good.'

* * *

'They've finished processing Eric Morton's car,' said Sutton an hour later. 'Nothing to link the vehicle to Winnie Palmer.'

'But?' asked Warren.

'The carpet that covers the spare tyre in the boot is not the Vauxhall original.'

'Now why would he do that?' asked Hardwick.

'Don't get too excited,' cautioned Sutton. 'The carpet is so battered it could easily pre-date Winnie Palmer's death. The previous owner is dead, so there's no way to tell if they were the ones that replaced it.'

'We'll put it to him,' said Warren. 'If he squirms, it might tell us something. Rachel, where are you with Abacus Cabs?'

'The threat of prosecution has put the wind up them,' said Pymm. 'We have the paper ledger recording all their off-the-books jobs. We're working backwards from New Year's Eve for any mention of Winnie Palmer or jobs in her street, and forward for any references to the Culverhouses. We'll cross-reference any potentials with the location data from his phones, assuming he left them turned on.'

'Morton is due in front of the magistrate for driving whilst disqualified,' said Warren. 'Whether or not they decide to revoke his bail for the assault charge against his partner, he's out of the picture for a while.'

* * *

'I can see how Eric Morton could pass for his brother Kyle,' said Richardson. It was last thing and she'd just finished interviewing the older brother. At first Kyle had tried to claim he knew nothing of his brother's driving ban and had arranged the lease payments on his brother's behalf because Eric had a dodgy credit record.

Richardson blew that argument out of the water in seconds. Morton consistently refused a solicitor, doubtless worried that word of his predicament might get back to the law firm he worked for. Within five minutes, he was telling Richardson everything she wanted to know.

'So Eric's on the sofa bed in the living room, and everything that his ex didn't take to the tip is in the family garage,' she summarised.

'And he hasn't stayed anywhere else since New Year?' asked Warren.

'Apparently not.'

'What about access to a lock-up or garage?' asked Sutton.

'Not that he's aware of.'

'What's your gut telling you?' asked Warren.

'I think I believe him,' said Richardson. 'When I gave him the search warrant and explained what it was in relation to, I thought he was going to puke.'

Sunday 11th March

Chapter 29

'Come on, Warren, we'll be late!' called Susan.

Warren slipped his phone into his pocket, pushing aside the feelings of guilt. No emails needing his personal attention had come in overnight and today had been in his work calendar for months. As much as he hated taking time off during an investigation, he hadn't had a rest day in over three weeks and as Tony Sutton had said to him just the day before, nobody ever lay on their deathbed and thought, 'I wish I'd spent more time at work.'

The fact was, in Warren's line of work, there was never a good time to take a break, and sometimes you had to accept that life outside of the job was equally important. And there was no way he was missing today.

If something major happened, he could be back within two hours of receiving a call.

Just one day, he prayed silently. *Just one day.*

* * *

'Surprise!'

Granddad Jack almost dropped his walking frame; fortunately, Dennis, Susan's father, had a steadying hand on his arm. The old man's look of confusion turned to one of delight as Warren stepped out of the living room to hug him. Susan joined him, kissing him on the head. 'Happy birthday, Granddad,' she said. Susan had lost her grandparents years before she met Warren, and Jack and his late wife, Betty, had been very moved when she took to calling them Nana and Granddad after she and Warren had become engaged.

'We know it's a few days early, but we wanted to do something special,' said Bernice, Susan's mother, as she closed the front door of the large house that she and Dennis had lived in since before Susan was born.

'You shouldn't have ...' managed Jack, as Dennis helped him remove his coat. The close proximity of Susan's parents to Jack was the reason Warren had not moved back to the Midlands. Ever since Nana Betty had died, they had taken his grandfather to their hearts. Warren's relationship with his in-laws had been strained at times – Bernice in particular could be a woman of strident opinions – yet he would forever be grateful for the way they had looked after Jack. This morning, they had collected him from his care home as normal to attend mass, then brought him to their house for Sunday lunch.

'And who have we got here?' asked Jack his face beaming as he was accosted by a four-year-old blonde whirlwind.

'Careful, Tiffany,' admonished Susan's sister, Felicity, as the little girl forced a large, helium-filled balloon with the number '94' written in childish handwriting on it into Jack's free hand. 'I made this,' she said proudly.

'Let the man sit down, Tiff,' said Jeff, Felicity's husband, taking his daughter's hand.

Warren felt himself smiling as he watched Susan's four nieces and nephews competing to be the first to hand their cards and presents to their surrogate great-grandfather. Catching her husband's expression, Susan slipped her hand into his. Warren glanced down at her swollen belly; God willing, after years of disappointment and false starts, this summer, Jack would finally have his first great-grandchild.

At this moment, one hundred miles away from the horrors of Middlesbury, and surrounded by the people he cared about most in the world, Warren couldn't remember the last time he had felt so happy.

* * *

'So you are actually running two murder investigations at the same time?' said Jeff. Susan's brother-in-law did something that Warren didn't really understand in international banking. His frequent overseas travel meant he couldn't always make it to family gatherings, and Warren was enjoying catching up with him, as the family tucked into one of Dennis' famous Sunday roasts. How the man juggled everything was a mystery to Warren, who found it stressful enough working alongside Susan to prepare a roast for four if they had Tony and Marie Sutton over. Including the four children, Dennis was currently feeding eleven hungry mouths, and by the looks of things, they would all be taking Tupperware containers away with them to reheat later in the week.

'Are the government cutbacks that bad?' Jeff asked.

'Well they certainly don't help,' said Warren, 'but to be fair it's not like you see on TV, where detectives drop everything and focus on one case at a time. It's normal to juggle multiple investigations, although they are typically at different stages. I have a very good team, and we're used to increasing our numbers at short notice with colleagues from Welwyn. Mind you, IT support have been complaining the building's wireless network is struggling to handle so many devices. Most of the seconded officers and civilian workers have a smartphone, a laptop and a tablet.'

'They never showed that on *The Bill*,' joked Jeff.

'Blimey, you're showing your age,' Warren said with a laugh.

'How many years has it been since that ended? Did they even have mobile phones then?'

Jeff's reply was drowned out by the piercing shriek of a smoke alarm. Dennis looked up in confusion.

'What's that?' he asked.

'The Yorkshire puddings,' said Bernice jumping to her feet. 'I knew there was something missing.'

She scurried out to the kitchen, her husband following behind.

'Why didn't you set the timer?' she could be heard, scolding her husband.

'I did,' he protested. 'The batteries must be going.'

'Some things never change.' Jeff chuckled as his mother-in-law continued to berate her henpecked husband.

Across the table, Felicity rolled her eyes. Beside her, Susan frowned.

*   *   *

'I wish we could stay longer,' said Warren, as he bid farewell to Bernice and Dennis. It got harder to leave every time. His mobile phone had remained resolutely silent all day and he'd managed to resist the temptation to check his email.

'Well, I think we'll need to take Jack home soon anyway,' said Dennis. It was seven p.m. and the old man was visibly flagging, having forsaken his afternoon nap to play with the children. Warren was unable to push aside a feeling of melancholy. Jack had turned ninety-four. How many more days like this would they enjoy?

Having been 'on call' all day, Warren had partaken in only a small glass of champagne to toast Jack's birthday, so he opted to drive back to Middlesbury, letting Susan rest. She was unusually quiet.

'Warren, can I ask you something,' she said. 'Did Dad seem normal to you?'

'How do you mean?' he asked.

'That whole thing with the Yorkshire puddings is still bothering me.'

Warren tried to make light of it. 'Yeah, I was a little disappointed as well – they'd have been lovely smothered in beef gravy. Mind you, I'm not sure I could have managed anything else. I'm absolutely stuffed.'

'And that's another thing,' said Susan. 'There was enough food for twenty adults, not seven adults and four young children.'

'Your dad always over-caters – you know that,' said Warren. 'And he knows how much we love bubble and squeak later in the week.'

Susan said nothing, but Warren could see she wasn't happy.

'What's worrying you?' he asked.

'I heard Dad ask Jimmy twice about how his rugby was going.'

'Well we all do that sometimes,' said Warren soothingly.

'But Dad hates rugby, and he was delighted when Jimmy stopped playing it to focus on his football last year.'

'I'm sure it's nothing,' said Warren, trying his best to reassure her. But now that she had put the idea in his head, little, inconsequential things that he'd easily dismissed over the past year or so started to come back to him.

'You know his mother died young?' she said.

'She died of a stroke, didn't she?' replied Warren. 'But she was a heavy smoker. Your dad is fitter than men half his age.'

'She was fifty-eight,' confirmed Susan. 'Apparently, she became very forgetful in the last six months or so. After she died, the doctors said they thought she'd had a number of mini-strokes over the previous year. They never did an autopsy, but they assumed she had vascular dementia.' Her voice caught. 'What if it wasn't that? What if it was normal dementia? It can run in families, you know.'

Warren reached over and squeezed her hand.

'Look, if you're really that worried, why don't you text Felicity?

They're staying for another couple of days; ask her to keep an eye on him.' He gave her hand another squeeze. 'It's probably nothing. He basically prepared a Christmas dinner today; that's enough to fluster anyone.'

Susan squeezed back, but remained silent for the remainder of the journey, staring sightlessly out of the window.

The sky was darkening, and with it Warren's mood. At least there had been no unpleasant surprises from work during the day.

Monday 12th March

Chapter 30

The phone dancing around on the bedside table rattled loudly against the wooden surface. Warren fumbled for the handset, the fog of sleep still enveloping him.

His eyes were too sleep-laden to focus properly and he couldn't make out the caller ID. The surge of adrenaline from a late-night call finally cleared his mind enough for him to hit the answer button before Susan woke.

'Jones,' he managed, his voice croaky.

'Warren, it's John.'

Immediately, Warren felt himself relax slightly. It wasn't the care home. Then he tensed again. His eyes now worked well enough for him to make out the time on the digital alarm clock: 2.56 a.m. Why was John Grayson phoning him on his personal number at this time? The man's voice was clear, not the thick-tongued rasp of someone awoken himself only moments before. In the background, Warren could make out the sound of police radios. His office-bound boss was outside somewhere, attending an incident.

'What's happened?' whispered Warren, tiptoeing out of the bedroom.

Grayson's voice was grave. 'We've got a situation.'

*　*　*

The country lane was blocked off for one hundred metres either side of the burgundy-coloured Jaguar. The luxury car's lights were on, the driver's door open, the engine turned off. All four tyres were fully deflated.

Blue lights splashed off the trees lining either side of the lane. A short distance ahead, a Ford Focus had two wheels on the grass verge. The driver, a young man, perched sideways on the driver's seat, his feet on the road, his hands wrapped around a cup of something hot and steaming.

Two Scenes of Crime vans were already present when Warren arrived. A third pulled up as he finished getting into his paper suit. They would be throwing everything they had at this.

The sight of Grayson dressed in a full scene suit had banished any lingering doubts that he was still dreaming. The only times Grayson had attended a fresh crime scene in recent years was after one of his officers had been killed … Warren forced away the memories.

'The driver of the Focus spotted the Jag parked at the side of the road as he returned from work,' said Grayson. 'He slowed down for a better look, then saw the body lying in the road in front of the car.'

'What time was that?' asked Warren.

'He says he called it in as soon as he realised what had happened. We logged the call at 12.58.'

'And they're sure it's him?' asked Warren.

'Reasonably. The first responders called in the vehicle registration, and he's the right size and build.' Grayson let out a puff of air.

'Let's go and have a look, shall we?' said Warren.

Grayson swallowed and nodded. Warren was struck by the fact he'd slipped automatically into the role of SIO, and Grayson had fallen in behind him. He'd need to be careful of that; issuing orders to his superintendent as if the man was a constable wouldn't look good for either of them.

The body lay face down on the tarmac, inches from the front

of the car. Dressed in a three-piece suit, he'd clearly not been expecting to spend a significant amount of time outside on a cold night.

'Has anyone been to see his wife?' asked Warren. 'If nothing else, we need to make sure he isn't tucked up in bed beside her, having lent his keys to someone.'

'I'm going there next,' said Grayson. 'We don't want the press getting wind of this on social media and doorstepping her before she's even realised he didn't come home last night.' He looked meaningfully towards the man who'd found the body, his face now illuminated by his phone screen. Grayson lowered his voice. 'As far as I can tell, he hasn't twigged who this is yet, so hopefully that'll give us a few hours' grace.'

Warren turned back to the body. The pool of blood encircling the man's head glistened in the headlights. 'It looks like he was shot from behind.'

Careful not to kneel in the blood, or touch anything, Warren bent down further.

'I can't see if the bullet went through,' he said. He hoped not, for the family's sake; exit wounds through the face made an open casket funeral impossible.

'He wasn't shot with a gun.'

Warren looked up at Andy Harrison, relieved to hear his voice. It stood to reason that the most experienced CSI in the county would have been told to either drop whatever job he was on or get out of bed and head to the scene sharpish.

Harrison shone his torch on the back of the victim's head. The beam reflected off something metallic, embedded in the skull.

'Bloody hell, is that a …'

'Yes. Easier to get a hold of than a handgun and just as effective at close range.'

Warren rocked back on his heels. 'Jesus …' he breathed.

Standing up, his mind whirred as he planned his next moves. Grayson wouldn't have called him out if the powers-that-be

207

weren't planning on him taking charge. The Culverhouse murders and Winnie Palmer were currently progressing at a slow slog as the team trawled through the mountain of evidence both cases had generated. He would reassign the daily grind to teams from Welwyn; he'd want the officers he knew best working on this.

At least the proverbial blank cheque, an urban myth in recent years, wouldn't be an issue.

In the meantime, one thing was certain: if it was him, Councillor Aldous Paddon would not be standing for re-election, and the Conservative Party had just lost the man touted as their next parliamentary candidate for the constituency of Middlesbury.

* * *

'Pending formal identification, Councillor Paddon's wife has been informed of her husband's death, but there is a news blackout until twelve,' said Warren. 'Scenes of Crime have confirmed the car's tyres were burst with a stinger device or similar. They found several detachable hollow spikes embedded in them. We are therefore operating under the assumption that Councillor Paddon was ambushed. Determining whether or not he was the intended target, or just unlucky, will be a significant thread in this investigation.'

He fixed the room with a stare. 'We will *not* be sharing details of the ambush or the weapon used with the press or family at this time.'

Five hours and three coffees into the investigation and Warren was holding an initial eight a.m. briefing. On the screen behind him was a headshot of the victim, taken from the council website. Pale-skinned, with full cheeks, the man was bald on top, with steel-grey hair either side.

He hadn't clapped eyes on Grayson since the man had left to wake up the newly widowed Doreen Paddon; he was currently down in Welwyn attending a crisis meeting with the chief constable.

A few years ago, Grayson would have been ecstatic to have been involved in such a high-profile case; one last chance to finally prove himself worthy of promotion to chief superintendent, with the privileges and pension boost that came with such an advancement. But now, only weeks from retirement, that ship had sailed.

So far they had determined that Paddon had been attending a charity evening to raise money for terminally ill children, at the Reverend Hardingham Community Centre, affectionately known by the locals as 'the Rev'.

'Why wasn't his wife with him?' asked Hutchinson.

'Official line is she has been suffering from a cold and went to bed early,' said Warren. 'Unofficially ...'

They all knew the rumours. Councillor Paddon had a wandering eye and, allegedly, wandering hands. The *Middlesbury Reporter* had been filling column inches for the past few weeks with stories about an unnamed admin assistant who had recently left the council's employ. Despite not yet finding a new job, she was seen sporting a large and expensive necklace, and an even larger bump under her dress.

Paddon and his wife had dismissed the rumours as politically motivated and Mrs Paddon stood by her husband one hundred per cent, decrying the hurtful and untrue stories. Despite the couple's vehement protestations, the *Reporter* had continued to run the stories, suggesting there was enough truth in them that they had no fear of legal consequences.

It was the sort of scurrilous tittle-tattle that Warren normally flicked past whenever he bothered to read the local newspaper, but he'd spent half an hour skimming through anything he could find about the late politician in search of potential motives. As soon as the news embargo was lifted, they would be tracking down those who had reported the stories to see if they had any insight on the night's events.

'We'll look at potential motives in a moment. Let's concentrate on a timeline for the previous twenty-four hours,' said Warren. He drew a horizontal line on the whiteboard.

'Mr and Mrs Paddon live in Stenfield. They attended their local church, St Peter's, between ten a.m. and eleven. Councillor Paddon had a brief chat with a couple of constituents, but his wife claims they were perfectly cordial. We'll track them down as a matter of course.

'After returning home for an hour, they walked to the Gamekeeper's Inn; it's their local and everyone knows them. She doesn't recall any discussion beyond a bit of chitchat with the landlord and a couple of the locals.

'After returning home at about three p.m., Councillor Paddon spent the remainder of the afternoon in his office, she assumes doing constituency business. He left for the charity event about six-thirty, on his own.

'Everything from now on comes from his campaign manager, Noah Tilstone. He claims Councillor Paddon arrived just before seven, which is consistent with the most direct route from his home, and includes the Middlesbury Road where he was found later that night.

'The dinner was officially seven-thirty for eight, and he got there early to speak to a few people privately before the press and other guests arrived. The meal was a three-course sit-down, finishing a little after nine-thirty.'

'Do we know who he sat with?' asked Sutton.

'There was a seating plan,' said Warren. 'During the coffees, Councillor Paddon gave a short speech then mingled. He spoke to a few people, some of them prominent business leaders, and some of them acquaintances. Tilstone said it was a pretty convivial affair and he's unaware of any arguments. They weren't the first or the last to leave, and he reckons they made their excuses about half past ten. They spoke briefly in the car park about their plans for the coming week and then went their separate ways. Tilstone claims to have arrived home at five to eleven. We'll need to confirm that obviously.

'Councillor Paddon's car was found three miles outside

Middlesbury, on the road back to Stenfield. Assuming he didn't take any detours, that means he probably arrived there between 22.45 and 22.55.'

'I've requested speed camera and ANPR data from the area,' said Richardson. 'But unless the killer or Councillor Paddon were speeding, we won't have anything on the road where he was found. We may get lucky with traffic light cameras if he left Middlesbury by the most direct route. We'll flag any vehicles that passed through the lights a couple of minutes either side of him.'

Warren switched pens and continued the line in red. 'The call came in at 12.58.' He drew a question mark beneath the red ink. 'The question we need to answer is what happened between him leaving the Hardingham Centre and him being found.'

'The car's GPS should tell us when the car was stopped, which will give us a window for when the ambush happened,' said Sutton.

'We also need to know if he was killed immediately after pulling over,' said Hardwick.

'The autopsy is starting soon,' said Warren.

'I know it was late at night, but it seems a bit risky to torture him at the roadside,' said Ruskin. 'If it was me, I'd either drag him into the bushes or I'd just kill him immediately and flee.'

The young DC sported two impressive black eyes. He'd been greeted by a stuffed panda on his chair, and numerous colour printouts of him, manipulated so he appeared to be eating bamboo, had been affixed around the office. There was no doubt in Warren's mind that Pymm had been the ringleader, but as there was no way she could have attached them herself, he wondered who had assisted her the previous evening? Ruskin had taken it in good humour and paid the appropriate cake penalty for his reckless actions.

'If the killer was waiting for him by the roadside, then there should be something there for the CSIs,' said Warren. 'The verges are soft soil.'

'Assuming it wasn't one of the guests at the charity event, who else knew he'd be there that night?' asked Richardson.

'There was a piece in the paper mentioning the event, and all his appointments are on his page on the council website,' said Warren. 'This could have been a planned attack, not a chance encounter.'

'The choice of murder weapon tells us that,' said Sutton. 'Who the hell carries a nail gun around with them on a Sunday night?'

Chapter 31

There was no dodging the midday press conference and so Warren made use of the bathroom downstairs. As he emerged, freshly shaved, his hair wrestled into some semblance of a style, he was greeted by Sutton, who'd found him a banana and a cereal bar. 'Take care with these – we wouldn't want you to get crumbs down your jacket, would we?' he said. He reached up and straightened Warren's tie. 'Who's a handsome boy, eh?'

'If you spit on a tissue and wipe my face, I'll give you a slap,' said Warren.

Despite the news blackout, the journalists knew there was something in the air, and the room was already full when they arrived.

'Rather you than me,' said Sutton, eyeing the assembled reporters through the window in the door.

'DCI Jones,' said a voice behind him. Turning, Warren recognised a writer with the *Middlesbury Reporter*. 'Can you tell me what today's press conference is about?' she asked.

During their previous encounters, she'd come across as ambitious, resourceful and very forthright; it didn't surprise him that she wouldn't be shy about ignoring the news blackout and trying to steal a march on her rivals.

'Sorry, Marcia, got to rush,' he said.

'DI Sutton?' she asked, more in hope than expectation.

'I'm in charge of hair and make-up.'

*   *   *

Despite his last-minute grooming, Warren felt underdressed. Flanked by DSI Grayson and Assistant Chief Constable Mohammed Naseem, Warren was the only officer not in uniform. Naseem and Grayson both wore their jackets, and the lights from the TV cameras reflected off their polished epaulettes.

The assembled reporters quietened as the men took their places at the long table, the presence of ACC Naseem communicating the seriousness of the news they were due to impart.

'Thank you all for coming at such short notice,' started Naseem. 'At one a.m. this morning, Hertfordshire Constabulary received an emergency call from a member of the public reporting a seriously injured person on the Middlesbury Road, between Middlesbury and Stenfield. Unfortunately, the person was pronounced dead at the scene and a murder inquiry has been opened.

'We have positively identified the deceased as Councillor Aldous Paddon. His family has been informed and our thoughts are with his loved ones at this difficult time. They are being supported by specialist officers, and we would ask you to respect their privacy.'

The assembled journalists were an experienced bunch, but the news took them completely by surprise. Warren tried not to blink at the sudden explosion of camera flashes. Already, some were hastily typing on their mobile phones; doubtless websites across the country would be updated with Breaking News banners within the next couple of minutes. They had definitely replaced the lead item on the one o'clock news bulletins.

'Do you know the cause of death yet?' shouted someone from the back.

The press office had prepared a statement, but nobody expected the assembled reporters to sit quietly whilst it was read out.

'As you can appreciate,' said Grayson, 'the investigation is at a very early stage and we are unable to release that information at the moment,' he said. It had been agreed that the cause of death would be announced the following day to the public as a 'shooting' with no further details. High-profile murders attracted calls from a large number of conspiracy theorists and other mentally unstable individuals; holding back details of the murder weapon would quickly eliminate those persons from the inquiry.

'DCI Jones, have you determined what time Councillor Paddon was killed?' Marcia Cooper had snagged a seat in the front row. 'How long was it after he left the fundraiser at the Reverend Hardingham Community Centre?'

So much for keeping quiet and letting the brass do the talking, thought Warren. It was interesting that she was so familiar with Paddon's movements. Had she been assigned to cover the fundraiser? He recalled seeing her by-line on some of the articles written about the late politician's alleged affair.

'We are still determining the exact sequence of events,' replied Warren.

'Do you have any suspects?' asked a familiar face from the local TV news.

'Inquiries are ongoing, but we would urge anyone with any information to contact us or Crimestoppers,' said Warren. 'If anyone recalls seeing a burgundy Jaguar XE between six-thirty p.m. and one a.m., we would urgently like to speak to them.'

'What about motive?' asked a woman in the front row.

'We are keeping an open mind at this time.'

'There will be another briefing tomorrow, when we hope to have more we can share,' interjected Naseem; if he didn't draw a line, the journalists would continue rewording the same questions in the hope something slipped.

'Before you go, I have a question for Superintendent Grayson,' said Marcia Cooper.

Warren's heart sank; beside him, Grayson kept his face neutral. 'Of course, Marcia,' he said.

'You are due to retire in a few weeks. Will you continue to lead the investigation, or will you hand it over to your successor?'

Grayson gave a tight-lipped smile. 'An investigation such as this is handled by a large team of officers. DCI Jones is the designated senior investigating officer, and he will be communicating his findings to myself and others.'

'Does that mean DCI Jones will be taking over the running of Middlesbury CID when you step down, Superintendent?' she persisted.

'This isn't really the time to discuss that,' said Naseem firmly. 'We will make an announcement on our website nearer to the time.'

Cooper directed a small smile at Warren. He had a sneaking suspicion that any help she gave the investigation would come with strings.

*　*　*

'You'll need to watch Marcia Cooper, Warren,' said Naseem after they'd left the room. 'She's had it in for Paddon for ages. If you speak to her, give her as little as possible and don't go off script. The last thing we want is Herts Constabulary quoted as a source in her next gossip piece.'

'Will do, sir,' said Warren politely, as he slipped on his coat. Out of the corner of his eye, he could see Tony Sutton standing next to Grayson, trying a little too hard to appear not to be eavesdropping.

'Before you go, Warren,' Naseem said, lowering his voice. 'I'd like to have a little chat with you. Just the two of us.'

'Of course,' said Warren, feeling his pulse increase. 'I can come up to your office now, if you want?'

'No, not today.' Naseem grimaced. 'I've got back-to-back meetings. I'll get my PA to clear some time in my schedule later in the week; we'll have a working lunch. She'll send you the details.'

'I look forward to it,' lied Warren politely, before joining Sutton. They exited the room, leaving Grayson chatting to the press officer.

'Lunch date with the brass,' hissed Sutton, barely able to hide his glee as they walked across the car park. 'Time to start choosing curtains for your new office. Ask Grayson if he's going to leave his coffee machine behind.'

'Don't be silly,' said Warren. 'You know it doesn't work that way. He probably just wants to make sure I don't say anything I – or rather Herts Constabulary – regret to the *Reporter*.'

Sutton grinned. 'Come on, you know you're at the front of the line.' He opened the car door and slid into the passenger seat. 'It'll be a pleasant change to have someone in charge who gives a toss about the future of Middlesbury CID, not somebody who just sees it as a stepping stone to greater things.'

Warren rolled his eyes. They'd been arguing about John Grayson's commitment to Middlesbury CID almost since the day Warren arrived.

'What would you like me to call, you?' asked Sutton. 'Shall I stick with Boss, or would you rather be called Superintendent?'

'Do you want to walk to the morgue, *Inspector*?'

* * *

'We must stop meeting like this,' said Professor Jordan.

Behind his mask Warren smiled tightly. He'd attended more post-mortems over the past few weeks than he had in the previous year. This time he'd strong-armed Sutton into joining him; payback for his friend dodging the unpleasantly graphic Culverhouse autopsy.

'No mystery about the cause of death,' said Jordan. 'Catastrophic brain damage.' He pointed a finger towards the back of his own head. 'The nails went in here, just below the occipital bone, destroying the brainstem. If it's any comfort to his widow, death would have been instantaneous. One nail might have been survivable, but not three.'

'Christ,' muttered Sutton.

'The hairs on the top of his neck are singed, which suggests it was a combustion-powered gun, rather than an electric one, and it was placed in contact with the victim.' He motioned to a metal dish. 'I've retrieved all three staples.'

'Bloody hell,' said Sutton. 'They must be three inches long.'

'And designed to punch through hard wood; he didn't stand a chance,' said Warren. 'The head of the nails have a logo. Perhaps we can track down the make of gun used?'

Jordan held one up as Warren took a photo on his phone and emailed it to Rachel Pymm.

'Is there any evidence he was restrained or if he fought his killer?' asked Sutton.

'No obvious defensive wounds or restraint marks,' said Jordan. 'I've sent off for a toxicology screen to see if he was incapacitated. There are superficial scrapes on his face but they're post-mortem. If I were to theorise, I'd say he was standing, perhaps slightly bent over, and the killer placed the nail gun to the back of his head and pulled the trigger. He then fell face-first onto the hood – sorry bonnet – of the car. He was dead, so didn't try to break his fall. He then rolled off, landing face down in the road.'

'Any evidence he was moved afterwards?' asked Warren.

'Nothing I can see. Lividity is consistent with the position he was in when the first responders arrived.'

'It was an execution,' said Sutton.

Chapter 32

'Very dapper, sir – you scrub up well,' said Rachel Pymm, the moment Warren and Sutton returned to the station.

'Did you do something with your hair?' asked Hutchinson.

'I think it was the make-up,' said Richardson.

'You can piss off, the lot of you,' said Warren; the banter of his colleagues, and the teasing of Sutton on the drive home, had lightened his mood. On the way to his office, he noticed that some joker had paused the BBC News at One on the large TV screen. He was glad he'd had time to shave; high-definition could be very unforgiving.

'Main briefing room, fifteen minutes,' he called over his shoulder.

* * *

Warren had forced a round of cheese sandwiches and an apple down his neck. The autopsy had killed his appetite but if he didn't eat now, it would come back with a vengeance and he'd find himself in front of the vending machine.

'Jaguar Land Rover are bending over backwards to help us,' said Pymm. 'I have the logs from the car's GPS and its on-board computer. He left the Hardingham Centre at 22.35 and took the exact same route in reverse that he drove on the way in. No detours or stops on the way, other than traffic lights.

'The car stopped where it was found at 22.48. The car's diagnostics recorded a sudden loss of pressure in all four tyres and triggered a dashboard alert eight seconds later. It looks as though it took him about twelve seconds to pull over. Given his speed, the stinger could have been up to three hundred metres before the place he stopped. The driver-side door opened about ten seconds later and stayed open.'

'He was killed Sunday night,' said Warren, a sudden leaden feeling in his stomach.

Sutton's eyes widened, as he realised where Warren was going. 'New Year's Eve was a Sunday,' he said. 'The Culverhouses were killed on a Sunday.'

Warren swallowed. 'Three killings, separated by time. The textbook definition of a serial killer.'

'And we have six days until he might strike again,' finished Sutton.

* * *

'Where the hell does someone even get a stinger?' asked Hardwick. Warren had just finished a crisis meeting with Grayson. The superintendent had pointed out that the fact that the killings appeared to have all happened on a Sunday could be a coincidence; nevertheless, the blood had drained from his face and he'd immediately jumped on the phone to Welwyn. The team were now brainstorming ideas, an air of controlled urgency in the room. Analysts in Welwyn were busy looking for other unsolved murders that might have been committed on a Sunday night.

'Surely you can't buy one off Amazon,' she continued.

'I'm running that down as we speak,' said Ruskin. 'But you're right, it's not the sort of thing Joe Public would have easy access to.'

'Were there any outgoing calls on Councillor Paddon's phone?' asked Warren.

'None,' said Pymm.

'So he didn't call the AA, he just got out of the car to see what the problem was,' said Richardson.

'He walked around to the driver's side front wheel,' continued Warren. 'Bent over to look at it, and that's when our killer shot him.'

'The stinger was removed from the road before the lad in the Ford Focus happened upon the scene two hours later,' said Sutton. 'What I want to know is how long was it laid down *before* Mr Paddon drove over it? I'm assuming we've not had any reports of other drivers losing all four tyres?'

'Good point,' said Warren. 'If we can find the last time another car travelled that route, it puts a window on when the killer must have laid it.'

'Perhaps they waited until they knew Councillor Paddon was on his way?' suggested Richardson.

'Which implies a second person,' said Ruskin.

'How long would it take to lay a stinger across the road?' asked Hardwick. 'Could the same person have followed him as he left, then overtaken him?'

'I could deploy one in under a minute when I used to work Traffic,' said Richardson. 'But if this person did overtake him, they would have been driving very fast. The GPS shows that Councillor Paddon was doing fifty-five to sixty-five for much of that journey, and he was only three miles down Middlesbury Road when the stinger was laid. If they left at the same time as him, and didn't go hare-arsing through town, they'd have had to travel upwards of ninety miles per hour to get there a minute before him.'

'Could have been a motorbike,' said Ruskin. 'It would be a bit more manoeuvrable through town. Unless Hutch was riding it of course.'

'I'll check all motorbikes on the ANPR,' promised Richardson.

'Any luck with the nail gun?' asked Warren.

'The logo on the nail is from a well-known brand,' said Pymm. 'They are expensive and it's unlikely somebody would buy those nails unless they used that make of gun. Our job would have been a lot harder if the killer had used generic staples. The good news is the three models of nail gun that the company sell are expensive. It would have been cheaper to buy an actual handgun; they sell hundreds rather than thousands each year.'

'Handguns are hard to get hold of in this country unless you move in the right circles,' said Warren. 'That might give us some insight into the killer. What's the bad news?'

'Well if it's that expensive, the question is whether the killer bought it for this ambush, or did they already own it? They've been on sale in this country for years, and there is a thriving second-hand market for them.'

'Can you hire them?' asked Sutton.

'Yes, I have a team working on that,' said Pymm.

'Who uses them?' asked Warren.

'Almost exclusively construction or really serious DIY enthusiasts. Domestic users would most likely hire one, borrow one, or buy one second-hand.'

'Just supposing we do find a suspect with access to a nail gun,' said Hutchinson, 'is there any way we can link the nails used back to it? Like they do with bullets and a gun?'

'Extremely unlikely,' said Pymm.

'Prof Jordan reckoned the nail gun was placed against the victim's head,' Warren reminded him. 'There may be transfer onto the end of the gun.'

'Let's just hope the killer wasn't careful enough to clean everything off,' said Sutton.

'Like I said, good news and bad news,' said Pymm.

Chapter 33

'Right, we've had twelve hours to get to know our victim,' said Warren. 'Tony, can you take this?'

Sutton projected the now familiar headshot of Councillor Paddon onto the screen.

'Aldous Paddon – known as "Al" to friends and family – was fifty-three years old. He was married to Doreen for the past twenty-eight years. They have one son, Rhys, aged twenty-five.

'He was first elected to the North Middlesbury ward as a Conservative councillor in 2011. He ran a successful property business until stepping down as its chair to concentrate on his political career, although he retains a controlling interest in it. As you are probably aware, Kenneth Falconer, the current Conservative MP for Middlesbury will be standing down at the next election, whenever that may be, and Councillor Paddon was almost certain to be chosen as the Tory Party's prospective parliamentary candidate in his place. He had no convictions or prior contact with police outside his duties as a councillor, and we have recorded no threats against him.'

'Thanks, Tony,' said Warren. 'Let's process what we have so far.'

'His wife,' said Hutchinson immediately. 'Presumably there is jealousy if rumours of the affair are true, but does she stand to gain anything by his death?'

'Nothing obvious,' said Sutton. 'From what the team have found so far, his business interests made him comfortable rather than rich. Most of their wealth came from her side of the family; her parents owned a lot of land in south-west England, which she sold after their deaths and *before* the 2008 financial crisis. Let's just say, he married well.

'Unfortunately for Mrs Paddon, the land didn't come with any titles and rumour has it, she *really* wants to be known as "Lady". She's not done anything to justify the title in her own right, so she was banking on her husband's political career.'

'What about the son?' asked Hardwick. 'Will he gain anything now, or does it all go to his mother in the first instance?'

'Good question – look into it,' said Warren. 'What do we know about the relationship between Aldous and Rhys?'

'There is some tension,' said Hutchinson. 'A piece in the *Reporter* a couple of years ago reported how his son supposedly "embarrassed" his old man, by speaking at a student rally denouncing Conservative Party policies that Aldous Paddon had given vocal backing to.' Hutchinson shrugged. 'You know the *Reporter*, take everything you read with a pinch of salt.'

'Good find,' said Warren. 'See if the article has any credence; it may have been reported elsewhere. Whilst you're at it, find out who wrote the original article; they may have material that they didn't publish. And whilst we're on the subject of family life, any insight into his supposed affairs, particularly this former staff member he has allegedly impregnated?'

'Just what I've seen in the *Reporter*,' said Sutton, barely hiding his smirk. 'I have the name of the journalist who wrote the stories, perhaps you could contact her directly? I'm sure she'd be happy to speak to you.'

'I'll take that into consideration,' said Warren, drily. He could try and fob her off on one of his more junior officers – a certain DI sprung instantly to mind – but he knew she wouldn't settle for that. 'Let's do a bit more sniffing around,' he continued. 'I'm wary about relying on what the papers have caught wind of. Are there other skeletons in his closet? And we need to confirm if he was paying her off.

'We've covered his personal and business life, so that leaves his political dealings. Noah Tilstone is coming in for a formal interview tomorrow. What do we want to know?'

'Any grievances from constituents,' said Hardwick. 'Did he hold surgeries with members of the public? It feels a little professional to be the local nutter pissed off about his neighbour's hedge, but you never know.'

Hutchinson snorted. 'To annoy his constituents, he'd have to interact with them.'

Warren turned to him. 'I forgot, you must live in his ward.'

'For my sins,' said Hutchinson. 'To put it bluntly, he's bone idle. I've written to him three times in the past couple of years. Each time, his reply just fobbed me off. He's good at hand-shaking, eating free lunches and getting his face in the paper or on TV, but it's clearly just a stepping stone to being an MP where he'll then get paid eighty grand, plus expenses, for continuing to do bugger all.'

'Perhaps it was that which upset the killer?' suggested Ruskin. 'Nobody likes being ignored. We should look at his correspondence and see if anyone stands out. Also, check his social media. My local councillor gets some real shit on Twitter.'

'If he's on the council, he must have responsibilities,' said Sutton. 'If he's chairing a committee that's in charge of closing services, he'll not be popular. Especially as he's a Tory, who a lot of folks blame for the budget cuts. I'll arrange interviews with the committees and see if that brings anything up.'

Richardson looked up from her tablet. 'I just looked up the boundaries of his constituency; Winnie Palmer is in a different ward, but both Derek Culverhouse's flat and his parents' house fall within it.'

* * *

It had been a long day; fourteen hours since Warren had been woken, and it would be another few hours before he could return to bed. He'd spent the whole day focused on the killing of Aldous Paddon, but it wasn't the only investigation.

'It doesn't look like there is much left for us at Eric Morton's former girlfriend's property,' said Hutchinson, reclining in one of Warren's guest chairs. 'She threw most of his stuff out and changed the locks when he was arrested for assaulting her. They shared a one-bedroom flat with no room for a chest freezer. There's no communal areas and, as far as she knows, he didn't have access to any outbuildings or rent any lock-ups. His only living family is his brother Kyle.'

'Does she remember any suspicious behaviour around New Year's Eve?' asked Warren, stifling a yawn.

'No. She confirms he was driving his taxi over that period. She'd been suffering with morning sickness over Christmas and New Year, so she just had a quiet night in with her sister and was asleep by the time he finished his shift.'

'Did she recall anything about the missing carpet from the boot of his car?'

'No. He kept the car very clean, but that's not unusual for taxi drivers. He never mentioned needing to replace the carpet.'

'Could she be covering for him?' asked Sutton. Despite everything, Morton was the father of her unborn child, and the relationship between victims of domestic violence and their abusers was often complex.

'Doubtful. She was interviewed by one of the officers from the domestic violence unit that she has known for a while and apparently, she's made a clean break. She wants him out of her life and is more than happy to cooperate; a lengthy jail term for murder would be a dream come true.'

'What about his brother's house?' asked Warren.

'All Eric's stuff is in the garage. The CSIs have bagged his clothing, but unless we can figure out what he was wearing that night, or the night Winnie Palmer's body was dumped, they don't really know where to start.'

'Anything that might have belonged to her?' asked Sutton. 'She was naked when she was found; whatever she was wearing must be somewhere.'

'Nothing yet. The garage has a connecting door with the rest of the house, and they store their chest freezer in there. But it's full of food. The CSIs have taken it for analysis, but I can't imagine the family have been using it for the past two months with Winnie Palmer frozen in there.'

'Plus, she was killed several weeks before he moved in with his brother,' said Warren. 'Where was he storing her before then?'

'Any evidence he has access to another property or a lock-up?' asked Sutton.

'Nothing obvious,' said Hutchinson. 'His keyring only has a front door key to his brother's place and his car keys.'

'He could use a combination padlock,' suggested Sutton.

'Well if he does have a lock-up, then he must be paying for it somehow. And unless he's running a generator, it'll need an electricity supply,' said Warren. 'Have Rachel scour his financial records for any regular payments that indicate he is renting one.'

Warren looked at the clock on his laptop.

'Thanks, Hutch.' He turned to Sutton. 'One more job to do today.'

Sutton looked grim. 'Let's get it over with.'

227

Chapter 34

Warren drove carefully up the well-tended driveway; beside him Tony Sutton had changed into a fresh shirt and tie. Behind them, motorised gates closed, obscuring the house from the gaggle of photographers and journalists hanging around outside. A number of constables had negotiated a clear area in front of the house's entrance, but it wasn't a crime scene and the pavement was a public right of way. Warren wondered what his legal position would be if he ran over the foot of one of them because he had been dazzled by a camera flash.

The family liaison officer assigned to Doreen, Aldous Paddon's widow, had contacted them to say she was ready to give an interview. Grayson and ACC Naseem had broken the news to her less than sixteen hours previously; they were going to have to tread carefully.

Until they were satisfied otherwise, Mrs Paddon was a potential suspect. However, she was also a recently bereaved widow and the added political dimension made it even more important that they didn't misstep. He covered his mouth as he yawned. He'd reached the point where caffeine had little effect. Barring any surprises that needed his immediate attention, Warren intended to write up his notes from the forthcoming interview whilst it was still fresh in his mind, and then head home.

He really hoped there were no surprises.

The door opened as soon as they emerged from the car. Warren recognised PC Kevin Lederer and was glad he had been assigned to the case; the role of the FLO would be critical. Not only would he provide support to the family and keep them apprised of the investigation's progress, he'd also feed back to the investigating team. Details that the family had forgotten, or perhaps deemed unimportant, could be channelled through him – and whilst Mrs Paddon and her family remained potential suspects, his observations and impressions might prove useful. Lederer had been in the role for years, and Warren valued his opinion.

A discreet CCTV camera was positioned above the door; given the expensive area, Warren was hopeful they'd retrieve plenty of footage from neighbouring properties.

According to Lederer, Mrs Paddon was alone. Her sister had been there for most of the day but had since returned home. Her son, Rhys, was still trying to get a flight back from Canada, where he was on holiday with his girlfriend. That was certainly a good alibi, although they wouldn't take it at face value.

After they'd introduced themselves, Warren accepted her offer of a cup of coffee. Sutton settled for a glass of water. Lederer immediately offered to make it, but Paddon insisted, and scurried out to the kitchen. The fresh tears that had sprung into her eyes as they had expressed their condolences suggested her offer of hospitality provided an excuse for her to compose herself.

'She's still in shock, but coping well,' was Lederer's quiet assessment. 'She's tougher than she looks.'

In contrast to her robust, six-foot husband, Doreen Paddon was a slightly built five foot. A few years younger than her husband, she could easily have passed for forty, although the stress of the last few hours had aged her.

As they waited for their drinks, Warren and Sutton looked around the living room, trying to get a feel for the family that had lived there for the past twenty-odd years. It was cosier than

Warren had thought it would be. He'd almost expected a large fireplace with a vase of perfectly arranged flowers and a carefully chosen picture of Paddon and his wife in classic 'politician's pose' – arm in arm, him in corduroy trousers and a woolly sweater, her in a modest flowery dress with a Labrador sitting obediently at their feet, and their house perfectly framed behind them.

There was certainly a large fireplace, but it was covered in framed photos, ranging from the Paddons' wedding photos to family holidays and dinner parties with friends; a still-life chronicle of a marriage that had lasted nearly three decades.

Whatever public political disagreements Aldous Paddon may have had with their son, he still featured heavily in the images, ranging from a new-born cradled in the arms of a tired-looking Doreen Paddon, through gap-toothed school photos, to awkward-looking snaps of him heading off to what looked like his end-of-school prom. The photos continued along the hearth, with Rhys in a university graduation gown, tossing his cap into the air, and smiling group shots of the three of them taken recently.

The one that stood out most to Warren was one of Rhys and his father; a candid shot seemingly taken unawares, both wearing Christmas jumpers and reindeer antlers. Aldous had his arm casually across his son's shoulders, with both men laughing at something off camera.

'That's one of my favourites; I just had to get it framed,' said Mrs Paddon, as she reappeared with their drinks. 'Rhys and his girlfriend spent Christmas and New Year with us this year for the first time. It was lovely.'

That meant the photo had been taken only ten weeks previously. Warren didn't like making snap judgements from one picture, especially one taken during the festive period, but it felt like a natural, comfortable father-son relationship. Was the image truly representative, or was there something dark lurking in the background?

'I realise this has been a terribly shocking event, Mrs Paddon, but I need to ask if you have thought of anyone who may have wished to harm your husband?' Warren started.

She shook her head. 'No, I've been racking my brain for hours and I can't think of anyone who would want to …' Her voice trailed off.

'So you aren't aware of any threats that your husband may have received?' said Sutton. 'What about strangers hanging around?' he persisted as Paddon continued to shake her head.

'Did his behaviour change recently?' asked Warren. 'Perhaps a little more worried? Taking extra care over setting the alarm system or locking the doors?'

'No, nothing. Everything seemed quite normal,' she said. 'I just don't understand why …' Again she broke off.

'I believe your son is away at the moment?' said Warren.

'Yes, he and his girlfriend flew out to Toronto last week to celebrate their second anniversary.' She gave a sniff. 'I'm so glad he isn't alone. When I phoned him this morning, it broke my heart. Talia is such a lovely girl – she'll look after him until he gets back.' Her bottom lip started to tremble, and she pressed a tissue to her mouth, mumbling through it. 'Al and I had a little bet going. I thought he was going to propose whilst he was out there. Al said he thought he'd wait until her birthday.' Her voice broke. 'And now Al will never know … He'll never get to give a speech at his wedding.'

'It sounds as if Rhys and his father were very close,' said Warren.

'Oh yes, they were like two peas in a pod. They would talk for hours on the phone at least twice a week, football, cricket, dirty jokes that Al would never share with me. It's going to be so hard for him.'

'What about politics?' asked Sutton.

'Yes, even that sometimes, although they hardly saw eye to eye.' Mrs Paddon gave a gentle laugh. 'I'm sure you've read about how Rhys embarrasses his father and denounces him publicly. Complete nonsense, blown out of all proportion. Aldous was

231

always very proud Rhys is willing to speak his mind, and they didn't disagree on the important things. God knows Al could probably have done without some of the headlines, but you know what they say about today's papers wrapping tomorrow's fish and chips. He thought it was all quite amusing; I think Noah was a lot more bothered about it than Al.'

'We'll be speaking to Noah Tilstone tomorrow,' said Warren. 'How involved were you in your husband's political life?'

'Not very,' she said. 'We'd talk about it of course, but most of it was rather dull. He was always very strict about separating work life from family life. First thing he'd do whenever he returned home was change into jeans and a T-shirt. He never did any council business outside of his office; he'd even walk in there to send texts or answer phone calls.'

'That must have been hard at times,' commiserated Sutton. 'Especially with him considering running as a member of parliament.'

Mrs Paddon sighed. 'I must admit, that did worry me, but Al insisted we'd manage. I suppose if he ever took on a ministerial post, we would have needed to rethink things ...' She stopped abruptly, as if realising it was all irrelevant now.

'Would we be able to take a look in your husband's office?' asked Warren. They could easily obtain a warrant, but he always preferred to ask.

'Yes, of course,' she agreed immediately.

'I believe your husband was seen as the most likely candidate to succeed Kenneth Falconer,' said Warren. 'May I ask how that was viewed by others within the party.'

Mrs Paddon gave a tight smile. 'Looking for a suspect?' She toyed with her mug for a few moments. 'I don't suppose it really matters now.' Her voice took on a bitter note. 'It's not as if party HQ can gag me anymore. Take a look at Harold Montgomery.'

'The councillor for Middlesbury East?' recalled Sutton, from his reading on the council website.

'Yes. He and Al have butted heads a few times on various issues. The problem is that Harold is a little behind the times, shall we say?'

Montgomery held rather strident views on a number of divisive topics and wasn't afraid to air them in the local paper or on the news.

'Well anyway,' continued Doreen 'Harold has been a councillor for almost thirty years, a loyal servant of the local Conservative Party. He and his friends assumed that – based on years of service alone – he was likely to be Ken's successor in the next election. He's in his sixties, so a term in parliament, perhaps two, would have been the perfect reward before he retires. But that ship has sailed. Ten or fifteen years ago, Harold's views might have been in tune with the party, but he's no longer the image they want to portray.'

'And was there any ... unpleasantness ... between them?' asked Warren.

'Yes,' she admitted. 'From both sides, I'm ashamed to admit. We're the safest Tory seat in the region, so it's quite a prize. Al was a lovely, kind man – but he could play dirty when he wanted to.' She paused. 'But I can't imagine Harold killing him, or even asking someone else to. For a start, I don't think he has the guts; he'd far rather talk about Al behind his back or spread lies.'

'What sort of lies?' asked Warren.

She snorted. 'About Al and some girl who used to work for him. About him getting her pregnant.'

'And you don't think that was true?' asked Warren carefully.

'Absolutely not. We've lived with this nonsense for months. First there were claims that Al had been a bit handsy with women at official functions. All unnamed of course, and no complaints were ever made to the police; just a quiet word to that rag the *Middlesbury Reporter*, so he can't even properly defend himself. Then suddenly some girl who used to work in the council office is let go – which was nothing to do with Al by the way; the councillors don't have any say in that sort of thing. Next thing you know, there are whispers she's claiming they had an affair and he got her pregnant, and that he's been paying her off.'

'Could you tell me the name of this young woman?' asked Warren.

'No. I didn't ask, and he didn't offer. I refuse to dignify her lies. I know my husband.' She gave a bitter laugh. 'I don't know what hold Harold has over the *Reporter*, but they'll print anything he says.

'I was so naïve. I should have just ignored that reporter when she doorstepped me to ask for a statement, but I didn't. I told her how I was sticking by him one hundred per cent; straight out of the wronged wife's playbook. I demanded she print it. She did, and promptly quoted "unnamed sources" who claimed we were sleeping in separate beds.' Doreen's cheeks flushed red. 'A complete lie. How on earth can anyone know what our sleeping arrangements are? We don't have a cleaner, or a gardener. None of our friends have gone sniffing around our bedrooms. It's complete rubbish.

'And I'll tell you another thing.' She pointed a finger at Warren and Sutton, no longer noticing or caring about the tears now flowing down her cheeks. 'I do the accounts in this house, and I can assure you that he hasn't paid a penny to anyone. If anyone is giving money to that slut, try looking at Harold Montgomery.'

* * *

'What do you think?' asked Warren, as they drove back to the station.

'That this is a lot more complicated than the *Middlesbury Reporter* have painted it,' said Sutton. 'Doreen Paddon strikes me as a grieving widow, not a jealous wife capable of orchestrating a cold-blooded murder.'

'I'm inclined to agree, as is Kevin Lederer,' said Warren. 'We'll pull her finances to check for any suspicious cash withdrawals that indicate she paid someone to do it and access her phone logs. We'll also check that Aldous Paddon didn't have any secret bank accounts he didn't tell his wife about – he could have spun his wife a pack of lies about this woman whom he supposedly got pregnant.'

'It seems strange that she didn't ask the accuser's name,' said Sutton. 'That's the one thing she said that I thought might be untrue, although why she would lie I don't know. She must know we can find out easily enough. Speaking of which, we should try and find out the identities of some of these other women he was supposedly inappropriate towards. "A bit handsy" is code for "sexual assault" in my book.'

Warren sighed. 'I'll phone Marcia Cooper first thing tomorrow.'

'She'll be wanting more than a phone call,' cautioned Sutton. 'I suggest you have your script ready and stick to it.'

Warren noted his use of the same phrase as ACC Naseem earlier that day. Sutton shrugged. 'Couldn't help it – the acoustics are better in that room than you'd think.'

'What about the son?' asked Warren. 'Doreen Paddon paints a rather different opinion of their relationship than the *Reporter* does.'

'Trickier,' said Sutton. 'I think we'll need to pull his financials and phone records as well. Assuming he hasn't told a really stupid lie about being in Canada, he'd have had to arrange for somebody else to kill his father. I'll speak to Hutch about interviewing his associates. I'll also get Karen or Moray to dig into his social media; we might be onto something if that Christmas photo was just a temporary truce and he's been bad-mouthing his old man to his friends online.'

'Which leaves Councillor Montgomery,' said Warren.

'Leaving the best until last,' groaned Sutton. He rubbed the bridge of his nose with his thumb and forefinger. 'I swear this headache started the moment she mentioned his name. I *really* hope it's not him, because if it is this case is going to be a political shitstorm.'

'I'll see what Noah Tilstone has to say about him when he comes in tomorrow. In the meantime we'll get warrants prepared for Montgomery's property, financials and phone records,' said Warren. 'But I'm not going anywhere near a magistrate with them; that's a decision well above my pay grade.' He gave a small smile. 'I'll let John deal with that. A little leaving present.'

Sutton was still chuckling as they pulled into the station car park.

'Don't take too much time writing up those notes,' he cautioned. 'It's been a long enough day for me, and I wasn't dragged out of bed at silly o'clock.' He gave an evil smile. 'And you'll want to be sharp and rested for your interview with Marcia Cooper.'

Tuesday 13th March

Chapter 35

'I'm not ready to dismiss Eric Morton just yet,' said Warren to the morning briefing, 'and Derek Culverhouse remains a person of interest. But we need to cast the net wider. Our eyewitnesses from New Year's Eve were somewhat unreliable, but let's assume there was a man acting strangely outside Winnie Palmer's house that night, and that he drove a dark-coloured five-door car. Let's also assume that this new friend she acquired in the months prior to her death may be involved.

'I've received authorisation for a large-scale trawl and follow-up of all the ANPR records in the area surrounding Winnie Palmer's house around midnight on New Year's Eve and the preceding months. Any matching vehicle picked up that night, and also snapped prior to then, is to be identified and, where possible, eliminated. We will also throw in data from the roads near the Culverhouses', Councillor Paddon's route to and from the Hardingham Centre and the area surrounding his home for the past few weeks.'

It was a huge undertaking that a few years ago would have been unimaginable. But the force had poured money into systems that could sift through the data automatically, using vehicle registration data from the DVLA. Nevertheless, the number of suspect vehicles generated would be immense, given the vague search criteria, so the final step – following up to identify those who didn't seem to be in the area for a legitimate reason – would be time-consuming, requiring human input.

Calling the meeting to a close, Warren headed back to his office. Despite his exhaustion the previous day, he'd slept poorly. Felicity had called that evening, and she agreed with Susan; their father was not himself. It would be a difficult conversation and they decided to broach the subject over Easter. Warren vowed to be there, no matter what stage the case was at, knowing Bernice wouldn't take it well.

It was hardly the ideal preparation for what he had to do next, but he couldn't put it off any longer. Taking a deep breath, he picked up his desk phone and punched in the digits he'd found on the internet.

'*Middlesbury Reporter*. Marcia Cooper speaking.'

*   *   *

Cooper settled back into the soft, padded chair in the smart interview room and closed her eyes briefly. 'I should come here more often – the coffee's a lot better than ours.' She smiled. 'I'm assuming this is different to what you offer guests occupying the interview suites?'

'Well it's certainly hotter,' said Warren. 'A face full of scalding coffee gets things off to a bad start.'

Cooper gave a short laugh, before taking another mouthful. Warren appraised her as she did so. She was a little younger than he'd first thought, perhaps late twenties, rather than early thirties. The *Reporter* was part of a consortium of regional papers. Her by-line listed her as a senior staff writer, which suggested she was doing a good enough job that the parent company had seen no reason to employ somebody more experienced from outside of Middlesbury.

'You've written a lot about Aldous Paddon in recent months,' said Warren.

'I have,' she said, her eyes giving nothing away.

'From your comments yesterday, I assume you were at the fundraiser Sunday night?'

'I was.'

'And did you see anything unusual?'

'No. It was a charity fundraiser. He spoke to families, shook hands, made small talk and enjoyed a free dinner, before earning his keep with a speech. All pretty standard fare. Say what you will about him, he can be a real charmer at these sorts of events.' She considered him for a second. 'Do you think his killer might have followed him from there?'

'We are keeping an open mind,' said Warren smoothly. 'Either way, it would help to know when he was last seen.'

'I saw Councillor Paddon and Noah Tilstone go out to the car park about ten-thirty and followed them. I thought I might get to speak with him.'

'And did you?'

She gave a short bark. 'No. Mr Tilstone told me, in the politest possible terms, to "do one". The two of them drove off and I decided to call it a night. There was nobody else in the car park and I didn't spot anyone leave at the same time as him. I got home just as the eleven o'clock news started on the radio. It's a twenty-five-minute drive roughly, so you can work out when I left from there.'

'How did Councillor Paddon and Mr Tilstone seem when you saw them in the car park?'

'They were chatting about something, but they stopped talking as soon as they saw me – I tend to have that effect.' She smiled ruefully. 'But for what it's worth, I didn't detect any tension, and Councillor Paddon gave him a friendly slap on the arm as they said goodbye.'

'Were you there all night?'

'Yes, I got there a bit before it started, to interview the organisers and take a few shots of the venue. I'll forward you everything, in case it's useful,' she said, anticipating Warren's request. 'I was a bit surprised to see Paddon already there. He and Noah Tilstone were chatting to Salim Khan, the owner of SK Precision Tooling; seemed quite intense.' Her face twisted into a wry grin. 'At least until Tilstone spotted me. Then they stopped.'

'Intense how?'

She puffed her lips out. 'Not aggressive, if that's what you're asking. More earnest. I think Paddon was making some sort of pitch to Khan. He has deep pockets and a fair bit of local influence, which is why he was at the fundraiser. If I had to guess, he was seeking backing for his bid to replace Kenneth Falconer as candidate in the next general election.'

'Speaking of which, what do you know about Councillor Paddon's parliamentary ambitions?' He tried to sound casual.

Cooper's eyes brightened. 'You think this may have something to do with his death?'

Warren shook his head firmly. 'No, I just need to get as full a picture of the victim's background as I can.'

'Did Doreen Paddon suggest you look into Harold Montgomery?' asked Cooper.

'No,' said Warren, masking his untruth with a hint of exasperation. 'And I'd appreciate it if you didn't spread those sorts of rumours.'

This was why he hated speaking to journalists. He really hoped the Harold Montgomery angle came to nothing; if Cooper realised he'd lied to her, it would come back and bite him.

'OK, if you say so,' she said, her eyes narrowing. 'Where to begin? Montgomery has been a councillor for thirty years, I guess. Rumour has it he naturally assumed that he would become the next candidate. But to put it bluntly, he's ten years too late. Frankly, it's just as well for him that social media wasn't around in the Nineties; politically, he's well to the right of Genghis Khan and says what he's thinking. Paddon was seen as a safe pair of hands – less likely to end up lead item on Channel 4 News or the front page of the *Guardian*.'

'How do you think Mr Montgomery took it?' asked Warren, knowing he was pushing his luck. He'd told her the police didn't regard Montgomery as a suspect; he doubted she'd be foolish enough to write anything contradicting that.

'Badly is what I've heard,' said Cooper. 'He was very supportive of Paddon back when he first ran for the council, and he saw it as a betrayal.' Her eyes glinted. 'He was delighted at Paddon's latest troubles, and to be honest he's crass enough to see his death as an opportunity, but I can't envisage him orchestrating it. The prize just isn't big enough. Montgomery has a massive ego, and he's an entitled bugger, but he's what? Sixty, sixty-one now? Unless something unexpected happens, the next general election is still four years away. He'd serve one, maybe two terms, probably as a backbencher. He's too much of a liability to be given anything more than a junior ministerial post in the department of "who gives a shit"; he's hardly going to be attending cabinet meetings or chairing select committees. Paddon was a much safer bet; he could probably have made a bit of a name for himself.'

'Assuming he wasn't tarnished by allegations,' said Warren.

Cooper said nothing, her expression neutral.

'Look,' said Warren, 'you know what I'm going to ask. It's a murder investigation – I have to look at every angle. You've been writing about these whispers of inappropriate sexual conduct for months. I need to know if there is anything in the stories and if there is any potential motive there.'

'I stand by everything I've written,' she said firmly. 'Don't be taken in by Doreen Paddon. She was as keen to see her husband running for parliament as him.'

Warren raised a placating hand. 'I wouldn't suggest otherwise, but at the moment the stories have very little detail. There are no names and no indication of where the information came from.'

Cooper chewed a nail. He wondered what she was going to ask for in return.

'You are scheduled to release more information later,' she said. 'I want to see it before the press conference.'

Warren pretended to consider. 'That's a big ask, Marcia.'

'The information is going to be out there anyway, what's the harm in letting me have a head start of a couple of hours? I won't name you as my source.'

He rubbed his chin. 'That's a bit unfair on other outlets.'

Cooper shrugged. 'It's an unfair world.'

'The best I can do is give you the press release now. You get the opportunity to write it up as a story, but you *cannot* publish it until after the conference ends. And you cannot use my name or reference Hertfordshire Constabulary as a source.'

'That doesn't give me much of an edge,' she said.

'Take it or leave it,' said Warren.

'OK. And what do you want in return?'

'Have you spoken to any of the accusers? They haven't filed any complaints with the police.'

Cooper looked away briefly. 'No. But I trust my sources,' she said quickly. 'And if the allegations were untrue, Paddon would have threatened the *Reporter* with libel.'

'I want the names of all the women making accusations. And your sources.'

She pursed her lips. 'You know I can't do that.'

'Can't or won't?'

'They have the right to anonymity,' she said.

'Public anonymity,' Warren clarified. 'Which is why you haven't printed their names in the paper. I'm assuming they gave their approval to the allegations being made public?'

'Yes, that's why they are so vague. I didn't want to accidentally identify his victims. I want to give them the opportunity to air their side of the story or even go to the police. Ever since #MeToo blew up, women like them are finally telling their stories. And people like Aldous Paddon are starting to get the message that their behaviour has consequences.'

'But you did give details about the woman he allegedly got pregnant,' said Warren. 'There can't be too many women sacked from the council when they were expecting.'

'That was different; she came to us. She was sacked because of poor job performance. She apparently approached him after that happened and basically said that if he didn't help her out financially with the baby, then she'd ruin his political career.' Cooper smirked. 'She was so naïve. She seemed to think she could get away with funnelling a couple of hints to the local paper and then sitting back and waiting for him to roll over. What did she think I was going to do? Sit by and wait for her to drip-feed me more information as and when she felt like it?'

'She didn't expect you to follow up on the story?'

'Of course not; like I said, naïve. I found her name out within an hour, but she's been ignoring my calls.'

'So why didn't you name her?'

'I considered it, but we decided it would make us look like we were potentially naming someone against their will. If she decides down the line that the relationship was more one-sided than was right, perhaps even abusive or coercive, then naming her paints us in a very poor light. #MeToo cuts both ways.' She made a face. 'And now it's a lot bigger story than "local councillor accused of extra-marital affair" or even "local councillor accused of sexual assault". Assuming they're willing to speak ill of the dead, they aren't going to be talking to me; it'll go straight to one of the nationals.'

Warren wasn't sure if she was more bothered about Paddon's alleged behaviour or the potential loss of a good story.

Cooper frowned slightly. 'I'd have assumed that Doreen Paddon would have given you her name.'

'She claimed not to know,' said Warren.

'That's interesting ...' said Cooper, her brow furrowed in thought.

'Look Marcia, we can find out who these women are by other means. But it's going to take us time and the more people we have to ask, the more likely it is people will figure out who they are,' he said. 'And you'll definitely lose your story then.'

He could see Cooper weighing up what he'd said.

'I'll give you their names, but not my sources,' she said eventually.

'Not enough. I need to know who told you,' said Warren. He thought it unlikely any of these women were directly responsible for the murder. But whoever was helping them ruin Aldous Paddon's reputation might have an axe to grind that had nothing to do with seeking justice for his alleged victims.

'Then I'll want a bit more from you,' she said firmly.

'I'm already giving you a head start on the press conference. I can't give you any more detail than we've already agreed to release without compromising the investigation.'

'OK, something else then,' she said. 'Winnie Palmer. Where are you with her investigation? Any suspects?'

'We're pursuing several lines of inquiry,' said Warren.

'Motive?'

'Again, we're pursuing several lines of inquiry.'

'Why wasn't a murder investigation opened when she first disappeared? A frail old lady disappears from her home at New Year and isn't seen again? Will there be an inquiry into failings in the initial investigation?'

'Now that I really can't help you with,' said Warren. 'My team only became involved when her body was found.'

'No opinion at all? Off the record,' she clarified.

'Off the record, there will be lessons to be learnt,' allowed Warren.

'OK, the Culverhouse murders. Is their son Derek still a suspect?'

'I really can't go into that,' said Warren. 'He is assisting us with our inquiries.'

'But he remains on bail.'

'Yes.'

She tapped her pen on the table. 'You really play your cards close to your chest, don't you, Chief Inspector?'

'Marcia, you know I can't risk compromising an investigation.'

'Then perhaps something different.' She frowned as if thinking. 'OK. Off the record. Are you going to take over from DSI Grayson when he retires?'

'Even off the record, I can't answer that,' said Warren. 'His replacement will be chosen on merit through a strict selection process.'

'But have you applied? Off the record.'

'Off the record, no comment.'

She burst out laughing. 'You're a tough nut to crack.'

Despite himself, Warren smiled; he admired her persistence.

'OK, let's try something else.' Her face become more serious. 'I am prepared to steer you towards my sources, on two conditions.'

'Go on,' said Warren, his tone making it clear he would not be making any sweeping promises.

'I want an exclusive interview with you when you solve the murder of Councillor Paddon. By all means make statements to the media outside the courtroom, but I want the full inside story.'

Warren thought it over, before nodding. It wasn't a big thing to ask, all things considered. 'What if we never solve the case?' he said.

She smiled. 'Then there won't be any story. But that's why I have a second condition. When ... if, you are appointed as John Grayson's replacement, I want to run an exclusive profile of you. Detective Chief Inspector – or would it be Superintendent? – Warren Jones, the most successful senior investigating officer in Middlesbury CID's history. What really makes him tick?'

*　*　*

Warren returned to his desk. In his absence, his mail had been placed on his desk. After discarding the usual junk mail, he tore open the remaining envelope.

Inside were two pieces of paper. One appeared to be a scrap of a label. A pale blue colour on one side, and white on the other, the only clue as to its identity were a few partial numbers, the edge of what appeared to be a large black letter, and a couple of vertical lines from a bar code.

The second sheet of paper was a neatly folded sheet of A4 computer paper. He opened it. Seconds later he was on the phone.

'I need a forensics team in my office, now!'

* * *

'It could just be a nutter,' said Sutton. 'God knows there are enough of them about.'

His forced cheer fell flat.

The envelope and its contents had been whisked away by Forensics for a full analysis. A CSI was currently in his office swabbing his desk in case any trace evidence had fallen out as he'd emptied it. They'd probably end up with a comprehensive inventory of everything Warren had eaten in there since Christmas.

Have you started to connect the dots yet, Warren?

The note had been unsigned, printed by what appeared to be a standard inkjet printer.

'It was addressed to DCI Jones, Middlesbury Police Station, and came with the normal mail,' said Warren.

'It's no secret that you are the SIO on these investigations,' said Sutton. 'And even with the limited information that we've released so far, somebody with an overactive imagination could easily see them as linked without being privy to all the details. It could even be a prank.'

'Yeah, you're probably right.' Warren sighed. 'This whole thing has got me jumpy. I just can't understand why anyone would post a random scrap of label to me.'

'Look, forget about it for now. We won't get anything back from Forensics for another day at least,' said Sutton. 'And look on the bright side, if it really is from the killer, the silly sod might have left their DNA or fingerprints.'

Chapter 36

From the way that Marcia Cooper had described him, Warren was expecting Noah Tilstone, Councillor Aldous Paddon's campaign manager, to be a gruff bear of a man; part bouncer, part political strategist.

Rather, the man occupying the same spot that Cooper had, barely two hours ago, was a slight, almost mousy man, with round spectacles and thinning hair.

'Al and I go back thirty years,' said Tilstone. 'It was me who persuaded him to run for the council. We went to university together; two North Hertfordshire lads in a posh Oxford college. I joined the Conservative Association when I was there and persuaded Al to come along with me. He never did much with it after he left uni, but I joined the local party wherever I happened to be living at the time.

'After I met my wife, we moved back to Middlesbury to be closer to my parents. Eventually we inherited their house. I got a permanent contract with Enderby Industrial Formulations and since we were going to be based here for the foreseeable future, I decided to do more for the party. I persuaded Al to get a bit more involved, and he agreed to run for the council in 2011. The rest is history.'

Tilstone took his glasses off and rubbed his eyes. They were bloodshot and swollen, the purple-black smudges beneath them standing out against his pale skin.

'I can't believe this has happened,' he said. 'I keep on thinking this is all some sort of nightmare. I mean who the hell would ambush and kill someone like Al? Are you sure he was even the target?'

'We're keeping an open mind,' said Warren, a phrase he was getting sick of saying.

'You are his campaign manager,' said Sutton. 'What does that mean?'

Tilstone gave a chuckle. 'Nothing official; or paid for that matter. Basically, when Al decided to run for the council, we weren't convinced the local party took the threat from Labour seriously enough. So I took over the day-to-day running of his campaign, rather than leaving it to the team in charge of all the candidates.' He gave a brief smile, showing tiny, sharp-looking teeth. 'It put a few noses out of joint, but when Al returned a bigger majority than his predecessor, they decided to let me continue.'

'Have you ever been tempted to run yourself?' asked Sutton.

'God no!' Tilstone laughed before sobering quickly. 'They say politics is show business for ugly people. Well, I'm no great looker, but I have no desire to make it in show business either. I enjoy the strategising and brainstorming, but I can't do all the other stuff.'

'Did Councillor Paddon mention any worries? Disturbing correspondence, run-ins with constituents, that sort of thing?' asked Warren.

'I've been thinking about that ever since I found out what happened,' said Tilstone. 'And I really can't recall anything significant. He gets the usual abuse on Twitter, but it tends to be general anti-Tory sentiment every time the government does something controversial, nothing personal.

'There are a few ranting letters or emails from the green crayon and All-Caps brigade, but it's usually about stuff Al has nothing to do with, like the chancellor's budget or Brexit. Those who don't find their way into the round file under the desk can usually be placated by a generic, "I'll pass it on to the relevant department" response.'

'We'd like to see any of his correspondence that you have on file, and we'll need his computer,' said Warren. As with Paddon's wife, he had a warrant if needed. They'd send the computer to Welwyn and ask for the full service, including recovery of any deleted files; better to be safe than sorry.

Tilstone frowned for a moment. 'Party HQ aren't going to be happy; they've got a real bee in their bonnet about data protection.' He gave a shrug. 'Sod it, better to ask forgiveness than permission.' He rummaged in his pocket and produced a key. 'Take what you need. You'll also want to see Al's home office if Doreen hasn't already let you.'

'Have you been helping Councillor Paddon make his bid to be considered the party's prospective parliamentary candidate?' asked Warren after thanking him for his cooperation.

'Of course.'

'And how was that going?' asked Sutton.

Tilstone chewed his lip. Warren could see the conflicting emotions behind his eyes. The man was a party loyalist; whatever disquiet existed in the local party, his instinct would be to keep it private. But on the other hand, his friend of three decades had been murdered.

'I realise this may be a sensitive subject,' said Warren, 'but we really need your help. What happened to Councillor Paddon was brutal, and clearly well planned. If we don't know why it happened, then there remains the possibility that the killer might have others in his sights. I assure you we will be as discreet as possible.'

Tilstone gave a small sigh. 'You probably know Harold Montgomery was unhappy that Al was likely to be chosen over him. He was actively briefing against Al within the local party, and he has a tame journalist desperate to make a name for herself. He's been feeding her all sorts of bullshit – none of it verifiable of course. Just enough that she can write some vague allegations and plant seeds of doubt.

'It's so frustrating,' he hissed. 'If they gave us something concrete, like "he touched her breast on this date, at this function", then we could give a proper rebuttal. I'm not even sure who some of these women are.'

'And you are confident that the allegations are untrue?' asked Warren, locking eyes with him.

Tilstone nodded vigorously. 'No question. He was so angry when that spreadsheet emerged last year listing Conservative MPs accused of being sexually inappropriate; to also be described as "a bit handsy" was a real insult. He's always been a little shy and awkward around women, and he's never been very tactile, even with close friends.'

'And what about Annalise Dell?' asked Warren.

For the first time since the interview had started, Tilstone looked uncomfortable. 'So you've got her name. Have you spoken to her yet?' he asked.

'Tell me what you know,' said Warren, side-stepping the question.

Tilstone puffed out his lips. 'Annalise Dell was employed by the council as an admin assistant. Anyway, back end of last year, she was let go. She'd been on a sticky wicket for a while; poor time-keeping, not completing her work, playing on her phone when she should be working, that sort of thing. That had nothing to do with Al. The councillors have absolutely no influence over hiring and firing, and she knows that.

'Anyhow, a few weeks after leaving, she suddenly announces she's pregnant and that Al is the father. She claims they had an affair before she was sacked, and that Al wanted rid of her to cover it up. She wants child support, including a big wad of cash up front before the baby is born.

'Al told her to get stuffed and denied he was the father. The next thing we know, she's parading her baby bump around and wearing new jewellery, telling anyone who'll listen that Al got her pregnant and he's been giving her hush money. Of course, she isn't named, so Al would actually have to publicly acknowledge her claims to deny them fully.'

'Forgive me, but why is this such a big deal?' said Sutton. 'Tory MPs caught with their trousers down is hardly a deal-breaker these days. Hell, one of the MPs tipped to be next prime minister when Theresa May finally goes is famous for it.'

'It still doesn't look good, does it? Why would the local party promote someone who already has that baggage? To their way of thinking, this could just be the tip of the iceberg. Say what you like about Harold Montgomery being a bigoted bastard, but as far as anyone can tell, he's not unfaithful.'

'Did Councillor Paddon deny that he had an affair with Ms Dell?' said Warren.

'Yes,' said Tilstone.

'And did you believe him?' asked Warren, again locking eyes with him.

There was a long pause, before Tilstone finally looked away. 'I don't know,' he said quietly.

Warren raised an eyebrow. 'You mean it could be true?'

'I genuinely don't know, but when I look back on it there were signs. Late-night meetings that weren't in our shared calendar, phone calls that he ended when I entered the room …' He gave a bitter laugh. 'He could probably hide an affair from his wife easily enough – she'd just assume he was doing council business. But he'd struggle to keep it from me.'

'If he was having an affair, why wouldn't he come clean, given what was at stake?' asked Sutton. 'Clear the air and beg forgiveness? The electorate are a lot more forgiving if you admit your mistakes up front.'

'Shame,' said Tilstone. 'We've been mates for thirty years. I was his best man and I'm godfather to Rhys. He knows I have a low opinion of people who play away from home. Plus, he really loves Doreen; you've seen how unquestionably she's accepted his denials. She trusts him implicitly, as does his son for that matter. He'd never be able to face the shame of letting us down.'

'And you think Councillor Montgomery is responsible for briefing the press with these allegations,' said Sutton.

'I'm certain,' said Tilstone. 'He won't have got his own hands dirty, but he's been in this game for a long time, and he has a close circle of friends with the right contacts.

'Look, who knows when the next general election is going to be? A snap election might only give us six weeks' notice, so the party are keen to have Kenneth Falconer's successor waiting in the wings, ready to hit the ground running.' He cleared his throat. 'This is confidential, you understand?'

'We'll be as discreet as possible,' promised Warren.

'There was going to be a closed-doors meeting next month to decide upon Kenneth Falconer's successor. The party knew it had the potential to get a bit scrappy, so they decided to do it out of public view and present the chosen one as a *fait accompli*.'

'And what will happen now?' asked Sutton.

'Assuming that party HQ doesn't decide to parachute in an outsider in need of a safe seat, Harold Montgomery gets it.'

* * *

The tables normally occupying the largest briefing room had been removed and replaced with rows of chairs from the canteen. Even so, there were still a dozen latecomers leaning against the back wall. Everyone present had either a notepad or a mobile device, with some balancing both on their knees. Looking out at the sea of faces, many of them unfamiliar, Warren felt like he was giving a school assembly.

'CCTV from the Paddons' house and GPS confirms he left

alone for the Hardingham Community Centre and took the most direct route,' started Richardson. 'He stopped briefly at three sets of traffic lights, all picked up on traffic cams, but he was still the only occupant of his car when he arrived.

'Leaving the event, we have CCTV from the lobby of the centre and the car park exit, but none overlooking his parking spot. Three groups of people, totalling eight individuals, left between eighteen and thirteen minutes before him, and three cars exited the car park within three minutes of them leaving. We're matching the licence plates to the CCTV to identify them.

'Councillor Paddon and Noah Tilstone walked out together at 22.31, followed two minutes later by Marcia Cooper. We then have Paddon's Jaguar leaving within sixty seconds of Cooper exiting, closely followed by Tilstone's Ford Focus, and then her Volkswagen Beetle, matching what she told DCI Jones. We pick up Tilstone on an ANPR camera four and a half minutes later, two miles away heading towards his address, so we're confident he wasn't with Paddon in his car. We also have Cooper's vehicle on the other side of town, travelling towards her home. I don't see how either of them could have followed him back to Stenfield.'

'What about his journey home?' asked Warren.

'The car's GPS shows he only stopped twice for traffic lights and took the most direct route. We have footage from four traffic cameras, including one of the stops. Nobody got into his car. The other stop wasn't on camera but lasted barely five seconds, the light must have just been turning when he arrived.'

'Not much time for someone to jump in,' noted Ruskin. 'What about vehicles before and after him at the lights we have on camera?'

'It was quiet that time of night, but we've logged everything in the fifteen minutes either side of him going through them. No interesting hits on the computer yet.'

'What about after they all left?' asked Sutton.

'Nobody leaves the front entrance for another thirteen minutes; that's after Councillor Paddon was ambushed.'

'What about other exits?' asked Hutchinson.

'There are two. The building alarm log and security cameras confirm the fire exit wasn't opened all night. The second exit leads from the food-preparation area to the bin store, again covered by a camera. We have staff in and out all evening, including a couple of smoke breaks, but everyone who went out came back in before Paddon left, and nobody jumped over the store's walls. All the ground-floor windows were locked, including the toilets, with no signs of forced entry.'

'So if he was followed from the Hardingham Centre, then it's unlikely to have been anyone in the venue at the time,' said Warren. 'Have we identified everyone present? Somebody could have tipped off the killer he was on his way.'

'We're matching seating plans and guest lists to the CCTV above the main entrance, the licence plates of any vehicles and the photographs that Marcia Cooper gave you,' said Richardson. 'The catering and bar staff are all from an agency and have worked previous events at the centre.'

'How are we doing with the CCTV from his street?' asked Hardwick. 'Were there any suspicious characters hanging around?'

'We've sourced footage from nine neighbours,' replied Richardson. 'Nobody seems to be loitering near his house that day; we're working backwards over the past few weeks. Unfortunately, there's a school around the corner and a parade of shops, so there are plenty of people and cars coming and going.'

'Every little bit helps,' said Warren. 'Rachel, how are you doing with the guest list?'

'Nothing on the PNC; all squeaky clean, including the catering staff,' said Pymm. 'I've also run their names through HOLMES and nobody is connected to any ongoing investigations. I'll do the same with any licence plates that come up and see if there are any known associates. If the killer did have an accomplice at the fundraiser who notified them when Councillor Paddon left, we might find a link that way.'

'Worth a try,' said Warren. 'What have we got forensics-wise?'

'They are still processing his car,' said Sutton. 'They've confirmed it was brought to a stop with a stinger, but was in otherwise good condition. Unfortunately, the only fingerprints on the car belong to Councillor Paddon, his wife, his son and Noah Tilstone.'

'No surprise,' said Warren. 'Let's move on and look at motives and suspects. I have the names of all the women who claim he assaulted them. Given the sensitive nature of the allegations, I have asked DS Kaur and her victim support team to reach out to them.'

Kaur cleared her throat and tucked an errant strand of hair behind her ear. 'There are four women named, and their allegations go back six years. This is in addition to Annalise Dell, the woman claiming that he got her pregnant. They will be treated with the same sensitivity as any other alleged victim of a sexual assault.'

Warren accepted her conditions; Kaur and her team had a fine line to tread.

'Given the sophistication of Councillor Paddon's murder, I think it unlikely that any of these women orchestrated it as some means of revenge. But, they could well have been pawns in an attempt to harm and discredit his political career.' Warren fixed the room with a stare. 'What we are about to discuss *does not* go any further than these four walls, without the explicit say-so of myself or DSI Grayson. Hertfordshire Police cannot be seen to be getting involved in party politics. If arrests are made or potential suspects contacted for questioning, then you are to make no public comment – not even off the record – without clearance from senior leadership. Understood?'

He waited until everyone in the room had signalled their assent.

'I don't have names for Marcia Cooper's sources – however, she has confirmed they come from the "inner circle" of Harold

Montgomery, councillor for Middlesbury East and the person, on paper at least, who stands to benefit the most from Councillor Paddon's demise. His name has cropped up repeatedly in the past thirty-six hours, so until we are satisfied otherwise, he and his closest confidants must be considered persons of interest.'

There was a palpable increase in tension in the room, and Warren hoped his warning would be taken to heart. There could be no compartmentalisation within the investigation; they would look fools if it transpired that a vital clue to the identity of the killer had been missed by someone not privy to Montgomery being a potential suspect. Warren just hoped nobody let the side down.

*　*　*

'The analysis of the paper ledger for Abacus Cabs is complete,' said Pymm. The dregs in the glass mug next to her computer mouse looked as though she'd been draining a septic tank.

'Hit me,' said Warren, although he could tell from Pymm's body language there wasn't much of any use.

'We've found plenty of jobs assigned to "Eric",' she said. 'And regular supermarket pick-ups, including several for somebody called "Winnie", but none for Winnie being picked up by Eric. That's not to say they aren't in there, but one of the dispatchers has appalling handwriting and didn't always list the customer's name. Sometimes they just wrote "Asda" and left it at that. Some jobs were also a free-for-all; whichever driver was in the area at the time.'

'So, inconclusive,' said Warren. He forced a smile. It was hardly Pymm's fault; her indexers could only work with what they were given. 'Good work. Now get yourself home.'

'Just a couple more things to tie up,' said Pymm.

'Tomorrow is another day,' said Warren, firmly. He knew Pymm hated to be mothered by him, but they had all been working extended shifts. She had a stubborn streak, and he knew from past experience that if he didn't watch her, she'd work herself to exhaustion and end up ill. It was his job to stop that happening.

For a moment, he thought she'd argue, but eventually she gave a grunt and switched off her computer.

Following his own advice, Warren locked his office and accompanied Pymm in the lift. It had been raining heavily, and she took hold of his arm as they crossed the car park. Her multiple sclerosis was largely stable, but it was progressive. Thus far, Pymm had resisted using her mobility scooter at work, but had reluctantly accepted that sometimes a little assistance from a friend was necessary.

'She's bearing up pretty well,' said Warren, in answer to her question about Susan. 'The morning sickness has eased a bit. I just hope there isn't a May heatwave. She's due to finish June half-term but the last couple of weeks of school could be miserable.'

'Tilly and Joey were both August babies,' said Pymm as she eased herself into the driving seat. 'Martin filled the freezer with ice lollies. I'd have preferred to add extra ice to my gin, but even back then, mother and baby groups could be really judgemental.'

Warren chuckled. As he turned to leave, Pymm stayed him with a hand on his forearm.

'Enjoy these last few weeks, Warren,' she cautioned. 'This is the last time you'll be alone as a couple; make the most of it.'

Thanking her, he crossed the car park. She was right of course. He'd been hoping his father-in-law might come down for a couple of days with his tool kit and help them prepare the nursery, but the universe had different ideas. Seriously? Three murder investigations?

Wednesday 14th March

Chapter 37

Taking Pymm's advice, Warren and Susan had marked out some time in their calendar for a bit of fun; Warren just hoped no more bodies turned up. In the meantime, he had to deal with the ones they already had.

'We've completed preliminary interviews with everyone who attended the fundraiser at the Hardingham Centre,' said Hutchinson, consulting his notepad.

'Any strangers in attendance?' asked Sutton.

'None. All the families are members of the same support groups and the landlord running the centre has confirmed that all staff are regulars.'

'What about outside? Anybody hanging around the car park?' asked Warren.

'Nobody that anyone saw, but once everything started, nobody left.'

Warren thanked him and turned to Pymm.

'I have Aldous Paddon's financial records,' she said. 'Almost all of them are jointly held with his wife.'

'What have you found?' asked Warren.

'Financially she didn't stand to gain much. Her inheritance, which she had sole access to, dwarfs his life insurance policy and the income from his property business.'

'Not actually needing more money has never stopped anyone from committing murder,' pointed out Sutton.

'A good point,' conceded Pymm. 'Regardless, their joint accounts seem pretty normal. What comes in more than matches what goes out; credit cards are cleared in a timely manner and neither of them has an overdraft. The mortgage on the house is paid off, as is the getaway in North Devon. It's been a while since they've helped their son out financially, the car repayments are up to date, and they haven't had a loan in fifteen years. There are no payments to casinos or suspicious cash withdrawals and certainly no standing order to Annalise Dell.'

'But …' said Warren, expectantly.

'It seems Mr Paddon had a little slush fund that only he had access to. All correspondence is online. The account has no direct debits or standing orders and there are no transactions on the debit card. The account was opened last July with a cash deposit of five thousand pounds, followed weekly by the same sum; twenty-five grand in total. There have been no deposits since, but there have been irregular withdrawals – a hundred or two, here and there, a little under four thousand all told, until six weeks ago, when there were four daily withdrawals of five hundred pounds in quick succession, with the first two twenty minutes either side of midnight.'

'He was drawing out cash as quickly as he could,' said Sutton. 'He could get his hands on twice his daily limit if he did that.'

'Two questions then,' said Warren. 'Who or where did he get twenty-five grand in cash from, and who or where was the cash going to?'

'And why did he keep the account secret from his wife?' asked Pymm.

'I can think of one obvious answer to my last question, and

I suspect it'll answer yours also,' said Warren. 'We need a little chat with Annalise Dell.'

*　　*　　*

'Annalise Dell's mobile phone is turned off, and she hasn't been seen by her neighbours,' said Hutchinson an hour after briefing. 'We're ringing around her friends to see if anyone has seen her. I don't suppose we can justify a warrant to check her phone's location history?' At Warren's look, he answered himself, with a sigh. 'Silly question. We'll keep doing it the old-fashioned way.'

He saw himself out of Warren's office as the phone rang.

'Have you found something?' asked Warren. He'd received the preliminary forensic report on the letter barely an hour earlier, such as it was. No fingerprints had been found, or trapped hairs or fibres. They'd swabbed everything for DNA, but even fast-track it would be some hours before they could eliminate Warren's own DNA, plus that of the office staff who had handled it prior to it reaching him. And he doubted the postie had been wearing latex gloves.

'Perhaps,' said the technician on the other end of the line. 'We'd already confirmed that the scrap of paper was part of a label from a tin. We ran the partial numbers and barcode through some retail databases and managed to find a candidate with the exact same shade of blue and a matching edge of printed text. I've emailed you the images.'

Warren opened the message and felt his blood run cold, even as he felt a flush of excitement.

The label was from a can of supermarket-brand dog food. The same dog food that Winnie Palmer had bought from the corner shop and had been left out in her kitchen. He quickly opened the scene report from the Culverhouse murders, scrolling quickly to the inventory for the kitchen bin.

The same brand of dog food had been left for the Culverhouses' elderly dog.

There was no way that anyone other than the killer could have known those details. And what's more, they wanted Warren to know they were connected.

Chapter 38

Warren held an emergency briefing to apprise everyone of the significance of the label from the tin of dog food, then retired to his office. Formally connecting the two murders would allow them to consolidate their resources.

Scrolling through his emails, he bit into an apple. His stomach complained loudly. His lunchbox contained two sandwiches made with half-fat cheddar; no matter how much pickle he added, the pseudo-cheese was still too dry and rubbery. Diet be damned, he decided. On the way home he was going to buy a decent block of Red Leicester. And some proper crisps. Susan had banned all his favourite flavours from the house, since the smell made her nauseous, but a month of eating nothing but ready salted was driving him insane. He'd buy a multi-pack of cheese and onion and keep them in his desk drawer and suck a couple of breath mints on his drive home. He fervently hoped her palate would return to normal after the birth.

Buried halfway down his inbox was an internal message received a couple of hours previously as he'd been dealing with the call from Forensics.

'Bugger!' He'd completely forgotten about his conversation with ACC Naseem. A window had opened in the senior officer's diary and his PA had booked a table for two in Stevenage. He didn't recognise the name of the restaurant, but it was on the high street; if he left now, he could just about make it. He smiled as he dumped the contents of his lunchbox in the waste bin; he could hardly turn down lunch with the assistant chief constable because he was only eating eighteen-hundred calories a day, could he?

'Can it wait, Tony?' he asked Sutton, who'd caught his eye as he left his office. 'Naseem has summonsed me for lunch. Muromachi in Stevenage, apparently.'

'Nothing that can't be emailed.'

Mags Richardson looked up as the elevator doors closed behind Warren.

'Do you think they're going to discuss …' She nodded towards Grayson's office, her voice lowering. 'You know what?'

'Fingers crossed,' said Sutton. 'Traipsing all the way out to Stevenage suggests Naseem might not want to be seen lunching with the chief, in case it looks too cosy.'

Richardson suddenly frowned. 'Muromachi. That's the new place on the high street. Do you think we should warn him?'

Sutton stared at her for a second, before his eyes widened. 'Oh, bugger. Well, it's too late now, he can't exactly look it up online whilst he's driving. He's not going to be happy …'

* * *

Warren found a parking space almost immediately, but he was still cutting it fine. He could probably guess why Naseem wanted to speak to him and he'd rehearsed his responses on the drive down.

He noticed the menu in the window at the exact moment ACC Naseem spotted him from the small table directly beneath it. Warren's heart sank and his stomach flipped.

Naseem waved a hand in greeting. For a brief second, Warren contemplated pretending not to see him; to carry on walking and take refuge in the warmth of the Indian restaurant next door.

Stop it, you're a grown man, he admonished himself.

An adult he may be, but suddenly it was as if he were a child again, faced with the anxiety that hit him every time he was invited to eat at a stranger's house. Fussy eater. Food-phobic. Awkward. Whatever the label, Warren still felt that flutter of hot shame.

Is there anything you don't like?

Better to ask what he would eat, rather than trying to guess what he wouldn't.

Friends and colleagues teased him when he removed salad from his sandwiches, or removed the garnish from a burger, but they knew what he liked, and it was rarely a chore to find something that they could all enjoy. Looking up the menu beforehand would usually alleviate any anxiety.

But today he hadn't had a chance.

If Naseem was deliberately trying to remove Warren from his comfort zone, then he couldn't have chosen a better restaurant.

Muromachi was a Japanese restaurant, specialising in sashimi and sushi.

Warren didn't like cooked fish; the very idea of eating it raw made his stomach churn.

He forced a smile and entered, scanning the room. Aside from rice and noodles, none of the other patrons were eating anything that looked remotely appetising, or even recognisable.

'So glad you could make it, Warren. I'm sorry about the short notice, but things are pretty hectic as I'm sure you can imagine.'

He gestured for Warren to sit down. 'I've been itching to try this place ever since it opened. I hope you're hungry!' Naseem gave a chuckle and patted his stomach. 'It's a lot healthier than curry, they say. Or at least that's what I tell the wife!'

Warren forced himself to laugh along with him, even as he struggled to breathe.

The waiter handed him a menu and took Warren's drink order. He stuck with sparkling water. The laminated card was quite liter-ally in a foreign language; even the English translations beside the Japanese script meant nothing to him and there weren't any pictures to help.

Warren pretended to study the menu. 'The chicken katsu curry sounds good,' he declared confidently. What the hell was katsu? It didn't appear to have fish in it, but he had absolutely no idea what combination of Japanese flavourings were in there. He liked curries, but Chinese curry was very different to Indian; what would Japanese curry be like?

'You'll forgive me if we skip the starter,' apologised Naseem. 'I need to get back to the office for a meeting.'

Warren was in a very forgiving mood, given that most of the dishes appeared to be either fish-based or contain vegetables he'd never tried before. Now was not the time to be over-adventurous.

'So, how is it going with the case?' asked Naseem once they had given their orders. 'I spoke to John yesterday, but I'd like your thoughts.' There was only one case that the assistant chief constable would be interested in.

Warren outlined their progress to date, including the possibility that the murder of Councillor Paddon might be linked to those of Winnie Palmer and the Culverhouses.

The grimace on Naseem's face confirmed that the news had already reached him.

'So far, almost everyone we've spoken to has cooperated,' said Warren. 'Except for the young woman who it is alleged Councillor Paddon got pregnant.'

'Annalise Dell,' stated Naseem, showing that he really was taking an interest in the case.

'We'll have to doorstep her and try to persuade her to stop playing silly buggers, but it doesn't look good if we're seen to be hassling a pregnant woman who just happens to have been alleging sexual wrongdoing against a well-regarded politician.'

'Quite. Well at least I don't have to tell you to tread carefully, Warren.' Naseem took a swig of water. 'Should we need to bring in any of Councillor Paddon's political rivals for questioning, then please go through John first, and I'd appreciate a heads-up.' He grimaced. 'Don't worry, I have no intention of interfering, I just like to be pre-warned if I or the chief constable will be getting an angry phone call.' He gave a smile. 'You can relax now.'

'Thank you for your support, sir, it's appreciated,' said Warren, unsure if Naseem was mistaking his anxiety about his food for worry that he was going to have the second-most senior officer in the force breathing down his neck.

Finally, the waiter arrived, balancing a selection of plates and bowls on his forearms. Naseem had slices of raw fish on a bed of rice, with what Warren assumed were some sort of pickled vegetables on the side. He liberally covered the fish with soy sauce, before tucking in enthusiastically with chop sticks. Warren tried not to gag.

The bowl the waiter deposited in front of him was filled with rice, and strips of what looked like fried, breaded chicken, with what he presumed was the curry sauce dribbled across it. He took a tentative bite of the chicken; he'd opted not to make a fool of himself and used a fork. To his relief, it was actually quite pleasant. He took another bite, feeling more confident. He'd definitely be able to finish the meal, and he made a mental note of the dish should he ever find himself in a Japanese restaurant again.

With most of his plate demolished, Naseem leant back in his chair. His tone became more casual, although Warren noticed his eyes remained sharp.

'You know, a case like this can draw the wrong sort of political attention.' He paused. 'But handled well, it can also generate the right sort of attention. I don't need to tell you that the superintendent ranks require a little more … diplomacy? Knowing the right people and the right things to say.' His eyes twinkled. 'Smooth-talking isn't everything of course – you still need to be a bloody good copper with a strong insight into the job. But you need to be able to broaden your focus to juggle several different cases and more operational matters. John has always been good politically.'

Warren was reading him loud and clear. A good showing on the Paddon murder case, whilst dealing with the Palmer and Culverhouse murders, would be noted and stand him in good stead, but he could just as easily blow it by upsetting the wrong people. More interesting was Naseem's qualified praise of Grayson; applauding his political acumen, but making no mention of his policing abilities. Tony Sutton would feel vindicated in his view that Grayson had spent too much time cosying up to the brass in pursuit of his next promotion, when he perhaps should have been a bit more focused on what his team were doing on the ground.

'There are several candidates for John's old position,' said Naseem abruptly. 'Some already have experience in that role; some are ready to step up. I'd employ any of them in a heart-beat – subject to formal procedures of course,' he clarified. 'But what I really want is someone who will build on what has gone before, who won't dismantle a very unique and effective team.'

Was he intimating that Warren was his favoured candidate in the hope he continued to build on the unit's success? Or was he instead suggesting he would rather Warren stayed where he was, doing what he did best? Warren's hands-on approach was unique; perhaps he didn't want Warren to move away from the front line?

'The cut-off date for the applications and references is the 29th, then we'll interview the following week,' said Naseem. 'We want to appoint John's replacement before he leaves, so that deadline must be strictly adhered to.' He looked at Warren meaningfully.

Warren was nonplussed. He'd submitted his application almost a month ago. Had Naseem not received it? The process was largely online, and he'd received an email receipt.

'You might want to give John's cage a bit of a rattle,' Naseem suggested.

Now Warren was completely confused. Grayson knew full well he was applying for the position and would be asked to supply a reference. Had he forgotten? It had been a busy few weeks after all. Perhaps there had been an administrative error?

'I'll do that,' managed Warren, deciding to speak to Grayson as soon as he returned to the station.

* * *

Warren was preoccupied with his missing reference all the way back to Middlesbury. Perhaps Grayson had yet to submit the documentation because he didn't think Warren was suited to the job?

The two men's relationship had varied somewhat over the years. They weren't close friends; they had little in common. But Grayson had shown Warren great kindness at times, insisting Warren take extra leave to get over the death of his grandmother, and even inviting Warren and his family into his home during the Delmarno case some years previously. Was he still offended that Warren had once been worried that Grayson might himself be corrupt? Surely not.

So was Grayson dissatisfied with his performance? He had never said so in Warren's appraisals. Grayson allowed him free rein to run cases as he saw fit, and enjoyed the reflected glory from the team's successes, but there were occasions when Grayson had been asked to account for their actions.

Could that be what this was about? Warren's record wasn't spotless. Again, choices he had made in the Delmarno case had left a black mark in his file, and a more recent lapse of judgement had arguably contributed to the death of a homeless man. Warren had berated himself far more harshly than the standards board had.

Yet all of that was known to Naseem and he still seemed to be encouraging Warren to apply.

So what was Grayson's problem?

Warren really hoped it was all due to an administrative error, because otherwise he and Grayson would be having a full and frank exchange of opinions when Warren arrived back at the station.

* * *

273

'He left for Welwyn about fifteen minutes ago,' said Janice, the support worker who acted as Warren's unofficial PA. He and Grayson had probably passed one another in opposite directions on the A1.

After thanking her, he returned to his office to brood. On reflection, it was probably just as well that Grayson wasn't there. By the time Warren had pulled into the car park, he was ready for a showdown with his boss; an urge that was probably due to stress from the last two weeks and the double espresso he'd had before leaving the restaurant.

It was far better that he took a night to sleep on it and talk it through with Susan. Unfortunately, there was no way to tell if Grayson had received the request.

He'd just have to ask him about it tomorrow and take it as it came.

Thursday 15th March

Chapter 39

Warren waited until Grayson had removed his coat and settled in before knocking on the superintendent's office door. He'd spoken at length to Susan the previous night. Budget cuts at her school had seen her over-ruled on more than one occasion when the person she believed was best suited for the job was side-lined in favour of a less-experienced, but cheaper, newly qualified teacher.

'Make sure it isn't an admin cockup first,' she'd warned Warren, before working through the reasons why Grayson may not think him suitable for the position. In the end, there was nothing that the two of them could think of that Warren hadn't already considered. On her advice, Warren had printed out his previous appraisals to use as ammunition, should Grayson try to claim he had concerns about Warren's prior performance.

Warren really hoped it was an oversight; he had no desire to get into a dispute with Grayson in the man's last few weeks on the job. A carefully placed word with one of Grayson's golfing buddies could easily find its way back to Naseem.

'Morning, Warren, what can I do for you?'

Grayson was fussing with his coffee machine.

'I had lunch with ACC Naseem yesterday.'

'Yes I heard about that,' said Grayson. 'I imagine there was a plea to tread carefully with this Councillor Paddon business?'

'Yes, I'll be certain to keep you in the loop, in case any toes need stepping on.'

'I appreciate it. I think,' said Grayson as he headed back to his desk. 'I hadn't planned on spending my last few working days massaging bruised egos and placating irate local politicians.'

'Naseem seems to think that my reference hasn't made it to the appointments board. Could you double-check that it hasn't gone AWOL and resend if necessary, please?'

Grayson carefully placed his mug on a coaster with 'World's Best Grandad' emblazoned on it. He gave a sigh. 'I'm sorry, I meant to sit down properly with you when I first got the request, but then the bodies started stacking up …' He gave an awkward smile.

'Is there a problem, sir?' asked Warren stiffly. 'Do you not think I am the right person for the job?'

Grayson gave a shake of his head. 'No, it's not that at all. You could do this job standing on your head with one hand tied behind your back.'

'I don't understand.'

Grayson stood up and walked over to the window overlooking the main office.

'The question you should be asking, is not "Am I the right person for the job?" but rather "Is this the right job for me?"'

'What do you mean?' asked Warren, moving to join him.

'Our team has some of the best officers in the force – in any force. It has been my privilege to work with them, but their results are *your* results.' He turned back to Warren. 'The best decision I ever made, notwithstanding proposing to Refilwe of course, is giving you a free hand. I haven't always agreed with some of your choices, and we've had our run-ins, but you are still one of the finest interviewers I have worked with and your investigative instincts are first-rate.

'In fact, I don't think you should even be a chief inspector, and in any other setting, I'm not convinced you'd have lasted the distance.'

'Sir?' Warren wasn't sure if he had just been insulted.

'I think that after twelve months, you'd have requested a reduction in rank. Not because you can't do the job, but because you would be no longer doing the job you love. The job that you are so good at.'

'I see,' said Warren, for want of any better response.

'Middlesbury is unique – we keep on saying it, because it is true. I know not everyone is convinced I appreciate that.' He snorted. 'God knows Tony Sutton isn't. Whatever. The point is that we – you – need to fight to keep it that way. Whoever takes over from me needs to understand that.'

'Then isn't that all the more reason for me to apply for the position?' asked Warren. 'I know you have fought for our independence behind the scenes. Will whoever takes the role be so keen?'

'I don't know,' said Grayson. 'Perhaps if you are promoted, you will be able to keep yourself on the front line. Perhaps you could request another DCI to help spread the load, but with the budget cuts …'

'But if I don't apply for the position, will whoever takes over let me run around playing sergeant, instead of sitting in my office like a good DCI?' said Warren, surprising himself with the bitter tone of his own voice.

'I genuinely don't know,' said Grayson. 'My recommendation to my successor will be for them not to change a damn thing, but we both know how that will be received.' He gave a thin-lipped smile. 'I can tell you now, that if you want to sit at the big boys' table, you have to be seen to be implementing change and bringing in new ideas. Hell, it doesn't even matter if they don't work.

'If you want that reference, then I will send it. I wrote it weeks ago and it's the best I've ever written. But think this through, Warren.'

Warren nodded. This morning it had all seemed so clear-cut. He'd applied for a job he was confident that he was qualified to do, and he had been affronted that Grayson may feel otherwise. But now he was conflicted.

Did he want to apply for a promotion that may or may not allow him to preserve Middlesbury CID as it was, yet would almost certainly mean that he had to give up much of what he loved about his job?

Or did he want to risk someone else taking over who may decide that Middlesbury needed to become more 'mainstream' and who might believe that chief inspectors had no business interviewing suspects and confronting murderers?

The deadline for Grayson submitting the reference was two weeks away. Warren had that long to decide whether or not to continue with his application or withdraw.

* * *

'I've been doing some sniffing around,' said DI Jason Sacker. Sacker was leading the team interviewing members of Middlesbury Council and the local Conservative Party. Warren and Sutton were with him in Grayson's office, everyone except Sutton enjoying a cup of his finest roast. 'Firstly, all of his fellow councillors, regardless of party, appeared shocked at what's happened, Harold Montgomery among them. Nobody can understand why someone would want to kill him or recalls him mentioning any concerns.

'His fellow Tories spoke of him fondly. Politically, he didn't rock the boat, rarely said anything too controversial and delivered a comfortable majority. Interestingly, nobody brought up his rivalry with Montgomery. I don't know if that means the disagreements have been exaggerated, or they don't want to air their dirty laundry in public. We remembered our instructions and didn't bring the subject up ourselves.'

Warren only knew Sacker tangentially but had heard much

about him. Rachel Pymm knew Sacker from when she worked out of Welwyn and had attended training courses with him when her multiple sclerosis diagnosis had necessitated a change in career direction.

Her assessment was: 'Smooth and charming – too charming if you ask me.' She had conceded, however, that he was a natural diplomat and probably the best suited to such a sensitive role in the investigation. 'I mean, it's not like we could send Hutch or Tony; they'd spend more time telling everyone what they are doing wrong than interviewing them.' Neither man had disagreed.

'What about his political opponents?' asked Sutton.

'Not as much rivalry as you'd think, if you only listen to them in the run-up to an election,' said Sacker. 'The Tories only control the council by two seats, so they all have to work together on a day-to-day basis. They won't go out of their way to publicly praise a colleague from a different party, but things aren't as febrile locally as they are nationally. One of the Labour councillors summed it up as: "Local councils have been served a shit sandwich by the government. That wasn't Aldous' fault, and nobody blamed him or the other Tories on the council for the mess the country's in nationally."'

'Have any of the other councillors received threats or abuse?' asked Grayson.

'They have a safeguarding team who screenshot anything disturbing on social media,' said Sacker. 'They're sending us everything, but nothing stood out to them. However, he was a member of several committees, all of which have made some tough decisions over the past few years.'

'You think he might have upset someone?' asked Grayson.

'Possibly. He was a member of the Council Works and Maintenance Committee – the group in charge of maintaining public buildings. They recently renewed the contract for the next five years; including a two-million-pound refurbishment of the town hall.'

'He was shot with a nail gun,' said Sutton. 'Just the sort of thing somebody involved in building works would have access to. Was somebody sending a message?'

'It certainly crossed my mind,' said Sacker. 'And his appointment wasn't without controversy.'

'In what way?' asked Grayson.

'Bearing in mind the source, one of the Labour councillors claims his position on Works and Maintenance raised a potential conflict of interest. One of the firms competing for the contract was employed by Paddon through his property development business. No prizes for guessing which company undercut all the others and landed the gig. Paddon claimed he had no business partnership with the firm, he just used them as subcontractors, and that he had always been very satisfied with the standard of their work. He voluntarily disclosed that he and the managing director of Mankin Property Development were friends, but denied passing details of the rival bids to him.

'Three months after Mankin's appointment, they found a significant amount of asbestos that had somehow been missed in their initial survey of the town hall, causing them to revise their estimate upwards; the projected job cost is now more than any of their rival bidders forecast – at least one of whom had costed in a contingency for just such an occurrence.'

'Dirty bugger,' muttered Sutton. 'If Paddon did come to some dodgy deal with his old mate to get the contract, then that could be motive enough for someone to kill him and might account for that mysterious twenty-five grand he suddenly came into.'

'Perhaps, perhaps not,' cautioned Grayson. 'We only have the word of one of his political rivals; we need to be careful not to be seen to be endorsing their allegations without evidence.'

'I agree,' said Warren. 'But Tony's right. Even if it was entirely above board, perception counts. We should look into the rival bidders and see if any of them were suitably aggrieved.'

Friday 16th March

Chapter 40

Annalise Dell had been determined to avoid questioning, to the point where Warren was starting to wonder if they could justify a warrant for her arrest. Therefore, it was something of a surprise when she presented herself first thing, solicitor in tow, at the main reception desk.

'Any idea why she's been avoiding us?' Warren asked Kaur after she'd taken her statement.

'Reading between the lines, she's worried about the impact this might have on the case she's filing for constructive dismissal,' she said drily. 'You'll need to confirm it, but it sounds as if her alibi is solid for that night, and really she has nothing to gain by killing him. She doesn't see it this way, but she was pretty much blackmailing him. Murdering him would have killed the goose that laid the golden egg, and she's far too clever to do that. Even if he stopped paying her hush money, when the child was born she could have demanded a paternity test and received child support. As it stands, she may be able to sue for a piece of his estate – assuming she can get a court order to prove paternity – but it's hardly guaranteed. Frankly, she's up the proverbial creek without a paddle.'

Despite everything, Warren felt a twinge of sympathy for the woman. He and Susan were facing a massive upheaval in a few months' time; he couldn't imagine how much harder that would be without the support of a loving partner.

'What about his other accusers?' asked Sutton. 'The ones where it allegedly wasn't consensual?'

'My team have interviewed all of the women that Marcia Cooper named,' said Kaur. 'I'll send over my report by close of play today, but all have alibis that should be verifiable. Again, leaving aside revenge – which wasn't the vibe that my officers got from any of them – Councillor Paddon's death wasn't in their interest. If they had decided to pursue it legally, it would have been largely "he said, she said" and without him to defend himself ... I'd be surprised if it is even settled out of court. Who would they sue?'

Warren thanked Kaur and turned back to Sutton. 'Not a big surprise,' he said. 'It was a staged execution. Even if somebody decided to settle the score, it was too elaborate. A knife in the ribs in a dark alleyway would be much more likely.'

'No argument from me,' said Sutton.

* * *

The findings of DI Sacker provided more of a motive for Paddon's death than the fallout from his alleged sexual misconduct. But even then, Warren wasn't entirely convinced.

'There was unquestionably a lot of ill feeling over the awarding of the maintenance contract to Paddon's old buddy,' said Sacker. 'And even more, when Mankin Property Development allegedly took the piss and asked for more money.'

'Enough to stage an ambush and shoot him in the head with a nail gun?' asked Warren.

'Money can make people do extreme things, but I'm not sure what they would have gained from killing him. The job has already started; killing Paddon won't stop it. I spoke to the other three bidders. Two of them are long-established firms. They were

286

certainly annoyed by Mankin's shenanigans, but as one of them said, it isn't the first time a dodgy politician has engineered a lucrative contract for one of his mates, and it won't be the last.'

'What about the third bidder?'

'They're new to the game; it was a consortium of smaller businesses that teamed up to take a punt. They always knew they were at a disadvantage against the big players, but the bloke I spoke to was pretty hacked off they had been undercut by MPD because they were honest enough to highlight potential over-runs if the asbestos turned out to be more widespread than the plans showed.'

'Are there any more big contracts in the pipeline?' asked Warren. 'If one of the bidders thought that the same thing was likely to happen again, they could have arranged for him to be taken out.'

'I don't know,' said Sacker. 'I'll look into it.'

Warren thanked him and leant back in his chair. Outside in the main office, everybody had their jobs to do. Nobody was short of work, and judging by his inbox, Warren wasn't either. So why did he feel as if he was doing nothing?

He looked at the clock; Grayson had disappeared some hours ago. He was probably already on the golf course. Did Warren need to still be there, or was it just presenteeism? Sod it, he decided. When the baby came, he would need to be more disciplined about his work hours, particularly at the weekend, and if he did end up in charge of the unit, he should lead by example and try and maintain a healthy work-life balance. The coming weekend was going to be stressful enough as it was.

Saturday 17th March

Chapter 41

The post arrived at its usual time and Warren was alerted immediately to its presence in the mail room. The printed label on the front of the envelope matched the one he'd received previously. This time there was something small and hard inside.

Warren and Sutton watched as the package was carefully opened by a gloved CSI, who upended the contents onto a sterile sheet.

The clues are all there. Have you connected the dots yet, Warren?

As before, that was all that was written on the printed note. But this time, instead of a scrap of paper, there was a small, hollow spike made from black plastic.

It was confirmation of what they already believed.

Councillor Paddon had been killed by the same person who had murdered Winnie Palmer and the Culverhouses. And they would probably strike again soon.

Chapter 31

Sunday 18th March

Chapter 42

Warren flip-flopped between hope and trepidation. So far, there were still no obvious links between all three murder scenes, other than the dog food label, the Sunday night connection and the killer's taunting. Winnie Palmer and the Culverhouses were elderly and vulnerable; but Councillor Paddon was middle-aged. Winnie Palmer had died of a broken neck, then been stored in a freezer. The Culverhouses had been shot with Stanley Culverhouse's own shotgun in a staged murder-suicide, whilst Aldous Paddon had been executed with a nail gun after an ambush.

Even if it was a serial killer, they had yet to identify anyone whose orbit overlapped the three sets of victims. Derek Culverhouse lived in Councillor Paddon's ward, but they had found no correspondence by him or his parents to indicate that he had any animosity towards the man. In fact, it was believed that he had voted for him in the last council election. They had found no indication that he had ever met Winnie Palmer.

Callum Harradine and his ne'er do well mate had been seen drinking around the time that Paddon was being killed. Spencer Aspinall made his usual Sunday night phone call, the handset locating to his home, and Activision confirmed that he spent several hours actively playing *Call of Duty*.

Eric Morton remained Warren's number-one suspect; they had yet to rule out the erstwhile cab driver and unlicensed doorman, but by the same token they still didn't have anything concrete.

As he scurried from briefing to briefing, Warren envied his team. They all had their jobs; important work that hopefully brought them closer to apprehending their killer.

But it was slow and methodical.

Too slow.

They *needed* a breakthrough. If their fears were correct, then the clock was ticking ever louder. As the day wore on, the anxiety in the office increased. Would the killer strike again? Would there be another body?

By the time Warren went to bed that night, there had been no reports of anybody missing or any unexplained deaths. But that didn't mean anything. Was their killer out there at this very moment, adding to their toll?

Or were they finished?

That was the question that rattled around Warren's head, as he stared into the dark; even the deep, comforting breathing of his wife beside him failing to quell his fears.

Monday 19th March

Chapter 43

The body was propped naked against a tree. Again, the grisly discovery was made by an unfortunate early-morning dog walker.

After receiving the call on his car's hands-free kit, less than a mile from work, Warren had angered his fellow commuters by executing a tight U-turn and racing for Farley Woods, just off the A506, a couple of miles outside Middlesbury.

He parked behind the open doors of a Scenes of Crime van and had almost finished wrestling his way into a paper scene suit, when DCI Carl Mallucci's BMW ground to a halt; he must have really put his foot down on the A1.

'Yeah, it's him,' confirmed Mallucci after the two officers had carefully picked their way through the trees.

The drug dealer's one good eye stared sightlessly straight ahead, the other a bloody mess.

'It looks as though he didn't kill his brother and go on the run,' Mallucci continued, swallowing hard. He looked away.

'He could have been dumped here anytime in the past three days,' said Meera Gupta, the most senior CSI on shift when the call had come in. 'That's the last time the woman who found him walked this way. He's started to decompose, but I can't be any more specific.'

Warren could see for himself that the man's bare feet were too clean for him to have walked here, and his nose told him the rest.

He looked over at Mallucci, who was unhealthily pale under his mask.

'He looks different, because his skin is a lot darker, obviously,' said Warren, standing up, ignoring the trembling in his legs. 'But now I know what I'm looking for, there's no doubt; he was killed then stored frozen, before being left to thaw out. He was killed by the same person as Winnie Palmer.'

*   *   *

We're going to need a bigger briefing room, thought Warren as he squeezed his way to the front.

Carl Mallucci was updating the team on what they knew about that morning's victim.

The murder of a drug dealer a month previously, by a single shot to the head as he sat in his car had initially been Middlesbury's case, due to its location. However, Nick Lagdon had been well known to the drugs squad and the case had quickly been reassigned. Their prime suspect was Lagdon's brother, Bobby, who had disappeared immediately after the killing. Nobody questioned would admit to seeing him, and none of the mobile phones he was associated with had been used. Those who had spoken to the police professed to being perplexed as to motive. The brothers were famously tight-knit, having even spent time together behind bars.

The killing was premeditated, with Lagdon subdued by a TASER and incapacitant spray before his car was moved to a secluded area of woodland, and he was shot with what they believed was his own handgun.

'The motive for the killing bothered my team,' admitted Mallucci. 'They were foot soldiers; neither of them were involved in the supply end where the real money is. Even on a good

300

night they won't have earned running-away money. Furthermore, Bobby wasn't the brightest bulb in the chandelier. For him to plan such an execution and then successfully disappear for so long seemed improbable. We always suspected there was more to it.'

'Now we know there was,' said Warren. 'It's too much of a coincidence that Bobby kills his brother, then stumbles across our serial killer. What did you recover in the way of forensics from the crime scene?'

'The CSIs found a couple of fairly long, grey head hairs on the rear of the passenger seat headrest. The Lagdon brothers, as you know, are twenty-something black men of Afro-Caribbean heritage; these hairs were not theirs. There were no follicles unfortunately, so DNA is unlikely; we might get a match to a suspect using mitochondrial DNA, but we can't trawl the database.

'The hairs had been cut, suggesting that the person involved may have had a haircut recently, or had at least been wearing those clothes when they went to the hairdresser. From their placement, one scenario is that the person sat behind Bobby in the passenger seat and leant forward, transferring the hairs from their clothing as they did so.

'Unfortunately, there's so much other dirt and fibres in there, we can't even be certain these hairs are linked to the killing. They could have been there for months.'

'Well it's more than we had yesterday,' said Warren, before turning to address the team.

'Whilst we will of course be keeping our options open, our working assumption is the same person killed Winnie Palmer and Bobby Lagdon, which by extension links them to the Culverhouses and Councillor Paddon. Nick Lagdon could have been killed for unrelated reasons, but it's a pretty hefty coincidence if he was.

'First priority is to establish any points of contact between the Lagdons and our other victims. A lot of planning is going into each of these murders; we're not talking about somebody randomly shooting people on the street. If anyone has any suggestions as to why our killer has targeted an elderly, church-going widow; two pensioners; a local politician; and two twenty-something drug dealers, I am all ears.'

'There is one potential link,' said Mallucci. 'The Lagdons dealt all sorts. The toxicology report that you sent me is still being analysed, but the chances are that if the Culverhouses were sedated with illegally sourced oxycodone, then it's from the same batch that has been on our streets for the last few months. As to whether or not the killer got it from the Lagdons ...' He gave an open-handed shrug.

'That could mean that the Lagdons are outliers,' said Sutton. 'They were only killed because our murderer didn't want the Lagdons to identify them as a customer.'

'Do we think Nick and Bobby were killed at the same time?' asked Hutchinson.

'Impossible to know,' said Mallucci. 'Our initial investigation of Nick Lagdon's killing did find significant traces of Bobby's blood on the passenger side of the vehicle, but it wasn't enough to determine if he had been killed or just injured during a fight with his brother.'

'We know Nick was violently subdued, bundled into the boot, and then placed back in the driver's seat before being shot,' added Warren. 'Bobby's post-mortem may tell us if there was a significant period between his death and his being frozen, or if he appears to have been held prisoner before he was killed.'

'Where does this leave Derek Culverhouse?' asked a sergeant from Mallucci's Welwyn-based team.

'On the face of it, no change,' said Tony Sutton. 'The only link between his parents' deaths and Winnie Palmer is the brand of food left out for their dogs. The only link to the Lagdon killings is the presence of oxycodone at their house that may or may not have come from them. However, we know that Bobby Lagdon and

Winnie Palmer were almost certainly killed by the same person because of the way the bodies were dumped. So if we tie him to one murder, he looks good for the others.'

'We recovered drugs from his flat,' Hardwick reminded them. 'The Lagdons could have supplied them.'

'This makes our efforts to establish a link between Derek and the other victims even more urgent,' interjected Warren. 'But let's not place all of our eggs in one basket. We have a number of potential suspects from the other murders. I'm still not happy with Eric Morton. Let's continue cross-referencing all of them and looking for any overlaps.'

* * *

Warren phoned Grayson with the results of Bobby Lagdon's autopsy last thing that evening. He was exhausted; the day had been a treadmill of endless meetings and conference calls, and then he'd popped home, before visiting the morgue. He'd at least been gratified to find that Carl Mallucci disliked autopsies even more than he did.

'Murder weapon was a thin-bladed knife, similar to the ones I'm told are used to fillet fish. In through the eye, through the hole at the back of the eye socket and into the brain. That may have been survivable, but the killer gave it a wiggle for good measure.'

That was the part of Prof Jordan's explanation where Mallucci threw up.

'Death was close to instantaneous, which is why there was so little bleeding.'

'Any idea how long he'd been dead before freezing, or how long he'd been left in the woods?' asked Grayson.

'No. The prof is satisfied he was probably dumped during the three-day interval between the dog owner taking her walks but that's it. However, he was happy to suggest that Bobby was inca-pacitated for a shorter period before death than his brother, and there was no pre-mortem bruising consistent with him bouncing around in the car boot like Nick.'

Warren's tone became heavier. 'Which suggests that if they were attacked at the same time, Nick may have shared the boot with his brother's corpse.'

'Oh, the poor bastard,' said Grayson. The Lagdon brothers weren't exactly fine, upstanding citizens, but the thought was heart-breaking.

'Of course, Bobby's body might have been removed before the car was driven away with Nick in the boot,' said Warren.

'In which case, there may have been two killers,' finished Grayson.

Tuesday 20th March

Chapter 44

At Warren's request, he was notified the moment that the mail arrived and he'd left the morning briefing immediately.

The meeting had focused on links between victims. Former taxi driver and unlicensed doorman Eric Morton was certainly shady enough that Warren had no problem believing he may have known the Lagdons. If they could establish that he killed the two dealers, then that might lead back to Winnie Palmer. Derek Culverhouse claimed his father had mentioned a 'funny-looking bugger' who had taken Mrs Culverhouse to her social club. Would Morton's twisted jaw be enough to elicit such a comment?

Then there was Derek himself. He stood to gain from his parents' death, but where was the link to Winnie Palmer? The oxycodone may have come from the Lagdons, and he had grey hair that might match that found in the back of their ten-year-old Renault Megane, but it seemed an elaborate way to dispose of somebody just because they may remember him. Then again, if they were dealing with a serial killer, then the motives might not make a lot of sense. On the other hand, serial killers often used the same method each time. These deaths had some similarities and overlaps, but otherwise were very different.

By the time he arrived at the mail room, the CSIs were already on their way. The envelope and its printed label were the same as before, but the package was heavier. The CSI opened the envelope and carefully removed the contents: a black notepad and what appeared at first glance to be a wireless earbud. Leaning closer, Warren saw that he was mistaken. He'd seen a device like it before when visiting Granddad Jack. It wasn't the earpiece from a set of headphones, it was a hearing aid.

* * *

Forensic Document Services had arrived moments after the CSIs. Everything needed to be taken away and processed for trace evidence, but Warren really needed to see the contents of the notebook before it disappeared to the lab; who knew how time-critical it might be?

A compromise was quickly brokered, with the CSIs carefully lifting the notepad onto a disposable sterile sheet, and the document examiner gently opening its pages with forceps whilst Warren stood over her shoulder and photographed it with her camera.

'The hearing aid looks similar to the one found on Stanley Culverhouse's bedside table,' confirmed Sutton, from the doorway. 'The CSIs noted one was missing and looked for it, but the killer must have taken it with them. We'll know for sure if it's his when the DNA comes back.'

Unable to contain his curiosity anymore, Sutton entered the room and looked over the examiner's other shoulder. It was fortunate that she was so short.

The notebook was a reporter's-style pad with an elastic strap to keep the black, leather-effect cover closed. The forty or so lined pages were a cream colour, with a margin on the right-hand side. The cover was blank. The documents team would use a range of high-intensity light sources to identify any fingerprints or indentations, but Warren's gut told him that the killer had been too careful.

'It would have been too easy for us if they'd given us a hand-writing sample,' grumbled the analyst.

The author had eschewed a pen and instead printed the text on pieces of neatly trimmed paper, glued in the centre of each page.

Warren swallowed as he read the words; the envelope had been addressed to him directly, and as before, there was something disturbing about the personal nature of the correspondence.

It looks as though you need some extra help, Warren.

The examiner carefully turned the page over. Warren took another photograph before forcing himself to read what was written.

'The damn thing's a bloody confessional,' breathed Sutton.

'Greed makes man blind and foolish, and makes him an easy prey for death.' – Rumi

The Persian poet Rumi lived in the thirteenth century, but his words are still true of twenty-first-century drug dealers.

Nick and Bobby plied their trade on the Chequers Estate. I'd been buying from them for months. Some weed two or three times a week, pills and coke at the weekends. A little extra on bank holidays.

Pretty soon, they thought they knew me: lots of money, 'professional', in denial about my problem and willing to pay above the odds. I know they fleeced me, but I never worried about them mugging me. Why beat me up for whatever I have in my wallet that one time, when they know I'm going to be back again and again?

They thought they were cultivating me – of course it was the other way around.

'He's boasting,' said Sutton. 'He's proud of what he's done.'
The analyst turned the page.

The night I did it, I had everything prepared. They park in the same spot most evenings, as regular as clockwork. All the junkies know their schedule, but the police don't. They rely on intelligence from informants, but who's going to rat out their supplier? Most of their regulars are there as soon as they turn up. The wasters can't get down the job centre for their interviews, but they're bang on time for their fix. I always timed my visits for just before they move on, and as far as I can tell, I'm always their last customer.

The car's parked in shadow of course, hidden from any CCTV cameras. Good for them, even better for me; I don't want them asking why I'm wearing latex gloves or catching a glimpse of the paper forensic suit under my street clothes. They'd never commented on my rubber bathing cap before, so I felt confident it was hidden under the wig I always wore.

The team would go through every word in the notebook, but Warren couldn't stop himself from dictating notes to Sutton as he read the notepad aloud.

'We have a potential location for the killing. Double down on witness interviews in that area,' instructed Warren.

'Wigs, gloves and a bathing cap – they'll be a forensic dream,' said Sutton. 'But if he chucked them away that night, they'll be long gone.'

They drive a crappy Renault – they aren't daft; two young black lads in an expensive car? That's going to get pulled over; we all know what the police are like. And how would they pay for it without someone noticing and wondering how two losers like these guys can afford a BMW or a Mercedes?

In their own way, they were quite smart, I suppose.
But still greedy.

'The psychologists will have a field day,' said Sutton, 'but I've not spotted any spelling mistakes yet, and he's laid the text out carefully. This is not the ranting of some nut-job.'

'He's also switched tenses,' noted Warren. 'It's like he's reliving it.'

The day before, I WhatsApped them; told them I was having a birthday party and I'd need extra. I'd been buying from them for ages by then, and they knew I was good for it.

Two hours before they turned up, I stashed my gear behind the bins in the alleyway opposite where they park.

Beside him, Sutton scribbled down instructions to search the alleyway without being asked. Five weeks had passed, but there might still be something.

I've been buying from them for months but chucking the pills and the coke away. A bit of weed to chill out in the evening is one thing, but I'm not a fucking idiot. I'm not getting hooked on any of the other shit like the losers that form the bulk of their clientele.

But tonight, I need to be top of my game, my reflexes sharp. So a dab of coke before I cycle up. Not enough to get high, just enough to get my pulse racing.

They recognise me on sight. Better dressed than most of the dossers they sell to, with my mini-commuter bike and leather man-bag; it's why I don't get stopped. The police know who they are looking for if they're going to do a stop and search, and I'm not that person. The man-bag is ideal for storing my drugs and cash; even better for storing everything else I need tonight.

'Mini-commuter bike and a man-bag – somebody must recognise him,' said Sutton.

'I'm sure that Forensics said there were multiple bicycle tracks up where the car was found,' said Warren. 'See if they can identify marks from one of those fold-up bicycles; I can't imagine somebody taking one of those dinky little things up there for a bit of off-roading.' He frowned. 'Didn't Derek Culverhouse describe oxycodone users as "losers"?'

'I think you're right,' said Sutton.

The routine is simple. Pull up to the passenger window, wait for Bobby to roll it down, then swap the drugs for the money. Easy-peasy. Nick sits in the driver's seat, the car in gear, his right hand on the gun that he keeps between the seat and the door.

So I shot him first.

Private ownership of TASERs and other stun guns is illegal in the UK. Probably a good thing – you wouldn't want them getting in the wrong hands 😉. But the dark web and Bitcoin get you pretty much whatever you want these days. Pay a little extra and you can get a multi-shot version juiced up to give a bigger kick than the maker intended.

'Jesus, the sick bastard is using a winking emoji?' said Sutton, aghast.

Whilst Nick was flopping around in the driver's seat, I shot Bobby, right in the neck. That was the easy bit. Stun guns don't knock people out, they just confuse and disorientate, so you have to be quick. I bought super-strength pepper spray and handcuffs from the same website. Two big squirts in both their faces and the last thing Nick was thinking about was his gun. Speedcuffs are a piece of piss to apply and these guys made it easy, with both their hands clawing at their eyes. I took Nick's gun; I didn't want him getting any ideas. According to the timer on my watch, I had both sets of cuffs on and the gun in my bag in well under the fifteen seconds I'd allocated. Adrenaline and cocaine – an unbeatable combo!

I guess you people are now realising that the man you've been hunting for the past few weeks isn't Bobby. He didn't kill Nick, I did. But Bobby died first.

The technician turned the page.

One of the advantages of a Renault Megane is that it has five doors and a large boot space. I slid along the rear seat. My two victims were so busy trying to work out what was going on, they probably didn't even realise the back door had opened.

I imagine your CSIs found some of Bobby's blood on his side of the car, but not enough to assume he was dead or mortally wounded; number-one suspect I imagine. A six-inch blade through the eye socket will do that. Dead instantly with very little bleeding, especially if you wrap a towel around his head immediately.

Another page.

Nick was a little trickier – you see the last thing I wanted was to kill him there and then. Shoot him in the head and I'd be driving around in a clapped-out Renault with a broken driver's side window and his blood and brains all over the door. So out came the stun gun again. Did you know that some models come with a 'Drive Stun' capability? It's a nasty little feature designed for 'compliance through pain, rather than incapacitation'. My juiced-up model did both. By the time Nick figured out what had happened to him, the pillowcase was over his head and his mouth stuffed with rags. The press of his own gun against his forehead and a bit more encouragement from

313

the stun gun and he was happy to get into the boot. Amnesty International has expressed concern about the 'Drive Stun' feature. I agree with them, and I imagine Nick had strong feelings on the subject also. 😄

Bobby was the next problem. Fortunately, he's pretty small and he fitted easily enough into the decoy bag; a bit heavier than some I'd carried in it, but I could lift it onto the back seat of the car without too much hassle and cover it with a blanket, with enough room left over for my bicycle.

'Who is the other person he's carried in his bag?' asked Sutton. 'Winnie Palmer? She's a lot lighter than Bobby Lagdon.'

'I hope so,' said Warren. 'Otherwise, there's probably at least one more victim out there we don't know about.'

I guess you've already found Bobby; that area is full of dog walkers. I won't insult your intelligence by explaining how he's stayed so fresh; although from my reading it would appear that as soon as he started to thaw out, nature will have taken its course quite quickly. Sorry about that – it can't have been the most pleasant scene you've attended.

Similarly, I won't insult you by detailing how Nick met his end. A bullet from a handgun, point blank against the temple. It doesn't do as much damage as, say, a shotgun under the chin, but it did the job quite nicely.

Of course, I'd staged it to look as though Bobby had shot his brother Nick from his seat on the passenger side. There was some of Bobby's blood on his side of the car, so you probably figured out he'd been injured also – maybe a bit of a fight? Didn't know I had him in the freezer, did you?

But how many of the inconsistencies did you spot? Obviously the pinpricks from the TASER probes. Did you wonder why Bobby subdued him first? What about his wrists? I'm sure there must have been some bruising from the handcuffs. What

about the rest of his body? We went over a couple of speed
bumps – faster than was strictly necessary, which was a little
unkind to poor Nick in the boot. I'm sure the development of
those bruises will have told you he didn't live for much longer.

Have you joined the dots yet, Warren?

The examiner turned the page over and flinched. 'I didn't need
to see that before lunch,' she said.

The next few pages were colour photographs of the two
brothers, probably printed with an inkjet printer.

With the notebook completely documented, Warren and
Sutton left his office. Sutton looked how Warren felt.

Word had got out and most of the rest of the team were gathered around Rachel Pymm's workstation as she downloaded the
photographs from the document examiner's camera. Grayson was
less than five minutes away, having immediately made his excuses
and abandoned his meeting with ACC Naseem; Carl Mallucci was
also racing up the A1.

'Main briefing room, one hour,' instructed Warren as he and
Sutton headed for Grayson's office.

The hearing aid had now unquestionably linked the
Culverhouse and the Lagdon killings, and Bobby Lagdon and
Winnie Palmer had both been frozen after they were killed. The
envelope containing the broken-off spike from a stinger had
been identical to the others, bringing in Councillor Paddon.
Nick Lagdon had been shot in his car on a Sunday evening, and
his brother's body might have been dumped on Sunday night.

Today was Tuesday. So far, they knew of six victims. There was
no doubt in Warren's mind that if the killer wasn't stopped, that
number would increase in the next five days.

Chapter 45

Grayson and Mallucci read through the confession in silence.

'The language is polished, with few errors I can see,' said Grayson, 'although some of our current crop of politicians have proven that erudition shouldn't be confused with intelligence.'

'And confident use of semi-colons,' noted Warren. 'This guy is pretty well educated.'

'What about this quote from Rumi?' asked Mallucci. 'Could it be a sign of a classical education?'

'Not necessarily,' said Sutton. 'I googled it and the first hit was a meme. The killer could have spotted it on Facebook.'

'Let's not draw too many conclusions yet,' said Warren. 'The analysts will give us a fuller understanding of his likely education level. I'm more worried about who the killer's audience is.'

'It was addressed directly to you and used your first name at the end,' noted Sutton. 'That creeps me out a bit.'

Warren shrugged. 'I was named as SIO at the Culverhouse press conference, and the envelope is simply addressed to DCI Warren Jones, with the street address for this building.'

'But I'm the SIO for the Lagdon murders, and the confessional is all about them,' said Mallucci. 'Why isn't it addressed to me? Not that I'm feeling left out, you understand.'

'Anyway, that wasn't what I meant by his audience,' said Warren, steering the conversation back from its tangent. 'The confession is almost instructional. I don't think this is aimed solely at us. I think he wants it to go public.'

*　*　*

'If you are right about the killer wanting the notoriety, then that's exactly why we don't go public at this stage,' said ACC Naseem, his voice firm over the speakerphone. 'We'd be giving him exactly what he wants. Announcing there is a serial killer at large will cause panic and a press storm; the sick bastard will absolutely love that.'

'I see what you are saying, sir, but don't we have an obligation to keep the community safe?' pressed Warren. 'Let's face it, the killing of two drug dealers isn't going to give them sleepless nights. The random killing of a couple in a farmhouse is a tragedy, but could have been the result of a family dispute. A little old lady goes missing, then turns up dead; worrying, but that's modern life. A politician assassinated on a country lane; probably bent.'

'But if you link these together it means anyone could be next. Probably this coming Sunday. Perhaps people need to think about taking precautions?'

'What sort of precautions?' asked Naseem. 'The Lagdon brothers were killed whilst sitting in their car dealing drugs. The Culverhouses were murdered in their beds, with no sign of forced entry. Winnie Palmer probably let her killer in, and Aldous Paddon was ambushed. What would you have us tell the public?'

Grayson's mouth twisted and Warren could see he wasn't happy with what he was about to say. 'I agree with ACC Naseem,' he said. 'We also haven't verified any of the details written in the notebook. It sounds as though he's a smartly dressed man, possibly white, wearing a man-bag and riding a fold-up bicycle. But do we know that for sure? The killer could actually be a scruffy black

317

female, so releasing those details to the public could derail the entire investigation. We'd be playing right into the killer's hands.'

'The hairs found in the back of the Lagdons' car were grey, so probably from an older person and were almost certainly not from a person of Afro-Caribbean heritage,' Mallucci reminded them.

Grayson glared at him. 'OK, a scruffy *white* female. Assuming they were actually from our killer; mitochondrial DNA won't even tell us if they were male or female. Hell, we don't know that it's just one person carrying out these killings. There could be a gang of them.'

'Yeah, but what are the odds of two sick fucks like this finding each other and deciding to join forces?' asked Mallucci.

'You'd be surprised,' said Warren. 'Siblings, best friends drawn to each other because the other kids wouldn't play with them, lovers … Studies suggest as many as twenty per cent of serial killers are part of a pair.'

'And a third of those pairs are male and female,' interjected Grayson.

'Point taken,' said Mallucci.

'And we're assuming the killings aren't linked, other than by the voices in the murderer's head,' said Grayson. 'It could all be a way of distracting us from the real reason behind one or other of the murders. That motive could point in the direction of the killer.'

'I'm not sure what's more worrying,' said Sutton. 'Victims chosen at random by a madman, or one genuine target with everyone else viewed as "collateral damage". That's a special kind of cold.'

'Then it's settled,' said Naseem. 'We keep the fact it's a serial killer to ourselves for the time being. We can revisit that decision once Forensics have finished their investigation. You never know, we might even get lucky and find a fingerprint leading us right to the killer, although I for one won't be holding my breath. In the meantime, I think we need outside help. I want you to look into bringing in an expert on serial killings. Speak to the Major

Crimes Unit, John, see who they recommend.'

'What about our team, sir?' asked Warren. 'Everyone in the office knows about the notebook, and we need to keep them in the loop.'

'Warren's right,' said Mallucci. 'And we need to think about how it will look in six months to outsiders blessed with the benefit of twenty-twenty hindsight. If there is another killing and it transpires we missed an opportunity to apprehend the suspect because the left hand didn't know what the right hand was doing ...'

There was a pause at the end of the line. 'I don't suppose we have much choice.' Another pause. 'OK. Brief everyone but make it absolutely clear that until they get my personal say-so, *nobody* utters a word of this outside the investigation. It is strictly need-to-know. No hints to reporters, no chatting about it down the pub, not even pillow talk. Am I clear?'

'Crystal,' said Grayson. Sutton, Warren and Mallucci signalled their assent also.

Walking back into the main office after the call ended, Sutton muttered in a voice that only Warren could hear. 'With six victims and a ticking deadline, I don't know when Naseem thinks we're going to have the time to chat about this down the pub.'

Wednesday 21st March

Chapter 46

Forensics had worked around the clock, and Tony Sutton shared their preliminary report during the morning briefing. The team had pored over the confession the previous day but had been able to surmise little more than Warren and Sutton.

'The sender of these letters is forensically aware,' said Sutton. 'No fingerprints on the envelopes, the notebook, or the hearing aid; not even Mr Culverhouse's. Fortunately earwax, or rather the skin cells trapped in it, is a good source of DNA; who knew? Pending those results, and because of the less than subtle references to blowing Mr Culverhouse's head off with a shotgun, we'll take it as a given it's his.

'We're also going to assume that given the overlap of the probable timings of the victims being killed, stored and then left for us to find them, that Bobby Lagdon wasn't the victim of a copycat killer who found out about Winnie Palmer and decided it sounded like a good idea.

'The killer claimed to have carried the bodies in a decoy bag. These are large bags, used by hunters and gamekeepers to transport dead animals, so are hardly common purchases in urban areas. Either the killer already had access to one – in which case that may give an indication of where he lived or his lifestyle – or he needed to buy one.'

'Anything Forensics can tell us about the materials used?' asked Warren.

'Plenty, but little of any use,' said Sutton. 'They could have picked up a pack of the envelopes from any supermarket any time in the last ten years. The stamps are self-adhesive first-class, so no need to lick them. There's no date or price, and no way to tell where they were bought. The address labels are also self-adhesive, and the most popular brand sold.

'The ink on both the labels and the accompanying letters are standard HP formulation, used in almost every inkjet printer they've made for the past ten years; don't even ask about the paper. They are looking at the printed text and images for microscopic artefacts that might allow matching to a specific cartridge, but we'll need a suspect first. The pages were glued into the notebook with a Pritt Stick.'

'What about the notebook?' asked Hutchinson.

'That's a bit more promising,' said Sutton. 'They are only sold online or through specialist stationers. You might find them in a very large WHSmith, but you wouldn't get them in a supermarket.

'Forensics have found no fingerprints, trapped hairs or skin cells. They've taken some random swabs to look for contact DNA, but I'm not hopeful.'

As always, Warren was impressed with the amount of detail his colleagues in Forensics had unearthed but they'd need a suspect. By using common or generic brands, anyone of interest who possessed such materials could simply quote sales figures for each item and let the jury make their own minds up.

'What about the postmarks?' asked Hutchinson.

'They passed through the Middlesbury sorting office, but that depot serves us and all the surrounding villages.'

His report finished, Sutton sat back down.

'First task, continue cross-referencing every person of interest from each murder,' ordered Warren. 'Flag anyone who comes up in more than one investigation. Identify anybody with a potential alibi for any of the murders so we can decide if we can eliminate them once and for all, or they need to stay in the mix—'

Warren stopped speaking as the door opened; his stomach lurched. He could only think of one reason Janice would interrupt a briefing.

'Sir, you need to come downstairs to the mail room.'

* * *

'The envelope and the label appear to be a match,' announced the forensic technician who had arrived within fifteen minutes of Warren seeing the small envelope isolated on a table in the small office that processed all of the mail arriving at Middlesbury station.

The previous package had been sterile forensically, but there was always the chance that the sender had slipped up this time. Warren should really have left the woman to get on with her job, but he hadn't been able to bring himself to leave. Neither had Sutton.

'Go ahead,' he instructed. He'd donned a pair of latex gloves, although he doubted he'd handle anything personally. The knot in his stomach tightened.

The CSI carefully slit the envelope open, before reaching inside with a pair of tweezers. The small notebook was identical to the one received yesterday and Warren's mouth became even drier.

* * *

Warren had printed photographs of the notebook and distributed them to the team. As before, the taunting letter was accompanied by pictures, taken at night, but harshly lit by the flash of a camera phone.

'That poor woman,' said Pymm quietly. They had all seen the images taken by the CSIs when Winnie Palmer was discovered, but there was something especially disturbing knowing that this had been captured by the person responsible for the elderly woman's death.

Again, the killer's statement started with a quote.

'I must be cruel, only to be kind.' – William Shakespeare

They say that loneliness is a killer. I suppose it is. Society values a person by the contribution that they make. But what happens when we no longer have anything to give? When we grow too old to produce anything deemed worthy? Do we just forget about these people, leaving them alone to live out the rest of their days in obscurity?

When everyone you loved and who loved you has gone, who is there to mourn your passing? To even notice you have disappeared? I think Winnie Palmer felt that way. No husband, no children, a handful of friends who are themselves on the scrap heap. Who would even notice she was missing? For months, the world assumed that she had just … left. Unmissed by anyone except her dog.

I guess that's why she was so open to friendship. To conversing with a stranger who took the time to return her purse, which he convinced her he had found in the street. She hadn't even noticed it was gone.

She cursed her carelessness of course; how many times had she been told not to leave it perched on top of the battered trolley that she dragged around to the shops each week? But the pocket on the front was torn, its zip broken. It would have fallen out of there just as easily as she assumed it had fallen off the top.

Would she have invited me in for a cup of tea and a slice of cake to say thank you if she hadn't been so starved of company? Maybe, maybe not. But it didn't take long to strike up a friendship. The offer of a few household repairs, a story about how she reminded me of my own late grandmother, and that was all it took. By the time I popped around uninvited to wish her a Happy New Year, she opened the door to me without any hesitation; Benny had long since stopped barking and growling whenever I appeared – he trusted me as much as his owner did.

Why did I kill her? What was so special about her that I chose her?

Well, figuring that out is what they pay you for, Warren. Are you sure you're up to the task?

Warren heard the door to the briefing room open. He looked up to see Grayson leaning in; he looked furious. He had quietly left a few minutes earlier, after Janice had whispered something in his ear.

'Warren, my office. The shit's just hit the fan.'

Chapter 47

Grayson rotated his computer, so Warren could see it clearly. The door made a shucking noise as it closed behind him.

'Fuck,' said Warren as he read the headline shouting at him from the *Middlesbury Reporter*'s website.

'ACC Naseem expressed a similar sentiment when he called,' said Grayson.

Middlesbury Rocked By Serial Killer

Warren scanned the story, the blood running cold in his veins, even as his cheeks flushed. The story had been published online a little over two hours previously. The weekly print edition wasn't due out until Monday.

'She's linked the Lagdon brothers, Winnie Palmer, Councillor Paddon and the Culverhouses,' he breathed. The 'she' in question was Marcia Cooper, and the story, though sensational and short on facts, had successfully identified that the killer appeared to favour Sunday nights. The story heavily implied that there could be another victim that weekend.

'Shouldn't she have contacted us for comment before running this?'

Grayson scowled. 'Apparently, she phoned the press office last thing yesterday and asked if any of the recent deaths were linked. Her inquiry was extremely vague, and the media team weren't on the need-to-know list, so they fobbed her off with a generic "inquiries are ongoing and there is no specific intelligence to link them".'

'Which bolsters her claim that we are deliberately misleading the public.'

Warren felt a surge of anger. Marcia Cooper hadn't wanted to tip them off that she was going to run such an inflammatory piece in case they managed to secure an injunction.

Grayson read his thoughts. 'Legal are looking into whether we can shut it down as a matter of urgency, but the cat's already out of the bag. Two hundred tweets at the last count using the hashtag #MiddlesburySerialKiller, and the switchboard has been fielding calls from national and international media outlets. Naseem is doing his nut.'

Warren could well imagine. The assistant chief constable wasn't named in the article, but ultimately it had been his decision to keep things quiet. Cooper and her editor had bent, if not broken, the guidelines that they were supposed to follow in these situations. But any official censure would be months away, and the paper had clearly made the judgement that any penalties would be a small price to pay for the increase in readership and click-through-advertising revenue.

The press office would be in full damage-limitation mode. One thing was certain though: if she thought he was going to give her an exclusive about the Paddon murder now, she could damn well think again.

* * *

Professor Elizabeth Swann looked exactly as she did on the TV. Her blonde-grey hair was trimmed in a neat bob, and she wore a smart blouse and jacket. The only surprise, as she was invariably filmed seated at a desk, were the bright orange trainers.

'My sciatica's flaring up,' she'd apologised, as she motioned at her garish footwear. Her slight embarrassment was at odds with the confident and assured persona she projected as she gave her opinion on whichever deviant killer was being profiled on the true crime documentary series that Warren and his co-workers privately referred to as *Britain's Biggest Bastards* and its companion show they'd dubbed *World's Worst Wankers*.

'Thank you for coming here at such short notice,' Warren greeted her, as she signed in at reception.

'Not at all – I've finished my contribution to this semester's teaching and my PhD students are pretty self-sufficient. Besides, Middlesbury is only a short train ride from London.'

'Have you checked into your hotel yet, Professor?' asked Warren.

'Please, call me Lizzie,' she insisted, her accent a curious hybrid of Birmingham and London, with lingering traces from the years she'd spent working in the US. 'And no, I decided to come straight here. When you travel as much as I do, checking into a hotel is a well-oiled procedure.'

Prof Swann had been recommended by the Major Crime Unit in Welwyn. The criminologist had aided numerous police forces around the country and abroad, taught classes and supervised graduate students at UCL, and had written three textbooks and two best-selling paperbacks. She'd even given guest lectures at the FBI's famed Behavioural Analysis Unit.

All of this Warren had gleaned from her UCL staff page, the website for *Britain's Biggest Bastards* and Wikipedia.

He was in two minds about what Prof Swann could contribute. Another pair of eyes wouldn't hurt, and serial killers were rare enough in the UK that any insight from somebody who specialised in their study could certainly be useful.

On the other hand, several high-profile investigations had been sent down the wrong track when the senior investigating officer had relied too heavily on advice from a profiler that had later turned out to be naïve, speculative or simply oversold.

In the end, a profiler was just another investigative tool, no different to forensics, witness statements or the artificial intelligence behind the HOLMES2 case management software. He would consider whatever insight Swann could provide and use it as he saw fit.

'I've read everything you sent me, and I'm keen to see what you are already thinking,' she said as they climbed the stairs to Warren's office. Reaching the landing, they were greeted by Tony Sutton and John Grayson. After introductions, Grayson made his excuses and left. Sutton rolled his eyes. As usual, Grayson wasn't going to work any later than he had to. Warren and Sutton, on the other hand, had phoned their respective wives to let them know it was going to be a late one.

'Coffee?' asked Warren. At least Grayson had left his office unlocked so they could impress their guest with his private stash.

Thursday 22nd March

Chapter 48

Lizzie Swann worked like a demon. Her initial pizza-fuelled session with Warren and Sutton had gone on until late, and her caffeine intake was nearly as impressive as Warren's. He'd dropped her off at her hotel, and it was clear she'd stayed up even longer; the presentation she'd loaded onto the briefing-room computer was new to him.

Her enthusiasm was understandable; she would be dining out on this case for years. Lectures and academic papers were just the tip of the iceberg. Warren suspected that at the very least an episode of *Britain's Biggest Bastards* would be in the offing, possibly even a book. He wondered if he would be invited to participate; he wasn't sure how he would feel about that.

'I'll start this briefing the way I always do,' she said, after being introduced to the team. 'Criminal profiling *is* a science, but it has its limitations. We're dealing with human nature and a mercifully small data set. That means there are a lot of generalisations that we need to be cautious of; I will try and grade my observations in terms of reliability, to help you make up your own minds.'

Her frank admission had the desired effect. The polite scepticism softened, much as it had with Warren and Sutton the night before.

'First, much of what we know about the minds of murderers – in particular serial killers – comes from interviews with them; I'm sure you're familiar with some of the big names. The problem is we are limited to those who engage with us after their arrest and conviction. That inherently biases the interviews towards those who are willing to talk about themselves, and haven't evaded capture or killed themselves. For every narcissist loving the attention, there is a quiet person who refuses to even acknowledge the interviewer. Unfortunately, that is sometimes overlooked when looking for patterns in behaviour. Worse, it can become something of a self-fulfilling prophecy. The persistent stereotype that serial killers are typically white, middle-aged males, choosing victims who have the same ethnicity or background, can lead us to pay less attention to potential suspects than we should.

'And this is why this killer is especially interesting.'

She changed the presentation to a white background, using a remote pointer to populate the screen with bulleted points.

'Our killer is a narcissist; there is no rational reason to contact DCI Jones and explicitly link these disparate crimes. He – and I believe it is a he, probably singular – is boasting. He wants recognition. And he thinks he is clever; cleverer than you, certainly.'

She took a sip of water.

'But this is what worries me. I think our killer is an aficionado. I think he is obsessed with serial killers and wants to be recognised as "one of the best", if you forgive that phrase.

'I believe he has studied whatever he can easily get his hands on and is trying to confound us by playing against stereotypes. But it shows. He has to rely on what he can find on the internet, on TV and in books. And so some of those lazy stereotypes have influenced his choices.

'Take this example. One of the most basic – and publicly documented – ways to divide serial killers is into organised and non-social, versus disorganised and social. The killer can't do anything about his social skills, his education level, intelligence

336

or childhood of course, but he has taken care to vary his methodology across both categories. He left the Culverhouses and Councillor Paddon at the scene but moved Nick Lagdon before leaving him to be found. He took Bobby Lagdon and Winnie Palmer away, concealing the fact of their deaths whilst he stored them in a freezer, before depositing them where they could be easily found weeks later.

'Then there is "uses seduction to restrain", versus "attacking in a blitz". We believe he talked his way into Winnie Palmer's house. But by his account, he took the Lagdon brothers unawares, ambushed Councillor Paddon, and it appears that he entered the Culverhouses' property covertly and attacked them without warning.

'The next attributes are a little more tricky to fake, and this is why I think our killer is deliberately trying to muddy the waters. Organised killers leave a controlled crime scene, with little physical evidence. Disorganised do not. Winnie Palmer was regarded as a missing person for months, with no evidence of foul play. But the Culverhouse scene was messy, and the CSIs flagged it as murder within twenty-four hours. That appears to be disorganised. Again, the original Lagdon and Paddon crime scenes were clearly murders, with some forensics left behind; again disorganised.

'But look deeper. The *physical* evidence from the Culverhouse scene hasn't actually pointed you towards anyone. Then look at the Lagdon killings. The killer successfully made Bobby Lagdon the initial suspect in the killing of his brother.

'The killings also appear to be very controlled. The victims haven't been beaten and there is no evidence of sexual assault; if he is aroused by his actions he's dealing with it away from the scene. This is all the very antithesis of disorganised. All of this at least points us toward an organised killer, for whatever use that is.

'So, what kind of profile can we build? I've said one male. We can't rule out the assistance of another person, but I see no direct evidence of that, and the letters appear to be written by the same individual. At the very least, the writer is probably the dominant partner. Perceived wisdom is that serial killers typically limit their victim pool to one ethnic group. In this case, the Culverhouses, Councillor Paddon and Winnie Palmer were Caucasian, but the Lagdon brothers were black men of Afro-Caribbean heritage, so again he is subverting stereotypes. From references in the letter about the Lagdons – where he expresses confidence that he won't be stopped by police – I am going to lean heavily towards our suspect being white.

'He is clearly very intelligent. The killings are meticulously planned and the use of language in his communications suggests above-average literacy. But that doesn't mean he necessarily has educational qualifications. The quotes are easily found on the internet, so we can't read anything into that. In fact, his apparent need for approval from the police indicates there is insecurity and a desire for recognition. So we are probably looking for someone who may believe they haven't reached their full potential. I wouldn't be at all surprised if our killer has a massive chip on his shoulder when it comes to how he feels that "the system" has let him down.

'Which leads on nicely to age. Again, he has sought to be different. The Lagdon brothers were in their twenties, the Culverhouses and Winnie Palmer elderly, and Councillor Paddon in his fifties. As to how old he is, this is tricky. He is an adult, and young enough that he can physically subdue his victims; he will have had to move quickly to take down the Lagdon brothers if his description in the letter is accurate. Unfortunately, the language used doesn't have any obvious indicators, such as current slang to indicate a younger person, and it appears to be fairly generic English spoken widely in this part of the UK. People in their twenties, and those in their late forties and above, will have been taught a high standard of grammar in schools.' She smiled apologetically. 'Those closer in age to DCI Jones and myself were less

well schooled in grammar, after some very questionable education policies by the Conservative government of the 1980s. But a
keen reader may have absorbed some of those rules organically,
and there are an increasing number of software plug-ins that can
modify a writer's style.'

Warren returned her smile; his dissertation supervisor at
university had openly admitted that he had been given additional guidance on how to support Warren's cohort. The older
Tony Sutton had thought that hilarious.

'Presentation-wise, I think he is likely to be socially awkward,
but not so much that he can't interact when necessary. If he is
the person who befriended Winnie Palmer before she was killed,
then he has to have at least some social skills. Plenty of serial
killers have maintained apparently normal intimate relationships.
He will need somewhere to keep the freezer for the bodies, and
perhaps some of his other equipment, but that doesn't tell us if
he lives alone, has another secure location, or if his family just
don't go into the garage. What I will say is that he has access to
at least some disposable income, and is technically quite savvy,
apparently using Bitcoin and the dark web.

'It's almost certain that the victims were all killed, and Bobby
Lagdon and Winnie Palmer's bodies were dumped, on Sunday
night or early Monday morning That indicates that perhaps our
perpetrator works during the week or is otherwise occupied.

'You've probably heard of geographical profiling: the theory
that a serial killer lives or works somewhere close to where their
victims are killed. Perhaps even inside the area bordered by their
kills. Our killer is almost certainly local, as he appears to be
demonstrating local knowledge, but given his habit of subverting
expectations, I'm not going to be any more specific.

'You have been working on the assumption that the individual
spotted outside Winnie Palmer's home on New Year's Eve is a likely
suspect. The limited details available – a white, tall male between
twenty and fifty – would fit our profile. The apparently deformed

jaw might indicate a difficult childhood – many serial killers are known to have been bullied as children, but that's speculation; the damage to his jaw may have been acquired in later life.'

She paused, looking towards the door as it opened. Warren felt himself tense as Janice entered the room. She looked at him apologetically, before nodding her head at his mouthed question.

Warren turned to Swann who, along with everyone else in the room, had divined the reason behind Janice's interruption.

It was that time of the morning again.

There was another letter.

Chapter 49

Warren had invited Swann to accompany him and Sutton to the mail room. Grayson joined them, keeping headquarters apprised of the situation by mobile phone.

The small room was becoming more crowded every day, with the same forensic technicians already busy at work. There was only just enough space for them all to fit in.

Warren watched Swann out of the corner of his eye. He could see her excitement, even as she tried to hide it. He couldn't blame her. Her role in an investigation typically involved sifting through existing evidence, usually at some remove. Here she was at the very heart of an active case, seeing results unfold in real time.

This time the familiar envelope contained just a notebook. The killer had again glued in his printed confession, alongside graphic pictures of the crime scene. Warren took photos and they returned to his office to read through it.

> *'It is forbidden to kill; therefore all murderers are*
> *punished unless they kill in large numbers and to*
> *the sound of trumpets' – Voltaire*

'Another easy to find quote from the internet,' noted Sutton. 'I think Voltaire was talking about war, but I guess our killer's referring to something else.'

'I agree, but *who* is he referring to? The victim or himself?' asked Swann. 'Is there any indication that Councillor Paddon had blood on his hands? Literal or metaphorical?'

'Nothing literal,' said Warren, 'but he has voted in favour of some quite punishing austerity cuts, which probably indirectly led to deaths. Could our killer be impacted by them?'

'Something to consider,' she said. 'Otherwise, he's referring to himself. Paddon makes six victims that we know of. In serial killer terms that's a good number, but not really that impressive compared to some …' She trailed off and cleared her throat. 'Sorry, I have got into the habit of viewing these consultations as an academic exercise. I didn't mean to depersonalise the victims.'

'That's OK, we understand,' said Warren gently. Swann had spent years examining some of the worst examples of human behaviour ever witnessed. For the sake of her own mental well-being, she would need to step back from the impact of the offenders' behaviour and reduce each case to its bare facts.

Warren just wished that was an option for him and his team.

'This reference to trumpets,' said Grayson. 'Could he be referring to that piece in the bloody *Reporter*? You said he is a narcissist; could he see that article as trumpeting his "achievements", for want of a better word?'

'There's certainly something in that idea,' said Swann. 'Obviously, no normal person – and frankly, between us professionals, I have no problem using the words "normal" and "abnormal" to divide the world – would see anything praiseworthy in that story. But our killer wouldn't see it that way. There's no doubt in my mind he'll save that article. I wouldn't be surprised if he's also following the different hashtags being used on social media to describe his crimes.

'The timing would have to be pretty tight though,' said Warren.

'It was published yesterday. He'd only have a couple of hours to reference it in this letter before catching the last post.'

'Maybe we'll get lucky and he was rushed enough to leave us some forensics,' mused Grayson as they moved on.

Another clue, Warren. How many more do you need?

'First name again,' muttered Sutton. 'It's giving me the creeps. And I don't like the taunting – it feels personal.'

Warren tried to sound nonchalant. 'We've already discussed this. I'm the SIO and my face is fronting the investigation.'

'Regardless, I want you to be careful,' said Grayson. 'Vary your route home. Make sure the alarm is set and the windows locked. Is Susan still at work?'

Warren raised a finger. 'Don't even suggest it, John. You know what she's like – there's no way she'll take time off so close to the exam period. She did a personal safety course after the last time and her school is like a fortress; I'd rather she was there than at home to be honest.'

Swann raised an eyebrow, but Warren ignored her. The Delmarno affair still caused the occasional bad dreams for both him and Susan, even years later, and he had no wish to rehash the details.

He turned back to the letter.

Nobody is really safe in the twenty-first century, even – especially – our public figures. Aldous Paddon's official Facebook page is followed by over 300 people, any of whom could see what his plans were for that night, and the coming month. His page on the council website lists his official engagements between now and the local elections, and his personal webpage is filled with grinning photos of him with the great, the good and the not-so-good.

Did you know that when somebody stands in an election, an address is listed? Some candidates give their constituency office – a clever way of hiding the fact that they don't live anywhere near the folks who will be voting for them – but Councillor Paddon is a man of the people! He wants voters to know he lives locally. That he understands the issues facing the good people of Middlesbury. That he doesn't reside in a big mansion in leafy Cambridgeshire.

Of course, he doesn't exactly live on the Chequers Estate, seeing for himself the devastation his political friends' policies have wrought on the poorest in society. Nor do his cronies, getting fat off the public money funnelled their way with a nod and a wink, gaming the system to freeze out the competition. No, he lives in the nicest part of Stenfield, which is only part of Middlesbury for electoral purposes.

He isn't daft enough to give his full address – he wouldn't want anyone undesirable tuning up on his doorstep unannounced. But there's enough there to know that the only sensible route home from the Hardingham Centre is by that dark, lonely country lane.

'He's boasting,' said Swann. 'He's showing us – you – how easy it was. But perhaps here we also see some suggestion of motive.'

'A bloody great chip on his shoulder?' suggested Sutton. 'That would tie in with the quote. He could be referencing Paddon's role in the budget cuts. Perhaps we should be looking for someone who feels especially pissed off?'

'There are also indications in the Lagdon letter that he is politically switched on,' said Swann. 'The references to the police being more likely to choose black men for a stop and search or for driving a nice car, even his references to Amnesty International's concerns over his use of a stun gun, all point towards someone with a strong political awareness.'

'So why Paddon?' asked Grayson. 'He was hardly the most extreme council member.'

'Then it must be more specific,' said Swann. 'More personal, even. I'd continue looking at correspondents or constituents that he had contact with. Look for unresolved grievances. It's interesting that he refers to "cronies getting fat off public money", given the controversy over the town hall renovations.'

'The Culverhouses lived in his constituency,' Sutton reminded them. 'Could this be the real motive? Are all the other deaths just there as a smokescreen so we think Paddon was targeted randomly?'

'I'm not sure. The other killings are very sophisticated. I think that the act of killing – and doing it better than anyone else – is his primary motivation. That being said, he has to choose his victims somehow, so why not select someone who he feels has done him wrong?'

'If the killer is Derek Culverhouse, then surely his parents weren't just "collateral damage?"' said Grayson.

'I'm really not sure,' admitted Swann.

'What about these women that Paddon supposedly assaulted or had affairs with?' asked Warren.

Swann shook her head. 'Certainly not the women themselves. If there is any link, I would expect it to be an upset partner. Assuming that the killer is aware of the allegations and even cares, I would think it is likely simply another justification for his target.'

'At least we know how he staged it,' said Grayson. 'And if what he says is true, he really puts the effort in. No wonder he has to do it at the weekend.'

'Again, he wants us to know how clever he is,' said Swann.

Did you know, that between the hours of ten p.m. and one a.m., on a typical Sunday night, between one and three cars pass that spot every hour? So the odds that somebody else would fall into my little trap were relatively slim. It takes between eighty-five and ninety-five seconds for me to deploy the stinger. And a little over half that time to retrieve it so nobody else needs a new set of tyres. So three minutes notice from when he entered that road gives ample time to roll it out, jog to where I estimate his car is likely to stop, and hide myself.

The mobile tracking app that I installed on my phone is accurate to within one hundred metres. At sixty miles per hour, he would travel that distance in just under four seconds, so I could pinpoint exactly when he would hit the strip, plus or minus four seconds.

It's tempting to let you chase your tail and waste hundreds of man-hours trying to find out how I got hold of his mobile phone to install the tracking software, but I'm feeling generous and I know that budgets are tight. I'm not James Bond. I didn't steal his phone or send him an infected email. I just bought another phone, glued a magnet to it and stuck it to the bottom of his car 😄 Keep It Simple, Stupid xx 😄

'I wonder if there is anything we can use from what he's told us,' said Warren. 'If we do a cell mast download, we could identify all the handsets being used in that area. Even if he was smart enough to use burners, we might get a lead back to him.'

'I'll get onto it,' promised Grayson. 'Magistrates can be a little funny about warrants that indiscriminately pull in members of the public, but I think they'll play ball on this.'

I notice you haven't told the public exactly how I killed him. If he'd sat tight, locked the doors, and called the AA, he'd probably be alive now. A woman almost certainly would have done so, stranded on a pitch-black country lane. But he was a middle-aged bloke obsessed with cars, so I figured the odds were better than even that he'd get out and have a look. He never saw it coming. You could say I had him NAILED! 😄

346

So there you have it, Warren.
I've given you everything you need.
Are you really as good as they say you are?

'More fucking emojis,' growled Sutton. 'He's a lot less funny than he thinks he is.'

'It's all a game to him, isn't it?' said Grayson, his tone similarly bitter. 'They're just bits of meat for his sick fantasies.'

Chapter 50

Swann's insights cast doubt on many of the potential suspects that the different investigations had identified, but were not enough to rule them out entirely. So the most important job was to whittle down the combined suspect lists.

Warren had borrowed as many wheeled magnetic whiteboards as he could get his hands on. All of the suspects and persons of interest, from each of the murders, were attached to the boards. Piles of printouts and statements occupied the main briefing table, with Rachel Pymm the room's epicentre.

'We can exclude anyone for whom we have a confirmed alibi on one or more of the Sunday nights we know a victim was definitely killed,' explained Warren to Grayson and Naseem, who'd decided that what the busy team most needed right now was a visit from the senior brass. 'As we can't be certain exactly when Bobby Lagdon and Winnie Palmer were dumped, we are only accepting alibis covering the entire period when the bodies could have been left. Similarly, although we are fairly confident the person spotted outside Winnie Palmer's house on New Year's Eve is involved somehow, we are keeping an open mind as to exactly when she was killed. DS Pymm and Prof Swann are prioritising anyone who remains in the mix.'

'Sounds sensible,' agreed Naseem. 'What about Councillor Paddon's colleagues?' he asked, revealing the real reason he had decided to brave the traffic on the A1. The possibility that Aldous Paddon might have been killed by a political rival was bad enough; the idea that an elected politician might be a serial killer was enough for the Home Secretary to take a personal interest.

'We are treating them exactly the same as any other persons of interest, but we are prioritising them.'

'What other lines of investigation are you following?' asked Naseem.

'We have teams in Welwyn looking for overlaps between POIs and victims, be it through social media, vehicles, mutual acquaintances and intelligence already on the system.'

'How is the list looking?' asked Grayson.

'We've culled a few names already – and added a few more mutual acquaintances,' Warren pointed at one of the whiteboards. The photos at the centre had been crossed out.

'Callum Harradine became a POI when he matched an e-fit of the man seen by witnesses outside Winnie Palmer's house on New Year's Eve. He confessed to a burglary that we know happened on the night the Lagdon brothers were killed.'

Grayson grunted. 'He never struck me as sophisticated enough.'

'That's also Professor Swann's assessment.'

'Spencer Aspinall spends his Sunday evenings playing video games in the family garage and on the phone.'

'What about Eric Morton?' asked Grayson.

'Definitely still at the top of the list. He's not academically bright, but he's intelligent in his own way and Swann thinks he could fit the profile,' said Warren. 'He regularly works Sunday nights as a taxi driver, so he's out and about. He's unlicensed, so not all of his jobs have been properly logged. We have his phone location data and some ANPR, and we're trying to track down some of his fares from any of the nights in question to see if they can verify it was him who picked them up. Unfortunately, his solicitor successfully got his bail reinstated, so he was free the night Councillor Paddon was killed.'

Naseem's phone vibrated. Glancing at the screen, he mouthed an apology and stepped outside the room.

Grayson raised an eyebrow and lowered his voice. 'Judging by the way he's been nodding his head, you're definitely making the right impression.'

Warren gave a tight smile. He knew exactly what Grayson was hinting at, but the last thing he needed right now was a discussion about his career plans. There were still a few days before he had to decide whether or not to tell Grayson to submit his reference, but he had been so busy he hadn't had a chance to properly discuss it with Susan. His decision would affect both of them, and the future of their unborn child.

Chapter 51

'Derek Culverhouse is looking unlikely,' said Sutton. 'The mito-chondrial DNA from the hair in the back of the Lagdons' car doesn't match him and we have two good CCTV captures of him driving his car near War Memorial Park that show he'd have really had to have been flying to make it to his parents' and back the night they were killed.'

'He never really fitted my profile,' said Swann. 'I can see why you were looking at him for his parents' murder, but I struggled to reconcile him with the other killings. Aside from Nick Lagdon, none of the other deaths came with an obvious perpetrator; the killer even tried to conceal they were murders. If he killed his parents, he would have to know that he would be the number-one suspect, but he made no attempt to fabricate an alibi. And why would he send us clues ensuring if we nail him for his parents, he goes down for all of them?'

'OK,' said Warren, 'I can buy that, but you know we need more. Anyone who does the things he's doing has to be crazy – in the popular sense of the word, if not the clinical sense – can you really know what is going on inside that head?'

'No,' said Swann, 'and you are right to be sceptical.'

'Fortunately, we have hard evidence,' said Sutton. 'First of all,

351

New Year's Eve. His parents had a get-together, including his dad's brother and wife; they all stayed over until the second. They both confirm that Derek was definitely up with them until the early hours, and around the following day, and his uncle backs up the story about him nearly falling off the wagon and drinking that whisky.'

'OK, so it wasn't him outside Winnie Palmer's house,' said Warren. 'But he didn't fit the description anyway. He could have sneaked out when everyone else was in bed and the man getting dressed in the street at midnight is a coincidence.'

'True. But we can also rule him out for the Lagdon murders. That Sunday he took his two oldest boys to the football. They stayed over at his flat and he drove them to school in the morning. We have WhatsApp messages with the mother and boys confirming the arrangements, and time-stamped photographs of him and the lads eating pizza and watching movies until late. The boys slept on a sofa bed in the living room that blocks the only door to the flat. Realistically, there's no way he could have snuck out without waking them. On top of that, his phone never left, and we have CCTV from his neighbour showing that his car doesn't move all night.'

'Works for me,' said Warren.

Friday 23rd March

Chapter 52

Warren had been in since shortly after seven a.m., having picked up Lizzie Swann from her hotel. The woman was indefatigable; her first act after accepting a coffee was to print a spreadsheet summarising the work she'd continued after Warren had dropped her off the previous night.

'Today's job is establishing alibis for all those remaining on our combined suspect lists,' Warren told the ever-growing team of officers assembled in front of him. With the largest meeting room now given over to Rachel Pymm's team, the main office was the only space, aside from the canteen, that could hold so many bodies. This was now the biggest investigation Warren had ever coordinated; in addition to those present, there were scores of specialists working down in Welwyn.

'DS Pymm has compiled a priority list, which we will work our way down in order. Use every tool we have, including support from Welwyn. Any pushback, mention *Operation Riviera* – that'll bump you to the top of their job list. Bang on doors and run up the phone bill. Speak to friends, family and work colleagues but keep it vague – we don't want to tip the killer off. Stick to the elimination criteria and escalate anyone you can't prove is not our man.'

Warren closed the briefing with another admonishment not to discuss the investigation outside of the team. Marcia Cooper's latest piece had been full of speculation, and criticism of the investigation, but no inside information. He wanted to keep it that way.

Returning to his office, Warren retrieved the small tub of antacids from his desk drawer. He'd lain awake for much of the past few nights, and the extra-strong coffee he'd been using to compensate was taking its toll on his stomach; his agreement with Susan to cut back on caffeine was on hold.

He rolled his head, wincing at the crunching from his neck. He was missing his regular early morning swims. Never one for fashionable mental health fads such as mindfulness, he nevertheless found that the enforced boredom that came from an hour with no stimuli beyond the rush of water past his ears helped reset his brain, leaving him clear-headed and able to focus on the coming day.

In a couple of hours the post would come. What would it reveal? Another letter? News of another addition to their killer's grim toll? He'd tasked a small group of analysts to reopen all murders or unexplained deaths and reinvestigate missing person cases from the past five years. Swann was on the fence as regards Winnie Palmer being the killer's first victim. The murder had been meticulously executed, but mistakes were made; namely being spotted on New Year's Eve. Was that just bad luck, or a sign of his inexperience?

'Boss, you need to see this.'

Warren jumped. He'd barely registered Sutton's tap on his open door.

The DI thrust his tablet computer at him.

'Shit,' groaned Warren as he read the latest headline on the *Reporter*'s online edition.

CLOCK TICKING AS POLICE NO CLOSER TO FINDING
MIDDLESBURY SERIAL KILLER

Below, a smaller subtitle made his gut clench.

Famed TV Profiler Brought in to Assist Investigation

'Jesus, they've even got a photograph of her,' said Warren, aghast.

Had Marcia Cooper placed a target on Lizzie Swann's back?

*   *   *

Swann took the news better than Warren expected.

'It comes with the territory,' she said. 'My TV work makes me recognisable and I get threats on social media from those who object to me campaigning to increase sentencing for stalkers. I'm not going to let it affect what I'm doing here.'

'Regardless, I'm not happy about you being alone in that hotel,' said Grayson. 'ACC Naseem has authorised a protection detail. They'll drive you to and from here, and there will be somebody stationed outside your door overnight. That's assuming you want to remain. You can always return to London and consult remotely.'

'No, I would much rather be here.'

Warren wasn't surprised – Swann clearly wasn't one to take fright easily. And he'd seen the gleam in her eyes. Leaving aside future TV and book deals, she was fully invested in the case. She wanted to catch the killer almost as much as he did.

'What do you think the effect will be on our killer, now that he knows you are involved?' he asked her.

'I think he is going to be ecstatic,' she said. 'In the last letter he openly questioned whether you are good enough to catch him. Bringing me in is vindication we are taking him seriously.' She looked apologetic. 'My public profile will stroke his ego. It's almost guaranteed he's watched some of the documentaries I've consulted on, maybe even read my books.'

'We need to get ahead of the story and cut Marcia Cooper off at the knees,' said Grayson. 'I'll speak to Naseem. I'll recommend we level with the public; the cat's already out of the bag anyway.' He stroked his chin. 'I'll see if media relations can tap up a few tame reporters and offer them some exclusive details that the *Reporter* doesn't have. I'm damned if I'm going to let Marcia Cooper further her career off the back of this.'

* * *

By the time Warren and Sutton left Grayson's office, it was mid-morning.

'Shouldn't the post have arrived by now?' asked Sutton.

'You're right,' said Warren, crossing to Janice's desk.

'Mail arrived at the usual time.' She gave a nervous smile. 'Nothing for you or anything suspicious for the rest of the investigative team. I'm guessing that's a good thing?'

Warren let out a deep breath. 'Maybe.'

He turned to Sutton whose face shared the same mixture of emotions that Warren felt.

'Perhaps there are no more victims?' Sutton suggested. 'Councillor Paddon could have been the last one.'

'Or he hasn't chosen his next victim yet,' said Warren grimly. 'Today is Friday.'

'And he kills on a Sunday,' said Sutton.

Chapter 53

'We have downloads for all the cell masts on the route between Councillor Paddon's home and the Hardingham Centre for the night he was killed,' said Pymm. 'It's going to take us time to trawl through – there are literally thousands of records.'

Warren had feared as much. 'Put as many people on it as you can.'

'Already done. The words *Operation Riviera* are like a magic spell. We've already got a couple of potentials.'

'Tell me more,' said Warren, leaning on the edge of Pymm's desk.

'We know from the letter that he was using tracking software, probably the same type that parents use to keep an eye on their kids. That means a smartphone with an internet connection to send the location updates. I figured that only handsets making regular data connections during that time would be of interest. One would probably be more or less static in the vicinity of where Councillor Paddon's car came to a stop. The other handset would be moving along his route, as it was attached to his vehicle.'

'That makes sense.'

'The handset was attached to the bottom of a moving vehicle with a magnet, which might have caused an unstable connection, so including partial matches, we have one candidate for the static phone and three for the moving phone. We've no idea how frequently the tracker will have been pinging the server with its GPS coordinates, so can't determine if any connections are from the app or just normal network traffic.'

'Any information on ownership?'

'Two of the moving phones are registered. They roughly follow Councillor Paddon's likely route through town but connect to the network infrequently. I can't determine if that was due to a spotty connection or just the phone pinging social media for updates. I've put in a request for their usage history.'

'What about the other two handsets?' Warren knew Pymm well enough to know that she would save the best for last.

'Unregistered, pay-as-you-go. Both connected to the network for the first time that evening; neither has connected since then. They were briefly in the vicinity of each other when they first connected at 20.37, close to the Hardingham Centre.'

'The meal would have been well underway by then,' said Warren, excitement mounting.

'Exactly. One phone remained stationary and turned on until we know Paddon left, when it travelled directly to the spot where his car was ambushed. It was turned off roughly three minutes after the car was brought to a stop. The other handset was turned off a couple of minutes after it first connected, before reappearing on the network about an hour later, close to the ambush spot. It was turned off permanently at the same time as the one we think was attached to the car went dark.'

'Prioritise them,' said Warren.

'Already on it. The network are trying to identify the handsets by their IMEI numbers, and the SIM cards by their serial numbers, so we may be able to track down sales. If they were sold online, we might get a customer directly. If they were sold over the counter, we might be able to identify the retailer and pull up CCTV from point of sale.' She frowned. 'Maybe it's time for a bit of good luck?'

'I sincerely hope so,' said Warren. 'In the meantime, we have pretty much an exact time that the killer must have been in the Hardingham Centre's car park to attach the phone to the car. He also had to get himself back out to the country lane to set up the ambush. Get Mags and Hutch to pull CCTV from the surrounding area and start looking for witnesses, so we can place any future potential suspects there.'

'Will do, but it was dark and the car park is around the back of the centre.'

'Do what you can,' said Warren.

*   *   *

Although there would be no let-up over the weekend, sending Swann back to her hotel room on a Friday night with nothing more than the TV, a takeaway, and a burly police officer in the corridor for company seemed rude at best.

It didn't take much to persuade her to at least eat that takeaway with him and Susan in the comfort of their living room. He'd drop her back at the hotel later.

'Wow, how long until the big day?' asked Swann at the sight of Susan's swollen belly.

'Longer than it looks,' said Susan, as she pecked Warren on the cheek. He brandished the paper sack filled with the finest fare their local Indian restaurant had to offer.

'There was a mix-up with the order number and it sat on the side for ages. I said I'd give everything a quick blast in the microwave, rather than wait for him to cook again from scratch.'

'Good call, I'm gnawing my arm off,' said Susan. Lately, her appetite had become insatiable. How she could wolf down a whole madras curry and pinch more of his, but would turn green at the merest whiff of cheese and onion crisps, was a mystery that could only be explained by hormones.

He sent the two women into the lounge whilst he dealt with

the food. There was a half-empty bottle of white wine in the fridge, and he poured Swann a glass, with only a small one for himself so he could drive her back to the hotel later.

They had decided that for the next few hours at least, talk of work was off limits. He was pleased to hear through the open door that the rule was being followed. Swann's sister had just had a baby, and she was recommending a maternity range she swore by.

Waiting for the food to reheat, he leafed through the pile of mail.

Most of it was either junk or bills, and he separated them into piles to be dealt with or shredded before recycling. He opened a shiny black envelope, its brightly coloured address label promising an 'exciting free gift'. More plastic crap for the recycle bin he suspected as he tipped it out on the surface so he could dispose of it.

He had no idea how long he stood there in shock before Susan startled him.

'Hmm, I'm not really sure you're DzzleGrl's target demographic,' she said, reaching for the lurid green lipstick.

'Don't!' said Warren, snatching her hand away. The brand of cosmetics couldn't be a coincidence.

There was another victim.

And the killer knew his home address.

Chapter 54

Grayson had arrived at Warren and Susan's house moments after the CSIs. Several patrol cars, lights flashing, blocked the ends of the street, and uniformed officers in stab vests stood in the rear garden. Warren could only imagine what the neighbours were thinking – he suspected that the Joneses were headlining the neighbourhood WhatsApp group.

'The letter appears to have been delivered by Royal Mail, so there's no evidence the perpetrator has been to your house,' said Andy Harrison, his voice slightly echoey over the mobile phone's speaker.

Warren, Susan, Tony Sutton and Elizabeth Swann were seated around Grayson's dining table. His response had been immediate, and he'd brooked no argument. His wife, Refilwe, was a prominent international human rights lawyer. Over the years, she'd annoyed enough undesirable characters that the Grayson family home, whilst not exactly a fortress, was protected by the best security system on the market. With all of the couple's children now living independently and Refilwe herself overseas, there was no shortage of space.

This evening, that security was supplemented by armed patrol officers. Naseem had authorised their immediate deployment; they'd deal with any longer-term arrangements tomorrow. The whole situation was rather too reminiscent of the Delmarno affair some years previously, and Warren could see his wife was thinking exactly the same thing.

'Get Mags to run through whatever CCTV is available, just in case,' said Grayson. Warren nodded and relayed the password for the digital video recorder in their home office. The numbness had finally worn off, to be replaced by a growing ball of anger in the pit of his stomach.

'No letter this time,' said Swann. 'I wonder why?' At Grayson's insistence, she had retrieved her overnight bag from her hotel room and joined them.

'Are we sure it's even the same person?' asked Tony Sutton. He'd driven straight over as soon as he'd heard the news. 'It could be a copycat. After all, it's come to a different address, and the stationery is different.'

'Christ, that's all we need,' said Grayson.

'We need to assume it's genuine, until we can prove otherwise,' said Warren.

'Has anyone told the poor girl's family yet?' asked Susan.

'We've informed the Missing Persons Unit, who are sending over a support team,' said Sutton, letting out a big sigh. 'But I don't know what they're going to say. That a lipstick from the make-up company she endorses was sent to the SIO of a serial killer investigation? The main thing is just to prepare them for the media storm.'

That it would end up as front-page news was in no doubt, and the timing was not coincidental. The *Reporter* had been following the disappearance of reality TV star Charlotte Gibson since the day she had disappeared. Had the team clicked on the article immediately below that morning's latest revelations from the unknown informant, they would have seen another piece by Cooper about the unexplained disappearance of the DzzleGrl spokesperson. Grayson currently had the article open on his tablet and a copy of the missing persons report on his laptop.

The family of Charley Gibson have renewed their appeal for any information regarding the whereabouts of the Hertfordshire-based TV presenter on the two-month anniversary of her disappearance. The former reality TV star, who has spoken publicly about her long-standing battles with alcohol and drug addiction, and her ongoing mental health issues, was last seen on January 23rd. Her final Instagram post, two days before her disappearance, was on the eve of the first anniversary of her father's death from colon cancer. In it she thanked her 650,000 followers for their support, and said she was taking a break from social media to think about her father.

Her distinctive pink BMW was later found in a church car park in the village of Aust, South Gloucestershire, about ten miles north of Bristol. The church is a short walk from both the Severn Bridge and the banks of the River Severn, leading to speculation that the troubled star may have been travelling to the notorious suicide spot. A spokesperson from Avon and Somerset Police said that an extensive search of the river and the area surrounding it had failed to find her body and she is currently listed as a missing person.

The case of Gibson bears eerie similarities to the 1995 disappearance of Richey Edwards, guitarist with the Welsh band the Manic Street Preachers ...

'It fits the pattern, if we assume she was killed on the Sunday,' said Swann. 'The two-month anniversary is of the last sighting of her car on the M4, which was the Tuesday morning, the day before she was reported missing.'

'So where is her body?' asked Sutton. 'If she was killed on the Sunday night, and the killer drove her car to Gloucestershire on the Tuesday morning, then that leaves thirty-six hours unaccounted for. Did the killer take her body down to the River

Severn and dump her in the water, or is he storing it in a freezer somewhere? Are we even certain he's killed her? Could he be keeping her alive someplace? I don't like to say it, but unlike his other victims, she's a very pretty young woman and a celebrity to boot.' He let the implications of what he was suggesting hang in the air.

'I think he has almost certainly killed her,' said Swann. 'There's no evidence he kept any of his previous victims alive for longer than necessary, and there are no indications of sexual assault. Sexually motivated serial killers tend to be all or nothing. Aside from incidental victims that may have got in the way, they will assault or abuse all of their targets.

'As to whether he transported her body to the River Severn, that would again seem unlikely. All his previous victims were either left where they were killed or dumped in this area. Aust is near Bristol, so it's what, 150 miles away? It doesn't fit his pattern.'

'But we know he is trying to challenge those stereotypes,' said Warren quietly.

Swann conceded the point.

'If he did take her there, how did he get her body into the water?' asked Sutton. 'The bridge and surrounding roads are covered by CCTV to try and catch anybody feeling suicidal. There's no way her bright pink Beamer wouldn't have been spotted. If she committed suicide, there are secluded places along the riverbank that she could have walked to and jumped from. There's no CCTV at the church where her car was left, and it is theoretically possible to make it to the river without being captured on camera.'

'I think Tony's right,' said Grayson. 'I think he did what he needed to up here and then drove her car down to Gloucestershire as a diversion.'

'And it worked for two months,' said Warren. 'Camilla Wong says that they were starting to wind down the investigation, assuming she was either a suicide or had decided to disappear.'

366

'He certainly chose his victim well,' said Susan. She'd been scrolling on her phone. Her involvement in the discussion was somewhat irregular, but in the past, her insights had proven useful. Besides which, the whole investigation was irregular.

She turned her phone around. 'Her Instagram feed is full of posts cataloguing her battles with mental health, alcoholism and prescription drug abuse. I can see why it was believable that she'd kill herself.'

She switched apps. 'Her publicly available Spotify playlist is full of angst-ridden Nineties bands, including lots of early Manic Street Preachers.'

'An easy win for the Missing Persons Unit,' said Grayson. 'I understand why they wanted to close it and move on, but on top of the Winnie Palmer debacle, it doesn't look good for them.'

'We need to start from scratch,' said Warren. 'Full forensics on her house; it's a murder scene until we can rule it out. She was alone that weekend and her phone apparently never left there until it was turned off just after she posted she was taking a break. Did she do that or the killer?'

'You'd think that would have been a warning that things weren't right,' said Susan. 'She was a young woman in her twenties, who pretty much lived on social media. With her history of problems, surely radio silence for that length of time must have raised a flag? Why wasn't she reported missing until the Wednesday?'

'A question I'm sure her loved ones have been asking themselves ever since,' said Warren. He knew from experience that they would forever feel guilty.

'We can submit that last Instagram post to Forensic Linguistics,' said Sutton. 'They might be able to determine if she wrote it, although autocorrect might mess that up if her phone has learnt how she normally types.'

'We also need to fully process her car,' continued Warren. 'There may be trace evidence from when the killer drove it down to Gloucestershire. If he used it to transport her away from her house, then her scent may be in the boot.'

'The case isn't closed yet, so the vehicle should still be secure,' said Grayson.

'How will he have returned home?' asked Swann. 'If he drove down there in her car, he would need to have got back somehow.'

'Good point,' said Warren. 'If we still assume he works alone, then he will have needed to use public transport or hire a car.'

Sutton reached for the tablet. 'Nearest train station is Bristol Parkway. He could go via London, or if he wanted to dodge the security on the underground, he could pay more and change at Birmingham. Alternatively, he could have used the National Express and caught a coach, again from Bristol.'

'How did he travel from Aust to Bristol?' asked Susan.

'Cab or bus is most likely,' said Grayson. 'We'll get Mags to pull in everything from that area.'

'We should also check any CCTV in Aust or at the stations for cyclists,' said Warren. 'We know from the Lagdon killings that he has one of those folding commuter bicycles; not great for long distances but I'm sure it'd do the job.'

'And he'd fit right into the morning rush hour,' said Sutton. 'The last time her car is recorded is just after six a.m. Give him half an hour or so to park and clean the vehicle, then an hour to cycle to Bristol and he'd be turning up at the bus or train station at peak time on a Tuesday morning. I'll get in touch with the Transport Police for anything they have on the trains or the stations. Fingers crossed we can still access any video after two months.'

'If this is really what took place, then the whole thing was meticulously planned,' said Swann. 'How did he know about the lack of CCTV coverage in the area? Or whether it would be plausible for her to walk from where he left the car to the river? He won't have left anything to chance, so was Google Street View good enough, or did he go on a reconnaissance expedition?

'These letters in the post are just his way of boasting. I don't think they are the culmination of his killing spree. If anything, I think he wants us all on edge, waiting to see what he does next.'

She didn't need to say anything else. Sunday was less than twenty-four hours away.

Saturday 24th March

Chapter 55

Warren's eyeballs felt and looked as though they had been rubbed with sandpaper. He'd spent the night wondering how the killer knew his address. They weren't listed in the telephone directory, nor on the publicly available electoral roll. Had the killer followed Warren home?

Fortunately it was a Saturday, so Susan didn't have to worry about going into work, but they would need to inform her school of the potential threat before Monday. The killer wouldn't make it through the locked gates during school hours without an appointment, but hundreds of children would be walking to and from school – could the killer snatch one of them as his next victim? So far, he had only targeted adults, and Swann felt it unlikely he would switch to younger people, but he seemed intent on confounding expectations, so it couldn't be ruled out.

Warren, Swann and Grayson had left early, leaving Susan in the company of the armed officers standing outside. She had insisted Warren join them; the only way to be truly safe was to catch the killer and for that he needed to be with his team. She'd had the presence of mind to grab her laptop the previous evening and was going to try and distract herself with schoolwork, although Warren doubted she'd be successful.

News of the previous night's events had already done the rounds and there was an almost frightening intensity in the office. Even though there was no evidence that the killer had been on their property, it still felt like a violation. He could tell by the handshakes and occasional hug that his close-knit team felt the same way. Although every resource available was being thrown at the searches, preliminary forensics on Charlotte Gibson's house and vehicle weren't due for some hours.

'Nothing of any use on the envelope or the lipstick,' reported Sutton to the morning briefing.

'We've eliminated most of the persons of interest on our combined lists,' said Pymm. 'All of the women that Councillor Paddon was alleged to have assaulted have been cleared. Similarly, we can account for the whereabouts of all his political rivals and their teams on several of the nights in question.'

'That's something at least,' said Warren, although the potential fallout from Paddon being killed by a rival politician bothered him less this morning than it had done yesterday.

'Where are we with the man seen changing clothes outside Winnie Palmer's house?'

'We still can't eliminate Eric Morton,' said Hutchinson. 'Abacus Cabs don't do any jobs for respite centres, but Derek Culverhouse seemed to think the drivers were volunteers anyway, so he could still be the "funny-looking bugger" his dad mentioned. His phone location data shows he was probably out and about in his cab on most of the nights in question but we've yet to track down a customer for any of the nights we're interested in.'

'Not good enough,' said Warren. 'Given that the car he illegally drives is registered to his brother – who is also the person whose identity he used when signing up for work at the cab firm – we can't be sure it was him driving.'

Warren tapped his teeth. Resources were no longer an issue for this investigation, and the killer was likely to strike again within the next day or so. 'I think we have enough to justify putting him under surveillance,' he said. 'Hopefully he'll lead us to wherever he is keeping Charlotte Gibson. If nothing else, we may prevent him committing another murder.'

* * *

Warren felt exhausted, and not just from lack of sleep. He'd met with Charley Gibson's mother and boyfriend before the press conference and their grief was raw. They'd given several press conferences and interviews over the past two months pleading for Charley to return, refusing to accept that she had committed suicide. Now they were in an even worse limbo – was she dead, killed at the hands of a serial killer? Or was she being kept alive by some sick and twisted individual? Was the link even real? The package with the lipstick had none of the earlier signatures, such as the self-printed labels, the black notebook and the supermarket envelope; it could all be some sick joke.

For all they knew, Charley Gibson could have killed herself that fateful Tuesday morning, or just decided to walk out of her life, seeking space to deal with whatever demons plagued her.

But most terrifying of all, could she have been killed by some-body else who was now using their serial killer to cover his or her tracks? Was there another murderer out there that they weren't even aware of?

Chapter 56

'Preliminaries are in from Forensics,' announced Sutton to the afternoon briefing. 'The cadaver dogs have found nothing in Charlotte Gibson's BMW. Subject to a couple more tests, they are prepared to state that there is no evidence her body was transported in her car. The regular sniffer dogs were less conclusive. Unfortunately, there was an old coat in the boot and the handlers can't say with any confidence whether they were picking up on that, or if she had been kept in there alive.

'The original fingerprinting revealed only her prints on the car's controls, which was expected as nobody else was allowed to drive it. The passenger side had those of her boyfriend, mother and her two closest friends. No unknowns. They've now swabbed for DNA.'

'So, two possibilities,' said Warren. 'Either he drove the car and wore gloves. Or he made her drive the car, whilst he was a passenger. Do we have any CCTV to show if there were one or two occupants in the car on its way to Gloucestershire?'

'Sorry,' said Richardson. 'It was dark then and the ANPR footage on the motorway is at the wrong angle.'

'What about her house?' asked Warren.

'The initial search when she first went missing found no

obvious signs of disturbance,' said Sutton, 'but it was a missing person investigation, so it didn't get the full treatment. They've had the blood dogs in, and they were interested in the bathroom adjoining the master bedroom. It is *very* clean. When she's been depressed previously, she's tended, in her mother's words, "to let things slip a bit". The rest of the house isn't dirty, but she'd clearly neglected the housework for a while. It seems unlikely that she cleaned just that room before deciding to take herself off.'

'What about luminol?' asked Ruskin. 'Surely if the killer stabbed her in there and cleaned up, he didn't remove every trace? That's practically impossible.'

'Nothing on any of the tiled surfaces or the shower tray,' said Sutton. 'They are going to dismantle the shower later today and take up the floor to see if anything seeped down there.'

'So, until we hear otherwise, we can't assume she was killed in her house,' said Warren. 'She could have been transported else-where, although I am strongly leaning towards her being killed up here and her body stored, with the trip to Aust a diversion. Hutch, tell us what we know about her living arrangements.'

'She bought the house about fifteen months ago. It's a converted farmhouse, isolated in a rural setting with the neighbours well out of earshot. Quite the place for parties, according to the tabloids.

'It needed a lot of work done, so she stayed with her mum in Hertford initially, and helped care for her father. She moved in last year, a few months after her father passed away, and was joined shortly after by her boyfriend, the boxer Joey Kirkhouse. He was in LA when she disappeared. He isn't listed as next of kin – that's her mum – and he isn't named in her will.

'The other significant men in her life, including her manager and publicist, all have alibis for that period. The initial investi-gation determined that there was no evidence of forced entry to the property. The alarm system was armed when her mother finally came over to check why she wasn't returning her calls. Unfortunately, it's a basic unit that doesn't record when it was set.

There's also no CCTV. Apparently, Kirkhouse had been promising for months to arrange installation of a decent system but hadn't got around to it.'

Warren winced. Video cameras could have answered so many questions about what happened to the TV presenter and perhaps even deterred the killer from taking her; he suspected her boyfriend would be living with that guilt for the rest of his life.

'What about trace evidence?' he asked.

'Luckily, Kirkhouse hasn't stayed there since he flew back from the US after she went missing,' said Hutchinson. 'He just collected some clothes and a few personal belongings under the eagle eye of her mum, so the house is largely untouched. Unfortunately, no tyre tracks were taken the day she was reported missing.'

'What about her electronic footprint?'

'All went dark the Sunday she was last heard from,' said Pymm. 'No social media posts or other communications. She hasn't used any of her bank accounts. Her TV last accessed Netflix Sunday evening. Her last trip to the filling station was the previous Friday, with no evidence of any other lengthy trips, so it was probably close to full when the killer took it.'

'What about the lead-up to her disappearance?' asked Grayson. 'Any changes in her usual patterns?'

'Nothing obvious,' said Pymm. 'They looked into all of that when she went missing. They also looked into anyone creepy on social media. She was a high-profile young woman, so she received plenty of misogynistic abuse on Twitter, most of which her management team blocked or reported. You know how it is with these faceless keyboard warriors, most of them are just weirdos with no social skills who get a sick thrill out of upsetting people. Instagram was also quite cruel, although most of that was just the normal cattiness and bitchiness from other women about her appearance whenever she posted a selfie.' She paused, her voice cracking. 'Listen to me. When did that sort of behaviour become normal?'

Beside her, Ruskin squeezed her shoulder in support. Pymm's fifteen-year-old daughter, Tilly, had been dealing with online bullying for the past six months. The devastating effect on the previously bubbly teenager had been upsetting for the whole family.

Pymm gave him a smile and continued, her voice a little thick. 'There is a team looking into any persistent trolls. Unfortunately, because of her public profile, her posts are visible to anyone, not just followers. If the killer didn't comment or like any of them, there's no way to tell if he was reading them.

'She had a tendency to overshare. She posted a selfie outside her house on the day the sale went through. There weren't many properties for sale in this area of Hertfordshire at that time matching the helpful description and price published by *The Sun* newspaper. It's still archived on the estate agent's website, complete with a photo taken from the same angle as the selfie. Easy pickings for a stalker.'

Warren thanked the team, then turned to Swann.

'There are clear parallels with the Culverhouses here,' she said. 'Converted old properties, limited security, remotely located … However, the only other case where we believe that the killer entered the home was Winnie Palmer's. That was in a residential street with neighbours so that could just be a coincidence.'

'The social media angle is worth pursuing, as it may be how he identified her and perhaps even found out when she was especially vulnerable,' said Swann. 'The tone of her posts in the run-up to her father's anniversary clearly indicate, at least with the benefit of hindsight, that she was struggling with her mental health. We also know the killer used Councillor Paddon's public Facebook page to determine where he would be that evening.

'But the Culverhouses and Winnie Palmer had no social media presence, and the Lagdon brothers were hardly Instagram stars. Our killer is practised and methodical, not impulsive, so I doubt he has left us a breadcrumb trail by liking or commenting on her posts.'

Warren thanked the two women. 'Right, people, Charley Gibson is another piece of the puzzle. Re-interview anyone initially spoken to and widen the net. The initial interviews focused on her mental health and motives for disappearing. Now we know she was taken against her will, dig deeper. Was her change in demeanour before she disappeared solely due to the upcoming anniversary of her father's death, or was something or somebody else worrying her?'

He took a sip of water.

'Our next question is why did our killer target her? What is so special about her? Look into her history and day-to-day existence. Look for any overlap with our other victims and record any names or places. Rachel, I want you to let HOLMES work its magic on her phone and financial records. The connection between our victims could be something as tenuous as shopping at the same store or a visit from the same washing machine repair engineer. Maybe the algorithms can make that link.'

Warren knew he was asking a lot. HOLMES was one of the most sophisticated computer systems of its kind, designed for just this sort of challenge. Its constantly updated dynamic reasoning engine could make links that a couple of decades ago would have required hundreds of person-hours or sheer blind luck. But even in the twenty-first century, where it seemed that everyone on the planet was connected to one another by invisible, electronic filaments of data, most interactions between individuals still went unrecorded, or were inaccessible to the database.

Warren's gut told him that the person they so desperately needed to find knew enough to stop those connections being made.

Chapter 57

The caller ID on Warren's desk phone showed a familiar-looking internal number that his tired brain just couldn't recall.

'DCI Jones,' he answered, stifling a yawn.

'Sir, it's DS Mickie from the Social Media Unit. I've emailed you a link. You need to check it out, right now.' The woman's voice was unfamiliar, but there was no mistaking the urgency that accounted for her abruptness.

Right on cue, an email appeared in his inbox. He opened it and clicked the link, which the Force's software had already scanned for viruses or other malware.

'Son of a ...'

* * *

'The "Sunday Night Slayer" is what he's calling himself,' said Warren.

'That's crap,' said Sutton. 'He'd have been better off with the "Middlesbury Murderer"; at least both words begin with the same letter.'

'It's not about the name. He's trying to control the narrative,' said Swann. 'He's a narcissist. It's not unprecedented; Dennis

Rader gave himself the moniker BTK – Bind, Torture, Kill. I think he's banking on the name being memorable.'

'It's definitely legit,' said Ruskin. 'There are details here we haven't revealed to the press.'

The website had been flagged by the Social Media Unit, who'd been monitoring tweets with hashtags relating to the killings. The Twitter account had been set up just hours previously and sent only a single tweet – a link to a website located on a free hosting site based in Eastern Europe. The unit were now racing to get posts sharing the link across other social media platforms removed, but it had already gone viral.

'He's uploaded everything he's sent us, word for word,' said Ruskin, who'd been trawling through the crudely designed webpages. 'It's all here, complete with photos.'

'Anything about Charley Gibson?'

Ruskin manipulated the mouse. 'Yes, there's a blog post dedicated to her.'

Warren swallowed the bile that threatened to burst forth. 'Show us,' he managed.

Ruskin clicked the link. 'Fuck …' he breathed.

* * *

Warren sat alone in his office, with only a single desk lamp for illumination. Those remaining from the day shift were taking a break at Warren's insistence. He closed his eyes and massaged his temples, the paracetamol he'd scrounged off Rachel Pymm ineffective. Poor sleep, too much coffee and constant stress were the causes of the problem; along with avoiding the optician. Like it or not, he was in his forties and reading glasses were beckoning.

He still tasted the bile that he'd swallowed.

'Could this be about me?' he'd asked as the confessionals had again taunted him by name. The sight of his own picture at the top of the blog post dedicated to each victim had sent horrified gasps around the room. The image was an old headshot, posted on the force's website years ago, but it was still chilling.

In the years since first coming to Middlesbury, he'd worked many cases and inevitably his public profile had increased. Press conferences, interviews appealing for witnesses, even statements read out on behalf of victims' loved ones after the courts had delivered their verdict. The thought that he might be seen as some sort of worthy adversary to a deluded killer – a killer who sought his attention by murdering innocent people – made him nauseous.

'Could I even know this person?' he'd asked.

'Not necessarily,' Swann had said. 'He started sending letters long after you were named as SIO. It's quite possible that had somebody else taken charge, he would be addressing them.'

She'd made perfect sense, but that couldn't quash Warren's sense of shame, or fear.

'You'll need to add me into the mix,' he'd managed, his voice steadier than he felt. 'Look at the cases I've worked since I started here. There are plenty of people who might hold a grudge against me, but nobody still out on the streets who would ...' He'd trailed off, unable to voice the thoughts.

Derek Culverhouse had been formally cleared earlier that evening; it should have brought relief, but hearing that his parents had been the victims of a deranged serial killer had destroyed him. The blood on the dashboard of his car had been from a particularly persistent nosebleed exacerbated by his father's blood thinners. Karen Hardwick had tracked down the woman at his father's bowls club who'd called Derek to come and take him to A&E the previous month.

Warren thought back to the horrific website. The details contained within its pages had confirmed much of what the team had deduced for themselves, but still left one vital question unanswered.

Why had he done it?

The rambling musings about how the Culverhouses had nothing to live for anymore, with lives beset by pain and illness, had struck him as a desperate attempt to justify the unjustifiable; Swann had agreed. And how had he chosen them? His boasts had contained little concrete information on that score. Could it be because revealing that connection would lead them to his door?

Again, Warren felt the anger rising within him. The killer had written about the elderly couple's meaningless lives, dressing it up as a social commentary. But he had been wrong. The Culverhouses faced challenges, and in the case of Mrs Culverhouse a short and painful future. Her adoring husband doubtless spent sleepless nights contemplating the suffering he was powerless to alleviate, and the inevitable loss of the person he loved most in the world.

But even in that darkness, there was hope. The couple had a close circle of loved ones, and they were planning a party to celebrate fifty years of marriage.

Winnie Palmer might have been lonely, still missing her husband, perhaps even regretting that they'd never had children. But despite what the killer saw on the outside, she too was loved. Her friends at church and the Wednesday Club missed her dry sense of humour and sympathetic ear. Her oldest friend, now in a home, had valued her visits. Even her dog, taken in by another member of the Wednesday Club, still pined for her in her absence.

And what about Charley Gibson? A young woman with her whole future ahead of her. She'd had her problems, but then who didn't? The trite quote from Voltaire that the killer had started her entry with, '*It is not love that should be depicted as blind, but self-love*', was a pathetic attempt to depict her as a vapid narcissist, feeding off the hollow adulation that came from so-called celebrity culture. Did the killer recognise the irony?

He'd boasted of the way he'd hidden his tracks for so long, laughing as the police believed the plot he'd so carefully constructed – a troubled young woman, with highly publicised demons, finally putting an end to her pain. He'd let himself into

384

her house, sneaking into the en-suite bathroom as she lay slumbering, alcohol and prescription antidepressants finally helping her blot out the world for a few precious hours. There he'd waited, until eventually she'd awoken to use the toilet. Still groggy, she didn't stand a chance as he cut her throat from ear-to-ear.

Again, he'd made no mention of how he had chosen her. Was she just a random celebrity he had come across on Instagram, or had he met her elsewhere? Was that the key to identifying him? And where was her body? Of all his victims, she was the only one whose whereabouts remained unknown. Was she still frozen somewhere or was she already out there waiting for an innocent member of the public to stumble across something they would never unsee?

The killer had regarded her relationship with her boyfriend as shallow; vacuous. A paper-thin construct conducted publicly for the benefit of their careers, validated by likes and comments from their followers on social media. But Warren had met Joey Kirkhouse. He'd been broken; as devastated as any loved one Warren had ever encountered. Would their love have defied the odds and lasted forever, or would it have publicly crashed and burned, its bones picked apart by armchair pundits? Who could tell? But then wasn't that uncertainty the same of any relationship, high profile or not?

The Lagdon brothers, or even Councillor Paddon if your personal politics were that important to you, could easily be demonised, yet they all had futures. What right did the killer have to take that away? Warren wasn't fooled for one second by his grandiose musings. They were boasts by a man who sought only attention. An audience to gratify his own ego.

If … when … they caught him, there would be attempts by some to justify his behaviour. To explain how a disrupted childhood, a bang on the head, even a genetic predisposition were the root cause of his social deviancy.

But Warren just didn't give a shit.

385

Chapter 58

It was getting late, but Warren held one last meeting with his team.

'At least he's confirmed that he killed Winnie Palmer on New Year's Eve,' said Sutton. 'So the man getting dressed in the street still has to be our main suspect.'

'We need to determine when their paths crossed,' said Warren. 'When did he steal the purse? Was it in the corner shop, or on her walk home?'

'We have CCTV from New Year's Eve,' said Richardson, 'but it sounds as though he started grooming her long before then.'

'Hutch, speak to that friend of hers again,' said Warren. 'The one who said she'd met a young man. See if she remembers anything else at all.'

'Will do, I'll also talk to the vicar, and I'll get a team to canvass everyone at her social club.'

Grayson looked thoughtful. 'My mum belongs to a club close to where she lives, but they regularly go on trips and socialise with other groups across the city. I'll bet the Hardingham Centre hosts a social group.'

'It's got to be worth a look,' said Warren.

'I'll take that,' said Hardwick. 'We think she let him in so perhaps he's a volunteer or works there?'

'Take another look at the staff working the night Councillor Paddon was killed,' said Sutton. 'The fire doors were covered by CCTV and alarmed, and the windows were supposedly locked, but where are the keys? Could somebody have climbed out a window in the store room or one of the toilets?'

'What about the Culverhouses?' suggested Richardson. 'Their paths didn't seem to cross with Winnie Palmer, but if it's a member of staff or a volunteer that's associated with several groups, that "funny-looking bugger" could be our man.'

'That still leaves the other victims,' said Hutchinson. 'I can't see the Lagdons hanging around a community centre, unless they were selling drugs.'

'Isn't their mother ill?' said Ruskin. 'Perhaps they used to take her to a social centre?'

'Which just leaves Charlotte Gibson,' said Grayson.

'Her father died of cancer,' said Pymm. 'Perhaps she sought support from the voluntary sector?'

'Hell of a gap, though,' said Sutton. 'Her dad died twelve months before she disappeared. Which suggests that the killer identified her as a target over a year ago. Could he have been planning it this long?'

Warren considered what they had all said. Could that be what connected them? A sick, depraved individual hunting his victims under the guise of a volunteer? The link appeared tenuous at best, but it had to be worth a shot; their killer would likely strike again within the next thirty-six hours. They couldn't afford to ignore any theories.

The call from the force's cybercrime department came just as Warren was dismissing everyone for the night, and he and Lizzie Swann were preparing to return to Grayson's.

'Bad news about the website,' said the technician. 'It's owned by a Moldovan "bulletproof" provider, and we can't raise a warrant to get it taken down or access its traffic logs.'

'Is there anything we can do to identify where he's connecting from?' asked Grayson.

'No, I'm sorry, sir. The host specialises in websites that are all but impossible to keep a track of. Even if we could get a court order to force UK-based internet providers to block users from accessing the site, it would be useless. It masks its true IP address with an encrypted redirection service. We can't even be sure what country its servers are physically located in.'

'What about the pictures he posted?' asked Sutton.

'The images have had their metadata removed. We can't tell what sort of device was used to take the original photograph.'

Warren wasn't entirely surprised, but it was still a bitter blow.

'How many people have accessed the site?' he asked.

'Impossible to tell for sure, but there are dozens of comments on each page.' He paused. 'Most are calling him a sick bastard, or words to that effect … but a lot aren't.'

'He's building an audience,' said Swann. 'In the Seventies and Eighties serial killers would sometimes contact newspapers and demand that their so-called manifestoes be published. These days they can speak to the world directly.'

It was a disturbing notion. Most of the anonymous internet users trawling the killer's archives were probably just the morbidly curious, sickened and enthralled in equal parts. But not all. Cybercrime had uncovered links to the site on message boards hidden on the dark web, the underbelly of the internet that most users were unaware of and unable to access through the usual portals cataloguing the so-called surface web. It was a vast, unpoliced playground welcoming predators like their killer with open arms. There was no doubt in Warren's mind that at least a few of the people reading through the sickening descriptions were getting a thrill … and perhaps even harbouring ideas of their own.

Sunday 25th March

Chapter 59

To say that Warren woke early on Sunday morning would be a misrepresentation. Rather, he decided it was a reasonable enough hour to roll out of the bed in John Grayson's guest room, and tiptoe downstairs for a coffee.

Grayson was already sitting at the breakfast bar, a stack of newspapers by his elbow. His eyes were as red as Warren's felt. Moments later, Swann arrived, mobile phone in hand.

'It's hit the papers,' Swann and Grayson said at almost the same moment.

Word of the killer's website had reached the local, national and even international press in plenty of time for it to dominate several front pages. If the killer wanted to make a splash, then he'd timed it just right; the Sunday tabloids were besides themselves with excitement.

'Nothing new on the website since we went home last night,' said Grayson, 'but plenty of so-called experts have had time to air their considered opinions.' Without asking, Grayson handed them both a cup of coffee. It was the extra-strong blend he kept for 'special occasions'. They were going to need it.

* * *

'What have Eric Morton's surveillance team got to report?' asked Warren in the team briefing. Authorisation for continuous observation of the erstwhile taxi-driver and bouncer who remained their number-one suspect had been granted without hesitation.

'They've been in an unlet apartment across the street from his brother's house since yesterday afternoon,' said Richardson. 'We have a confirmed sighting of him entering the property at four p.m. and he was still there at eight a.m.'

'What about his brother and family?' asked Warren.

'Uncertain. We believe they were already in the house when surveillance started. We have tentative IDs of his sister-in-law and children before they closed the curtains yesterday evening. No sign of his brother. His car is in the drive, and his mobile phone is in the house, but we haven't had eyes-on.'

It was the best they could hope for in the circumstances. Knowing the location of Morton eased the burning in the pit of Warren's stomach somewhat. If he left the house, the surveillance team would follow him. Pre-approval for Authorised Firearms Officers had been granted, on the grounds that the handgun used to kill Nick Lagdon was still outstanding. If Morton was their man, then hopefully he would be stopped before he could kill again. Ideally, they'd also secure enough evidence to prove his intent, but the preservation of life was the over-riding goal. If he was sufficiently spooked that he abandoned his plans for the evening, then that was a victory.

'Where are we with Charley Gibson's close contacts?' he asked Hutchinson.

'All her closest friends and family either gave new witness statements yesterday or are coming in today. We've also identified a few more close friends that weren't interviewed initially. Any names or details that make the interviewer's nose twitch will be flagged immediately so we can jump on them ASAP.'

'Forensics?' asked Warren, turning to Sutton.

'The floor tiles are up in the bathroom. They've found tiny

traces of blood that seeped through a gap in the grouting. Andy Harrison reckons it's the best clean-up job he's ever seen. It must have taken hours.'

'That probably accounts for the twenty-four hours or so between her murder and the sighting of her car on the Tuesday morning,' said Hardwick. 'Still ballsy though. After she posted that message on social media about feeling down, her mum or a friend could have come around unannounced to see why she wasn't answering her phone.'

'Probably just as well they didn't,' said Ruskin. 'I can't imagine he'd have taken kindly to a knock on the door whilst he was on his hands and knees with a scrubbing brush.'

'What else?' asked Warren.

'Alarm and lock specialists are at the Culverhouses' and Charley Gibson's,' said Sutton. 'It seems the bugger got in without triggering anything or forcing a door or window. Did he have access to the codes and copies of their keys? Did he bypass the system physically or by exploiting a flaw? Did he charm his way in, like he claims to have done with Winnie Palmer? Or is he lying to us and in reality, he set it off and just took them out when they came down to investigate?'

'That sort of lie wouldn't be inconsistent with his personality type,' interjected Swann. 'He has been desperate to showcase his cleverness. I have no doubt he is willing to exaggerate or even fabricate events if it makes him seem smarter. Being able to hack a burglar alarm or pick a lock would feed into that.'

Warren looked at the wall clock. Earlier that morning, it had felt as if the second hand was racing around the clock-face, counting down towards the moment that their killer next struck. Now it seemed to have slowed to a crawl, as they settled in for another day of waiting.

He concluded the meeting; his team were busy and they all had plenty to do, none of which would be accomplished in an overcrowded, stuffy briefing room.

'I don't know how you stand it,' said Swann when everyone else had left. She leant against the wall. 'I'm not going to lie, I always wondered what it would be like to work on a live investigation. But now that I'm here, contributing whatever small insight I have, I realise that I never really understood the pressure you are all under; knowing that not only is there someone out there who needs to be brought to justice, but that he is almost certain to kill again.

'How do you sleep at night?'

Warren gave a tight smile. 'I don't.'

Chapter 60

'That was the security specialists,' said Sutton as he hung up his phone. 'If the locks were tampered with on either house, any damage is insufficient to stand out from normal wear and tear. They are also as sure as they can be that there are no recently replaced windows in either property.'

'So the killer didn't break a window and then hide his tracks,' said Warren. 'What about the alarm systems?'

'Both properties had older systems made by different manufacturers, but they are in perfect working order, with no evidence that the sensors have been messed with. Neither have the control panels. There are no fingerprints other than the homeowners'; DNA is pending, but I can't imagine he'd have been that careless.'

'So either he knew their codes, or he charmed his way in,' suggested Hardwick from her workstation.

'There is another possibility,' said Sutton. 'Apparently, there are backdoor codes for both models to allow alarm engineers to gain entry if necessary. I asked if that implied that our killer might have links to alarm fitters, but he admitted you can find them on the internet.'

'So, to go back to what Karen suggested,' said Warren, 'assuming he didn't force his way in, then either he charmed them, somehow knew the alarm code, or already knew what sort of system they had so he could look it up on online.'

'Meaning the victims must have been linked to the killer in some fashion,' finished Sutton.

* * *

'I'm at the Hardingham Centre,' said Ruskin over the speakerphone. 'They were burgled about five years ago and upgraded the windows and the doors; all of them are double-glazed and lockable. However, the keys are in the kitchen; anyone who works at the centre knows where they are.'

'Are any of the windows suitable for getting in and out of there without being noticed? Particularly during a busy fundraiser?' asked Sutton.

'The disabled loo has a window that I reckon is big enough for someone my size if they stand on the toilet seat. It isn't covered by the outside cameras.'

'What about getting back in?' asked Warren. 'Everyone who attended that night, staff included, left by the main entrance, so the killer didn't hop out the window, stick the mobile phone to Councillor Paddon's Jag, and then leave.'

'Doable, I reckon,' replied Ruskin. 'There's a waste pipe outside you could use to boost yourself up.'

'Seal the area,' ordered Warren. 'I'm sending a CSI team down.'

Warren doubted the killer had been careless enough to leave fingerprints, but they might find a shoe print on the toilet seat or the waste pipe, or clothing fibres on the window frame.

Ending the call, he turned to Hardwick. 'How are you doing with the social club angle?'

'The Hardingham Centre hosts several different clubs; everything from the original Duke of Edinburgh group set up by the late reverend, to the WI and Pilates for Pensioners. There is also a group aimed at older members: tea and cake, bingo, guest speakers and days out. All of the clubs are run by volunteers, so I'm compiling a list.

'We've finally identified the respite centre that Jemima Culverhouse attended. I am also waiting for names of volunteers and staff associated with Winnie Palmer's Wednesday Club.'

'What about the others?'

'That's more tricky. Charley Gibson's dad wasn't that old, so he wasn't a member of any volunteer-run social clubs. His main interactions with charities or volunteer services were with Macmillan Cancer Support and the RVS coffee shop in the hospital. Charley or her mother drove him for appointments when he was too ill to drive himself.'

'Sounds unlikely,' admitted Warren. 'What about the Lagdons?'

'Their mum *is* ill, and they did drive her to hospital appointments. But her only social club is a more general group for the Afro-Caribbean community. The community policing team are trying to persuade them to share their volunteers and members list with us. But to be honest, even if they do, I'm not sure how useful it would be. They've confirmed that pretty much everyone is black or mixed-race, which doesn't fit our profile.'

'There is another problem,' said Sutton. 'Eric Morton was definitely not on the guest list for the fundraiser and Abacus Cabs swear he was no longer working for them by the time Councillor Paddon was killed.'

'Which means that either he attached the mobile phone in the car park without ever entering the centre,' said Warren, 'or we have a team of officers watching the wrong man, whilst our killer is free to plot his next move.'

Chapter 61

'I have an overlap between Winnie Palmer's club and the Hardingham Centre,' said Hardwick, her cheeks flushed with excitement.

Warren turned away from his laptop.

'Seth Lovesy. Forty-six years old and a volunteer minibus driver, with a day job as a freelance courier and a bit of taxi driving on the side. He owns a van and a dark blue, five-door Mercedes.'

'Sounds promising,' agreed Warren. 'Anything on the system?'

'Nothing, but that's not really a surprise,' she replied. 'He'd have needed an enhanced DBS check to work with vulnerable adults so any prior convictions or concerns would have been flagged.'

'Does he match the description of the man seen getting changed outside Winnie Palmer's house on New Year's Eve?'

'That I don't know,' said Hardwick. 'He's lived at his current address for so long, he's still got an old-style, paper driving licence, so the DVLA don't have a photo of him.'

Warren stood up. He'd have liked to track down a photo or description, but he knew that every second they wasted was another second their killer had to plan his next attack. For all they knew, he could be out there already, targeting his next victim.

'Bring him in.'

Behind Hardwick, the support worker who had been monitoring the surveillance team on Eric Morton popped his head around the door.

'Sir, the surveillance team on Eric Morton report movement.'

Warren took the radio handset from him.

'He's just exited the property and got into the driver's seat of a black Vauxhall Insignia,' came the quiet voice of the lead surveillance officer.

'So much for his driving ban,' muttered Sutton as Warren entered the main office.

'Was he carrying anything?' asked Warren.

'Negative. No bags and he's not wearing a jacket. His trouser pockets aren't bulging suspiciously.' She paused. 'He's starting the engine.'

Could this be what they had been waiting for? Was their killer about to make his move? If Morton was their killer, then he kept the bodies and any equipment he used somewhere other than his brother's house. Could he be driving to that location to get prepared for whatever he was planning that night?

'Follow him,' ordered Warren. 'Do not let him out of your sight.' He picked up the phone and dialled the gold commander in charge of the team of authorised firearms officers currently standing by. Having them on operational readiness for all this time wasn't cheap, but they couldn't risk a delay if their target presented a threat to the public.

Over the radio, he could hear a car engine; the surveillance officer kept up a running commentary, complementing the vehicle's GPS tracker.

'There are some lock-up garages about two miles further on, if he stays on this road,' said Pymm highlighting a digital map. 'That could be where he keeps his stuff.'

'If he has a freezer there, he'll need an electricity supply,' said Sutton.

'There are some privately leased, powered units up there,' said Pymm. 'But before you ask, I already had someone contact all storage companies within fifty miles of Middlesbury last week. They all require payment either by credit card or standing order from a bank account, so either our killer isn't on our suspect list, or somebody else is footing the bill.'

'Unit One: Suspect turning left left onto Redbridge Road,' interrupted the radio. 'Speed forty, no sign he's clocked us. Maintaining distance.'

'Unit Two: We're two cars behind Unit One. Maintaining visual contact.'

A moment later. 'Unit One: Suspect vehicle has turned left left onto Poplar Street, last-minute decision. Will continue on Redbridge Road and cut through.'

'Unit Two: We still have him, turning onto Poplar now.'

'Shit, do you think he's seen them?' asked Sutton.

'Unit Two: Suspect vehicle is continuing along Poplar Street, speed thirty. Continuing pursuit.'

'Unit One: We're parallel on Aspen, we'll try to get ahead and rejoin, but we'll have to go noisy.' The pitch of the vehicle's engine increased as the trained driver accelerated. The vehicle's sirens started. They had no choice; they were in a residential area on a pleasant Sunday afternoon; they couldn't go racing down the road without alerting other road users to their presence.

Warren bit his lip; he hoped they didn't spook Morton.

'Unit Two: Suspect is pulling into customer car park for the Sainsbury's Local.'

'I'll park up the street,' interjected the driver.

'ARV thirty seconds away,' cut in another voice, from the Armed Response Vehicle.

Warren swallowed.

'I have eyes on suspect,' confirmed the passenger in Unit Two. 'He's exiting the vehicle.'

'Follow him,' ordered Warren. The last thing they needed was for Morton to walk in the front of the convenience store and disappear out the back.

'Unit One on scene,' came the voice from the first car, its sirens now silent.

'Suspect is entering Sainsbury's,' came the voice of the passenger from Unit Two, accompanied by the sound of a car door closing. 'There are plenty of customers. I'll maintain pursuit.' Her voice was little more than a whisper.

The passenger from Unit One confirmed he was doing the same a few seconds later.

Warren closed his eyes, trying to conjure up the scene from the ambient noise over the officers' radio. A mechanical hum signalled the opening of the store's automatic doors, and the background noise changed to that of shoppers. He swallowed again as he heard the unmistakable pitch of a child's voice. A metallic rattle indicated Unit Two had picked up a basket to blend in better. 'He's in the snack aisle,' she muttered, 'loading up on crisps and nuts.'

What was he doing? Picking up junk food for an evening in front of the TV, or sourcing supplies to fuel him as he did whatever he planned later that night?

'He's now heading down the medicines aisle,' continued Unit Two.

'I've got him,' whispered Unit One. Warren pictured the two officers seamlessly handing over the pursuit to avoid being noticed.

'He's picking up paracetamol and ibuprofen,' relayed Unit One, then he went silent for a moment. 'Heading to the self-service checkout.'

'I'll wait outside,' came the voice of Unit Two. Warren heard the quiet clatter of the basket being replaced, and the hum of the automatic doors.

'Excuse me, madam, can I have a word?' The voice was male and firm.

'Shit, she's been stopped by security,' said Unit One.

'You are bloody joking,' groaned Sutton.

There came a few tense seconds as Unit Two tried to discreetly tell the overzealous guard to back off. There came the sound of a zip, as she produced her warrant card.

'Target is looking at his phone,' came the voice of Unit One. 'I don't think he's noticed what's going on. Which means he's the only bloody person who hasn't.'

Finally, Unit Two persuaded the security guard to let her go. 'I'm burned,' she said. 'I'm going to walk up the street away from my vehicle.'

Now there was only one officer in the small shop.

'Status, Unit One?' asked Warren urgently.

'All good,' he replied. 'He's next in line. I have my warrant card to hand, but it looks like Unit Two has warned security off.'

Back at CID, the team waited impatiently. How long did it take for someone to pay for a basket of junk food and painkillers?

'He's outside,' came Unit One's voice eventually.

'I have eyes on him,' came the voice of the driver from Unit Two. 'He's getting into his car.'

'ARV standing by,' confirmed the gold commander. The vehicle was parked in a side street, engine running.

'He's on the move, turning back the way he came,' said Unit One, accompanied by the slam of a car door.

'Where's he going?' asked Sutton of no one in particular.

'Turning right right onto Redbridge Road,' came the next announcement.

'That's in the opposite direction to the lock-ups,' confirmed Pymm.

'He's returning home, isn't he?' said Sutton. Moments later, Unit Two confirmed Morton's entrance to the street where his brother's house was situated.

'Unit One and Unit Two, return to base,' ordered Warren, concealing his disappointment. The surveillance team in the house could continue to watch him, whilst the pursuit team switched to new vehicles in case they needed to follow him again.

'Do you think he was testing us?' asked Ruskin.

'I don't know,' admitted Warren. If Morton thought he was being followed, then he would certainly not be going out that night.

He forced a smile that he didn't truly feel. 'If nothing else, then we know he won't be killing anyone later,' adding silently, *if he's even our man.*

* * *

'Not a chance,' said Sutton. They were watching Karen Hardwick interviewing Seth Lovesy. Their target had opened the door to his flat dressed in tracksuit bottoms and a scruffy *Star Wars* T-shirt. Which was ironic.

'He's certainly a funny-looking bugger, but if you painted him green, he'd look like bloody Yoda,' said Sutton. 'Unless he can use the Force, there's no way he's hoicking dead bodies around.'

It was a rather uncharitable observation, but not entirely inaccurate. Their suspect was barely five feet tall, had a bald head with whisps of hair, buck teeth, and prominent ears. He'd been alarmed by the presence of the forced entry team outside his door but had been more than willing to attend the station 'to clear things up'. Either the drunk couple from New Year's Eve had consumed something stronger than alcohol, or he wasn't their man.

Warren's stomach burned.

* * *

'No new witnesses for Charley Gibson,' said Hutchinson, slumped into Warren's visitor's chair. 'We've spoken to her nearest neighbours again, now that we know she was probably killed that weekend, rather than going missing two days later. None of them are close enough to see or hear anything, and nobody's CCTV extends beyond their own property.'

Karen Hardwick appeared at the door.

'Seth Lovesy's alibis check out,' she said. 'The Samaritans confirm that he takes calls overnight twice a week, including each of the Sundays we're interested in. They wouldn't release details because of data protection, but they have a log and he took several on each of those occasions. He uses his landline, so we can place him at home, which matches his neighbours' recollections.'

'Never mind,' managed Warren, concealing his disappointment. It was late and the tension within the team was increasing hour by hour as they approached midnight. If they were wrong about their suspect, then the killer could already have selected his victim. Would they get a call within the next twenty-four hours informing them of his latest atrocity, or would they have to wait for days until another body was found? Would he announce his latest action on his website, or send something in the post?

'You know,' said Hardwick, giving a tired smile, 'we deal with some of the shittiest human beings on the planet. It's easy to forget that people like Seth Lovesy exist. He really is one of the good guys.'

Warren forced a smile of his own. He shared her sentiment, but at the moment, he was a lot more worried about one of the bad guys.

Monday 26th March

Chapter 62

This time, Warren was the first downstairs. Exhaustion meant he had finally dozed for a few hours, but his sleep had been fitful, disturbed by unsettling dreams that he couldn't remember.

By the time Grayson and Swann joined him, he had the coffee machine on and bread in the toaster. It still seemed strange to be so at ease in his boss's house, but Grayson had been insistent that his three guests treat his home as their own. His wife had been overseas for almost two months; Warren suspected he was enjoying the company.

'No reports of any suspicious deaths or missing persons,' he informed them, 'and no sign of life at Eric Morton's brother's house overnight. The upstairs lights came on a few minutes ago.'

'His kids are still primary school age,' said Grayson. 'If it's anything like our house was, they'll be dragging them out of bed and hunting missing socks any minute now.'

Warren heard the creak of a floorboard from upstairs. Susan's school had agreed that for safeguarding reasons it would be inappropriate for her to attend school until a full risk assessment was completed. She would set cover work as if she was sick.

'So, have we dodged a bullet?' asked Grayson. 'Yesterday's jaunt to Sainsbury's could have been a test. If he spotted the surveillance, then perhaps he aborted his plans?'

His tone was upbeat, but the optimism didn't reach his eyes. If Morton wasn't their killer, then they had wasted hours watching an innocent man, whilst their target went about his business.

*　*　*

The call came shortly before midday.

'Everybody, main briefing room, ten minutes,' Warren ordered through the open door of his office. 'It looks like he's struck again. And this time there are two.'

*　*　*

'Glynn and Shona Bevan. Last seen yesterday evening, shortly after seven, by Mrs Bevan's mother, who was babysitting.'

A wedding photo of a couple in their early thirties had been projected onto the briefing room screen.

'They were only reported missing two hours ago,' said Warren. 'Fortunately, somebody on the ball at Missing Persons escalated it to me.'

He took a sip of water. 'So far we know that yesterday was Mr and Mrs Bevan's wedding anniversary. They had a baby seven months ago, and Shona's mother was visiting from Scotland for a week. Yesterday evening was the first time they had been out as a couple since the birth.

'Shona put plenty of milk in the fridge, with formula if it ran out, so Grandma told them to go and enjoy themselves, and have a lie-in this morning. Grandma slept in the nursery with the baby and had an early night. She got up a couple of times to do a feed but let the couple sleep.

'Shortly before ten this morning she finally decided that the baby really needed Mum, and discovered that their room was empty, and their bed hadn't been slept in. She called both of

408

their mobiles, checked her voicemail, even looked at WhatsApp. That was when she called 999.'

Warren looked around the room. 'Obviously, there may be other explanations for why the couple have disappeared, but these were new parents, anxious about leaving their daughter for more than a few hours. Shona phoned her mother twice from the restaurant to check everything was OK and texted to say when they were leaving. Unfortunately, her mother was already asleep, so didn't raise the alarm sooner.'

Ordinarily, Rachel Pymm would have made a quip about Grandma taking on more than she bargained for, but she said nothing; nobody in the room was in the mood for humour.

'It seems highly unlikely they will have decided to voluntarily leave their daughter, which leaves no happy explanations. Until we have evidence to the contrary, we have to assume they have been taken by the killer and we will proceed as if they are currently alive. I am liaising with Missing Persons and an emergency appeal for their whereabouts has been issued to the media. This is currently our number-one priority and Tony Sutton will be issuing job lists.' Warren looked at his watch. 'Team leaders reconvene for a status briefing in two hours.'

* * *

'Eric Morton was not involved,' said Richardson, hanging up her phone. 'He never left the house all night, there's no rear access to the property, and the surveillance team watched him accompany his sister-in-law walking the kids to school. Interestingly, they seemed rather closer than one might expect for in-laws.' She shrugged. 'Just an observation.'

Warren frowned. 'If Morton is having an affair with his brother's wife, then that raises some interesting questions about their domestic arrangements, given that he's been staying there since his ex kicked him out. I wonder if there's anything else they're sharing?'

'What are you thinking, boss?' asked Sutton.

'Have the surveillance team actually set eyes on his brother since they arrived yesterday?'

Richardson started scrolling through her emails.

Warren turned to Swann. 'You've read what little we have on his brother. Could we be looking at the wrong person? Could they even be working together?'

'I can't think of anything that would make Kyle any less likely as a suspect.' She paused for a moment. 'In fact, his brother's job would require a higher degree of literacy than it would appear Eric has. I could definitely be persuaded that he is more likely to be the author of those notes and the posts on the website.'

'And the car Eric used for his cab driving is actually registered to his brother,' Pymm reminded them. 'After that, most of our evidence against Eric is circumstantial, such as phone locations and traffic cameras. There's nothing directly contradicting his brother's involvement.'

'No reports of sightings of the brother at all during the surveillance op,' said Richardson.

'Then we need to confirm his whereabouts, immediately,' ordered Warren.

Chapter 63

'We have confirmation that Mr and Mrs Bevan arrived at the Piccola Venezia Italian restaurant just before seven-thirty last night, for a pre-booked table.' Richardson projected an image from a CCTV camera above the entrance. The main briefing room was only half filled, primarily by the team leaders for the different strands of the rapidly moving investigation.

'The restaurant was quiet, and we have clear footage of them throughout their meal. They interacted with nobody except the serving staff, and don't appear to have used the bathrooms at the same time as any other customers. We're tracing all staff and customers as we speak. They paid at their table and left at nine-fifteen.'

'How did they travel?' asked Warren.

'They used a pre-booked taxi from Abacus Cabs to get there,' said Pymm. 'I have a second phone call from Mr Bevan's mobile to the same firm at 21.08. Unfortunately, they were quoted a waiting time of forty-five to sixty minutes.'

'Could Eric Morton or his brother have got wind of that job call?' asked Sutton.

'We're checking now,' confirmed Pymm.

'We can see him phoning for a taxi on the CCTV, after which

they have a discussion, before leaving,' continued Richardson. 'It doesn't look as though he tried to call another taxi firm. I have spoken to the bus companies, and there was one due in ten minutes from the main stand on the high street that would have dropped them close to their house.'

'Then what?' asked Sutton.

'They never arrived at the bus stop,' said Richardson. 'We also have CCTV from three neighbours that shows they didn't make it home.'

'Can we track them any further?'

'Piccola Venezia is off the high street so there are no public cameras,' said Richardson. 'But Hutch has teams knocking on the door of every business along their most likely route, for footage of the pavements outside their premises. We're watching it in situ to save time. I'll let you know as soon as they find anything.'

'What about mobile phones?'

'That's what's worrying me,' said Pymm. 'I've got cell site data showing them en route to the restaurant and during the meal. Their call logs match what we already know. Both phones left the restaurant at the time shown on the CCTV and moved together at a brisk walking pace in the direction of the high street. Then they go dead. Neither phone has reconnected. I think that's when they were snatched.'

'How precise is the location data?' asked Warren.

'Within fifty metres,' she confirmed, 'and there are a couple of alleyways inside that radius. I have a search team on its way.'

* * *

'We have a warrant to search Eric Morton's brother's house,' said Grayson. 'If we have good reason to suspect that Kyle isn't present, then we can conduct a search to determine his whereabouts, given that there could be lives at stake.'

Grounds for a lawful search were strict and it looked as though

412

a sympathetic magistrate had been willing to interpret the rules in their favour. The problem would come if they found his brother absent and had to exercise the warrant – a canny defence might try and get anything seized that wasn't directly relevant to Kyle's disappearance declared inadmissible.

It was a calculated risk. The previous search, conducted after Morton had first come into the frame, had uncovered nothing linking him to the murders. The chances were that he hadn't been foolish enough to move evidence into the house since then, so there was unlikely to be any good forensics that might be kicked out. If they did find other evidence, then they could apply for another search warrant on stronger grounds. Either way, the priority at the moment was the safe recovery of the Bevans; they'd deal with any legal problems down the line.

* * *

'We've picked up the Bevans on CCTV from businesses they walked past,' said Richardson. 'I think we can be reasonably sure when and where they disappeared.'

Richardson's report was verbal, relayed directly from the officers on the scene.

'They are picked up by cameras outside the Watchmaker's Arms, which is two doors down from Piccola Venezia, then they are captured by a nightclub on the opposite side of the street, and under the canopies of two further shops seventy metres apart. *They do not* appear on the camera that they should next be seen on, which is a hundred metres further on.' She used her finger to draw a circle around a map of the area on her tablet. 'They disappeared somewhere within this stretch of street.'

'Good planning or good fortune by our killer?' asked Sutton. The area transcribed by Richardson had a narrow alleyway between a maternity shop and a curry house, neither of which had CCTV extending beyond their premises.

'We have a team in the alleyway now,' said Pymm, 'but if they were taken there, then they didn't make much of a fuss. There were several smokers outside the Watchmaker's and nobody heard or saw anything they thought worth reporting. None of the residents in the nearby flats recalled hearing anything.'

'My gut feeling is they were picked up in a car,' said Richardson. 'They couldn't get a taxi, and it's a long bus ride home. Could they have flagged down what they thought was a private hire cab? It's illegal, but we know plenty of people still do it.'

'For what it's worth, Abacus Cabs swear they haven't had any contact with Eric Morton or his brother,' interjected Hardwick.

'And we know the car he was using for his taxi driving never moved last night, so either they have access to another vehicle or they weren't involved,' said Sutton.

'Look into it,' said Warren. 'See if you can identify any vehicles that pass down the road at the same time they do. Cross-reference with any ANPR data from the surrounding roads and the previous killings.'

* * *

Eric Morton's sister-in-law had almost collapsed in fright at the sight of armed officers on her doorstep. The Lagdon brothers' handgun was still missing and they weren't taking any chances.

'Fuck off,' had been the succinct reply from Morton, shouted from the kitchen when he overheard the request to see his brother.

He'd changed his mind when he caught sight of the AFOs and pointed mutely upstairs.

Warren listened to the traffic over the radio. He could hear the thump of heavy boots on stairs, accompanied by shouts of 'Armed Police'. A few seconds later, he felt the tension drain out of him, to be replaced by a sense of frustration, then fear.

'Suspect is in bed. Repeat: suspect is present.'

Chapter 64

'Tucked up in bed, suffering with the flu,' said Sutton. 'Which explains his brother's trip to Sainsbury's for paracetamol and ibuprofen and his gallant offer to accompany his sister-in-law on the school run this morning.'

Despite Warren's best efforts, a dejected air hung over the team. Eric Morton and his brother had been their prime suspects, and now it felt as if they were back at square one.

It came as no surprise when Warren's desk phone rang.

'Get the website up on the screen,' he ordered after hanging up.

* . * . *

'Those who fail to learn from the mistakes
of their predecessors are destined to repeat them.'
– George Santayana

It doesn't matter how many times we're told not to hail a taxi in the street – people still do it. Too lazy to wait? Too stingy to pay full price? Or just too drunk to think straight? It doesn't really matter. I wasn't expecting to bag two last night, but I'm nothing if not adaptable, and I always carry extra gear, just in case.

It is amazing what you can buy online if you know where to look; mobile phone signal jammers are a really useful piece of kit. I might even start carrying one with me when I go to the cinema to stop idiots ruining the film by checking Facebook every ten minutes 😂!

To be honest, I probably didn't need it. They were so busy pawing each other, I don't think they even heard me when I told them there was a burst water main and we had to take a different route. Pro tip: signal jammers block your own handset as well, so make sure you download any maps for your sat nav before you turn it on. I didn't have a clue where the address was that they gave me! 😂

By the time the husband realised we definitely didn't need to go via a dark country lane it was too late. The child locks stopped them getting out, and a face full of pepper spray and a couple of quick zaps with my favourite toy stopped them breaking the window or climbing into the front.

I'll give the wife credit: she may have been half blinded and recovering from 50,000 volts, but she was ready to put up a fight when I opened the back door. But I showed her the gun and she decided not to be a hero.

Dealing with two of them at the same time was trickier than I thought and required a bit of jiggery pokery. In the end, I ditched the gun and stuck the knife in my back pocket. I got them to stand beside each other, squirted them both in the eyes, gave them another quick shock and then used the knife to stab them both. I think I did the husband first, but I can't remember. I still managed to slit their throats, so the plan wasn't a complete disaster, but I'll have to think it through more carefully next time I try and do a two-for-one!

Click the link for photographic evidence. (Not Safe For Work obviously 😂).

'Bastard!' shouted Sutton. 'Son of a fucking bitch.' He dropped into his chair and placed his head in his hands. Moray Ruskin jumped to his feet and started pacing angrily.

'OK, everybody, deep breaths,' Warren managed. 'Let's take a few minutes and get our heads clear.' He looked over at Swann who had turned a sickly green, covering her mouth and swallowing a few times. Mags Richardson snatched up a wastebin, but the profiler waved her away.

Warren managed to hold himself together long enough to ensure that nobody needed his immediate support, before walking stiff-legged to his office. Closing the door behind him he collapsed into his chair.

Pushing a fist into his mouth, he stifled a sob. Weeks of endless stress flowed out of him, along with red-hot tears. News of the missing couple that morning had come as a bitter blow to all of them, but the hope – no matter how faint – that they might still be alive had driven them onwards, forcing them to push their feelings to one side. Now that crutch was gone.

Warren had never met the couple; he'd only seen a single photograph of them. Twelve hours previously he hadn't even known they existed. Yet at that moment he felt as if he'd lost a loved one. He felt paralysed; there was so much he needed to do, but he couldn't order his thoughts.

The counselling he'd undergone to deal with the PTSD he'd developed after Gary Hastings' death had given him techniques he could use, and so he forced himself to close his eyes and breathe. After a few minutes, the helplessness started to subside, the grief turning now to anger; a white-hot glowing fury directed towards the faceless killer.

How dare he? How *fucking* dare he? What gave him the right to act like some sort of god, snuffing out innocent lives to satisfy whatever demons were speaking in his head? To destroy families? To make an orphan of a helpless baby? To threaten Warren's own wife?

Now, instead of pushing down the rage, he let it fill him. From now on it would drive him forward. For the first time in his life, Warren wished for the death penalty. He didn't care what justification the killer's defence team might dredge up for the man's sickness. Planet Earth would be a better place without him.

Tuesday 27th March

Chapter 65

There was no time for the team to lick their wounds. It was now Tuesday, and if the killer stuck to his routine, then somebody else would die that coming weekend.

'He's not going to stop on his own,' said Swann over coffee in Grayson's office. 'He's enjoying it too much and he regards it as a battle of wits between you and him.' She looked apologetic. 'I'm sorry, Warren, but every time he successfully kills someone, he sees it as a victory.'

'It doesn't help that the media are treating it like a circus,' said Grayson. 'At least the more responsible outlets have agreed not to use your photograph or mention where you are currently staying. Even Marcia Cooper has agreed to keep her mouth shut for the time being.'

'I'd stay away from social media, if I were you,' said Swann. 'The armchair detectives and the trolls are having a field day. Although it is good to see that a few people have called out the killer's incorrect paraphrasing of George Santayana's quote.'

Warren nodded. It had been a shock to see his own face – and Swann's – on some of the less reputable online news sites. How would that affect his future? That sort of notoriety wasn't always helpful for a hands-on officer like Warren. Not to mention that as far as he was concerned, every death was a personal failure.

He pushed the thought aside; now was not the time for self-criticism.

*　*　*

'Right, people, listen up!' Warren strode into the main office radiating more energy than he felt.

'Yesterday was a very shit day. But he's given us more clues; we will catch this bastard. Rachel, kick us off.'

'I was hoping we'd get lucky and find a phone in the vicinity that left the network the same time as theirs,' she said, 'but either he switched the jammer on before they got in the car, or he turned his phone off earlier.'

'What about the website?'

'Still no way to work out who is posting to it. The photos are just woodland, no clues to whereabouts and no metadata. We can't even zoom in without going grainy.'

'Mags?'

'We have every car that hit ANPR in that location six hours either side of when they went missing. Only a couple of vehicles have been identified that appeared near our previous scenes. We've also added all of the vehicles that loosely fit the description from New Year's Eve to the previous list for manual elimination, but it's slow going.'

'We know he took them out to a rural area to kill them,' said Sutton. 'What about ANPR on trunk roads leading out of Middlesbury?'

'Already in the mix,' confirmed Richardson.

'In that case, I won't keep you any longer,' said Warren.

Next stop was Welwyn for a crisis meeting with the chief constable, followed by a press conference.

He grabbed the tub of antacids from his desk drawer.

Wednesday 28th March

Chapter 66

It was three days since the Bevans' disappearance, and months since their killer had first struck, yet despite the team's tireless work, he remained a ghost. Warren was trying to be as upbeat as possible, but the slow progress was wearing on everyone. The chief constable remained supportive, but the press conference had been brutal. If he never saw Marcia Cooper again, it would be too soon.

The call came in just minutes after a frustrating morning briefing, and by the time he and Sutton arrived, the entire area surrounding the row of rental garages had been taped off. A yellow Ford Transit van was parked in front of an open lock-up, 'Herts Custom Storage' emblazoned on the side in red lettering. Paper-suited technicians on their hands and knees placed yellow scene markers next to tyre tracks on the concrete apron in front of the garages.

'Is it them?' Warren asked Andy Harrison.

'I only took a quick look, but there are two of them and they're stuffed in the same freezer, wrapped in separate plastic sheets. Guessing by the sizes, the wife is on top and her husband underneath.'

'What about the second freezer?'

Harrison's forehead wrinkled. 'Not nice; it's obvious the freezer has been turned off for some time. Unfortunately, that was the one the workers opened. She wasn't as well wrapped as the other two, so I had a bit of a look-see, and I'm going to say young white woman with blonde hair. She had a small tattoo of a broken heart on her left shoulder.'

'Charley Gibson,' said Sutton quietly.

Warren hoped he was right. Because if it wasn't her, then yet another family was going to receive some devastating news.

'I'll tell you something,' said Harrison, 'that place is kitted out like some sort of serial killer's paradise; it has to be seen to be believed. Fingers crossed, it's going to be a forensic goldmine.'

David Hutchinson joined the three men.

'I've spoken to the two blokes who opened the unit. They're Polish; their English is basic but serviceable. The owner of the company that the lock-up belongs to has just arrived.'

'Let's speak to them before we suit up,' said Warren. He was desperate to get inside the space where the faceless monster had planned his evil, but the priority had to be getting the ball rolling on their hunt for him. Now their killer's den had been discovered, he might step up his pace, trying to kill as many as he could before the net finally tightened, no longer limiting his murderous activities to the weekend.

Tomasz Albin was a pale-skinned, compact man in his forties. He brandished a pile of stapled sheets. 'I printed out everything I had in case you need it.'

'Thank you, Mr Albin,' said Warren. Sutton started emailing photographs of the sheets to Rachel Pymm so she could start working immediately.

'What can you tell me?' asked Warren.

'Such a terrible tragedy,' he said, shaking his head.

'Why don't you start by telling me why your workers were here today?' prompted Warren.

'Of course. We were repossessing the unit because the tenant hadn't been paying their rent and electricity.'

'And when did that start?'

'The rent is due on the first of the month. The tenant paid by direct debit, but the bank declined it. I emailed them but got no reply and their mobile phone number wasn't working. Eventually, I sent a final demand and cut off the electricity two weeks ago – that often makes them get in contact. There was still nothing, so this morning I sent Krzysztof and Stefan around with the bolt cutters.'

'What can you tell us about this ...' Sutton checked the document '... Nancy Rudd?'

'Nothing really. She signed up online back in November. I never spoke to her.'

'So how did you get the keys to her? Did she give you an address?'

'No need. We secure the unit with a combination padlock to stop squatters but encourage customers to fit their own. When a tenancy ends, they remove theirs and replace the combination lock. I send someone out to check things over, and if the unit is in good order, they get their deposit back, minus any outstanding electricity.'

'So you have no idea who is renting your units?' asked Warren, pointedly.

Albin shifted from one foot to another. 'Never been a problem before,' he muttered.

Warren exchanged a glance with Sutton. Criminals loved people like Albin; he had zero interest in who was using his units, or what was stored in there.

'What about security? I don't see any CCTV or alarms,' said Sutton.

Albin folded his arms defensively. 'It's a basic unit – you get what you pay for. Look, it's nothing to do with me what people keep in their garages. I run an honest business. I pay my taxes and provide a valuable service. If I see any evidence of criminality, I report it to the police.'

It's hard to see something, when you refuse to look, thought Warren. 'OK, Mr Albin, I think that's all we need for now.' He handed over his card. 'If you could email those documents to this address as soon as you can, it would be very much appreciated.'

Warren turned to Sutton. 'Let's suit up.'

* * *

'Bloody hell,' breathed Sutton. 'I've never seen anything like this.'

The lock-up was a windowless concrete box large enough to house a car, with enough space left over for a couple of bicycles or garden furniture. The front half of the unit, directly under the tilting metal door, had a cheap wooden desk with drawers and a plastic fold-up chair. Next to it stood a metal frame with canvas storage baskets. On the desk sat a laptop computer and inkjet printer. A dubious-looking daisy chain of extension cords and multi-plugs snaked across the floor from the single electrical socket. A CSI was photographing the contents of the top drawer of the desk, a stack of plastic evidence sacks in a pile next to her. Acting as a divider between the front and the rear were tall, open shelves filled with books and DVDs.

'It's like a bloody library,' said Warren, craning his neck to read their spines. 'Biographies of serial killers, forensics manuals, an introduction to criminology, even a couple of Lizzie Swann's books. It's as if he's studying for a degree in murder.'

'They do a good job of hiding the freezers,' said Sutton, as he peered around the shelves. 'Two of them, basic chest units. They look old, so probably second-hand.'

'Can you see if the serial numbers are still on there? If we can track down the original owners, we might find who they sold them on to.'

Sutton leant over the nearest unit, careful not to touch the surface. 'It looks like it, but you or I will never get down there to read them off. We'll have to wait until they pull them out to remove the bodies.'

Warren gave a shudder; in all the excitement he'd somehow forgotten what lay inside the appliances.

Chapter 67

'I've traced where those freezers were originally bought,' said Hardwick. By the time Warren and Sutton returned to CID, the smallest CSI had managed to get her arm behind the units and snap their serial numbers with her phone.

'According to the manufacturers, the Zanussi was bought online through Currys in 2007, and the LEC through John Lewis in 2009. I've contacted both retailers and we'll have customer details within the hour.'

'Rachel, where are you with the bank account paying for the lock-up?' asked Warren.

Pymm pushed her glasses back on her nose. 'I have a name, and it matches that of the customer. A Ms Nancy Rudd. But I doubt it's her; she's eighty-four. She opened a savings account forever ago, which has never done very much. She requested online banking in 2015 and opted for paperless communications. Then she apparently opened this new account last year. She was a pre-existing customer, so there was no need for any ID checks. This account has been quite busy of late, with a direct debit mandate to the storage company, multiple Amazon and other online purchases, and a cryptocurrency exchange, which allows the buying and selling of Bitcoin.'

'ID theft?' asked Warren.

'That's certainly one explanation,' said Pymm. 'Either way, I think somebody is squatting, using her account. The payments were irregular; cash paid in using envelopes in the drop boxes outside the branch, after close of business on a Friday, so several days' worth of CCTV will need checking. The last one was several weeks ago. The balance was close to zero, which is why the direct debit was declined.'

Warren rubbed his chin. 'I wonder why he stopped topping it up? Do the bank have an address for Ms Rudd? It'd be useful to speak to her. Maybe she can shed some light on who is using her account.'

'Yes, but she hasn't been on the electoral register at that address since 2015.'

'OK.' He turned and looked across the room. 'Moray, are you busy?'

* * *

'We've not been able to find any witnesses,' said Hutchinson. 'None of the nearby houses have a clear line of sight of the lock-up.'

It was now after lunch, although the smell from the lock-up meant Warren would have no problem sticking to his diet today. He noticed that Sutton's lunchbox hadn't moved from the top shelf of the fridge either.

After the morning's discovery, the team had pivoted to tracking down the former tenant of the lock-up. Every available body was now knocking on doors and chasing leads.

'Damn,' said Warren. 'What about customers renting the other units?'

'Ha! Those we've identified were somewhat cagey, but when they realised we weren't interested in what *they* were storing in there, they opened up. Unfortunately, nobody remembers seeing who used that unit.'

'Worth a try,' said Warren. 'Karen?'

'I've traced the original owners of both freezers, and they sold them online through the local listings pages of the *Middlesbury Reporter*,' said Hardwick. 'The Zanussi was advertised back in December, as part of a house clearance when the owner died. Their son remembers it was picked up by a large man with a white van, but can't be any more helpful. Naturally, he was paid cash. We're looking at his phone records to see if we can identify the buyer's number.'

'Much good that'll do us,' said Sutton. 'This guy must have a tree that grows burner phones. What about the LEC?'

'That was more recent, back in February. The owner helped the buyer carry it down the garden path and place it in the back of a white van.'

'Any description?'

'No, he arrived after dark and was wearing a coat and scarf; they didn't really speak. But he remembers he was a big man. He said he thought the back of the van might belong to a builder, as there were some tools and bits and pieces of wood. There was lettering on the side. Something Construction.'

It wasn't much to go on. If they could identify the mobile phone number used to phone the sellers, they could work out where it was when it made the call, although Warren feared it would just lead back to the lock-up.

'Talk to Mags,' he said. 'If the van belongs to a builder, it may be listed under a company name with the DVLA. Get her team to flag any white vans registered to construction companies within the vicinity of the sellers' houses the evenings the pick-ups occurred.'

* * *

'Ms Nancy Rudd is in a care home,' said Ruskin. 'The family living at her old address never met her.'

'Any forwarding address?' asked Warren. By now it was early

evening and the adrenaline fuelling him was starting to wear off.

'No. I spoke to the next-door neighbour; she remembered Ms Rudd but said they were never more than passing acquaintances. She lived with a man who they had assumed was her husband, but apparently they were never actually married. He died back in 2012 and she cared for him until the end. She fell ill herself a couple of years later with some sort of lung condition. They only had one child and he wasn't able to look after her, so they sold the house and she moved into a care home.'

'And the neighbour doesn't remember the name of the home?'

'No, but she thinks it was local.'

'OK, that's a start. Call around all the homes in the area and see if you can track her down. If she's no longer alive, question the staff and residents. She could have been the victim of ID theft, but I can't help asking myself who is in a better position to take over an elderly person's bank accounts than a trusted loved one?'

Thursday 29th March

Chapter 68

If he wasn't wearing a different tie, Warren could be fooled into believing that Ruskin hadn't moved since Warren had gone home the previous evening. He hoped that wasn't the case; the DC was jokingly referred to as the Duracell Bunny on account of his endless energy, but everyone had a limit.

'Who knew there were so many care homes within fifty miles of here?' asked Ruskin.

'It's an ageing population,' said Warren. He clapped Ruskin on the shoulder. 'So keep on earning the overtime, Moray; all the extra tax you pay will help fund DI Sutton's care when they put him in a home in a couple of years.'

Sutton's retort was cut off by the arrival of Karen Hardwick, her cheeks flushed.

'I have the inventory for the lock-up,' she said. Immediately everyone gathered around her.

'We'll have to wait for the labs to process everything before we get any DNA or fingerprints, but it looks like it contains most of what we're looking for and plenty more besides. IT are standing by to analyse the laptop and printer as soon as Forensics finish looking for trace evidence, but the printer model is consistent with that used on the parcels. There's also some interesting-looking equipment plugged into one of the multi-plugs that they are keen to examine.'

She fanned a set of printouts across the nearest desk. 'No doubt about it, it's definitely our man; the canvas baskets on the shelving units are filled with murder kit. Plastic sheeting, duct tape, latex gloves, disposable protective suits ... There's also washcloths, concentrated cleaning chemicals, a UV light source and a half-empty bottle of luminol.'

'That's how he managed to remove the blood from Charley Gibson's bathroom,' said Sutton. 'He scrubbed it clean, and then squirted the area with luminol to spot anything he missed.'

'It gets better,' said Hardwick. 'There's a stinger with missing spikes matching those embedded in Councillor Paddon's tyres and two phones, one of which has a magnet glued to it. There are also green pills that look a lot like oxycodone. In the desk drawer there is a half-empty pack of notebooks of the brand he sent us, envelopes, self-adhesive printer labels, stamps, paper and a Pritt Stick, along with two sets of what appear to be house keys, and scraps of paper with handwritten, four-digit numbers on them.'

'Burglar alarm codes,' said Warren and Sutton simultaneously.

'See if the keys and the codes match Charley Gibson's or the Culverhouses',' ordered Warren.

'If they do, then he definitely had some sort of connection to their two properties,' said Sutton. 'That could be the link we're looking for. I'll get Rachel to prioritise it.' He got to his feet.

'Don't you want to hear what else they found?' asked Hardwick.

'You have definitely been spending too much time with Rachel,' said Warren. 'You're picking up her bad habits.'

She produced a stack of photographs from the folder and spread them across the desk. 'Behold the mother lode.'

'Son of a bitch,' breathed Sutton. 'That's how he managed to avoid getting flagged by ANPR. He used a different set of licence plates each time.'

*   *   *

438

'That lock-up is a treasure-trove,' said Sutton, as he and Warren sat down with their respective choice of hot drinks. The DI had just returned from Stevenage, where he had witnessed the autopsies of the Bevans. The pathologist's preliminary report had matched the confession on the killer's website. Charley Gibson was scheduled for the following day; given the state of her body, he was half-seriously contemplating putting in a request for annual leave.

'He must have slipped up somewhere and left a fingerprint or DNA,' he continued.

'Which is only useful if we already have him in the database,' Warren reminded him.

'True, but loads of it has serial numbers. If we can trace it back through the online sellers, then it has to lead back to him at some point. Even if he used a locker, rather than getting it sent to his home address, they're always well covered by CCTV.' He took a long swig of his red bush tea. 'I tell you, mate, I have a good feeling about this.'

Warren nodded, but was unable to summon up his friend's enthusiasm. 'I'm pleased with everything we've found in there,' he said. 'But what really worries me, is everything we *haven't* found.'

Sutton's smile dimmed. 'Winnie Palmer and Bobby Lagdon's clothes, the stun gun and the decoy bag he moves the bodies around in.'

'And the Lagdon brothers' handgun.'

Chapter 69

'Pete Robertson in Forensic IT has taken custody of the laptop from the lock-up,' said Hutchinson. 'He'll contact us as soon as he has anything.'

'Anything on ownership?' asked Warren.

'Not yet. We ran the serial numbers from the laptop and printer by the manufacturers. They were both sold through Amazon, who are trying to link them to the customer that bought them.'

'Thank God for big data,' said Warren.

'In other news, IT reckon they've figured out how the killer accessed the internet,' said Hutchinson. 'The kit running off the multi-plug is a wireless extender. They did a scan of the area and were able to pick up a Wi-Fi signal leaking from a nearby house. The owner's router still had the default password. The extender boosts the signal strength enough for a laptop or other device to piggyback on their internet connection.

'But here's the thing. The extender is mains-powered, and Tomasz Albin claims he turned the electricity off two weeks ago. So how is he posting stuff to the internet?'

'Could he have written the blogs in advance and scheduled their release?' asked Ruskin. 'Alex is in charge of his company's social media accounts, and he does that all the time.'

440

'He only took Shona Bevan and her husband Sunday night,' said Warren, 'so he must have been able to use the printer and laptop within the last few days.'

'Well the laptop can be recharged, obviously, but interestingly the printer is a portable one with a battery,' said Hutchinson, 'which would make sense if he was worried about a reliable electricity supply. But that still doesn't answer how he used the internet if the wireless extender wasn't working. IT are pretty confident that the leaked Wi-Fi signal isn't strong enough without a booster.'

'He could have tethered his laptop to a mobile phone and used its 4G connection,' said Ruskin. 'Alex does that when he's travelling sometimes. It's expensive though, so that's probably why he was leeching off somebody else's signal.'

'So, what's to stop him updating his website using his phone?' asked Sutton.

Warren was frowning.

'Penny for them, Boss?' offered Ruskin.

'He must have known the electricity had been cut off,' said Warren. 'How long would one of those chest freezers remain cold for?'

'Forty-eight hours if you keep the lid closed?' answered Sutton.

'That's what I thought,' said Warren. 'I was thinking that maybe the power being cut was what spurred him to dump Bobby Lagdon's body, but why didn't he dispose of Charley Gibson whilst he was at it?'

'And why did he stick the Bevans in there, when he knew it wouldn't keep them fresh?' finished Sutton.

* * *

'We've run the indexes from the licence plates that we found in the lock-up,' said Richardson. 'According to the DVLA, they were all sold on within the past six months.'

'What does that mean?' asked Sutton. 'Surely he hasn't been buying up old bangers? There were eight different plates in there – that's a hell of a risk. Somebody would remember him.'

'And if the DVLA have recorded the vehicle as being sold on, then they must have a record of the new owner.' Warren paused. 'Please tell me it's that easy?'

'Sorry,' said Richardson. 'The new owners are scattered all over, with no obvious link. It seems that the plates are cloned and appear to have been made illegally by one of those online companies that don't require ownership documents.'

'Small ads,' said Sutton.

'*Autotrader*, to be strictly accurate. All vehicles have appeared on their website with photos that have the licence plate clearly visible.'

'He went to all that trouble for a reason, didn't he?' asked Warren.

'Definitely. Aside from one plate, which comes from a Renault the same colour as the one owned by the Lagdon brothers, all the others are from Black Audi A3 hatchbacks.'

'So if he gets pulled over, the plate matches the description of the vehicle,' said Sutton. 'Clever bastard.'

'Which means we know what vehicle the killer drives,' said Warren, his excitement growing.

'That's the good news,' said Richardson. 'The bad news is that the current model has been available for the past five or six years. If we can get some ANPR footage, we might be able to narrow that down a bit, since the car had a facelift a couple of years ago. But it's popular, especially in that colour. There are *a lot* of them on the road.'

'And if he's using a different plate each time he kills, to stop us building up a pattern of his movements, what's to stop him having a fake plate on his car the rest of the time, so if we do figure it out, it doesn't lead straight back to him?' asked Ruskin.

'Let's not get too pessimistic,' said Warren. 'This is a fantastic find. Mags, you're the expert – what do you propose? You can have whatever resources you need.'

'We run all the plates through ANPR and build up a pattern of his movements. Then we eyeball any video footage and log any dark-coloured A3s manually. He has to change the plates somewhere. Is he driving over to the lock-up? Is he doing it at home, or somewhere else? If we're lucky, we'll find some overlap where multiple plates crop up over time to give us a geographical area that our killer frequents. If we're *really* lucky, we might chance upon one of our indexes appearing or disappearing in an area at the same time as a different number we're not familiar with.'

'Which could be his real registration number,' said Sutton.

'How long?' asked Warren.

Richardson stared into space for a moment, a look of concentration on her face. 'How long is a piece of string?'

* * *

Moray Ruskin's voice was even louder than usual over the speakerphone when he called from the Hazelwood Care Home.

'Ms Nancy Rudd moved in here at the beginning of 2015, selling her house to fund her care. She was fully *compis mentis*, so she remained in charge of her affairs to the end, but her son set up online banking and bought her a cheap tablet so she could keep on top of things.'

'And no doubt made sure that he kept a note of the passwords for future reference,' said Sutton.

'Is she still alive?' asked Warren.

'No, she died in April last year, but get this. She died sooner than they expected.'

'What do you mean?'

'She had advanced COPD, and probably only had weeks left. Her son and his family visited every Sunday; the day she died, the son's wife appeared at the reception desk and said her mother-in-law had started having difficulty breathing. Since it was her long-standing wish not to have any more medical intervention, they just said their goodbyes and let her slip away.'

'And this surprised the care home?' asked Sutton.

'Officially, no. The doctor examined her and agreed she had died of natural causes, specifically asphyxia from her lung condition. Unofficially? One of the assistants, who wasn't involved directly in her care, recalls that they thought she probably had a little longer. However, she was in a lot of discomfort, and if one of her relatives decided to help things along a bit by disconnecting her oxygen for a little while or using a pillow ... well, she'd made her wishes perfectly clear. Better it happen with her family present, than alone in the middle of the night.'

'Jesus,' said Warren. 'And I'm guessing no autopsy, as it was recorded as natural causes?'

'Correct, and a cremation, so we'll never know.'

'Do we have a name for the son?' asked Warren.

'Yes, and you'll never guess who.'

* * *

The moment Ruskin gave them the name of Nancy Rudd's son, all the pieces started falling into place.

'I can't believe I missed it,' said Pymm, opening windows on her computer. She pointed at a bank statement. 'The Culverhouses had that kitchen fitted six months before they were killed. The work was done by a firm called FAB Construction.'

'Who probably had a key and the burglar alarm code so they could come and go,' said Warren.

'And I'll bet they have a nail gun,' said Sutton.

Pymm continued tapping away at her computer. 'Charley Gibson had her whole house renovated before she moved in.' She opened a different statement on a second screen. 'She was paying an outfit called Hertfordshire Renovations.'

Opening a fresh browser window, she started typing in Google. 'If this firm is anything like the one that has been adapting our house, then they probably subcontract some of the jobs out to local specialists.'

The firm's website appeared on the screen. Pymm navigated to a link entitled 'visit our trusted partners'.

Fourth down the list: FAB Construction.

Warren took his phone out, his hands shaking. Susan answered on the third ring.

'Sweetheart, it's me. You said you thought Spencer Aspinall's deformed jaw was congenital. What was his father's name, and does he have the same abnormality?'

Chapter 70

Waiting is hard; waiting when you aren't in charge is even harder. Warren and Sutton were parked in a quiet cul-de-sac almost half a mile away from the house Freddie Aspinall shared with his wife and son. A drive-by by an unmarked surveillance vehicle a few minutes before had confirmed that the white van used by Freddie Aspinall Building & Construction was parked on the family's driveway.

Warren had handed over coordination of the operation to the designated gold commander; he wasn't a Tactical Firearms Officer and so he and Sutton were sitting on their hands whilst the scene played out over the airwaves.

'Team One in position,' came the voice of the lead TFO in the unmarked van parked diagonally opposite the house, followed by confirmation from Team Two in their BMW estate car a few doors further down.

'Team Three in position.'

Should their target try to escape through the rear of the house, they would be met by a team of armed officers waiting in the access road behind the Aspinalls' back fence.

'Mobile Unit One, standing by.' A moment later a second patrol car, stationed at the opposite end of the street, also confirmed their readiness to block entry and exit to the road as soon as the word was given. They were taking no chances on Aspinall's escape, as well as preventing innocent members of the public driving into harm's way.

'Paramedics standing by.'

'All units ready, DCI Jones. Are we good to go?' It was a courtesy; the gold commander had final authority and wouldn't proceed unless he was satisfied, but it was Warren's operation.

'Yes,' said Warren.

'Go, go, go,' ordered the commander.

Immediately, the airwaves were filled with the metallic slide and thump of van and car doors, followed by heavy boots on tarmac. Moments later repeated shouts of 'Armed Police, stay where you are!' were accompanied by a crash as the steel ram made short work of the uPVC front door. A second crash and more shouts signalled the breaching of the side door leading into the garage.

Warren started the engine. Beside him, Sutton straightened his ballistic vest. Warren looked over; his friend was focused and grim-faced but there was no sign that the adrenaline surge was exacerbating his heart condition.

Warren shifted the car into gear. The seconds ticked by, the two men trying to picture the scene from the shouts and background noise over the radio. Finally the voice of the gold commander cut through the chatter.

'Scene is clear. Two detained. Repeat, scene is clear.'

Warren released the handbrake and popped the clutch, the car's tyres squeaking as he pulled away from the kerb. Turning right, they entered the Aspinalls' road and Warren accelerated hard, keen to join in the action. A few moments later, he ground to a halt outside the property and Sutton jumped out of the passenger seat.

'Who have we got?' he asked the lead TFO, who was exiting through the remains of the front entrance, his carbine resting on his forearm, his finger clear of the trigger.

'Two persons. One female, matching the description of Patricia Aspinall. A male in his twenties says he is Spencer Aspinall.'

'No sign of Freddie Aspinall?' asked Warren.

'No, sir. All rooms, including the garage are clear. Nobody is in the loft and Unit Three confirm the garden shed is empty.'

'There's no sign of the Audi A3 registered to Freddie Aspinall,' said Sutton, after a quick consultation over the radio.

'Shit,' said Warren.

*   *   *

'Tea and sympathy,' said Warren. 'Freddie Aspinall clearly went to great lengths to conceal what he was doing from his wife and son. If we are to get their cooperation, we need them onside.'

Warren was holding an emergency strategy briefing. So far there had been no sight of the Aspinall family car on ANPR within the immediate vicinity. The Traffic Unit had programmed the system to flag all licence plates belonging to black Audi A3s, in the hope that if he was driving the car using false plates he'd continued using registration numbers matching the same model of car. Richardson also had a team scouring the past few months of *Autotrader* for other vehicles that Aspinall might have lifted registration numbers from. If any of those vehicles popped up in the Middlesbury area, they would be given top priority. Unfortunately, many of the original cars were still on the road, and so legitimate vehicles were also being flagged by the system.

'We've spoken to his workmates, who said he texted them this morning to say he had a dicky tummy and wasn't coming into work,' said Ruskin. 'They were a bit pissed off, because it meant they had to make their own way to the job they're on and didn't have some of the tools they needed.'

'The text was sent at 06.22 this morning,' said Pymm, 'from a location consistent with his house. The phone then left the network.'

'What are his wife and son saying?' asked Warren.

'His wife is saying nothing; she just keeps repeating that there must be some mistake. She's downstairs waiting for the duty solicitor to arrive,' replied Hutchinson. 'She's not under arrest, but she seems terrified. Whether she was scared by us kicking her door in, is scared of her husband, or is scared we'll find out she knew something she should have told us, I have no idea.'

'What about Spencer?' asked Warren.

'He's been more forthcoming. We've kept him and his mother apart so they can't coordinate. He hasn't asked for a lawyer,' said Hardwick. 'He claims not to have seen his dad since yesterday. Apparently, he ate his dinner in the garage as he was playing video games until late and didn't come out until after his parents had gone to bed. He thought it a bit strange that his dad's van was still on the drive when he got up at eleven, but he assumed he'd taken the car for some reason.'

'What are the neighbours saying?' asked Sutton.

'The man who lives immediately next door is on his way to give a statement,' said Ruskin. 'He's lived there since before the Aspinalls moved in and seemed keen to speak to us.'

'What about the search teams? Anything jumping out?' asked Warren. It was early days, but they'd been in the property for over an hour and Andy Harrison had done a preliminary walk-through.

'Not much from the house yet,' said Hutchinson. 'They're bagging his wardrobe. There are some socks the same colour as the unknown fibres found on Winnie Palmer's carpet. They've also taken his hairbrush and toothbrush for DNA. They're going to compare hair samples with those found in the back of the Lagdons' car. We know Freddie Aspinall had grey hair, so that might be a match.

'The van is on its way to Welwyn for the full treatment. It looks as though there are some tools in there, so I've asked that they do an inventory as soon as it arrives.'

* * *

'I've spoken to the Aspinalls' next-door neighbour,' said Hardwick. 'Freddie is, in his words, "a complicated man".'

'What does that mean?' asked Warren.

'Apparently, he's a nice enough bloke most of the time, but he has a real temper on him, if you rub him up the wrong way. When he's off on one, he can be completely beyond reason.'

'That matches what Susan said about his interactions with the school,' said Warren.

'Well it's interesting that you bring up school. Apparently, Spencer's lack of motivation is a regular source of tension. Several times he's heard Freddie berating him for being lazy and squandering chances that "he would have killed for when he was his age". I asked him what he thought that might mean and he said it was obvious that Freddie was a very intelligent man, who could probably have gone to university, but his family couldn't afford it. He said he is a voracious reader.'

'That matches what I saw on the video Andy Harrison took,' said Hutchinson. 'There are bookcases everywhere. I only glimpsed a few of the titles, but it's a real mix, including some literary classics.'

'You said that whoever wrote those letters was very intelligent, but not necessarily formally educated,' said Warren, turning to Swann. 'Could this be significant?'

Swann pursed her lips. 'I certainly wouldn't dismiss it. The language in the letters is very fluent, with a really good grasp of vocabulary, and the punctuation and grammar are excellent. People can often overcome deficits in their schooling by absorbing good practice from reading.'

'There's more,' said Hardwick. 'Apparently, they used to have a family dog. Spencer was an only child and it was his constant companion. Anyway, it fell sick and was in distress. He heard Freddie explaining to Spencer, who was probably only eleven at the time, that it would be too expensive for the vet to cure her, and so putting her out of her misery was the kindest thing to do. Apparently Spencer tried to cajole his father into paying the vet, even offering his pocket money. Freddie came close to losing his temper.

'Lo and behold, an hour later, they're digging a hole in the back garden and Spencer is in floods of tears with some flowers. There's no way they could have taken it to a vet in that time.'

'So, unless the dog expired on its own, he thinks Freddie dispatched it?' summarised Warren.

'He didn't see or hear anything, but that's what he's always assumed.'

'Lizzie?' asked Warren.

'Farmers sometimes put animals down to minimise distress,' she said. 'But they're usually working animals, not family pets. They are also trained to do so humanely. Freddie Aspinall was a builder, living in a town. Where would he learn to do that? A lack of empathy towards animals is a trait many serial killers demonstrate. I'd be interested to hear if there are other examples, especially from childhood.'

'It also matches what we heard from the care home,' said Sutton. 'If he really did hasten his mother's death, then it sounds to me like a pattern of behaviour.'

'The killer spoke of the suffering of Mrs Culverhouse, and implied that Winnie Palmer was lonely,' said Hutchinson.

'It could be argued that some of these acts, if done humanely, show evidence he has empathy and is trying to relieve suffering,' said Swann. 'But the callous use of language in his letters doesn't strike me as especially empathetic. Rather, I think he kills because he wants to and it excites him. Keeping one step ahead of the police feeds his narcissism. He's just self-aware enough to try and justify it after the fact.'

Chapter 71

The case was building against Freddie Aspinall so fast that Rachel Pymm had to expand her team of indexers to help load the mounting evidence onto the HOLMES database.

She was briefing Grayson on what had been done so far.

'No fingerprints on the laptop found in the lock-up. DNA is still pending.'

'No surprise,' said Sutton.

'Digital Forensics have made a copy of the hard drive. Proper analysis will take days, but Pete Robertson has sent over a summary of the software installed and any search history that he hadn't erased. Recovering deleted data is their top priority.

'There are bookmarks and visits to sites that deal with disposing of bodies and cleaning up crime scenes, as well as forums dedicated to serial killers and notorious murderers.'

'Christ,' muttered Grayson. 'I can't believe this stuff is out there for sick bastards like Freddie Aspinall to trawl through and pick up ideas.'

'To be fair, most of the visitors tend to be crime writers researching their next book, but I get your point,' said Pymm. 'He also has encrypted TOR software installed so he can access the dark web. Obviously, that doesn't have a search history.

'But what does have a search and purchase history is Amazon, and he was too lazy to remember his password and use two-factor identification, so his account is wide open.'

Warren resisted the urge to pump the air. 'I take it you've had a look?'

'Oh yes. The account is in the name of Mr Sunday Slayer – obviously Amazon don't care what you call yourself. There is one payment method – the same card used to pay for the lock-up – and there are two delivery addresses. One matches the house his mother lived in when she opened those bank accounts years ago – although nothing has ever been delivered there as far as we can tell – the other is a collection locker in Stevenage where everything seems to be sent.'

'Get Mags to pull the CCTV from the locker and anything surrounding it,' said Warren. 'And use ANPR to see if we can place the family car or his van in the vicinity when he picked his parcels up. Have you had a chance to look at what he was actually buying?'

'I have someone matching all those DVDs and books to his purchase history, but the highlights are the laptop and printer, a fold-up commuter bike, stationery and office equipment matching what we found, plus what appears to be those distinctive notepads he's been posting to you. There are also boxes of disposable gloves, paper forensic suits and a large decoy bag used by game hunters. The description suggests it is big enough to hold a small person.'

'A decoy bag that he's probably got with him,' Sutton reminded them.

'What about banking apps or websites?' asked Warren. 'We need a complete chain linking the items in the lock-up with the finances used to purchase them.'

'His history shows that he visited the same bank his mother's accounts were held with. I've applied for a warrant for their records. If we can show the laptop was used to access his mother's account, then I think we've closed the loop.'

'What about CCTV footage of him making the cash deposits to service the account?' asked Grayson.

'Mags is on it.'

'Any physical forensics from the search of his house and van, or the lock-up?'

'Headline news is that they found a nail gun in the back of his van. The staples it uses match the ones used to kill Councillor Paddon, and there are blood spots inside its tip. It's covered in fingerprints, including ones matching those found on his hairbrush. They are arranging for prints from his workmates for comparison, so we can rule out any defence that it isn't the property of his business.'

'Anything back on those keys?' asked Sutton.

'Yes, one set each for the Culverhouses and Charley Gibson, and the numbers we found match their alarm codes,' she replied. 'Derek Culverhouse confirms that Freddie Aspinall Building & Construction fitted the kitchen and he lent him a key and gave him the alarm code so they could come and go. They returned the key when they finished, but obviously Freddie got a copy cut and Derek never thought to change the alarm code. It was the same set-up for Charley Gibson. Hertfordshire Renovations have confirmed they employed FAB Construction to do the kitchen and bathroom.'

'The bodies of that poor couple speak for themselves, but are there any forensics linking him to the Lagdons or Winnie Palmer?' asked Grayson. 'We have his confessions in those damn letters, but you know how much the CPS and juries like physical evidence. I want the bastard charged and tried for everyone he's killed; no exceptions.'

'We know Bobby Lagdon and Winnie Palmer were stored in a freezer; that may yield something. A pair of muddy trainers at the back of his wardrobe might match some partial impressions at the dump sites and the local soil. The shoes are pretty well worn, so hopefully there will be DNA or fingerprints linking them back to Freddie. There are also some red fibres similar to those found on Winnie Palmer's carpet and the socks that they found.'

'So, he was smart enough to take his shoes off in her house, but didn't think to dispose of those red socks, or ditch the trainers he was wearing after he dumped her,' said Grayson.

'Aside from possibly suffocating his mother in the care home, this was probably his first kill,' said Sutton. 'We know he's made mistakes, like being spotted on New Year's Eve. Plus, he may have bought the socks as part of a multi-pack, dumped the ones he was wearing, but forgot there were more identical pairs in his undies drawer.'

'What about the bicycle?' asked Warren.

'There were lots of bicycle tyre impressions near where the Lagdons' car was left after Nick was shot. They are too degraded for a definitive match and most come from mountain bikes, but at least one set is consistent with the smaller wheels found on a fold-up bike of the type he ordered online.

'Now we know who we are looking for, we should see if he crops up on the CCTV at Bristol Parkway train station or the National Express depot,' said Warren. 'If we can get a clear image of him turning up on a fold-up bicycle, it's another link to the lock-up and places him in the vicinity of where Charley Gibson's car was left.'

Chapter 72

'We're still not getting anything from Patricia Aspinall,' said Hutchinson, after a fruitless forty-five minutes with Freddie Aspinall's wife. 'Her solicitor has clearly told her to keep her mouth shut. All I got from her before she completely clammed up was that it was all a big mistake and her husband was in the house with her on every evening that we asked about. But she's shifty and very scared; she's lying to us about something.'

'I suppose we can charge her with assisting an offender if we prove that she's not telling the truth,' said Sutton.

'I wouldn't bet on that,' said Warren. 'He's gone to such great lengths to hide his activities that I imagine her defence will claim she went to bed before him each night and had no idea he was out and about.'

'Except for New Year's Eve,' pointed out Hutchinson. 'Supposedly all three of them saw the new year in together, before Spencer went back to the garage to finish off the game he was playing. If that was true, then Freddie couldn't be the person spotted by that drunk couple around midnight.'

Warren rubbed his chin. They really needed Patricia Aspinall to admit to her husband disappearing on Sunday evenings. But how could they persuade her to do so?

'You said Spencer hadn't asked for a solicitor,' he said. 'I reckon he's going to be the weak link here. I suspect there's also at least some resentment, given what the neighbour has told us. I think it's time to lean on him.'

*   *   *

Warren had thought long and hard about whether he should interview Spencer Aspinall, given that his wife had taught him. If Aspinall made the connection, would that sour the interview, or would he be able to use it? In the end, Warren decided to go with his gut. He'd take Karen Hardwick along with him, and if he felt his presence was hindering, rather than helping, he'd make an excuse and leave her to it.

Mindful of his earlier 'tea and sympathy' edict, he entered the interview suite with some fresh coffee and a packet of biscuits.

'Sorry to keep you here so long. You must be starving,' he said. 'If you like, I can ask someone to pop across the road and fetch some sandwiches?'

'No, thank you,' said Aspinall. Warren appraised him carefully as the young man opened the biscuits.

'Have you found my father?' he asked, his eyes downcast. The man's shoulders were slumped in defeat, a marked contrast to his defiant and arrogant air when Hardwick had brought him in previously. *He knows, or at least suspects, something*, Warren decided.

'I'm afraid not. We really need to speak to him urgently. Do you have any idea where he might be?'

Aspinall shook his head. 'No, sorry.' He returned his eyes to the table.

Hardwick cleared her throat and ran through the necessary preliminaries. When Warren formally introduced himself for the tape, Aspinall looked up. 'You're Mrs Jones' husband, aren't you? The science teacher?'

457

Warren steeled himself but forced a smile. 'Yes, that's right.'

'I always liked Mrs Jones. She really knew her stuff – you could ask her anything and she'd try to answer it. Not every teacher likes being interrupted by questions.'

That somewhat contradicted Susan's account of their relationship, but former students often had selective memories.

'You spoke to me at our sixth form careers day.' He gave a shy smile. 'You probably don't remember me. I had long hair then.'

'There were a lot of people there,' admitted Warren. He'd ended his talk a little sooner than planned, having been distracted by a number of important emails coming through on his phone.

'It was an interesting talk.'

'Thank you.' He took a chance. 'Not interesting enough to make you sign up though?' He softened the comment with a wry smile.

'I've thought about it.' He gave a snort. 'I imagine a career with you guys is off the table now?'

'Why do you say that?' asked Hardwick.

'I'm not daft. I know why you came crashing into our house today. And why you pulled me in three weeks ago.' Despite the harsh words, his voice held no edge.

'Is there anything you think we should know?' asked Hardwick gently.

The man sighed. 'I lied the last time I was here,' said Aspinall. 'About New Year's Eve.'

'How do you mean?' asked Warren, keeping his tone even.

'I said that I spent New Year's Eve speaking to someone on the phone, then went and saw the new year in with my parents, before I went back to the garage to carry on playing *Call of Duty*. It was true, except for the bit about seeing in the new year with Mum and Dad. We had a row.' He shrugged again. 'You know how it is; Christmas, stuck in the house, and a bit too much to drink. Dad had been on at me all week about 2018 being the year I "finally did something with my life".' His voice became bitter. 'Whatever the fuck that means. Anyway, I wasn't really bothered

458

– it's just another mark on the calendar. Half the people I play against aren't even in the UK; it was still mid-afternoon on the west coast of the US at that time.'

'So why did you lie?' asked Hardwick, her tone non-judgemental.

'I was scared. You'd just turned up asking about what I was doing that night. I knew that if I said I was in the garage all night and my parents didn't see me, you'd think I sneaked out and … you know …' He looked down at his hands. 'Sorry.'

'Was your father in the house that night?' asked Warren.

'I don't know. Really, I don't. I had my headphones on.'

It wasn't enough to prove to a court that Patricia Aspinall had lied about her husband's whereabouts. Her previous claim that they were all together had been unwitnessed.

'Spencer, I'm going to show you some dates,' said Warren. 'Could you try and remember if your father was around on those evenings?'

Aspinall looked at the list. 'Sorry, they're all Sunday nights. I tend to stay in the garage and play games at the weekend.' He frowned. 'Hang on. Is it OK if I look at the calendar on my phone?'

'Of course,' said Warren.

'This date.' He pointed at the sheet. 'Mum was away that week. She was visiting her sister in Leeds. Dad doesn't really get on with her, so he stayed and worked.'

'And did you see him at all?' asked Warren.

'I suppose so. Maybe?' Aspinall looked unsure. 'Unless he wants me to come on a job with him, he's usually gone by the time I'm up. I sort myself out for dinner if Mum's not around. He doesn't usually bother me if I'm in the garage.'

Warren and Hardwick kept their faces neutral. If Patricia Aspinall was away that week, she would have no idea what her husband was up to on the Sunday that Charley Gibson had been killed, nor what he was doing on the Monday or the Tuesday, when her house had been cleaned and her car driven down to Gloucestershire.

* * *

Aspinall had gone for a toilet break.

'I requested the *Call of Duty* server logs from Activision when we first brought him in for questioning,' said Pymm. 'His computer was logged on, and we already established he was on the phone that evening, with the handset localised to their house.'

'So it looks as though he was definitely in when he says he was; he just claims to have lied about seeing in the new year with his parents,' said Warren. 'Which would mean his mother also lied when she told us he was in with them watching the fireworks on the BBC. Therefore, she might have lied about her husband being there.'

'Hutch, we really need her to admit that she can't give her husband an alibi. Go and press her. Tony, go with him. A DS and a DI will show her we mean business. Bring up her week away with her sister and make it clear that we will verify.

'In the meantime, I think Spencer has had long enough in the bathroom. Let's not let him dwell too much on whether he is chucking his father under a bus.'

* * *

'The relationship between Dad and I has always been a bit, you know … difficult.' Aspinall had re-entered the room surrounded by a fug of stale cigarette smoke. He seemed in a more contemplative mood. 'Mum says it's because we're so alike. Maybe she's right, I don't know. I do know she'll never hear a bad word said against him. Even when he's being an arsehole, she'll defend him. Even against me.'

'That must be hard,' said Hardwick.

'What was he like when you were younger?' asked Warren.

'Strict; he never gave an inch. He always used to say that he'd have killed for the opportunities that I had and he couldn't understand when I didn't push myself like he thought I should. When it became clear I wasn't going to go to university – at least not yet – he tried to get me to work with him. To learn a trade, instead of "sitting on my arse all day, trying to be a writer". I help him out sometimes; you know, a bit of cash in hand if they need some extra muscle, but I can't imagine doing what he does for the rest of my life.'

Aspinall looked at the ceiling lights, and Warren noticed a glistening wetness in his eyes. 'The really daft thing is that he loves reading. He always has a book on the go. In the evenings he sits with headphones on to block out Mum's soaps so he can read in peace. He even says that when he retires, he'll write something, but he scoffed at me when I said I want to be a full-time author.' His voice became angry. 'I mean seriously, where the fuck does he think books come from? Some of his favourite writers have been churning out novels for over forty years. Does he think they all sat down on their sixty-fifth birthday and decided, "right, it's time for a second career", and are still going strong when they turn a hundred?'

'What was your father's relationship like with his parents?' asked Warren carefully.

Aspinall gave a tight smile. 'I know exactly why you're asking.' His face crumpled and he pushed his fist into his mouth. 'I always thought … but you know nobody ever wants to believe that. But after what he did to the dog when I was a kid … well if you can do that …'

'I'm not sure what you mean, Spencer,' said Warren gently.

Aspinall sniffed, and wiped his nose on his sleeve. He cleared his throat.

'When I was a kid, we had a dog, Sandy. She got sick, but Dad said we couldn't afford to take her to the vet's, so she had to be put to sleep. I begged him not to, but he wouldn't listen. He got really angry and said it was the kindest thing; that it would be cruel to keep her alive. He took her into the garage. I could hear Sandy whimpering, then that was it. A couple of minutes later he came out with her in a carrier bag and said, "She is at peace now. No more pain."

461

'The next week, they sent me to my grandparents as Dad was taking Mum away on a surprise holiday. He called it "the honeymoon they never had", because they were so young when they got married, they couldn't afford to go away properly.'

Aspinall bared his teeth. 'That's why he couldn't afford to take Sandy to the vet's; he spent all his money on first-class flights, champagne and bloody oysters.'

'That must have been very distressing,' said Hardwick. 'But what does it have to do with your grandparents?'

Aspinall blinked, as if jerked back to reality.

'Sorry.' He took a deep breath. 'Nana was in a care home. She was ill. We all knew she only had a few weeks left. One afternoon, she was in a lot of pain, struggling to breathe. We were all there; it was a Sunday. Dad asked us if he could have a little time alone with her. Mum and I went for a coffee. When we came back, Dad was coming out of the room in tears. I'll never forget his words: "She is at peace now. No more pain".'

Chapter 73

'Patricia Aspinall is insisting her husband was with her every Sunday night we asked her about, including New Year's Eve,' said Sutton. 'She's admitted that she lied about Spencer being with them but is adamant that Freddie watched the fireworks with her on the BBC.'

'What did she say about visiting her sister?' asked Grayson.

'An honest mistake,' continued Sutton. 'She thought it was the week before. I agree with Hutch's earlier impression, though; she's definitely hiding something, and she's obviously terrified.'

'What about the dog?' asked Warren.

'Refused to comment.'

'She's protecting him,' said Hutchinson. 'She knows it'll look bad if she admits he dispatched the family pet.'

'What about the death of his mother?' asked Grayson.

'Claimed it was natural causes; refused to say any more when I asked her who was with her when she died.'

Grayson rubbed the bridge of his nose vigorously. 'Shit. There's no way we can justify arresting them. All we've got is that lie about New Year's Eve, which any half-competent defence will claim was just an overprotective mother looking out for her son.'

'Has she given us any idea where Freddie might be?' asked Warren.

'No,' replied Sutton. 'She claims that as far as she was concerned, he went to work as normal this morning. She admits she went to bed before him, and never actually heard him join her, and that he was gone when she woke up.'

'Had his side of the bed been slept in?' asked Grayson.

Sutton gave a tight smile. 'Can't remember. She's not giving us anything concrete that might come back and bite her on the arse if we prove it's a lie.'

'What about his van still being on the driveway, and the text message he sent to his co-workers saying he was ill?' asked Warren.

'Doesn't know anything about it. She just assumed it wouldn't start, or he decided that he didn't need all his tools, so took the car, which is usually parked down the street. She did try to call him at lunchtime to ask him to pick up some milk, but it went straight to voicemail.'

'Convenient,' said Warren. It was frustrating, but getting a wife to speak out about her husband was always difficult. At the moment, their house was being turned upside down by a team of CSIs. Given what they had already found in the storage unit, and the stack of forensics already being fast-tracked, he was confident it would only be a matter of time before they had enough to charge him with, if and when they finally found him.

'Cut them loose,' said Grayson.

'Where to?' asked Warren. 'They can't go home, obviously. But I'm worried that Freddie is still out there. We've seen what he's capable of; from where he's standing, they're two potential loose ends.'

'Arrange for them to go to a hotel for a couple of nights. I'll get authorisation for a protection detail; I imagine the chief constable won't be happy if we turf them out and Freddie Aspinall kills them.' He clapped Warren on the shoulder. 'In the meantime, it looks as though you and Lizzie get to enjoy another couple of nights at the Hotel Grayson.'

Friday 30th March

Chapter 74

Warren drained the dregs of his coffee, before calling the morning briefing to order. It was Good Friday, but everybody had cancelled their plans for the bank holiday. The faces in front of him were drawn and grey; he wasn't the only person who'd lain awake worrying about what Freddie Aspinall was planning next. His disappearance showed that he knew they were on to him, and so it had been decided to go public. A press conference fronted by John Grayson and ACC Naseem was scheduled to start within the hour, but all major media outlets had already been furnished with up-to-date photographs of Aspinall, and details of the missing Audi.

'How are we doing with CCTV?' Warren asked Richardson.

'The good news is that Amazon have footage from his last couple of visits to the locker. We also have video from one of the cash deposits that serviced the bank account.' Her voice was croaky and she took a swig from her water bottle.

'And the bad news?'

'He was wearing a baseball cap and dark glasses with his collar turned up; he kept his face turned away from the camera the whole time, and there are no logos on his cap or jacket. I have a couple of shots from other locations, but they aren't much better. I've sent it all off for image analysis, but they aren't miracle workers; if there's nothing there, there's nothing there.'

'What about ANPR?'

'Inconclusive. The family Audi was snapped entering and leaving the general area of the locker both times, but over an hour either side of when the parcels were picked up. The same with the bank run. There are dozens of businesses around there he could have been legitimately visiting, or he could have just parked in a side street and waited an hour to muddy the waters. Rachel has been using his phone's location history, but surprise, surprise, both times it was sitting at home. I have teams collecting more CCTV but it was weeks ago, most will have been overwritten by now.'

'Keep at it,' said Warren. 'All we need is one identifiable image of him wearing the same clothes as the person using the Amazon locker.'

He turned to Ruskin, who had been showing Freddie Aspinall's headshot to potential eyewitnesses.

'I spoke to the couple who we think saw him on New Year's Eve. The boyfriend lingered over Aspinall's photo, but ultimately went for Callum Harradine. His girlfriend went straight for Eric Morton.'

'Hardly surprising, since both of those fine gentlemen were identified from the e-fit they generated,' said Warren. 'Did Mr Kirkby mention that he'd had quite a bit to drink that night?'

'He might have brought it up,' said Ruskin.

'What about the original owners of the freezers?'

'No use,' he said. 'Too dark and too long ago.'

Warren pushed out his lips. 'He's not making it easy for us, is he? Rachel, anything on his financials?'

'Nothing. The account in the name of his mother has recorded no activity for weeks. The joint account he shares with his wife has had nothing since a fifty-quid cash withdrawal last Saturday. Neither has his business account. There is no obvious correlation between withdrawals and the cash amounts deposited in his mother's account. Which means he has – or at least had – another source of funding we know nothing about.'

'Anything from his mobiles?' asked Sutton.

'Nothing from the SIM cards or the handsets. His car's telematics are also offline, so we can't trace it that way. We're mapping all of his known movements over the past few months, including those of the phones from the lock-up, to see if we can identify any boltholes, but nothing yet.'

'If he does have a place to hide, you can bet he hasn't been visiting it regularly with his phone turned on,' said Sutton.

'What about his online activities?'

'No activity on the Sunday Night Slayer website since Monday, or any of the associated social media accounts,' continued Pymm. 'He maintains a low online profile in his day-to-day life, just a personal Facebook account that mostly shares photos and dodgy memes. FAB Construction has very basic business accounts on Facebook and Instagram with contact details and pictures of completed jobs. The text to his colleagues is the last thing we have.'

'Hutch, anything from the search teams?'

'Nothing significant. It looks like he did a really good job keeping his two lives separate. IT have seized all electronic devices in the house, but the laptop and the phones we found in the lock-up suggest that he probably maintained a clear boundary. Any overlap that proves the lock-up is definitely his could take weeks to find.'

Warren acknowledged him with a nod. 'At this stage, our number-one priority must be finding him. Tony, visit the Aspinalls' hotel and see if the dawn of a new day has brought any insights. Based on what we haven't found, we know he is probably armed with a stun gun, possibly a handgun, and maybe incapacitant spray. We've also not identified any knives consistent with the ones used to kill Bobby Lagdon or the Bevans. The decoy bag we believe he used to transport the bodies is also missing.

'Professor Swann and I think that he probably had a contingency plan in case his hideaway was discovered. Now he knows we've identified him, he might step up his pace. Today is Friday, but we cannot assume that we have until Sunday to find him before he kills again.'

Chapter 75

'It looks like we've uncovered his motive for targeting Councillor Paddon,' Warren had told Grayson as soon as the superintendent returned from the press conference. ACC Naseem joined them via conference call. 'DI Sacker has been examining correspondence related to the Maintenance and Works Committee that Paddon was involved in. They recently awarded a multi-million-pound contract to Mankin Property Development to refurbish the town hall. A contract Freddie Aspinall Building & Construction also bid for, in partnership with two other small firms. The partnership was only formed to bid for this job and dissolved again afterwards. FAB Construction were only a junior partner and Aspinall never spoke to DI Sacker's team, so we didn't find the connection immediately.'

'These things happen,' said Naseem; a generous allowance that Warren hoped was echoed in the inevitable review of the investigation. 'Am I to assume Mr Aspinall did not believe it a coincidence that the job was given to a firm owned by someone Paddon considered a close personal friend?'

'He certainly did not,' said Warren. 'He was banking on the contract to help him expand his own company and was really disappointed when Mankin undercut them and won the bid.

471

And, according to his workmates, he "did his nut" when the links between Mankin and Paddon were revealed in the *Reporter*. He was "absolutely fucking furious" when Mankin went back to the council, cap in hand, after an "unexpected" cost over-run that the partnership had factored into their bid, meaning they were undercut.'

'Which is why Paddon was killed with a nail gun,' said Grayson.

'Which begs the question as to whether the other targets have a similar personal connection?' said Naseem.

'It's an angle we've been actively pursuing since the outset,' said Warren, 'but we have nothing so far. I'm leaning more towards convenience. By all accounts he had little to no interaction with Charley Gibson, and his firm are one of several that Hertfordshire Renovations subcontract to; he had no influence on their decision to take on the work. He did deal with the Culverhouses, but according to his workmates there was nothing unusual about the job. Payment was on time, and they were unaware of any disagreements. However, in both instances he had access to their properties, which were conveniently isolated.'

'But he seems to have groomed Winnie Palmer,' said Naseem.

'That's true, but we can find no evidence of their paths crossing prior to the run-up to Christmas, when she mentioned a new friend. We have no idea how he first identified her as a potential target.

'In terms of his other victims, he needed access to oxycodone, so a dealer was necessary. He was probably worried they could identify him if they were ever asked.'

'So the Lagdons became loose ends,' supplied Grayson.

'And if he's going to dispose of them anyway, then he may as well make them part of his plan,' Warren continued. 'I think the Bevans just ticked the right boxes; he planned on picking somebody up Sunday night and they were just unlucky.'

The sorrow in Naseem's voice was evident. 'So utterly, utterly senseless. We see a lot of wicked people in this job, but this man

472

is the closest to pure evil I have encountered. Catch this bastard and bring him to justice.'

Walking back to his own office, Warren felt a swirl of emotions. Sorrow at the senseless tragedy and a glowing anger towards the man who had done this. But he disagreed with Naseem in one fundamental way. Freddie Aspinall was not evil; evilness was orchestrated by the Devil. Warren's complicated and evolving personal faith had left him questioning in recent years whether the Devil was any more than a construct devised by man that he could blame for his own shortcomings. It was a debate that he and Tony Sutton had occasionally explored over the years, and one that they had never satisfactorily resolved.

Of one thing he was certain: there could be no apportioning of blame in this case. 'The Devil made me do it' was not an acceptable excuse or explanation.

This was all on Freddie Aspinall. Nobody else.

* * *

'It looks as though he took a header off the bridge and smashed his skull open on the rocks,' said Andy Harrison.

The call had come in just after five p.m. Hikers had spotted the abandoned vehicle shortly after lunch; it took two hours to assemble an armed search team and half that time again to find the body floating face down in the river cutting through Barrington Woods.

Warren let out a long, shuddering breath.

'It's over,' Sutton said quietly. He was as stunned by the sudden conclusion to the manhunt as his friend.

'He took the coward's way out.' It was a phrase Warren normally abhorred. Most people who killed themselves were worthy of sympathy, not accusations of cowardice, their final desperate act a way to end their suffering. But Freddie Aspinall deserved none of that. He had denied his victims' loved ones the chance to see

473

him answer for his crimes.

Emotions warred within Warren as the CSIs manipulated the body onto a stretcher. Relief that the rampage had finally come to an end. Sorrow that it hadn't ended sooner. And anger that a man like Freddie Aspinall had believed his sick desires were more important than another person's chance to live their lives.

But above all, there was an overwhelming sense of reassurance that the person whose very existence would forever be a danger to Warren, Susan and their unborn child was no longer a threat.

'Let's go home,' said Warren.

Saturday 31st March

Chapter 76

Warren felt reinvigorated. He and Susan had returned home shortly after midnight. With the threat now gone, Susan had been desperate to sleep in her own bed.

Warren felt the same way, and the five hours between his head hitting the pillow and his alarm sounding were the deepest, most fulfilling sleep he could remember in recent times. Susan had barely even stirred as he'd got up. Resting his hand on her bump, he'd felt a slight kick beneath his palm. 'Rest well, kiddo,' he'd whispered quietly.

The briefing had a slightly shell-shocked feel to it; everyone had been ready for a lengthy search. However, there was too much tragedy for anyone to feel triumphant.

'The family liaison team broke the news to the Aspinalls last night after we confirmed his identity,' said Hutchinson. 'His head was pretty bashed in, but his face was largely untouched.'

'How did they take it?' asked Warren, pushing aside the image of Aspinall's body face down in the water, his long hair drifting in the current. Despite his team's understandable feelings towards Freddie Aspinall, Warren was conscious of the fact that the man's wife and son were also victims.

'Spencer was resigned to it,' said Hutchinson. 'Patricia … not so much. She insists it's all a big mistake. She was so agitated, they called a doctor; she wouldn't even speak to her son.'

'Unfortunately, we are going to need statements from them both,' said Warren. 'Can you speak to the FLO and see if we can get them in when they're ready? Perhaps Patricia will have a change of heart when we show her some of the evidence against him. Speaking of which, where do we stand?'

'We have both a visual and mitochondrial DNA match between the grey hairs found in the Lagdons' vehicle and those taken from Freddie's hairbrush,' said Ruskin. 'Additional hairs have been taken from his head for further confirmation.'

'Aspinall's phone has been recovered from the Audi and is being fast-tracked,' said Pymm.

'CCTV from the National Express depot in Bristol, shows nobody that could be him with a fold-up commuter bicycle, or a bag he could hide it in, catching a coach the morning that Charley Gibson's car was left in Gloucestershire,' said Richardson. 'We're still waiting on Bristol Parkway train station, but there are a lot more cameras, so it's going to take a while longer.'

'Well it sounds as if we have plenty to do to keep us busy,' said Warren. 'But before you all leave, we have one other thing to discuss.'

* * *

Warren drove Swann to the train station. Her two-or-three-day trip had turned into ten, and she needed to return home. 'The last time I left my cat to be fed by my neighbour for this long, the traitorous princess punished me by refusing to eat anything I served and going next door to beg. It was bloody embarrassing.'

'Thank you so much for everything you've done, Lizzie,' said Warren. 'You've gone above and beyond.'

'No, *thank you*.' She turned to look at him. 'To be at the centre of an investigation like this … well it's put it all into perspective.' She grinned. 'Of course, if you really want to show your gratitude—'

'I'll think about it,' Warren interrupted her. 'And I'll have to get permission to appear on screen. I'm still a serving police officer.'

'Fair enough,' she said as Warren pulled into the short-stay drop-off zone. 'I'll email you some more thoughts later this week. Pass on my love to Susan and keep me posted on the baby.'

Warren promised to do so.

Before she exited the car, she turned back to him, her face serious. 'Something still bugs me. Throughout this case, Freddie Aspinall has sought to control and manipulate everyone involved, us included. So it kind of makes sense that he would end it on his own terms.'

'Why am I waiting for a but?' asked Warren.

'He was also an extreme narcissist who loved the attention he received. His trial would have had global coverage; documentaries and books would have been produced about him. Until the next one comes along, he'll be the most infamous serial killer in the world. So why didn't he stick around to see it?'

* * *

Freddie Aspinall's post-mortem had brought closure of sorts for Warren. External examination of his body had revealed no surprises; cause of death was massive trauma, consistent with a head-first fall from height, onto sharp rocks. A belly full of whisky and oxycodone had made doubly sure.

Driving back to Middlesbury, Warren and Sutton had brainstormed what needed to be done. The sooner they could conclusively link Aspinall to all of the killings, the sooner they could end the limbo for those left behind. Teams of family liaison officers had broken the news to the victims' loved ones, making sure that they were fully informed before the formal press announcement scheduled for tomorrow.

'There was nothing in the boot of the car, and his house and van have been turned upside down, but there's no sign of his bicycle, the decoy bag or his gun and TASER,' said Sutton.

'Which suggests that unless he disposed of them, he has somewhere else where he was stashing things,' said Warren.

'Another lock-up?' suggested Sutton.

'I really hope not,' said Warren. Because another lock-up was another potential place to store a freezer. Were there more victims out there that they didn't even know about?

Chapter 77

'You really didn't have to do this,' said Grayson, from the passenger seat of Warren's car. 'Susan has had a stressful enough few days as it is, she shouldn't be cooking a meal for me.'

'It was her idea,' said Warren. 'You've been so kind to us. Besides, Refilwe's away for another week – we can't have you sitting around on your own.'

'Well, it was my pleasure,' said Grayson. He looked out of the window and gave a big sigh. 'Despite everything, I'm going to miss all this. You. The team. Being a part of something so important. I'm not sure what I'm going to do with myself, come next month.'

'You'll find something, John,' said Warren, pulling into his driveway. 'And if you don't, there's always golf.'

Grayson gave a quiet chuckle. 'I wish. Refilwe's list of jobs is so long I may as well be starting a second job. I'm going to get more involved in some of the charities that she works for. She's supported me so much over the years, despite the demands of her own career; it's time I paid her back.'

'You'll bring a lot of useful skills, I'm sure,' said Warren as the two men walked down the garden path.

Unlocking the front door, Warren, stepped aside. 'After you.'

Grayson entered the hallway, the smell of fresh cooking wafting out of the kitchen.

'In here, John,' came Susan's voice from the living room. Grayson wiped his feet and headed for the open door.

'Surprise!'

'You git,' was all Grayson could manage.

*   *   *

'Can I have everyone's attention, please?' announced Warren, after filling Grayson's glass with a generous measure of single malt. The Joneses' living room was crammed with the core team from CID. Rachel Pymm sat in an armchair, interrogating Hardwick about her new boyfriend, whilst balancing a glass of red wine on one knee, and a sleepy Oliver Hardwick on the other. Opposite them, Mags Richardson and David Hutchinson shared the sofa, cradling bottles of Newcastle Brown Ale; the resurgence of his Newcastle accent suggested it wasn't his first that evening.

'Uh-oh, it looks like the Chief is going to make a speech,' Sutton directed at Ruskin in a loud stage whisper. 'I'd pull up a chair and get yourself comfortable, Moray.'

'Behave yourself, Tony,' admonished Susan, 'or I'll tell your wife you've been drinking.' She handed him a half-glass of prosecco, an indulgence in which he partook only on special occasions.

Ruskin took a swig of his bottle of lager and settled himself on an ornate wooden dining chair. It creaked alarmingly. The chair was one of a set Granddad Jack and Nana Betty had bought second-hand after they got married. Granddad Jack had two, whilst Warren had taken the remaining four after they emptied his house. They could have fetched a good price at auction, but they evoked too many memories for him to contemplate selling them.

'Whoa, careful,' said Warren, as Ruskin leapt back to his feet. 'I don't think they had someone your size in mind when they made that.'

'Sorry, Boss,' said Ruskin, his face flushing the same colour as his beard.

'Now, if you've all quite finished,' continued Warren. 'It's been a hellish few weeks, and there is much left to do. But I wanted to gather you all here to thank you for your hard work, and because somebody here has a special birthday soon.'

'Not you, silly,' said Hardwick to her son, who had perked up at the word *birthday*. 'That was last week.'

Warren turned to Grayson. 'I know it's a bit early, and there will be plenty of formal events to mark your retirement, but I thought today would be a good time for us to present you with this.'

Warren reached behind the sofa. 'Your good lady wife tells me you've been eyeing this for a while,' he said as he wheeled out a monogrammed golf bag and trolley.

'I don't know what to say,' said Grayson, swallowing at the sudden lump in his throat. 'I really don't ...' His voice dried up.

The awkward silence stretched for a few seconds, before being broken by the tinkle of Pymm's wine glass as Oliver wriggled off her knee to take a better look at the exciting-looking contraption in the middle of the room.

'Careful, Oliver!' called Hardwick, torn between her rampaging child and the red stain spreading on the white rug.

'No, that's me being clumsy,' said Pymm. 'I should have placed it on the coffee table.'

'Don't worry,' said Susan hurrying to the kitchen for a cloth. 'I'm sure there'll be plenty more spillages when the baby comes.'

Ruskin started picking up broken glass, whilst Grayson scooped Oliver up to stop him treading on it.

'Fetch some salt,' Hutchinson called after Susan.

'No, white wine,' argued Richardson.

'Baking soda, I heard,' said Ruskin.

'Perfect timing,' Grayson whispered in the bemused toddler's ear.

Sunday 1st April

Chapter 78

The get-together at the Joneses' house had continued until late, and it was Easter Sunday, so the office was quieter than usual. But today was the first Sunday that Freddie Aspinall would not be adding to his dreadful tally or depositing the body of a previous victim.

News of Freddie Aspinall's suicide still dominated the headlines, with the *Middlesbury Reporter* getting in some sly digs about the effectiveness of the investigation.

'The Video Analysis Unit have a potential sighting of Freddie Aspinall outside the front entrance of Bristol Parkway train station the day that Charley Gibson's car was abandoned,' said Richardson. Sitting beside her ever-present bottle of water was a cup of coffee and a blister pack of aspirin.

She pointed at her screen. 'This is a small shop selling travel accessories, including luggage. Unfortunately, the angle is poor and the person we believe to be Aspinall is wearing a baggy hoodie and a baseball cap, and keeps his head down.'

A large man wearing a backpack entered the shop.

'Annoyingly, the shop's own footage from this date was erased a day before the Transport Police requested it, so we have nothing from inside.' She smothered a yawn as she fast-forwarded four minutes. The same man emerged, head still down, carrying a large electric-blue suitcase.

'We have him going back up the street, still no face shots, then he disappears for another six minutes.' She ran the video at full speed again. 'We believe this is him again.'

The man she pointed at was the same size and build, but his hoodie was a different colour, as was the baseball cap. But the electric-blue suitcase was clearly the one bought minutes earlier.

'That case is easily big enough for a fold-up bicycle,' she said.

'Any idea where he goes next?' asked Warren, fighting not to yawn himself, now Richardson had set the ball rolling.

'They are collating the video now. We should be able to follow him across the platforms and work out which train he catches. We may even get some video from inside the carriage.'

'That's great work,' said Warren. 'I don't think it'd stand up to cross-examination in court, but fortunately, there isn't going to be a trial.'

'Hutch, see if the Aspinalls' FLO can persuade them to attend a final interview. That blue suitcase is another item we haven't recovered. If he did have some other place he stashed things, we need to know about it. And whilst you're at it, set up some more interviews with his workmates; see what else they remember.'

Returning to his office, he was snagged by Janice. 'Sir, I have the editor of the *Middlesbury Reporter* on the line.'

Warren gave a dismissive snort. 'Tell him to speak to the Press Office. If he thinks he's going to get anything from me that is printable, he has another thing coming.'

Entering his office, he snagged his mug off the desk, before heading back out. It was mid-morning and he was going to need coffee and custard creams to sustain him until he went home for lunch.

'He says it's urgent,' said Janice. 'He sounds worried.'

Warren gave a sigh. 'Put him through to my phone.'

He took a moment to compose himself before picking up the handset. The last thing he needed was an ill-tempered quote splashed across the *Reporter*'s website.

Three minutes later, he was heading to Grayson's office.

* * *

'Tell me again why I should give a shit that Marcia Cooper isn't answering her phone?' said Grayson. The superintendent wasn't usually a big drinker, but Warren had all but poured him into the taxi that had taken him home after the party. 'Kick it over to Missing Persons,' he instructed.

'I already have,' said Warren. 'But he says that she was supposed to be meeting an anonymous source who promised to spill the inside story on our investigation. She was really excited; apparently, they hinted there was lots to tell, whatever that means.'

Grayson groaned. 'Great, just what we need. But if this scrote is determined to keep their identity secret, then they probably insisted that she turned her phone off.'

'They have a strict policy that reporters meeting sources alone should do so in a public place and keep their phones on. They have tracking software installed on all of their handsets.'

'Sensible,' said Grayson. 'Might she have disobeyed that rule?'

'Perhaps, but the meeting was scheduled for over three hours ago.'

'Any idea where they were supposed to meet?'

'McDonald's on the Copperston Road Roundabout. The GPS recorded her handset as arriving at 07.43, for an eight a.m. meeting. It stopped transmitting two minutes later.'

'They must have CCTV of the car park,' said Grayson. 'Well, if somebody is bad-mouthing us to the press, I want to know who they are. I'll string them up by their bollocks.' He reached for his phone. 'I think we have sufficient concern about her safety to justify a warrant for her phone records and real-time location tracking, wouldn't you agree?'

'I'd say so.'

*　　*　　*

'If the editor of the *Middlesbury Reporter* had called us sooner, we might have made it in time for breakfast,' said Ruskin as he and Hardwick entered the McDonald's takeaway. 'I could murder a McMuffin right now.'

Flashing his warrant card, he introduced himself to the duty manager.

The restaurant had both drive-through and seating facilities, and so the two officers divided the bank of surveillance cameras between them, with Hardwick focusing on the exterior and Ruskin on the interior. They knew from the GPS on Marcia Cooper's phone what time she arrived, and so started from that time point.

'I have her entering the car park exactly when expected,' said Hardwick. 'Damn, it looks as though she's parked on the far side of the car park, out of sight of the cameras.'

'Still no sign of her entering the seating area,' said Ruskin a few moments later.

'Whoa, there she goes,' said Hardwick. 'Her car's leaving already.' She looked at the timestamp. 'That's just over six minutes she's been here. The meeting wasn't even scheduled to start until eight.'

'Could she have received a text?' suggested Ruskin. 'She could have been using a burner phone.'

'Maybe. Or perhaps it was just a drop-off? A folder through the car window.'

'So why is her phone still off?'

'Something doesn't smell right,' said Hardwick. 'I'm going to call Rachel and Mags.'

*　　*　　*

490

'I have no sightings of her car on ANPR,' said Richardson when the conference call connected. 'Wherever she went, it wasn't by an arterial route or through the centre of town.'

'If she was using a burner, could you identify it?' asked Ruskin.

'Technically yes,' replied Pymm. 'I could request a cell mast download of every handset that has connected to the nearest tower, but that's going to capture dozens, perhaps hundreds of innocent users. I can tell you right now we aren't even close to justifying such a warrant.'

'I take your point,' said Hardwick. 'For all we know she might be doing an in-depth interview with somebody who is giving her the scoop of a lifetime. But if she is in any danger, then by the time we prove it, it could be too late.'

'I can request that the phone companies retain the information,' said Pymm. 'That way there's no delay if we do get a warrant.'

'I'll arrange for somebody to recover the CCTV footage for the Video Analysis Unit,' said Richardson. 'But in the meantime, keep on looking. If she did meet her source there, then there's a chance they're on camera. Run it for an hour or so each side of when she arrived to see if anyone interesting pops up. Log any licence plates that you see.'

Hardwick hung up and turned to Ruskin. 'Looks like we're here for the foreseeable. There's no way I can face that without coffee.'

Chapter 79

'Sorry about that,' said Hutchinson, returning to the gathering in the centre of the office. Warren was passing around a bag of doughnuts. 'That was the FLO for the Aspinalls. He's at their hotel, since he wasn't getting any answer when he phoned them.'

With Freddie Aspinall dead, and his wife seemingly in denial, that wasn't a huge surprise. 'Maybe they've turned off their phones?' Warren suggested.

'Well that's just it. He's standing outside Patricia Aspinall's room, and he's convinced he can hear a phone ringing inside. There's no response to knocking on either her or Spencer's door.'

'That sounds like a welfare issue,' said Warren. 'Tell him to go and ask for the manager to let him in.'

He turned back to the briefing. 'What do we still need answers for?'

Although there wouldn't be a trial, separate inquests would be held into each of Aspinall's victims, and they owed it to their loved ones to make sure that the man responsible for their deaths would be recorded as such, even if he was now beyond justice.

'I'm trying to pin down if he was absent from work the day Charley Gibson's car was driven down to Gloucestershire,' said

Hutchinson. 'They were on a job, but it was over two months ago, and nobody can remember if they saw him.'

'Speak to the client,' said Warren, distracted momentarily by his mobile phone buzzing in his pocket. He ignored it; he'd check his voicemail when he had a moment.

'What else?'

The phone stopped. Almost immediately, it started again.

'Sorry,' he said, 'let me deal with this.'

He stepped away from the desk and pulled it out. Susan. He felt his gut tighten. His wife was a schoolteacher – she knew better than most how difficult it was to answer the phone during work hours. Normally she just left a message. Accepting the call, he forced a positive note into his voice. 'Hi, sweetheart, everything OK?'

'I'm bleeding, Warren.'

His blood ran cold.

No, this can't be happening again. When they'd lost the twins, it had nearly broken them, and it had taken over a year before they had been ready to start trying again. This time, they were farther along, and only recently had Warren allowed himself to start believing this time would be different.

'Where are you?' he asked, his voice so calm it was as if somebody else was speaking.

'I'm at home.' She gave a little gasp. 'Please hurry.'

'Have you called an ambulance?' Everyone around him had fallen silent.

'They said it's not an emergency. I'll have to wait for one.' There was a fear in her voice that he couldn't remember hearing before.

He could see Sutton mouthing 'Go!' at him.

'Hold tight, I'll be home as soon as I can.'

'Please hurry,' she said, ending the call. Warren stood for a moment staring at the silent handset, dazed.

'Do you want me to drive you?' asked Sutton.

'No, I'll be OK,' managed Warren. Richardson appeared beside him, pushing his suit jacket into his hand.

'We've got everything covered,' said Sutton. 'Go and be with Susan.'

Not trusting himself to do more than nod his thanks, Warren took off for the stairs at a fast jog.

Sutton collapsed into his chair. 'Shit,' he said quietly.

* * *

'Come on, pick up,' Warren urged Susan, as he voice-dialled her mobile again. Once more, it went straight to voicemail. She must be using it; was she speaking to the hospital?

'Call home phone,' he instructed the car's hands-free kit.

The landline started ringing. '*Pick up, pick up, pick up,*' he repeated quietly, as he navigated a roundabout, his tyres squealing. The phone eventually cut to voicemail.

'Damn it!' he swore, thumping the steering wheel.

Breathe, he ordered himself, deliberately easing off the accelerator; he would be no use to Susan if he wrapped the car around a lamppost.

* * *

Karen Hardwick stared at the split-screen CCTV monitor, trying to ignore the steadily mounting throb in her temples. The source couldn't have picked a better time for a covert rendezvous, with a steady stream of vehicles entering through the main entrance. She noted each vehicle registration, the time that it entered and exited, and whether it went to the drive-through or the car park.

The VAU had specialist software that could do this far quicker than she could, but it would take time for someone to arrive and retrieve the data, return it to the unit down in Welwyn, and upload it in a usable format; far better that she and Ruskin had a quick look for anything obvious before they arrived.

She had soon got into a rhythm, splitting her focus between

the four different cameras, but her eyes were already feeling dry. Beside her, Ruskin stared unblinking at the faces of customers entering the restaurant. He thought it unlikely that the informant would have gone to all the effort of concealing their identity, only to enter a public restaurant for a coffee and a pastry, but there were also customer toilets inside.

Squashed as they were in the cramped office, Ruskin felt Hardwick stiffen beside him.

'What have you got?'

She rewound the footage a few seconds. 'There, see that?'

Ruskin squinted at her screen. The image was blurry, barely within the camera's field of view.

'Shit,' he breathed. 'Get on the phone – they need to know about this.'

*   *   *

'Marcia Cooper's phone just reappeared on the network,' said Pymm.

'What's she doing?' asked Sutton, striding across to her desk.

'Nothing yet, just a handshake with the nearest cell towers.'

'Any location data?' asked Grayson, joining him.

The two men waited impatiently as she connected to the necessary services.

'Got it. The phone appears to be static at present. It's travelled quite some distance from McDonald's. I've got it on the former Copperston Industrial Estate, about twenty miles away.'

'I don't like the sound of that,' said Sutton. 'I'm sure that's being redeveloped. I can't think of any good reason why an experienced reporter would meet a source there, especially on a weekend when there won't be any construction crew about.'

'Phone her,' ordered Grayson.

The seconds ticked by before Cooper's voice instructed them to leave a message.

'Given what Karen and Moray saw on the McDonald's CCTV, I'm requesting Armed Response to the Copperston Industrial Estate,' said Grayson.

'Shit!' Everyone jumped at the sudden expletive from the normally unflappable Hutchinson. 'The FLO assigned to the Aspinalls just called. Patricia Aspinall's dead.'

'What about Spencer?' demanded Grayson.

'No sign of him,' said Hutchinson.

'Rachel, has that warrant come through for Spencer Aspinall's phone?' asked Grayson. He had requested it as soon as Ruskin and Hardwick had called. A large man on a fold-up bicycle, wearing what appeared to be a massive decoy bag on his back, had entered the McDonald's car park thirty minutes before Marcia Cooper was due to meet her informant. They had not found any footage of him leaving again.

Her car had left over four hours ago. Close examination of the footage by Hardwick, in a futile attempt to determine if it was her driving, had revealed that the car's licence plate no longer matched the one that her distinctive green Beetle had been sporting when it entered the car park just moments before.

Traffic cameras had captured the car travelling well above the speed limit on the main road towards Copperston.

'Data is coming through now,' said Pymm.

Grayson dialled the number for today's gold commander. He doubted very much that Aspinall was using his regular phone.

'Thirty minutes,' promised the chief superintendent at the other end of the line. 'But it's a big site – any chance you can narrow down her location? We can't hit every building simultaneously.'

Grayson turned to Pymm.

'Well bugger me, he must have run out of burner phones,' she said, before he got a chance to ask her. 'I've found his registered handset. Right next to hers.'

'How precisely can you locate them?' he asked.

She pursed her lips as she concentrated. 'Sorry, even with data from two handsets the best I can do is a circle with a radius of roughly eighty metres.' She squinted at her screen. 'That's nine buildings.'

'Sirs, I've just got a call from the Social Media Unit,' called out one of the civilian analysts. 'Two hashtags #SundayNightSlayer and #TheGrandFinale have started trending on Twitter. They include a link to the SNS website.'

'Open it,' ordered Grayson.

The familiar homepage rendered quickly. An embedded video player displayed a bright yellow banner: 'Stand by For Livestream'.

Sutton grabbed the rear of the analyst's chair for support, a wave of dizziness passing over him, the taste of copper in his mouth. He knew exactly what was going to happen.

'He's going to kill her live over the internet.'

Chapter 80

'We can't block his website without cooperation from the hosting service, and they haven't answered a single email since we contacted them,' said Pymm.

'If he's going to upload the video from his own camera phone, can we shut it down at source?' asked Hutchinson. 'If we persuade his network provider to disconnect him, will that work?'

'Yes,' said Pymm. 'And if he realises he's lost his audience, he might hold off whilst he tries to fix the problem.'

'Get on it,' ordered Grayson. 'We can't have that poor woman being butchered live.'

Pymm quickly dialled a number, relaying her request.

'Armed Response are on site,' said Grayson after another brief phone conversation. The teams had planned their assaults en route, using maps made before the developers had started demolishing the site. They were going in half-blind, but they had no choice; Aspinall had forced their hand.

Suddenly a spinning blue circle appeared on the video player.

'Shit, he must have another phone that he's using to upload the video from,' said Pymm.

Moments later, the player came to life.

Seated on a wooden chair was a terrified Marcia Cooper.

Resting on her knee was an open notepad, in her trembling right hand, she held a pen. Behind her hung a black drop cloth, a bright light source off-screen providing illumination. Opposite her was another, empty chair.

'He's built a bloody TV studio,' said Sutton, realisation dawning. 'The fucking narcissist wants her to interview him.'

*   *   *

Ruskin drove, whilst Hardwick streamed the video live on her phone. 'I can't believe it. Do you think he's going to kill Marcia Cooper after she's interviewed him?'

Ruskin said nothing. The man on the screen had killed more victims than he could count off the top of his head.

'Wait, Moray, pull over and look at this,' said Hardwick suddenly.

Ruskin did so immediately, eliciting a chorus of angry horns from other drivers surprised by his sudden manoeuvre.

He took the device from her, instantly seeing what she had spotted. 'Shit!'

There was no need to say anymore. Ruskin jammed the car into reverse and mounted the kerb, executing a clumsy three-point turn. More horns blared.

Hardwick dialled Sutton on her work phone. 'They're not at the industrial estate, Tony,' she said.

'We know,' interrupted Sutton. 'The AFOs found Spencer Aspinall and Marcia Cooper's smartphones sitting in a derelict warehouse alongside what appears to be his victims' missing property and clothes. It looks as though he's been using it for storage. We're trying to figure out where he's taken her.'

'Look at the video. The chairs match the one that Moray nearly broke last night, and at the edge of the shot is the white rug Ollie spilled wine on. You can see the stain.

'He's in Warren and Susan's house.'

Chapter 81

Warren cursed his stupidity again. How could he have missed all the clues? And why hadn't he paused to ask why the curtains in the front room, which he'd opened that morning, were drawn again?

Of course, he knew why.

Spencer Aspinall had played him, just as he'd been playing everyone since he'd killed Winnie Palmer.

He should have realised something was amiss when he heard Susan's voice on the phone. She'd been terrified. He'd naturally assumed it was because she thought she was losing the baby. But Susan rarely panicked. In fact, when they'd they lost the babies previously, she'd been so calm she'd argued against calling an ambulance, even as she collapsed.

But the real red flag had been days before, when they located the lock-up. He'd dismissed it as the dumb luck that sometimes broke a case. But with hindsight, it was too convenient. The electricity had been allowed to run out and the rent go unpaid: Spencer had wanted it to be found, the first in a series of breadcrumbs leading them towards his father.

With a suspect in the frame, they'd seen what he wanted them to see, ignoring inconsistencies such as the grey hairs in the back of the Lagdons' car. The ends had been cut, as if the person had just had their hair trimmed. But Freddie Aspinall had a flowing mane of hair. It didn't look as though he'd been to a barber for months, which didn't match the description – such as it was – given by the drunk couple who'd spotted the killer on New Year's Eve. Looking at Spencer now, Warren was struck by the physical resemblance between father and son.

And then there was the sophisticated use of the dark web, the hacking into an unsecured Wi-Fi network, and the setting up of a website using a provider that protected and concealed his location. Freddie Aspinall was a builder; he didn't even have a business website and his Facebook page was as basic as it could be. Spencer had an A level in Computer Science.

Spencer sometimes worked for his father; he was insured on both of the family's vehicles and had full access to his father's tools and almost certainly the keys and alarm codes to the properties they worked on. Yet even there, Spencer had laid out the clues, choosing victims that his father's construction firm had links with. For Charley Gibson's renovations and the failed council bid, FAB Construction's involvement was concealed by its role as a subcontractor or partner. Was that deliberate? A ploy to make the connections, once uncovered, more convincing?

Yet the killings, or the dumping of the bodies, took place late on Sunday nights, probably lasting until the early hours of the following morning. Freddie Aspinall was a manual labourer, up and out well before seven a.m. Spencer supposedly stayed up all night playing video games, rolling out of bed when he felt like it.

Warren wasn't sure how he had faked the phone calls he had used as an alibi, but there were apps for everything these days. How hard would it be to set up his handset to automatically answer a call from an unregistered burner and leave it at home?

Spencer had described how his father had callously despatched the family dog, a memory that still clearly affected him. Yet the killer of the Culverhouses and Winnie Palmer had laid out several days' worth of food to tide their dogs over until they were found.

Swann had had her reservations: their killer was a narcissist, loving the thrill of the chase. How likely was it that he'd kill himself before he got a chance to revel in the attention?

* * *

Warren's memories after he was tased when he opened the front door were hazy. He recalled Aspinall effortlessly carrying him into the front room and sitting him down on one of his grandfather's wooden chairs, before securing his hands to its frame with two pairs of old-fashioned, chain-link handcuffs.

'I'm so sorry,' Susan had said, her face streaked with tears. She was similarly manacled, but he could see no obvious signs of physical harm.

'I have to say, DCI Jones – or can I call you Warren? – that Mrs Jones was braver than I thought she'd be.' Aspinall had chuckled as he pulled a black handgun from his waistband and pointed it towards the couple. 'The language she used when I put this against her head and told her to call you, was a real eye-opener. I'll bet you don't even speak like that in the staffroom when there are no pupils nearby, eh, Mrs Jones?'

His tone had turned serious again. 'But of course, pregnant women have a weakness.' He'd flicked the gun towards her swollen belly. 'It's probably an evolutionary thing.'

'Let her go,' Warren had pleaded. 'It's me you want.'

'Is it? You know, I hadn't even thought about who might be SIO on the investigation, and Jones is such a common name I didn't make the connection at first. That talk you gave was years ago. But when I realised who you are married to … well it was just too perfect.' His mouth had twisted, the effect exaggerated by his misaligned jaw. 'Of course you don't remember speaking to me, the way you humiliated me. I queued patiently for ages to speak to you, but you had one eye on your mobile phone.'

'I'm sorry, Spencer,' Warren had said. 'I don't remember—'

'Of course you fucking don't!' shouted Aspinall. 'I asked you about joining the police, but that fucking bell-end Toby Spackman said that the police would make me cut my hair and take a bath. And what did you say?'

'I honestly don't remember,' Warren had replied, a sinking feeling in his gut. He'd been very distracted. What had he said without thinking?

'You said that the rules about appearance were a lot stricter when you joined up.'

'I'm sorry, I really didn't mean anything ...'

Aspinall had ignored him. 'For months I was teased that I smelled so bad that even the pigs wouldn't have me. The twat even poured a bottle of shampoo on my head from the top of the sixth form stairs.'

Warren had opened his mouth to apologise again, but Aspinall had already turned his attention to Susan.

'Some of my schoolmates will be graduating university this year, but not me. I was probably the brightest kid you ever taught, and yet the school fucked me over by predicting me D grades at A level and writing a shitty reference. Now I'm stuck living with my parents and working for my dad with his moronic mates, who talk about nothing but football, beer and women. I could have been a doctor or a scientist, but you couldn't see beyond your stupid rules.'

Warren had shot a glance at his wife, who'd looked affronted. Now was not the time to defend herself and her colleagues against baseless accusations.

'Why are you doing this, Spencer?' Warren had asked, desperate to keep the man talking. As far as his team were concerned, he was at the hospital with Susan. Even if they did decide to try and contact him, Aspinall had smashed his phone.

'I've someone I'd like you to meet,' Aspinall had said, leaving the room. Warren had immediately tried to stand, but the chair had an ornate horizontal bar joining the front legs, and he couldn't get his feet far enough under to balance his weight.

He'd ceased his efforts when Aspinall re-emerged, dragging the large, canvas decoy bag Warren dimly remembered seeing in the hallway.

After unzipping the bag, Aspinall tipped it onto its side, depositing the bound form of Marcia Cooper on the floor with an ungainly thump, before dragging her limp form onto a third chair. The rip of the duct tape from her mouth jerked her back to her senses.

After reaching into his trouser pocket, he'd produced a folding knife, its blade encrusted with dried blood. Cooper's eyes widened in terror, as he held it in front of her face.

'There's no need to hurt her,' Warren had said, desperately.

'That's very gallant of you, especially after all the grief she must have caused you.' Turning to Cooper, he'd sneered. 'I can't believe you were so dumb. An anonymous source phones you out of the blue and claims he has the inside scoop on the biggest story of your career, and you didn't even think to question why they reached out to you, instead of one of the national newspapers? I'll bet you thought all of your Christmases had come at once. Book deals, TV documentaries, a job on a proper paper …'

He sliced through the tape binding her wrists.

'Don't worry, I'm not going to hurt you. I need you to do something for me.'

* * *

Ruskin was parked a few doors down from the Joneses' house, behind Marcia Cooper's Volkswagen Beetle. 'He's changed the plates again,' he observed.

'Uniform are on their way,' said Hardwick, juggling her work handset with her personal phone. 'But Armed Response are still out in Copperston. The nearest available unit is coming from Welwyn, at least fifteen minutes away.'

On screen, Spencer Aspinall was talking to Marcia Cooper.

At the edge of the shot, Warren said something that the camera phone didn't pick up and Aspinall spun angrily, pointing the handgun towards the couple.

'You were telling me about why you are doing this,' interjected Cooper quickly. As swiftly as it had come, the anger disappeared.

'Wait here,' said Ruskin, opening the car door.

'What? Where are you going?' asked Hardwick.

'Around the back. I need to get a look at the layout for the Armed Response Unit.'

'Are you crazy? Wait for backup, Moray, he's armed.'

Ruskin shook his head and started dialling Hardwick's work phone. 'You know how it works: uniform will get here, secure the perimeter and then wait for armed response. Who will then send someone in to get eyes on the target, before finally figuring out how to enter. How long is that going to take? The bastard is flapping in the wind like a flag. Every second we waste, is another second he could flip out and shoot everyone in the room.'

He inserted the earpiece from his hands-free kit. 'Keep the call active, so you can hear what's going on.'

'Seriously, Moray, this is a really bad idea,' she said.

'I know, but it's better than anything else I can think of.'

He closed the car door and started jogging towards an alleyway leading to the rear of the row of terraced houses.

'Shit, Moray,' said Hardwick.

She turned her attention back to the video.

* * *

'... it's basic psychology, you see,' said Aspinall. He'd been speaking for several minutes without pause, lounging on a wooden chair, the handgun resting on his knee. 'If you kill only one, then it's all about the victim. You're just the person who murdered Joe Bloggs. Nobody remembers *your* name. But if you kill more, then it shifts. Do enough and there are too many for the public to

505

remember, and so *you* are the person they recall. Dennis Nilsen was convicted of killing six men; they suspected fifteen. Who remembers their names?'

'Their families,' blurted out Warren, unable to let that go unchallenged. 'They were individuals, with people who loved them.'

Aspinall ignored him. 'They tried Peter Sutcliffe for thirteen deaths.' He gave a shrug. 'Nobody except for true crime fans can name them all, and don't get me started on Harold Shipman. Fifteen that they could prove, hundreds more they never managed to pin on him. But he doesn't count anyway.'

'What do you mean, he doesn't count?' asked Cooper.

'In the league table of Britain's most prolific serial killers, he was an anomaly. He was a doctor; that gave him special access. He didn't have to work for it. Bruce George Peter Lee is listed because he did twenty-six, but they were technically manslaughter because he was insane, and eleven were overturned on appeal. I'm not insane. I won't get "diminished responsibility". I've put too much planning into this. There'll be no dispute over whether I knew what I was doing.'

Warren felt sickened; he couldn't believe what he was hearing. 'You did all this to get on some league table?'

'Go big or go home, right?' said Aspinall. He turned back to Cooper and raised an eyebrow, as if waiting for her next question.

'How many have you killed?' she asked eventually.

'Twelve,' he said with what could only be described with pride. 'One less than Sutcliffe. Sorry, Mrs Jones, one *fewer*.'

Warren did the sums. They had investigated nine victims. Unless there were others, as yet undiscovered, there was only one conclusion.

'You killed your father.'

'Of course, he'd served his purpose.' Aspinall giggled. 'And you fell for it hook, line and sinker. It'll take weeks for the blood toxicology to reveal that he had far too much whisky and oxycodone in him to have killed himself.'

'And it was you who smothered your grandmother, wasn't it?' said Warren.

'Yes. I think Mum figured it out, but she thought I'd done it as a mercy. To be honest, I just wanted to see if I had the stomach for it.'

'That's why she lied; claimed that she died naturally,' said Warren. 'To protect you.'

'No!' snapped Aspinall. He turned to Susan. 'I know what you all thought at school. That Spencer's mummy wouldn't hear a bad word said against her little boy. That she'd protect him at all costs. But it was never about me. She didn't want you judging *her*; thinking *she* was a bad parent.

'You probably thought I'd arrive home after parents' evening and Dad would beat me black and blue, but he didn't. It was all Mum.

'Oh, she'd never lay a finger on me; how could she? I was six feet tall before my fifteenth birthday. But she'd tell me in this quiet voice how I was a failure. How I was the cleverest person she'd ever met, but I was too lazy. That I squandered my chances. That *they'd* had no choices, because she fell pregnant with me before they could really live their lives but she didn't want me to end up like my father: stuck in a job he hated, angry at the world because he never got to fulfil his potential.'

He looked at Susan. 'But I had a plan. I was going to go to university, I was going to be *somebody*. Not just the weird kid with the fucked-up jaw that everyone made fun of. But YOU stole that from me.'

Warren racked his brain furiously; he had to divert Aspinall's attention away from Susan.

'What about your dad?' he asked.

'He was a coward. He'd yell and shout, and he was so big it scared people, but it never meant anything. He'd try and sound all tough at parents' evening, but when we got home, he'd just put his headphones on and bury his nose in a book.

507

'You know it was Mum who killed the dog, right? Everyone believed it was Dad, because why wouldn't they? Mum was so quiet and timid, they probably thought he beat her every night.' He wiped his nose with the back of his hand. 'Dad was going to take Sandy to the vet's to get her put down, but Mum said not to be silly. She'd spent summer holidays on her uncle's farm ...'

He cleared his throat and looked away, as if embarrassed at his momentary show of weakness.

'She was so predictable,' he continued eventually. 'She insisted Dad was innocent, despite the evidence against him. How could she admit that she had a serial killer living under her nose? What would that say about her?

'You know, just like you, she really thought I was in the garage every Sunday night.' He gave a smile. 'It was easy to stop her coming in and finding out I was gone. I just lit a couple of cannabis joss sticks, logged onto a porn site and cranked the volume up. No mother is going to knock on the door if she thinks her son is doing that. You guys were even easier to fool. Do you know you can actually pay people in India to play video games for you to improve your rankings? They'll even mimic your IP address to stop your account being blocked.

'Of course, when she finally started to realise that if her husband wasn't guilty ... well, now she's *raised* a serial killer, not just married one! The ultimate example of bad parenting.'

'So why did you kill her?' asked Warren, now certain that Patricia Aspinall was victim number twelve.

'She was going to shop me. I could see it in her eyes. I couldn't let that happen; it was too soon.'

'How long have you been planning this, Spencer?' asked Cooper, her journalistic instincts briefly overcoming her desire to disappear into the background.

'Years.'

He leant forward, his voice taking on an earnest air. 'Do you know why most serial killers fail?' He didn't wait for an answer.

'Because they're chancers. They don't have a vision. They let this—' he pointed to his heart with the gun '—over-rule this.' He tapped his head. 'Even the planners; they kill once, and they get away with it. So a few months later they do it again. And again. But they're just lucky. They might get away with it five times, six times, maybe more, but finally their luck runs out. They don't have a goal. Even Harold Shipman got careless in the end.'

'What's your goal?' asked Cooper, unable to help herself.

Warren closed his eyes; he knew what the answer would be.

'To be the best.'

* * *

Ruskin breathed a silent sigh of relief. It appeared Susan had been in the middle of hanging out some washing when Aspinall arrived, the back door still ajar. His plan, such as it was, had almost failed at the first hurdle when he'd found the rear gate locked. Fortunately, some bricks from next door's partially completed garden wall had provided him with enough additional height to boost himself over the fence, although a protruding nail had ruined his suit jacket.

Crouching beside the open door he peered into the kitchen, listening intently as Aspinall ranted about the shortcomings of other serial killers. He recalled from the previous night that the kitchen led directly into the hallway, with a straight line of sight to the front door. The living room was about halfway down the passageway, to the left from his current vantage point. Light from the powerful lamps Aspinall had used to set up his impromptu TV studio shone through the open doorway.

Tactically, the safest way for the firearms team to storm the house would be for them to smash in the front door, whilst a second team simultaneously entered through the rear. The open kitchen door would facilitate that.

He was about to return to the garden and relay his findings to Hardwick when something caught his eye. Hanging from some hooks on the far wall were several sets of keys. a large silver one, sharing a ring with one for a padlock, appeared to be the right size for the back gate.

It was a no-brainer. The firearms officers would lose valuable seconds, and the element of surprise, if they had to smash the back gate in and make it down the garden path before entering the house. Who knew what Aspinall would do in that time?

He crossed the room as silently as he was able.

In the living room, Aspinall continued pontificating. No shadows crossed the light spilling out of the living room.

Ruskin closed his fist slowly around the keys, tightly grasping them to prevent them from jangling. Eyes fixed on the pool of light on the hallway carpet, he carefully withdrew his hand.

The protruding nail that had ruined his jacket, had torn the sleeve along the seam from the elbow downwards, stopping only at the cuff. It was this that caught a bunch of spare car keys on the next hook, sending them clattering onto the hardwood floor.

Immediately, Aspinall fell silent.

Ruskin froze, unable to decide if he should run out the back door, or if he should throw caution to the wind and hurl himself blindly into the living room and meet Aspinall head on.

The moment for action passed in a blink of an eye, and then it was too late. Spencer Aspinall emerged from the living room, the handgun pointed directly at Ruskin's chest.

* * *

Karen Hardwick had placed her work phone on speaker, so that the uniformed officers gathered around the handset could listen to Ruskin's call.

He'd been correct; the first thing the attending officers had done was seal the street, ushering curious residents back inside.

They were now awaiting armed response. In the meantime, her friends were facing a dangerously unhinged psychopath alone.

The video had been streaming continuously throughout the affair, and Hardwick had propped her phone on the roof of the car so she could see it clearly. She frowned in concentration. 'Something's not right here,' she said. She restored the volume on the video, which she'd muted once Ruskin had entered the house, finding it too distracting to try and listen to the open phone call and the video simultaneously.

Jogging over to a DS watching the video on a tablet, she checked it against her phone. The two feeds were identical. Which left only one explanation for the mismatch between what she was seeing, and what she was hearing over Ruskin's phone call.

'Somebody warn Armed Response; there's a delay on the video feed!'

* * *

Ruskin stepped across the threshold of the living room, hands raised, his torn sleeve flapping traitorously.

'It's over, Spencer. You're surrounded.' His voice was calm, despite the staccato rhythm of his pulse. 'There are armed officers waiting for my signal. Put the gun down and nobody needs to get hurt.'

Aspinall laughed. 'Nice try. You expect me to believe that heavily armed tactical firearm officers with body armour would send in somebody wearing nothing but a cheap suit?'

He gestured with the gun. 'Come on, don't be shy; make sure the camera gets a good shot of you. And you can turn your phone off and throw it over here whilst you're at it.'

Ruskin complied, his teeth grinding as Aspinall stomped on it and tossed it into a pile of similarly broken handsets.

'The fact that you're here tells me you've seen through my little ruse with the mobile phones out in Copperston.' Aspinall smiled. 'I'm not going to lie, I'm rather proud of that one; a simple timer app that switches flight mode on and off, so you can get the phone to appear and disappear from the network at will. I'm amazed no one else has thought of it before.'

'Even if DC Ruskin arrived alone, you can bet the Armed Response Vehicles aren't far behind,' said Warren. 'Leave now and you'll probably get away unharmed.'

'Who says I want to get away?' said Aspinall. 'Anyway, they're not going to shoot me.' He gestured towards the front windows. 'Nobody can see in, so they can't take me out with a sniper. The moment they come crashing through that door, I'll drop the gun.' He pointed towards the mobile phone on its tripod. 'And there's my insurance policy. No body-worn cameras mysteriously failing to record the moment an unarmed man is executed; it's all being streamed.' He turned around to face Cooper, who was staring wide-eyed at events. 'And if that doesn't work, I'm sure our journalist friend will ensure the truth is revealed.'

Moray Ruskin was not only two stone heavier and an inch taller than Spencer Aspinall, but he was also a keen sports player and obsessive gym-goer. His rugby tackle lifted Aspinall clean off his feet and the two men crashed through the black cloth Aspinall had rigged up as a background for his interview. The wooden mantelpiece above the fireplace gave way under the impact and they tumbled into an ungainly heap, the gun skittering across the floor.

Acting on instinct, Warren braced himself and tipped sideways to his right as hard as he could. Just as he'd hoped, the wooden chair, which had already been several decades old when his grandparents had bought it seventy years previously, gave way with a splintering crack.

Ignoring the pain in his arm, he rolled onto his left side, feeling the right handcuff break from the frame of the chair. He started crawling towards the gun.

Ruskin was on his knees, a dazed expression on his face, blood flowing freely from his scalp.

Aspinall rolled onto his back, planting both feet in Ruskin's chest.

The young Scotsman flew backwards, knocking the tripod supporting the camera phone over.

Ignoring Ruskin for the moment, Aspinall started scrambling towards the gun.

Looking back, nobody could ever really say if Warren made the right decision at that point. All he knew was that there was no way he could reach the gun before Aspinall. Perhaps it wouldn't have mattered. Perhaps he could have knocked the gun out of his hand before Aspinall brought it to bear on the person Warren loved most in the world. But Warren's instincts told him otherwise.

He turned back to Susan, who remained handcuffed to her chair.

Time slowed.

Behind him he heard the crashing of bodies and the smashing of furniture. In front of him, Susan's eyes stared at him as he threw himself desperately towards her.

The deafening retort of the gunshot came at the same moment Warren made impact with his wife, toppling her backwards, his body shielding her as best he could. As they crashed to the floor, he closed his eyes, breathing a silent prayer. It would be the cruellest of ironies if his actions harmed the unborn child lying trustingly inside his wife.

Opening his eyes again, Warren's breath caught in his throat.

'*No!*' he gasped.

Blood was splattered across his wife's face, her eyes closed.

The world stopped.

Warren's heart stopped.

* * *

Armed response were still several minutes away when Ruskin's phone stopped broadcasting. Hardwick barely made it three steps, before a sergeant twice her size yanked her back.

She was still arguing with him when the shot rang out.

*   *   *

For what seemed like an eternity, Warren stared in horror at the face of his beautiful, wonderful wife. His soulmate, his best friend and the mother of his unborn child.

'Call an ambulance,' someone shouted behind him. He dimly recognised the voice as that of Marcia Cooper, her tone panicked. 'Please, somebody call an ambulance,' she repeated. 'DC Ruskin has been shot.'

Warren's heart restarted with a jolt.

Susan's eyes opened and she gasped in pain. 'You're kneeling on me.'

Warren rolled to one side. All he wanted to do was take his wife in his arms and tell her how much he loved her. But he didn't have the time.

The scene was absolute carnage. Moray Ruskin lay on his back, eyes closed, blood spreading across his shirt. Spencer Aspinall also lay insensate, framed by a broken coffee table that somebody, presumably Cooper, had brought crashing down on his head.

The gun lay on the floor between them. Warren picked it up and placed it safely in his pocket.

With a deep groan, Ruskin's eyes opened. Warren knelt beside him. The man's eyes were glazed, and his skin felt clammy. His pulse was weak.

'We need a fucking ambulance,' screamed Cooper into Aspinall's camera phone.

Warren carefully peeled back Ruskin's shirt. With an effort, Susan knelt down beside him, the remains of her chair still hanging from her wrist.

'Hey, Moray, speak to me,' she called loudly into his ear. Ruskin's eyes closed again.

'The camera phone's broken,' said Cooper. 'I don't think anyone can hear us.'

'Go to the front door and call for help,' instructed Warren. 'There should be a set of keys hanging in the kitchen.'

'I don't know how bad it is,' said Susan. 'He's in shock. Moray? Can you hear me?'

'Marcia, make sure you open the door slowly, with your hands visible,' Warren called out; if there were firearms officers outside, the last thing they wanted was for her to be shot.

There came a groan from the direction of Aspinall.

Leaving Ruskin to his wife's care, Warren moved over to the man who had caused so much pain and misery.

So many victims, each of which Warren could name. They weren't just numbers.

Aspinall's eyes fluttered open. Seeing Warren standing over him, his mouth twisted into a smile. 'Shit, second place,' he croaked. 'I should have just shot Cooper and matched Sutcliffe.'

Suddenly, the rage was back. The man at his feet had brutally killed innocent people in a pathetic attempt to achieve notoriety, before crossing one final line; he'd threatened the life of Warren's wife and their unborn child.

Warren knew what would happen next. Aspinall would be arrested and charged. His name would be splashed across every media outlet in the world. He'd plead not guilty to ensure there would be a trial, breathlessly reported on for weeks. He'd insist upon taking the stand to give evidence in his own defence, the jury another audience to preen in front of.

And it wouldn't end there. There would be documentaries, films, books and articles; salacious and academic. Swann would doubtless be called upon to relay her own, intimate knowledge of the case. And Aspinall would love every damn second.

Before this, he was a man of no great consequence, known only

515

to those around him. Now his name would never be forgotten. And he was right; few would remember the identities of all his victims, but the name Spencer Aspinall would continue long after they locked him up and left him to rot.

By his own measure, he had still won.

Tears filling his eyes, Warren removed the gun from his pocket and raised it.

Monday 9th April

Epilogue

It felt strange to have Naseem seated opposite in Warren's own office. However, the ACC was already in Middlesbury, and it was the first time the two men's schedules had aligned. This was definitely one of the cases that would feature in the man's memoirs, once he finally retired.

'So Aspinall had been planning the whole thing since before his grandmother even died?' Naseem was aghast.

'The seed of the idea probably goes back to when he left school, but the pace really started to increase in the last couple of years. She'd left him a sum of money that he could only access if he went to university, or failing that, when he reached twenty-one. That gave him the funds he needed to start buying everything and renting the lock-up.'

'And all of that to top some bloody league table,' Naseem said with disgust. 'Why?'

'I think that's one for the psychiatrists,' said Warren. Lizzie Swann had already been in contact, although she wouldn't be allowed access to Aspinall until after he had been medically assessed before his trial. That being said, Aspinall had probably been correct when he'd predicted that he wouldn't be judged

519

insane. As Warren had predicted, he'd entered a plea of not guilty, thus guaranteeing a full jury trial.

'How is DC Ruskin?' asked Naseem.

'Getting better – that shot was one in a million,' said Warren. 'The bullet missed an artery by just a couple of millimetres.'

'What's the long-term prognosis?'

'It's not like the movies; shoulder wounds are normally permanently disabling. Another centimetre or so to the left and it would have blown out the joint. As it was, it smashed his collarbone and continued through. Hopefully he'll make a full recovery.'

Warren felt a little sick, even as he forced himself to sound upbeat. The CSIs had recovered the spent bullet; from its location, they believed that had it not been deflected by Ruskin's shoulder it would almost certainly have hit Susan.

'And mentally?' continued Naseem.

'Harder to say. I think Moray is dealing with it pretty well, all things considered, but his husband wants him to quit.'

Naseem grimaced. 'I can't say I blame him, but Moray is just the sort of officer we need to retain.'

Warren knew what he was hinting at, but he had no intention of pressuring Ruskin either way. 'You can speak to him yourself, sir; he's coming in later.'

Naseem looked at his watch; there were still a few minutes left. 'And how are you and Susan?'

'Susan's OK. The baby's fine, but we're looking into moving house. There are too many unpleasant memories there now.'

Naseem smiled sympathetically. 'I can't really say I blame you.' He leant back in his chair. 'Between you and me Warren, I'm amazed at your self-control. A truly wicked serial killer invades your house, threatens you and your pregnant wife, and then shoots your friend. There are plenty of men who would have taken that handgun and shot him dead; and we both know that given the circumstances, they'd have gotten away with it.'

Warren smiled tightly. 'He'd fired his only bullet, sir. I couldn't have shot him, even if I wanted to.'

'Ah, yes, I remember that from the ballistics report. By the time he'd despatched Nick Lagdon, he only had a single round left and no way to get any more.'

'One was enough,' said Warren quietly.

Naseem looked at his watch. 'Look at the time. We'd better not keep folks waiting.' The two men stood and shook hands.

'Congratulations on a job well done.'

Thanking him, Warren gestured for his guest to go first.

'Oh, just one more thing, Warren,' said Naseem, his hand resting on the door handle. 'Remind me to ask you one day exactly how you knew there were no more bullets in that gun.'

* * *

Naseem was at the centre of the room. He was just finishing a speech that had left John Grayson blushing and chuckling in equal measure.

'Now, there is another reason we are gathered here today. John will leave a big pair of shoes to fill, but I have every confidence in the officer who will be stepping into that role. It was a very strong field of candidates, and the position of superintendent is not one given out lightly – despite what some of you may think.'

The room laughed politely.

'However, this appointment was a unanimous decision. Middlesbury has had some tremendous successes under John, and I know that under the direction of Detective Superintendent Ashley Roehampton, you will continue to make Hertfordshire Constabulary proud.'

'Any regrets?' Sutton asked Warren quietly as the team politely applauded.

To outsiders, the decision to withdraw his candidacy was understandable. The pressures of juggling a new job with a baby, the strain of moving house, and the uncertainty of his father-in-law's diagnosis would make anyone think twice.

But as always, it was the opinion of Susan that had swayed him.

'You'd think that I'd be delighted for you to be promoted to a position where you are no longer so hands-on,' she'd said. 'But that night in John's kitchen, watching you leading that investigation – even feeling a part of it – I finally understood what it means to you. I can't ask you to give that up.'

The question was whether or not he would be allowed to continue doing the job he loved so much. Only the future would tell.

Warren answered his friend with more confidence than he felt. 'None at all.'

Acknowledgements

Wow, it's hard to believe that it's that time again – writing the acknowledgements for another DCI Warren Jones! Twelve books in and it still seems unreal. Thank you so much to everyone who has taken the time to read one. As always, it's humbling when I look at the number of copies sold or borrowed from a library, and realise just how many people have seen my stories.

The team behind me gets bigger with every book, and I always worry that I will forget to thank somebody. So I am going to give a big shout out to everyone who has helped and supported me along the way, including the authors, bloggers and Facebook users who have shared their wisdom, thoughts and grammar tips.

Of course, a big thank you must go out to the team at HQ Stories and HarperCollins, in particular my two editors for this book, Abi Fenton and Dushi Horti. It has been a delight working with everyone again and as always, the book is immeasurably improved every time you give feedback.

Before it reaches HQ, three more sets of eyes have scrutinised the manuscript: Cheryl, Mum and Dad. Thank you so much for your input.

As always, I have sought the expertise of those more learned than myself. My favourite lawyers, Caroline and Dan, have kept me on the straight and narrow for years when it comes to police and legal procedure. My sister, Kate, shared her expertise regarding opiates (she's a doctor, not a drug user), which gave me ideas for a useful plot point.

Andrew Fowlie very generously donated the use of his name for a character through the annual CLIC Sargent Good Books auction (now renamed Young Lives vs Cancer www.younglivesvs-cancer.org.uk), which supports young people affected by cancer. I hope you enjoy your appearance, and thank you so much for supporting such a wonderful charity.

This book was written and edited during the ongoing pandemic, so again I want to thank our wonderful NHS and the keyworkers (including the police) that have kept the country running. I tip my hat to the researchers and those manning the vaccine centres, who have brought the light at the end of the tunnel closer.

Finally, it has been another difficult, and at times disappointing year for everyone, but I know that it would have been far harder without my beloved Cheryl. I love you, and fingers crossed *it* will have happened by the time readers see these acknowledgments!

Best wishes,
Paul Gitsham
Essex.
March 2022.

A Letter from the Author

Time for another thank you to my readers! Whether you have been with Warren and the team since his first appearance, or this is your first experience of the series, then I hope you have enjoyed it.

It's been another difficult year! If you haven't read the book yet, let me reassure you that the novels in my series are typically set three or so years before their publication date, so the big C has yet to make an appearance!

Please, enjoy the journey, and if this book helps distract you for a few hours, then I've done my job.

Keep safe and thank you.

Paul.

The Last Straw

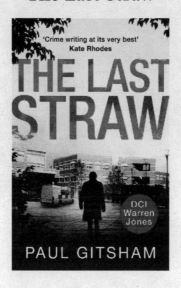

'Crime writing at its very best'
Kate Rhodes

THE LAST
STRAW

DCI
Warren
Jones

PAUL GITSHAM

When Professor Alan Tunbridge is discovered in his office
with his throat slashed, the suspects start queuing up.
The brilliant but unpleasant microbiologist had a
genius for making enemies.

For Warren Jones, newly appointed Detective Chief
Inspector to the Middlesbury force, a high-profile murder is
the ideal opportunity. He's determined to run a thorough and
professional investigation but political pressure to resolve
the case quickly and tensions in the office and at home
make life anything but easy.

Everything seems to point to one vengeful man but the
financial potential of the professor's pioneering research
takes the inquiry in an intriguing and, for Jones and
his team, dangerous direction.

No Smoke Without Fire

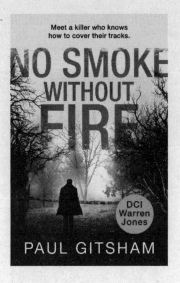

Meet a killer who knows how to cover their tracks.

NO SMOKE WITHOUT FIRE

DCI Warren Jones

PAUL GITSHAM

DCI Warren Jones has a bad feeling when the body of a young woman turns up in Beaconsfield Woods. She's been raped and strangled but the murderer has been careful to leave no DNA evidence.

There are, of course, suspects – boyfriend, father – to check out but, worryingly, it looks more and more like a stranger murder.

Warren's worst fears are confirmed when another young woman is killed in the same way.

The MO fits that of Richard Cameron who served twelve years for rape. But Cameron never killed his victims and he has a cast-iron alibi.

Then personal tragedy intervenes and Warren is off the case. But the pressure is mounting and another woman goes missing. Warren is back but will the break he desperately needs come before there's another victim?

Silent as the Grave

It's DCI Warren Jones' coldest case yet…

The body of Reginald Williamson had been well concealed under a bush in Middlesbury Common and the murder efficiently carried out – a single stab wound to the chest. Reggie's dog had been killed just as efficiently. With no clues or obvious motive, the case is going nowhere. Then Warren gets a break.

Warren's instincts tell him that the informant is dodgy – a former police officer under investigation. But when Warren hears the incredible story he has to tell, he's glad to have given him a chance to speak. Suddenly, a wide criminal conspiracy, involving high-level police corruption, a gangster and a trained killer, is blown wide open…and Warren finds that this time, it's not just his career under threat, but his family – and his life.

Fans of Peter Robinson and Peter James will love *Silent as the Grave*, the third novel in Paul Gitsham's DCI Warren Jones series.

Dear Reader,

We hope you enjoyed reading this book. If you did, we'd be so appreciative if you left a review. It really helps us and the author to bring more books like this to you.

Here at HQ Digital we are dedicated to publishing fiction that will keep you turning the pages into the early hours. Don't want to miss a thing? To find out more about our books, promotions, discover exclusive content and enter competitions you can keep in touch in the following ways:

JOIN OUR COMMUNITY:

Sign up to our new email newsletter:
http://smarturl.it/SignUpHQ

Read our new blog www.hqstories.co.uk

🐦 https://twitter.com/HQStories

📘 www.facebook.com/HQStories

BUDDING WRITER?

We're also looking for authors to join the HQ Digital family!
Find out more here:

https://www.hqstories.co.uk/want-to-write-for-us/

Thanks for reading, from the HQ Digital team

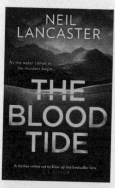

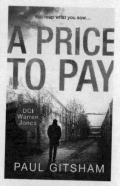

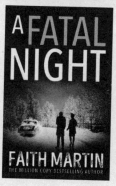

**If you enjoyed *Time to Kill*, then why not try
another gripping thriller from HQ Digital?**